MW00830486

PARADISES LOST

THE PASSAGE THROUGH TIME
1

Eric-Emmanuel Schmitt

PARADISES LOST

*Translated from the French
by Steven Rendall and Addie Leak*

Europa
editions

Europa Editions
27 Union Square West, Suite 302
New York NY 10003
www.europaeditions.com
info@europaeditions.com

Copyright © Editions Albin Michel – Paris 2021
First publication 2024 by Europa Editions

Translation by Steven Rendall and Addie Leak
Original title: *Paradis perdus. La traversée des temps – 1*
Translation copyright © 2024 by Europa Editionss

Library of Congress Cataloging in Publication Data is available
ISBN 978-1-60945-849-2

Schmitt, Eric-Emmanuel
Paradises Lost

Cover design by Ginevra Rapisardi

Cover image: Wenzel Peter, *Adam and Eve in the Garden Eden* (detail).
Photo 12/Alamy/Michal Hlavica

Prepress by Grafica Punto Print – Rome

Printed in Canada

CONTENTS

PARADISES LOST

A shiver.

First, a shiver.

Persisting, the shiver weighs, races, extends, cracks, divides, becoming two, fifteen, fifty shivers that take over the skin, awaken the senses.

The man opens his eyes.

Night . . . silence . . . coolness . . . thirst . . .

He looks into the surrounding darkness. The obscurity would frighten him if he didn't know where he was. Curled on his side on the damp limestone, he breathes in the tonic, reinvigorating air, which fills his lungs and revives him from the inside out. The pleasure of existing . . . How good a rebirth is! Better than a birth . . .

Their task accomplished, the shivers dissipate: the man has become aware of his body.

Abandoning the fetal position, he carefully turns over on his back and meticulously examines the various parts of his anatomy. Guided by his will, his arms rise above his face. His fingers bend, and their cartilage cracks; his hands descend, caress his chest, run over his belly, brush against the tuft of pubic hair, lightly touch his lukewarm penis. He commands his ankles to relax, lifts his feet, bends them left, then right, rotates them in a circle, then hugs his thighs to his chest. Everything works fine. Is he suffering any after-effects, any discomfort? His scrupulous physical examination confirms that he doesn't even have a scar. His twenty-five-year-old body has been returned to him intact.

"Noam . . ."

His name vibrates in the opaque cavity. Whew! His voice works, too.

He frowns. The syllables that bounced from wall to wall disturbed the atmosphere; with a word, a single word, humans, clans, peoples, nations, and history have burst forth, threatening and oppressive dangers, so remote from the animal happiness he enjoyed before. Noam. His given name oppresses him. Noam. Although that's what he calls himself, neither a mother nor a father whispers these sounds. Solitude. Extreme solitude. In this respect, a rebirth is less desirable than a birth . . .

He stands up. His skull strikes the stone of the grotto. Dazed for a few seconds, he rubs his scalp, calms down. Groping his way, he tries to leave this cavity to reach the neighboring one.

Where's the door? His palms explore the wall, find cracks, hollows, bends, but no opening. What then? Did the explosion that took place here cause a collapse that blocked the way out? Desperately, he persists. In vain. Is he trapped underneath blocks of stone? His heart beats faster, he pants, his forearms sweat.

Calm down. Begin again, methodically.

Kneeling, Noam establishes a starting point and examines the walls again. One pebble gives way, another, a third: he has found the way out.

He creeps into it. To the right.

He remembers putting his backpack down to the right. Provided, again, that the explosion hasn't . . .

The damp, almost living fabric touches his fingers.

Reassured, he takes a lighter out of the pack. After a few sparks, the flame springs up. Dazzled by this flare of fire, he turns his head away. He blinks; the cornea shrinks over his pupils. How long have his eyes gone without seeing anything?

He becomes accustomed to the light as he scans the walls. The rock has a skin, a shining, wet skin with dilated pores, pink, sensual, feminine, offering soft folds that attract him, sketching here a neck, an ear, an armpit, there a groin, lips, a clitoris, the mysterious darkness of a vagina. Noam was coiled up at the center of the earth, that belly where, over millennia, the liquid and the mineral merge. Dripping water has created these contours. What surrounds him has not been sculpted but seeped.

He finds himself getting an erection, and that amuses him . . . When did he last make love?

At the bottom of his pack, he finds a candle, lights it, and then, putting the lighter away, he grabs his clothes: pants, a linen shirt, sandals.

He laughs. He remembers that morning when he emerged naked from the caverns! It had frightened a group of peasant girls.

Dressed, holding the candle, he squeezes through the familiar bottlenecks. Crevices force him to slow down, to crawl on all fours, to hoist himself from one level to the next, to slip through a long passageway, until he finally reaches the hollow pit of the fissure.

An unusual light takes him by surprise. Noises.

What? Has his hideaway been violated? Usually, the only thing you can hear is the murmur of water. Extinguishing his candle, he creeps carefully toward the jagged opening.

Voices reach his ears. A motor hums softly in the distance. When he comes to the end of the winding artery, he looks out and can't believe what he sees.

The grotto has been invaded. Powerful spotlights illuminate the concretions. Attached to the escarpments, a path with an iron guardrail has been constructed, part dug-out road, part added gangway, occasionally widening to form a balcony providing a viewpoint. At the moment, certain individuals are following this path. A man brandishing a little flag is guiding a group and offering a commentary. In Arabic. In German. In English. In French.

Noam holds his breath. He'd never imagined that anyone would come so close. Careful! He can't be seen perched up here on this outcropping.

Crouching and protected by the darkness, he discovers, thanks to the lighting, an unexpected play of colors, from celadon to an orangish tint, passing through bronze and timid pastels. On the ceiling he discerns rigid, slender stalactites piercing the rocky skin like the scattered hairs that grow on the hard, leathery skin of elephants. In the distance, the surface becomes duller, more rounded, glossier, resembling solid clouds, petrified mists. Everywhere else, stalactites and stalagmites stare each other down, join, miss each other, fail to meet. Opulent Nature goes wild; drop by drop, century after century, with patience and imagination, it exudes an exuberant, abstract, figurative setting in which spheres, flows, nodules, piles, aggregations follow geometry, then liberate themselves from it to suggest a horn, a lion, a bull, an angry wrestler, a furious god. Here it builds chandeliers or melts candles; there it creates temples like the trailing tentacles of a jellyfish or chisels vertiginous organ pipes; on the remainder, it deploys hangings of calcite, interlaced draperies and cords.

Tense, Noam analyzes the ways out. Since the crack he knew about has been obstructed by the construction, he will have to find a different escape route. Time for improvisation!

As soon as the intruders leave the area, he comes nimbly down from the overhang, his pack on his back, leaping from one handhold to another all the way down the cliff.

"What are you doing?"

A voice has boomed out. It addresses him in German.

Noam makes out a red-haired Hercules wearing a flowered shirt, who is speaking to him from a platform. Continuing his climb, Noam replies in Arabic:

"I'm collecting samples for the lab."

"What?"

Since the giant doesn't understand, Noam repeats what he said in German, with an exaggerated Arab accent.

"Collecting samples for the lab."

"What lab?"

"The Lebanese Speleological Society."

Noam has thrown out that phrase without thinking. A silence follows. Only a few more meters to cross . . .

"Well, then," the German exclaims, "you're a hell of a climber!"

"Thanks," Noam replies, jumping onto the concrete pathway.

"How did you learn our language?"

"I studied in Heidelberg for a year."

Noam bids him farewell and quickly moves away. Where is the exit? The fact that his conversation with the first person he has met in several years comes down to a pack of lies exasperates him. Welcome to the human world! But it doesn't matter. The man who saw him climb down the precipice doesn't suspect him of having escaped from a secret chamber.

A group of tourists is approaching with the slowness of a herd of cattle. Noam slows his pace, greets them with a vague smile, and goes on, head down, trying not to slip on the wet ground.

Leaning on the guardrail, he becomes aware of a deep hole, a natural well that reveals the azure surface of the placid underground lake, made radiant by submerged spotlights. An electric, flat-bottomed boat is moving across it, carrying a dozen passengers. That's where the delicate sound of the motor was coming from. Noam infers that the two galleries are open for tours, the lower one by boat, the upper on foot. In the old days, only a few adventurers with helmets dared to go into the lower gallery, and no one suspected the existence of the upper one.

Gradually, the number of visitors grows. They chatter. A hundred idioms interlace. His eyes cast down, Noam is astonished by their get-ups: gawkers, hardly covered by short shorts or unbuttoned polo shirts, display their tattoos. What? Are they all sailors? All bandits? The women, too?

Noam shakes his head; he will solve that enigma later.

"Exit."

His heart pounding, he passes through a chrome-plated turn-stile, then plunges into an artificial tunnel made of cement. Ten meters. Twenty. Sixty. What if he's mistaken? Eighty. Ninety meters. As he moves forward, he sees daylight, feels its warmth, breathes in an air saturated with fragrances.

He emerges on a little square crawling with tourists. The sun blinds him; the suffocating heat paralyzes him. Bewildered, he leans on a balustrade and tries to control his breathing.

Around him, natives are selling things; some offer cold drinks, others ice cream, pistachios, salted peanuts, souvenirs—rag dolls, notebooks, shawls, fans, cups, spoons. Paying no attention to these enticements, the tourists consult a small, flat box that they hold in their hands; some of them hold it to their ears and talk in a loud voice, apparently to themselves. Bizarre . . . Apart from teenage boys and girls flirting with one another, no one pays attention to anyone else. Which suits Noam fine . . .

Taking his canteen out of his pack, he drinks.

He assesses the situation: a cog railway and a cable-car now connect the lower grotto with the upper one, his, which was formerly unknown. Regretfully, Noam concludes that he is probably visiting for the last time this refuge he has loved so much. He'll have to find a new hiding place, in case he should have to . . .

Let's not even think about it!

He sighs.

Run away. Always, running away. And he's been running for such a long time . . .

Why?

*

His legs are pumping full speed. The muscles in his calves and thighs hurtle him down the path, full of life, excited, swollen with blood, close to orgasm. Noam needs to let off steam.

After leaving the site at Jeita, he ate apart from the crowd, gobbling canned tuna—one of the precious preserved foods in his pack—and now he's covering the eighteen kilometers that separate him from Beirut. In this pleasant valley, pierced with gray stones, stocked with olive and lemon trees and oaks, he has only to follow the iridescent Nahr al-Kalb River, the very one that has its source in the grottoes and provides the capital with drinking water.

The sun beats down. The cicadas chirp and creak with such fervor that one would think the land was crumbling.

No longer accustomed to the heat, Noam ties a kerchief on his head, shields his eyes with his hand, and stops frequently to drink. Around him, at the summit of the hills or on their flanks, there are convents, chapels, monasteries, devoted to one saint after another. On the horizon, a vast opalescence borders the land: the sea.

As Noam goes on, exhausted by the heat, he raises dust. The scorched bushes bear neither flowers nor fruits. The dry grass, yellowed, brittle, friable, breaks. As for the olive trees, the famous trees that have contributed to the region's glory for thousands of years, they have lost their leaves; their knotty, twisted trunks wriggle out of the rocky ground, crying for water.

The state of the river worries Noam: far from occupying the whole of its bed, it stays in the middle, a prudent flow that leaves, here and there, a few lonely puddles that quickly evaporate.

Is it a heat wave?

A dog interrupts Noam's reflections.

Long-legged, emaciated, it's sniffing the body of a viper in the brush when it perceives the walker's presence. It turns around. As their eyes meet, the man and the animal immediately connect.

Slowly, Noam crouches down; slowly, the dog approaches, gangly, good-humored, with a supple, oscillating gait, its tail wagging furiously.

"Hello, there!" Noam whispers, in a language that no one speaks any more, but that the animal understands.

His hand receives the dog's damp, warm nose. Then his hands spread over its chest, petting it. The dog sighs; it's in love. They exchange a long look, as if seeing each other again after a long absence, although they have just met. The landscape disappears. Time is suspended.

"You out walking all alone?"

Wrinkling its velvety forehead, the dog stares at Noam and reveals the whites of its eyeballs, which gives it a sad countenance.

"You're trying to charm me, aren't you . . ."

The animal enthusiastically gives itself over to the caresses, without restraint or shame.

"Rocky!"

A raspy voice has emanated from the edge of the wood.

Regretfully, the dog tears itself away from Noam and heads toward its master's voice.

"Rocky!"

Obediently, then exuberantly, it disappears behind the thorny junipers.

Noam remains squatting. He shivers. He has felt more emotion meeting this dog than he did meeting humans . . .

Who greeted him? Who joyfully welcomed him? Spontaneous good will shone only in the dog's eyes.

He chastises himself: Noam, you'll end up a misanthrope!

Shrugging his shoulders, he goes on his way. "Misanthrope" . . . The term no longer frightens him. The only person who doesn't hate people is one who loves them. The only person who doesn't castigate his fellows is the one who expects the best of them.

Roofs announce Beirut's suburbs.

What name should he choose? Which nationality? Which identity will allow him to go unnoticed? Because he doesn't know what has recently happened in Lebanon, that theater of all conflicts and all reconciliations, he has to inform himself before he's asked even the smallest question . . . He knows from experience that a single sentence can put him in danger.

The city has grown since his last expedition . . . Reinforced concrete cubes. Basic four-storied buildings. As always, the edges of the city are not full of architectural splendors. Among these structures, bulldozers rust, cables hang in the void, open dumpsters and garbage bins display waste that delights the crows.

Noam stops at the intersection, stupefied. What a din! In addition to the backfiring of the jackhammers and the growl of the generators that supply the neighborhood with electricity, he hears trucks, cars, motorcycles, and scooters competing in decibels, and the windows of the apartment buildings vomit at high volume the sounds of radios or televisions.

He enters Beirut and strolls through its streets. Bodies brush against one another. Taxis honk their horns to attract fares.

Without realizing it, Noam looks at the women and follows them, hypnotized by their slender silhouettes. When they turn around, he lowers his eyes, turns away, takes a different path.

No, that's not going to start up again! He scolds himself when he realizes what he's doing.

Every time, seeing them from behind, he hoped it was Her! Every time, facing them, he was sorry that it wasn't Her . . .

Banishing that thought, he tries to concentrate on what surrounds him.

The locals are fiddling with the little flat box that he noticed in Jeita. Before long, Noam deduces that it is a telephone, a telephone without a cord. Incredible progress in a few decades! But why are these people peering at their phones when they're not using them? By standing behind a veiled, myopic, very absorbed Beiruti woman, he discovers that this tool emits luminous images. Better yet: without a pencil, pen, or typewriter, this young woman is writing a message on the screen, a text in perfect typescript!

He continues his wanderings, meditating.

In front of a school, high school students wearing suits sit on the asphalt, blocking traffic. Their posters bear a slogan: "No future, no school!" Noam goes around a bald journalist with a camera on his shoulder who asks one of the protesters, "What are your movement's goals?"

"It's not a movement, it's a strike," the teenager replies in impeccable English, speaking in a deep, resonant, virile voice that contrasts with his spindly anatomy. "We're boycotting our courses to warn adults, to mobilize the people, to hold politicians accountable. Why should we go to school if the future is compromised?"

With the nonchalance of innocent children, he considers the conversation over and goes back to his comrades; the journalist follows him.

"Aren't you exaggerating? You're making pigs fly!"

"The people exaggerating are the ones with their eyes and ears covered, who go on working, governing, voting, consuming as if nothing were happening."

"You're imitating young people in Europe and America!"

"Exactly. The youth of the world are confronting old people everywhere."

"A conflict of generations: the young against the old?"

"The woke against the un-woke."

"Are you going to war?"

"Too late: we have all already lost."

The muezzin's call to prayer resounds.

Noam continues on his way. Although he has perceived tension, he has not yet grasped either its causes or its implications. It's urgent for him to figure out what's brewing.

I need money.

Zig-zagging among the pedestrians in the crowded, narrow streets, he reaches, after the St. Irenaeus dispensary, a coffee-roasting establishment emitting enchanting aromas; across from it he spies a boutique whose walls curve inward, crushed by the weight of the building.

Oof, it's still there!

The shop, whose curtains are drawn, is not adorned by any sign and has a small door below the tiled sidewalk.

Noam goes down the three steps and pushes on the door, which resists and then gives way all at once—triggering a deluge of little bells. He ducks to avoid hitting the doorframe and enters the warehouse lit by greenish neon lights. Everywhere there are locked glass-front cases, horizontal and vertical, in which countless articles are displayed; he recognizes the shelves of items in silver, gold, glass, and porcelain, along with a collection of those new cordless phones.

"May I help you?"

From the back of the shop, the merchant, jowly, fat, his few tufts of black hair oiled and combed back over his low forehead, watches him approach, his eyes inquisitive, his violet lips forming an improbable smile.

Noam slings his backpack onto the counter in a virile action that universally signifies, "Watch it, nobody cons me, or else!"

The shopkeeper's eyebrows quiver, impressed. In a dense silence, Noam takes a ring from his pocket, rolls it across his palm, exhibits it.

"Here."

The merchant picks it up between his pudgy fingers with an affectation that he imagines is distinguished and murmurs in an unctuous voice, "A jewel you inherited from your mother, I suppose?"

He puts on a skeptical face, which makes him look even more baby-like.

"Not fashionable these days. A kind nobody buys anymore. This kind of setting, the style . . ." He snickers. "As is, I'd never be able to sell it! The stone, on the other hand . . ."

"A ruby."

"Yes."

"A big ruby."

"Not so big . . ."

"A big ruby."

"To be sure, not ridiculous, but . . ."

"Don't try to screw me. I've consulted your colleagues."

The fat man examines Noam and grumbles, "Do you know what they call this shop? The Cavern of the Forty. Why? Because of 'Ali Baba and the Forty Thieves.'"

He points a minuscule, chubby index finger at Noam.

"Even if there are forty of you, I'm only one. You're all inter-changeable. I'm not."

"Do you take me for a thief?"

"Do you take me for a fence?"

They size each other up. Noam knows the rest of the scene by heart. He goes on . . .

"I showed the ring . . ."

"Which belonged to your mother . . ."

"Which belonged to my mother . . . to other philanthropists. In Damascus. In Nicosia. In Valletta. In Istanbul."

Suddenly alert, the merchant changes his attitude.

"You're not in a hurry?"

"Not in a hurry to make a bad deal. How much are you going to offer me?"

By reflex, the puffy man activates his fingers, manipulating imaginary banknotes.

"In American dollars?"

"Obviously!" replies Noam, who has no opinion on the question.

The man lifts his eyes to the heavens, rolls them around sev-eral times in their sockets, moving them like a Chinese abacus, calculates, and then says, "Twenty thousand dollars."

"Are you a shopkeeper or an ironmonger?"

"Twenty thousand, I said."

"Forty thousand!"

"Twenty-five thousand."

Calmly, without a word or a look, Noam picks up his ring, wipes it off, puts it away, turns on his heel, and heads for the door.

After he has crossed the sill, when the little bells ring, the merchant barks, "Thirty-five thousand dollars!"

Noam turns and grimaces as a kind of farewell. Just as the door is closing, the merchant rushes forward and thrusts his foot between the door and the frame.

"All right, forty thousand dollars!"

They shake hands and Noam gets a sudden whiff of patchouli. Panting, feverish, cloying, the merchant invites his guest to drink a cup of coffee or tea. Noam feels a tinge of regret; he's not sure how much his jewel is worth, but given the shopkeeper's satisfaction, he doubts he got a fair price.

"Could you recommend someone . . . who makes passports?"

The merchant doesn't miss a beat—Beirut is still the meeting place of spies and traffickers of all kinds—and gives him an address.

Noam leaves the shop. The noise of thousands of cars bewilders him. So does the abundance of colorful signs. He feels the need to rest.

Unexpectedly, he spots, descending from a limousine, two shapely, slender legs wearing golden sandals with elegant straps.

He trembles. He waits to see the body of this woman, but his emotions tell him: it's Her!

He leans against the wall, unable to breathe.

The feet touch the ground, unfold languorous hips, a supple torso, and then the face appears. A red-headed torch, staggering in her sensuality, gets out of the car, escorted by a lover with slicked-back hair.

It's not Her.

Noam struggles to recover. He's suffering from confusion. His feeling a few seconds earlier had contained as much fear as it did desire. And now—did he feel relieved or disappointed?

Her . . . It was always Her . . .

He left society solely to get away from Her . . . Is he returning to it solely to find Her?

*

He's dug up a place to stay. In this squat fisherman's shack near the rocks on the coast, the Widow Ghubril took him in without demanding either a passport or an ID card. Eager to get her roof repaired, she's not picky about legality.

"Here's the internet code," she murmurs.

Taken aback, Noam accepts the piece of cardboard with numbers on it without daring to ask what to do with it. He crosses a hall smelling of floor polish and deposits his bag in the clean, whitewashed little room, which contains a bed, a tiny desk, a stool, a TV set, and a coffee table. Behind the French doors, a balcony so small it can only fit a chaise longue looks out toward the sea. Although this furnished room is extremely modest, it does have a magnificent view.

With money in his pocket, Noam goes to the address given him by the fence. Procuring false papers is becoming urgent. During the day, the look he's gotten from hotel employees and apartment managers when he claimed to have lost his documents meant either "You're a scoundrel" or "You don't exist." And the money that Noam, in accord with an ancient tradition, tried to slip them didn't help matters. On the contrary. Society's tendency to check people's papers for any and all movement has gotten worse since last time; the system has become more important than the individual . . .

Noam stands before a scarlet door on the first floor of the little house. He rings the bell. No answer. He rings again. He knocks. He calls out.

On the second floor, a middle-aged woman with her hair in a tight bun sticks her head out of the window and shouts, annoyed, "It's closed. My husband will come back from Byblos tomorrow."

Noam thanks her and walks away. Too bad. And so much the better . . . This will give him time to determine which nationality will work best in the present. Speaking a score of languages, he knows he's capable of taking on various identities. He goes into a bookstore that offers him a selection of the international press and buys about forty newspapers; in the bazaar, he purchases soap, toothpaste, cookies, oranges, a cluster of dates, a bottle of arak.

Back at the widow's boarding house in the Mar Mikhaël neighborhood, he lifts a glass of milky anisette to his lips, a way of celebrating his return to the world; then, stretched out on the bed, he grabs the newspapers and skims their headlines. Young people are rebelling. Everywhere! All over the planet, primary and secondary school students are boycotting their classes, university students are deserting their campuses; pounding the pavement, they're demanding that steps be taken to limit global warming.

"Global warming?" Noam doesn't know what that means.

After reading a few articles, he understands: the temperature of the world is rising. Deserts are expanding; regions that used to be temperate are disintegrating, subject to storms and heat waves. While plant and animal species are disappearing daily, enormous changes in the weather are becoming regular. The unforeseeable is becoming the rule. Either there is a water shortage and nothing grows, or it pours down and devastates everything. Photos alarm Noam: alpine glaciers that he climbed have melted; the polar bears he hunted, huge, athletic, menacing, are now dragging their miserable bodies around the outskirts of cities.

Night brings Noam one terrible revelation after another. Eight billion people now live on Earth! Eight billion people pumping oil and gas, driving cars, taking trains, traveling in planes, consuming electricity. Eight billion people throwing away plastic bags that soil the landscape and pollute the oceans. Eight billion people expanding urban space and reducing the space available for vegetation. Eight billion people clamoring for food when the earth, bled dry, is exhausted. Eight billion people demanding meat, more of it than animals provide. Eight billion people counting on an industry that dirties the sky, fills our lungs with dust, poisons rivers, destroys flora and fauna. Eight billion people polluting the atmosphere. Eight billion people thinking only of their profits, their pleasures. Eight billion people who don't want to change anything while everything changes. Consumerism, the worship of profit, the frenetic conquest of new markets, and the doctrine of free trade have caused a disastrous ferment.

Noam rubs his temples. During his hibernation, careless humanity has provoked its own extinction. Dripping with sweat, he returns to the first articles in the local paper, *L'Orient-Le Jour*, *The Times*, *Der Spiegel*, and *Le Monde*, all of which explain the student movement. After isolated warnings sounded by scientists who were mocked by sensible society, young people condemned the poisoned gift bequeathed by earlier generations: this way of life destroys life, Nature is no longer natural, the future has no future. Usually, young people feel anger, but these express their distress by ceasing to study. As they see it, the state of the planet confirms the bankruptcy of politics. Whatever the government, the quest for profit guides those in power. The price at any price!

Overwhelmed, Noam throws the newspapers to the foot of the bed. He knows it's a juvenile act—as if rejecting the messenger would do away with the bad news!—but reality oppresses him.

Why?

Why did he "wake up" just to find this? What good did it do to return to such a world? He's experienced many atrocities during his existence, but this one seems to him especially cruel . . .

He turns on the TV. Landing on Channel 31, he thinks there must be an error. Thirty-one channels? Impossible. This must be the Lebanese national channel, "31" referring to some date worth celebrating . . . Using the remote, he surfs more than eighty channels, flabbergasted; during his last trip, there were no more than two or three.

Reports show floods, typhoons, cataclysms, climate refugees, animals fleeing, ice floes drifting, coastlines eaten away by oceans whose levels are rising. He turns off the TV and sighs.

He will not sleep. He will remain motionless on the sheets that he has not even turned back. He will vegetate there for hours, awaiting dawn without illusions: sunlight won't calm his torment, answer his questions, or soothe his anxiety; it will merely justify his ceasing to be prostrate. It looks like the night will be hellish.

An idea suddenly makes him sit bolt upright.

He hesitates. He's afraid of going astray.

Should he . . .

The idea persists, sinks in, becomes embedded, established.

Yes. That's it. I have to.

*

Noam can no longer put up with anything. Neither sleeping nor waking. Neither himself nor others. Neither consciousness nor oblivion.

This week, he has entered into dialogue with the idea that devastated him. As obvious as it is, he resists it; as strong as it is, he rejects it; as interesting as it is, he turns away. His life has always been constructed in opposition to this idea. Giving in to it would mean surrender.

Every morning, he goes to a bar in the popular, trendy Mar Mikhaël area and tells the waiter to bring him sweets—cookies with pine nuts, pistachios, cinnamon, almonds, walnuts, coconut, all dusted with powdered sugar—and, smelling honey, rose, orange blossom, he studies the international press.

The false ID manufacturer has not returned from Byblos. His wife rants as she tells Noam this, and he can see from her face contorted by exasperation that she suspects he's cheating on her.

Noam has to wait. And this allows him to think about his next false identity . . . For years, to the question "Who are you?" he has been replying with a lie.

Cafés are the soul of a city. Without them, it would suffocate, lacking places to dream. Under the blades of the ceiling fans, among the people smoking water-pipes and the old men playing cards, Noam listens to what's being said. After a few sessions, he has distinguished the man of leisure who devotes his time to wasting it, the universal quibbler for whom thinking means criticizing, the pseudo-intellectual who finds satisfaction in repeating fashionable theories, and the true intellectual who is uneasy and tormented. Information pours in, reporting the impoverishment of natural resources, the disasters caused by industry, the irreversible rise in temperatures.

"You can refuse to listen to us," the intellectual at the bar concedes, "but you can't reject science. It's telling us that Nature's going to implode."

Noam, who is rediscovering the delight of being lazy, eating, and drinking, is ashamed of his hedonism.

Before long, this world will no longer exist. I'm one of the last to contemplate it.

Then his thought perceives the abyss.

Before long, *the* world will no longer exist.

Every second becomes uncomfortable. At the heart of happiness, he receives a dagger's blow: soon, we'll sweat, suffocate, die of hunger or of thirst.

Never again . . .

The present is tinged by nostalgia.

At these moments, the idea returns, the idea that illuminated his night. It doesn't provide a solution; it proposes an act. If he carried it out, he'd be fighting emptiness.

Beirut has retained its vigor. In spite of the torrid summer that has led wealthy Lebanese to retreat to the mountains, the city shimmers, snarled, noisy. The terraces of the bars and restaurants are constantly full. Young people show their disenchantment by day and enjoy themselves by night. Their pessimism, far from preventing them from living, incites them to go on: they go out, have fun, drink, brag, show off, move from one party to another, parade down the streets in convertibles that bellow their favorite music. As their parents used to do . . . And their ancestors before . . . One particularity marks this city: the pleasure it takes in existing. It eternally cherishes the ephemeral. From century to century, from generation to generation, the people of Beirut have been dancing on a volcano. What's the difference between yesterday and today? It used to be this neck of the woods that was in danger; these days, it's the whole Earth.

Mixing with the crowd, Noam is very fond of this *now* full of buried worlds, this *here* full of elsewhere. In this dense everyday life, he senses countless presences, peasants who have been cultivating this vale of milk and honey, Phoenician businessmen, importers of raw materials, exporters of artisanal masterpieces, Alexander the Great's Greeks, Egyptians of Ptolemy's dynasty, Romans, Arabian Muslims, crusading European Christians, the Druze, Turks of the Ottoman Empire, Italians from the republics of Venice and Genoa, French, English, Palestinians, Syrians . . . The continents converge on this narrow strip between sea-foam and snow, a trading post that brings together products from Asia, Europe, Africa, and the East, the meeting place of a hundred different roads. Strolling through the streets, Noam takes pleasure in noting that here there is no single language, no single politics, no single religion. Everything settles here, but nothing is set. The city stays in motion, animated. Seeing the fresh produce cart pulled by a haughty old man, he realizes that fruit is sectarian, too, with the Catholic grape, the Orthodox olive, the Maronite apple, the Sunni orange, the Shiite tobacco, and the Druze fig.

He admires this country, whose destiny is forever to skirt the abyss without falling in.

In the evening, he's moved by the women. All the women. The plump woman with satin-smooth shoulders and protruding breasts, the slender one with refined features, the touching petite one, the elegant giantess, the young woman with taut skin, the mature woman with kohl-lined eyes, the brunette, the blonde, the redhead, the white-haired woman, the bovine woman, the burlesque woman, the slow one, the lively one, the chatty one, the silent one, the one who dances, the one who drinks, the one who smokes, the one who laughs . . . Each seems to him a captivating secret; each holds a mystery he dreams of approaching. Beirut infatuates him with its merry-go-round of dazzling princesses. Sometimes their eyes meet. Women find him handsome. He knows that. Since he was twenty years old, his hard, sculpted body, clean-cut features, beard-framed mouth, green eyes, and long eyelashes have attracted them. He doesn't try to pick them up, though, even when encouraged by their flirtatious glances.

Because of Her?

He rejects this idea. She's not the only one! She's never been the only one. He has to forget Her.

No, he tells himself, if he refuses to begin a relationship, it's to preserve his integrity. In Beirut, he desires women, not a woman. Like an adolescent, he desires in general, not in particular.

How long will I remain honorable, he wonders, more tempted every evening.

At midnight, when the blood runs hot in his body, he flees his desire and seeks to avoid losing control by returning to the Widow Ghubril's house, but there, too, he finds himself skimming the newspapers to see if by chance they might have a photo of Her.

The rest of the time, he prepares; he becomes accustomed to the idea. Or perhaps the idea is becoming accustomed to him. On Tuesday, he bought a notebook; on Wednesday, three pens; on Thursday, a dictionary. After his shower, he sits on the stool, in front of the little desk, and imitates someone obedient to the idea: this ritual, though it lasts only a few minutes, might lead him to enact it.

On Friday, he sits on the rocks battered by the wind, the incoming tide, the salt. He contemplates at his feet the indigo of the water, the tall weeds that bend and straighten with the movement of the waves. He meditates. How could Nature disappear? It's still stronger than humans, those microscopic, ridiculous ants who, even when insane or out of control, cannot modify the cosmos.

A change in the light makes him look up.

To the north, the sky has grown dark; gray clouds, then black ones, are invading the horizon, climbing so high that they repaint midday as twilight. Behind him, sirens are wailing. In the distance, a humming sound announces the arrival of several airplanes.

What's going on?

He stands up.

Emerging from the adjacent houses, Beirutis are gathering, scrutinizing the coast. Noam joins them and listens.

"Look at the smoke!"

"It's coming on so fast."

"Horrible . . ."

"The firemen said the blaze had been under control for a week, but it's started up again."

"The firemen . . . How many of them are there?"

"It's because of the drought; everything is burning."

"The wind is fanning the flames."

"Worse, it's carrying sparks. Neither the asphalt roads nor the stone walls are stopping the fire. It's spreading."

"Six fire-fighting planes will never be enough!"

"The authorities have already evacuated three neighborhoods."

"Fuck, it's coming this way."

"It's urbanized here; the fire will stop before it reaches us."

"In the meantime, we can't breathe!"

Everyone is coughing. Noam holds a handkerchief to his nose to avoid inhaling the cinders that are falling from the sky.

All around him, people are reacting in their own ways; some touch their blue stones to protect them from bad luck, some tell the beads of their rosaries, some press rabbit's feet, some fiddle with their religious medallions, some stroke their hand of Fatima amulets.

A police car suddenly appears on the scene, and its driver barks orders with the help of a megaphone: "Go home. Close your windows. Seal your doors. Wear cloth masks. Children and the elderly should avoid unnecessary movement. I repeat: go home, close your windows, seal your doors . . ."

Nervous, the crowd disperses.

Noam, his throat irritated, his lungs attacked, hurries back to his lodging. Going down the hall, he passes the kitchen, where the Widow Ghubril is throwing melted lead in a pan of boiling water. It crackles, whistles, smokes, and then she utters the incantatory formula that averts danger and attracts good luck. Noam goes away on tiptoe. Beirut is attached to the supernatural to protect itself against despair.

He enters his room. Beyond the balcony, the sky and the sea have gone dark: the obscurity is spreading, even though it's midday.

This time, the idea wins.

Noam sits down at the desk and begins.

PART ONE
THE LAKE

1

I was born several thousand years ago in a country of streams and rivers, on the shores of a lake that had become a sea. Whether by modesty or by prudence, I would have preferred never to write that sentence: it discloses a destiny I've kept secret. Taking countless precautions, I've concealed my truth from others; I have avoided them, lied to them; I have fled, traveled, wandered, adopted new languages; I have hidden, isolated myself, changed my name, disguised and mutilated myself; I have pursued anonymity, endured deserts of solitude, and sometimes even wept. It didn't matter. They had to forget me, lose all trace of me. What was I afraid of? My longevity would not have failed to interest them because, since time immemorial, people have sought immortality, in heaven, under the earth, on the earth, in religion, in science, in posterity; but my longevity—which is incomprehensible—would've filled them with hatred. My fellows would have realized that they were not . . . my fellows. Once they had gotten over their astonishment, they would have resented me for being myself; they would have reproached themselves for being what they were. My sincerity—I was convinced—would have elicited only spite, jealousy, rancor, violence, in short, an avalanche of woes. I feared the consequences. For them, not for me.

I was born several thousand years ago in a country of streams and rivers, on the shores of a lake that had become a sea.

Whether by modesty or by prudence, I would have preferred never to write that sentence or any other, because I came into the world in an age that still lacked any alphabet. People listened.

They remembered. They strengthened their memories. When writing was invented, I was already four centuries old—later, I will recount the effect that produced for me. Although today I write in twenty languages, some still spoken, some forgotten, I consider this ability to capture reality on a sheet of paper an extraordinarily bold development.

I was born several thousand years ago in a country of streams and rivers, on the shores of a lake that had become a sea.

Whether by modesty or by prudence, I would have preferred never to write that sentence for the benefit of humans, those animals haunted by nothingness. A German proverb says: "As soon as a child is born, it is old enough to die." Let me clarify: as soon as a consciousness awakens, it dreads its disappearance. From the outset, it cannot tolerate its most basic feature, the knowledge of its mortality. The conclusion? Frustrated by Nature, inconsolable by essence, human beings are doomed to distress.

And what about me, I who have survived such a long time, have I experienced happiness? Allow me to develop my story, and you'll have my answer to that question.

I was born several thousand years ago in a country of streams and rivers, on the shores of a lake that had become a sea.

Whether by modesty or by prudence, I would have preferred never to write that sentence.

But this evening, I wrote it.

Why did I make up my mind to break my silence?

I'm scared.

For the first time in dozens of centuries, I'm scared . . .

*

I've been told that it was raining. A gentle, soft, warm rain. A rain that displayed all the colors of the rainbow to come.

In our lakeside home, Mama's water broke. As quickly as a fish, I slipped out of her, caught by the weather-beaten hands of Mamacha, my grandmother. Although I was my mother's first child, the birth did not take long.

"I'm made for it," Mama always said, pointing proudly to my ten sisters.

Perhaps, thanks to her magnificent rounded hips, she had been conceived to give birth, while I, for my part, proved especially fitted to being born. Slender, supple, lightweight, with smooth skin, I was moved by a desire to live that is as strong as ever.

What day was I born? The day it rained. Which month? The month of cob, the one following the month of sowing. Which year? A hundred and thirty-four years after the Battle of Ilodé. When I was a boy, people no longer remembered the Battle of Ilodé, but they counted the years on the basis of it.

Thus I was born in the year 134, several millennia ago. Too many kingdoms have perished, too many societies have collapsed, too many civilizations have disappeared for me to stretch the genealogical tie by attaching it to a known calendar. I appeared in an age when people measured time less than they do today. There were no birth dates or baptisms, no registry offices or fetishism surrounding birthdays, just shared memories. The lack of such things did not prevent us from coming into the world, living in it, benefitting from it. One morning, a baby was born: a celebration was improvised. One evening, someone died: another celebration was organized.

I looked like a normal human being, born of a normal mother and a normal father; I was first a normal child, then a normal adult who was wounded, bled, feared danger. It took that episode on the little island for . . . But let's not get ahead of ourselves.

When does an individual's life begin? When they're born: as they emerge from their mother's belly?

No, because they've spent months there.

When they're conceived: when the male seed fits itself into the feminine mold?

No, because the sperm and the egg were part of the father's and mother's flesh long before they met.

When the father and mother were born, then?

No more than the rest, because the father and mother themselves come from parents, who proceed from their parents, who spring from their parents, who . . . Heredity goes back endlessly. Is it possible to determine the second when genes begin their trajectory? Do we have to go back to the first man and the first woman? We will find neither an initial man nor a primordial woman . . . In us, millions of pre-existing elements make us exist. No life begins; it results. Before what is, there was always something.

Nevertheless, I know when my life began. With certainty. It started when I met Noura. The sparkling Noura. The superb Noura. The terrible Noura. After my mother, a woman who gave birth to Noam, a woman who . . . Sorry, I'm getting ahead of myself again. Please forgive my clumsiness; I don't often practice the writer's art. But then . . . how can I continue without mentioning Noura?

In my time, childhood was short. We didn't learn to read or write; no educational calendar cut up our years. But although we didn't go to school, we learned a great deal: how to respect the gods and the spirits; how to hunt edible animals and eliminate the harmful ones, protect ourselves from hostile ones, and train domestic ones; keep watch over herds of goats; milk bighorn sheep; pick berries and seed plants, cultivate them, water them, defend them against predators, harvest them, and preserve them. Our education also included hygiene, body-painting, and hairdressing. In addition, we learned to cook, weave, sew, fight, and make tools.

Childhood was soon over. When boys began to grow a beard, they became men; as soon as girls began to menstruate, they became women. Ceremonies marked this transformation—precise, extreme, sometimes cruel rituals that, as children, we had looked forward to as much as we dreaded them. When puberty came, couples were constituted, chosen by the parents of the two families.

At thirteen, I was married to Mina. At thirteen, my penis penetrated a vagina. At thirteen, my sperm poured into a uterus.

I felt a mediocre pleasure.

I dedicated myself to it, of course, but I felt more joy playing with the dogs, capering with the goats, herding the sheep, observing the flow of mountain streams, and even—I admit it—tussling with my friends. Though it did not revolt me, copulating did not exactly enchant me. This half-heartedness was not a problem for me or my friends. We didn't have wives for the sake of exploring sexual pleasure or ecstasy; we had wives because a male was attached to a female as soon as their bodies matured. Pleasure or displeasure—those nuances were not part of either our conversations or our thoughts.

At the time, I summed up my indifference to Mina in a few private revulsions: the smell of my semen—a week-old dead fish—embarrassed me, and its appearance disconcerted me—why did its whiteness turn transparent, then yellow, and how did a pasty substance dry out so fast? On the other hand, I found nothing to reproach in Mina, whose internal odors disgusted me less.

Because of my innocence, laziness, obedience, or habits, I didn't suspect the constraint to which I was subjected: our community had incited me to make love even though I felt no inclination to it. Though my beard had grown, my desire had not. To be sure, camouflaged behind the bushes with my friends, I had spied on the breasts, buttocks, and pelvises of the neighborhood women as they bathed along the banks of the stream . . . But is spying the same as coveting? Does uttering lewd words among pals suffice to transform them into mental images, obsessions, fantasies? I felt no lust. To really go for Mina, I'd have to need women; my ardor would have to need her in my arms, between my thighs, before I could find our intercourse intoxicating.

Society had given me satiation before I felt thirst. Married at the age of thirteen, I slept with my spouse; it was not a question of pleasure but of a rule.

However, I had known carnal wonder, I had experienced orgasm not long before, but . . . No, I'll talk about that when the time comes. Sorry, I'm closing this digression; otherwise my narrative will lose its way.

Noam prospered alongside Mina in his village.

I didn't consider myself an important person.

I didn't consider myself a person.

I didn't consider myself at all.

One after another, the days went on, the seasons went on. We participated in a collective movement. I was not living my story, but our story, among my people, like my people. I did not expect—I think—anything in particular from life, except that it would continue.

Mina gave birth to a son, to a daughter, then to twins. Which means that I received a son, a daughter, and then twins.

None of them lived more than a year. Mama, who was so proud of her eleven children, had given birth eighteen times to reach that score. Perpetuating oneself was turning out to be a difficult, thankless task riddled with failures. You got a wailing bit of flesh, took care of it, provided it with food, drink, and rest, but ensured that the bond, which was in danger of being broken, became neither strong nor tight. If you wanted to be attached to a child, you waited until they were seven years old, when they had survived childhood illnesses. Today, some people call the seventh year "the age of reason"; in the past, it represented the age at which people dared to love a child with reason.

Are people obliged to love their children? Many around me did not; all they had to do to win the community's esteem was to raise their offspring, feed them, and get them to puberty. Why love? Does loving make paternity or maternity any easier?

Mina adored her children, which made her very unhappy.

Every death caused her to weep, rendered her prostrate for long periods during which she wouldn't let me touch her. Instinctively, faced with infants, I had sealed myself up in an efficient, functional availability that committed me very little.

On rereading these lines, I note that I am describing my life at that time with detachment.

Nothing sounds more on the money than this detachment . . . I was living detached. I didn't know that Noam could differentiate himself, individualize himself, secrete ideas of his own, singular tastes, ambitions, or rejections. I was not an other, but the others.

I had to meet Noura for everything to change . . . No! Once again, I'm galloping ahead. Let's return to the story.

In the village, we led a hard-working, uneasy life. Our bellies were full, but our hearts were alarmed. If, thanks to the merciful gods and spirits, to the Lake and the rivers abounding in fish, to our fertile fields and our plump animals, we didn't fear hunger, we feared the Hunters, the ones who suddenly appeared alone or in organized groups. Peace didn't exist, and neither did hope for it; we lived constantly on the alert. There was no guarantee of order and security, we had to be wary, vigilant; we had to defend ourselves and fight, because if we didn't we would be pillaged and massacred.

In those times, people died like flies. To be sure, we had only one life to lose, but we perished for various reasons. We died as a result of a bear attack, a charge by wild boars, a wolf's bite; or as a result of falls, injuries, fever, indigestion; we died from our heads, mouth, teeth, guts, ass; we died from a broken bone, a swollen leg, a suppurating wound, yellowing skin, scabs that covered us, buboes that swelled our viscera; we died of weakness, exhaustion, infection, the enemy's blows. Nobody died of old age. Time didn't gradually disseminate death; there wasn't time for that . . .

The Peoples of the Lake got along well with one another. Our everyday activities unified us, but so did our devotion to the Invisibles: we shared the Lake and its spirit, the rivers and their souls, the springs and their nymphs, whose rites we celebrated. Since Nature's luxuriance did not incite us to compete with each other, the villages formed cordial bonds. They exchanged objects and women. Why objects? Because one stone-cutter made excellent axes, while his cousin made razor-sharp arrowheads; one jeweler created exquisitely refined bone collars; this weaver produced many-colored fabrics; and that tanner softened hides to perfection. Why women? Were they any better in the neighboring village or somehow exceptional in a remote village? Well-established, this custom was imposed by a silent necessity, the reason for which escaped us.

What did we know about the rest of the world? None of us had traveled even three days' distance from the lakeshore—or if someone had, they never came back. Occasionally, an excited, garrulous traveler to whom we granted our hospitality described for us other lakes, lakes from which one could not drink, with turbulent, capricious, roaring, deadly waves. We listened to these wild imaginings to relax, without believing the story, from which we drew only two conclusions: we lived at the center of the universe, and no other people was our equal.*

---

* I didn't know there was such a thing as salt water. For us, living far from seas and oceans whose existence we never guessed, the distinction between waters was drawn differently. There was the *living water* of springs and streams, the *sleeping water* of the Lake, and the *falling water* from the sky. They expressed separate divinities, the beneficial nymphs, the protective Lake, and the spirits of the sky, and we established no connections among them. Moreover, they didn't taste the same . . . As diverse in quality as they were in quantity, these three waters performed different functions: *living water* gave us something to drink, *sleeping water* gave us something to eat, and *falling water*, which was more ambiguous, provided us with either a reward or a punishment, depending on how the gods, as wise parents, reacted to our behavior. We would never have supposed that these were all one single liquid that evaporated from the Lake to make clouds that, letting their showers fall on the Earth's surface, created water tables from which emerged springs that fed the streams and rivers that formed the Lake. This continuity escaped us. We classified things in accord with their appearance and their utility for us. Today, this circulation of fluids, proven by scientists, elicits in me a still greater giddiness. Who conceived all that? What superior hand avoided all the traps and succeeded in constructing this harmony? If it was chance, then chance was a genius!

Humans have always known how to practice racism; my several millennia of experience testifies to that. I can discern nothing as spontaneous—not to say natural—as one group's scorn for another one.

On the shores of the Lake, we believed that we Sedentaries formed a humanity superior to the vile race of the Hunters. They didn't speak the language (ours) but made animal cries they pretended to understand (Don't even dogs grasp the barking of other dogs?). And then they smelled bad, hardly washed, were flea-ridden, and ate poorly. Finally, they slept outdoors, or else in caves, like wolves, at best in huts made of hides that they put up and took down, ignorant of con-structed houses and content with killing, chewing, fornicat-ing, and sleeping. Animals! Capable only of slaughtering their prey or picking fruit from trees. Once they had pillaged a place, they left it; they came back, years later, when the flora and fauna had been regenerated, and they pillaged it again. Plunderers! Instead of learning to observe plants in order to cultivate them, rather than creating flocks that would provide milk, leather, and meat, they doomed themselves to eternal wandering. They destroyed; they didn't produce. We, the Sedentaries, had stored grains and smoked fish that got us through the difficult months, whereas they lived from day to day. The cleverest among them sometimes carried a bag of hazelnuts, but the stronger ones murdered the clever ones to seize their provisions.

"Anyway, they kill their children," Mama would murmur as she stroked her amber amulet, the one that warded off demons.

The "child killers": that's what we called the barbarians. We didn't know whether it was a legend or a truth; when we saw mother hunters or father hunters prepared to do anything to feed the child they held close to them, we had difficulty imagining that they killed their progeny.

"They eat them," said Abida, my younger sister.

"That's horrific!" cried Bibla, my last sister. "Humans don't eat each other."

"The Hunters aren't humans!"

We argued about this subject so often that one evening Pannoam, my father, offered us an explanation: "The Hunters reproduce less because they can't move around with multiple children. Each parent carries a baby on him. They don't encumber themselves with a newborn until the preceding child can walk on his own.* They never found big families like we do."

My father tried to be just, even when talking to the Peoples of the Lake about the Hunters, the object of our terror.

When my grandfather Kaddour died at around thirty of an illness that had swollen his belly, my father became the village chief.

"Pannoam? There's no one better!" people said.

Pannoam had the qualities of a leader, and better yet, they were obvious at first glance. Not only was he of imposing height—long legs, broad shoulders, sculpted muscles, all of which I inherited—but his face radiated a controlled serenity. Although his thick neck, vigorous jaw, and temples with protruding, violet-colored veins indicated a temperament capable of aggression, his high forehead suggested intelligence, and his eyes expressed gentleness and his lips sensual delight. On his own, and as soon as he appeared, he embodied what people expected of a man, what one hoped to find in a chief.

"See and foresee, Noam," he repeated over and over. "You have to see and foresee. Don't limit yourself to what is; concern yourself with what will be."

So great was the reach of Pannoam's attention that he made a number of changes.

He ordered his people to abandon their wooden houses on

* The mothers nursed their babies for a long time, and that reduced their risk of getting pregnant again.

stilts at the edge of the Lake, houses we built during the low-water winter months in the mud.

"Why change? We've always done it that way!" the inhabitants protested.[†]

"The water is rising."

"That depends on the seasons."

In the course of the year, the height of the Lake varied by as much as the height of two men. In the autumn, the surface of the water crept up the stilts, reaching the floorboards of our houses and even submerging some of them. The Peoples of the Lake saw these floods as expressing the spirits' wrath and reacted simply by making sacrifices and offerings. When the level dropped, they saw in this the result of their piety, which had appeased the divinities.

According to Pannoam, the average level was rising, although many denied it. Since a house lasted about ten years—a little longer if made with oak instead of pine—each family had to move farther from the Lake to rebuild it, never being able to replace it at its original location, a proof that the water was slowly eating away at the land.

"It's not fate, Noam; it's a change."

"What's the difference?"

"You're subjected to fate. You adapt to a change."

"But we're praying to the spirit of the Lake and the souls of the rivers."

"I doubt that the conduct of the spirit of the Lake or the souls of the rivers is governed by the desires of the Sedentaries. If the divinities have decided to expand, they'll expand, in spite of humans. It's up to us to obey them, Noam; they control us."

He succeeded in persuading the inhabitants, just as he convinced me, to erect buildings in a dry, steep-sided, protective valley that overlooked the Lake. And the whole village moved.

---

† The lakeside villages were probably the first permanent settlements because the lake provided an almost constant supply of food, thus eliminating the need to move around.

My father took advantage of this to prescribe the use of twofold construction, with a stone foundation and an upper part made of cob; the mixture of straw and clay made for walls that offered robust resistance to wind and bad weather.

Pannoam, who required me to accompany him everywhere in order to educate me, led the population to organize its struggle against external dangers. Although we already had a division of labor—peasants who devoted themselves to pottery, weaving, rope-making, and cutting stone or wood—he suggested that we expand it.

"Some people will be used solely to defend the village. Freed from routine chores, they will fight against solitary good-for-nothings and the hordes of Hunters."

The villagers were indignant: "The barbarians don't attack us every day! According to your plan, Pannoam, we—farmers and stockmen—are going to support idlers who will work only now and then?"

My father argued that the "idlers" would spend every day training with their weapons, improving their fighting skills, and perfecting their axes, knives, and lances. The community's efforts would pay for the fact that these men devoted their lives to defending it.

"You know as well as I do that not every man proves to be a good farmer or stockman. You know, too, that a good goatherd or barley farmer doesn't necessarily make a tough fighter. And we all know that one time of life urges us to rush about, be active, and fight, while another urges us to reflect. This distribution of roles allows excellence to flourish while respecting everyone."

Contrary to all expectation, Pannoam received unanimous support. Ten ebullient young men, daredevils whose muscles and humors were hot, formed an elite battalion that protected us, along with our fields, our flocks, and our granaries, from intruders and pillagers. My father had just invented the police and the army.

People were impressed and boasted, and the rumor circulated. The various chiefs around the Lake came to observe Pannoam's system, sometimes for months, and because he spoke to them about it cleverly, without excessive pride and with diplomacy, they reproduced it in their own communities.

Everyone admired my father. I loved him.

I loved him more than anyone. I loved him to the point of never questioning what he said. I loved him to the point of wanting to resemble him in every detail, even the tiniest. I loved him to the point of self-denial. Had he told me to kill myself, I would have done it.

At no time did I ever imagine that he might be mistaken, either in the decisions he made for himself or the choices he made for us. That's why I didn't blame him for having required me to marry Mina; I didn't reproach him for having condemned me to sex without savor. I accepted the destiny he intended for me—to succeed him—while cultivating a single doubt: the fear of not being able to equal him.

My mother had beautiful, chestnut-brown hair, a little curly; greedy teeth; and a shapely, healthy, carefree body. Cheerful and tall, she approached the villagers with a combination of affability and authority that made her as powerful as it did indisputable. The care she took with her appearance—jewels, painted nails, subtle make-up, elaborate hairdos, rose perfume—deprived her of none of her sprightly nature, but it elevated her above other women. She was imposing. Did she cherish her husband? She adored being his wife; she loved loving him, the proud man who was the chief. His glory reflected on her.

Noam, son of Pannoam, was quietly preparing to become the next Pannoam. Nothing separated the son from his father, except a few years—fifteen—and my future was taking form: noble, magisterial, settled, just like him.

And then there was Noura.

And then there were the storms.

For that matter, Noura herself was a storm.

And the son opposed his father.

*

"Don't look at me like that; I'll get pregnant."

That was the first sentence Noura addressed to me. We didn't know each other; I was strolling along with my friends, whereas she was entering a foreign territory. Despite that risk factor, she said to me in a velvety voice, "Don't look at me like that; I'll get pregnant."

I was dumbstruck, doubting that I'd understood.

Noura looked at me, amused, her eyelids half-closed over her sublime green eyes. Though she was slighter than I, it seemed to me that she was dominant. This was due to the irony of her eyebrows, so purely arched that they seemed painted, the precision of her features, the slenderness of her figure, the haughty delicacy of her limbs, and especially her haunted stillness—although she didn't budge, I sensed countless forces at work within her, forces that urged her to move but that she had tamed, forces that endowed her with density and presence, forces that, from time to time, surfaced on her skin in the form of shivers.

"Don't look at me like that; I'll get pregnant."

My body had immediately noticed her beauty: a flame had reddened my face, my lips had opened, my breath caught in my chest, my legs turned to stone. A shock. No thought passed through my head. At the same time as my flesh had been awakened, my consciousness had stupidly nodded off. For the first of many times, I was being subjected to the "Noura effect": the body alive, the mind numb.

When I succeeded in figuring out that her sentence targeted me—accurately—I worried that other people might have heard it, which would have deeply shamed me. A quick look around calmed my fears. On this market day, everyone was absorbed in pursuing their own work. Some sold blueberries from the foothills, some dealt in ocher, some displayed terra cotta dishes or pots, some sold bunches of hemp or nettles, some unrolled their fabrics, some hawked leather capes, some spread sandals and slippers on a mat. All of this, plus the peasants whistling as they walked toward their fields. How naïve I was! Noura's arrows—I didn't know this yet—were infallible: had she wanted to reach onlookers and traders, she would have projected her voice; she had modulated it for me, for me alone, thus establishing a complicity, even an immediate intimacy between us. We'd hardly approached one another, and already we shared a little secret.

In an attempt to recover my composure, I stammered, "My . . . my . . . name is Noam."

"I didn't ask."

She turned her face away and became absorbed in the conversation that her father had begun with mine, both of them sitting under the Linden Tree of Justice, the place where Pannoam usually listened to people's grievances. Taking advantage of this distance, I admired Noura's delicate little nose, a frivolous nose that told a different story from her high cheekbones—which were irascible—and her smooth forehead—which was virginal. Attentive, nodding her head, now approving, now disapproving, she was following their discussion.

I had ceased to exist for her, which quickly became intolerable for me.

I touched her wrist so that she would communicate with me again. She jumped, horrified, took a step backward, and gave me a severe look, one eyebrow raised, as if I were a child who had done something naughty. Bolts of anger shot from her gold-veined eyes.

Ignoring her irritation, I persisted: "You haven't told me what to call you."

"I'll tell you if I want you to call me anything."

Firmly, promptly, she pivoted away with a vigor that meant: "It's over! Don't bother me again."

I'd never been treated that way! Who did she think she was, this foreigner?

I stamped my foot. She batted her eyelids. I became indignant: "Do you realize that I'm the chief's son?"

"You have to be somebody's son . . ." she retorted, shrugging her shoulders.

She moved away, pointedly turning her back on me.

I'd been piqued; now a wave of hatred engulfed me. Incapable of listening to what the foreigner was explaining to Pannoam, I was overcome by the temptation to thrash this girl, yes, to slap her, throw her to the ground, to drag her by the hair until she cried for mercy. Then she would no longer be able to fake indifference!

Did she sense my growing hostility? Her delicate neck and her shoulder blades trembled, as if she perceived that my fists were itching.

Our fathers embraced, and then Pannoam held out his arm, pointing to the houses; opening an invisible door, he offered the village to the strangers, invited them to enter it.

The girl pirouetted, walked toward me, flattened herself against my chest, close, very close, breath against breath, and murmured in a throaty voice, with her eyes cast down, almost timidly, "Hello, Noam. My name is Noura. I'm delighted to meet you."

I stood there, blissfully happy. She smelled as good as the heart of a flower, emanating a sugary, peppery fragrance made intoxicating by a hint of resin. I felt like I was inhaling a secret.

"See you!"

Turning on her heel, Noura grabbed her father's hand and merrily, lighter on her feet than a kid, accompanied him down the path to where it narrowed to lead toward the lakeshore, between the willows and bulrushes.

That morning, the stagnant air was bitter and stifling hot. Over the pale Lake, the sky spread a ferocious blue.

Who was this Noura? In an instant, she had blown hot and

cold, was fifteen years old, thirty, then eight. In an instant, she had instilled in me astonishment, fascination, curiosity, spite, hatred, hope.

I went up to my father.

"Who was that?"

"Tibor the healer; he cares for people and animals," Pannoam replied.

I didn't explain to him that I was referring to Noura; instinctively, I sensed that the feverishness into which she had plunged me represented a danger.

"Why did Tibor come to see you?"

"To offer us his services. He was living in a village on the shore of the Lake, a few days from here in the direction of the rising sun, but it was destroyed by mudslides."

"Mudslides?"

"After heavy rains, part of the hill gave way. The earth tumbled down as far as the shore. Nothing is left."

I put myself in Tibor's place, the one in which people consulted my father. The countryside was marked by calm, dignity, a harmony that, borne by the sweet, calming aromas of the linden tree, encouraged contemplation. Now I felt like weeping, rolling about on the ground.

"Does this Tibor have only a daughter?"

"Yes."

His forehead wrinkled. I thought he shared my concern.

"Curious!"

"What's curious, Noam?"

"Only one child? No wife? That's how Hunters live. Sedentaries don't live that way. Could the father and daughter be Hunters? Barbarians! Do you suspect them?"

I suddenly ferreted out the source of my uneasiness: if this girl had aroused so many diverse, atrocious emotions in me, it was because she didn't belong to our race! Clearly, she was a Huntress in disguise, a Huntress who had been able to make herself clean, elegant, well-groomed, sweet-smelling, a Huntress who could use language, but a Huntress all the same! That was why she had seemed to me so distant, so foreign: I had detected in her the passions of a wild animal.

My father studied me indulgently.

"Tibor is traveling with his daughter. When the mudslide occurred, all the villagers died. His sons and his wife perished. Through the spirits' mercy, he and the girl were in another part of the valley, looking for healing plants. That saved them."

He laid his hand on my shoulder.

"They bear the burden of an insurmountable sadness."

I immediately felt compassion for Noura and pardoned her for hiding her distress behind a brusque façade.

My father looked at me, smiling.

"You're right to be wary, Noam. Always be on your guard. Be suspicious for your people; be mistrustful for the credulous, careful for the careless. In this case, however, your mistrust is unjustified. Tibor and his daughter do not pose a threat. On the contrary, they would benefit us a great deal if they joined us. We don't have a healer. We should keep them."

A wish for warmth, sweetness, and repose rippled over my skin. An image accompanied it: Noura snuggling up to me.

"Of course, Father. Where did they go?"

"To a cousin's house where they are staying, a day's journey from here. They'll be back."

"Are they going to settle with us?"

"I've suggested that to Tibor."

"Why would Tibor continue his life among us?"

I was assailed by contradictory thoughts. A moment before, I was afraid that the father and his daughter might stay forever; now I was afraid that they wouldn't. In both cases, these prospects struck me with the violence of a fever.

"He's heard about our village. People have told him good things about us."

Modestly, Pannoam was implying that our reputation was flourishing on the lakeshore, thanks to his achievements, which had been copied by everyone. I began to calm down. He added, "He took a particular interest in the market. Tibor would meet many patients there, and he could acquire herbs from far-off lands."

My father had invented our market a few years earlier, establishing it despite the slowness of people's minds, the inertia of habits. To help his village prosper and distinguish itself, he'd had the idea of bringing together craftsmen or peasants who wanted to exchange goods once a week. The market attracted crowds of people who came not only from nearby villages, but also from remote ones. At this point, everyone knew about our village, which now had thirty houses.

"Here, according to Tibor, mudslides will never bury us."

I scanned the panorama, just to confirm my father's assertion. Our village, built on a natural plateau a hundred feet from the Lake and ten feet above it, received water from two streams, one on the side of the rising sun, the other on the side of the setting sun. These streams had run for days through rolling plains with gentle slopes. No steep mountain rose behind us, and on clear mornings we saw nothing but low hills that were in no way comparable to the jagged, snow-topped peaks that stood at the place where the Lake narrowed, where Tibor and Noura had lived.

"I am assigning you the mission of welcoming Tibor and his daughter."

"You can count on me, Father."

I was jubilant that he had entrusted me with a task that would allow me to be near Noura.

"Let's go take care of the dogs!"

I escorted Pannoam to the meadow where we tamed animals. I loved working with him to domesticate dogs, one of his most prized innovations.

At that time, we still encountered fierce packs of wolves and wild dogs, and my father had noted that our perennial enemies, the Hunters, were making clever use of dogs they had succeeded in taming, who now lived with them.

"That's normal," Mama said. "Wolves live with wolves."

"They belong to the same pack!" Abida added.

"In any case, they share their fleas."

My father, instead of holding forth on the subject, had observed the four-legged animals and taught me to differentiate between dogs and wolves: broad-backed, shorter, half the weight, dogs did not sport ash-colored hair but instead a coat that varied from white to reddish; sociable, they approached humans, seeking contact, frightened but intrigued. They also ate the same things we did, including grains and vegetables in addition to meat, while wolves remained carnivores.

Next, Pannoam had shown me how dogs could take part in hunting, some tracking the animal by means of their super-sensitive sense of smell, others attacking it or carrying home its body. We had often gone with our pack, our bows on our shoulders, to hunt hares, deer, or boars.

Then he studied their abilities as guardians. Since dogs sounded the alarm as soon as a man or an animal approached their domain, Pannoam had imposed them on our little army; at night, a soldier and a dog kept watch over the entrances to the village.

"If the soldier falls asleep, the dog continues his job as a sentinel."

One obsession tormented him: teaching our dogs to guard our flocks.

"Can you imagine how much effort we could save, Noam? If it worked, we'd no longer have to accompany our stock to the pasture!"

That morning, we were trying an experiment: putting our sheep in the meadow and then releasing the dogs.

"What if they devour the sheep, Father?"

"I gave them a generous meal at dawn."

The sheep, scattered, were grazing on the grass, each preoccupied with its own chewing. Pannoam set the dogs free.

Barking, they ran toward the sheep. I paled. I was afraid the dogs would eat them. But I quickly saw that they were undertaking something quite different: they were gathering the sheep together! Either they drove them into a restricted space, or they regrouped them in a circle by running around them. As if they were obeying my father's orders . . . He was jubilant.

"It's marvelous, Noam! They'll make perfect shepherds."

He told me to disguise myself as a predator and then move along the edge of the field behind the brush.

I did as he said, wearing the stinking pelt of a dead fox.

As soon as the dogs caught the scent of an intruder, they bounded to position themselves in front of the sheep to defend them. They prevented me from coming any closer, growling, howling, and baring their teeth. One of them was about to attack when I took off my fur so he could recognize me.

"Zarro, stay!"

Pannoam calmed the dog and then, excited, ran toward me; even though we were the same height, he hugged me, picked me up, and carried me around in triumph.

Amid this euphoria, Mama suddenly appeared. For years, she'd been annoyed by the affection Pannoam showed his dogs, reproached him for spending time with them and preparing food for them, and took offense when he spoke to them or named them. On every occasion, she mocked him: "Do you think they really understand you? It's the tone of voice, Pannoam, the way you pronounce their names, the commands, that dogs grasp. Nothing else."

My father always let her go on without saying anything in reply, and this just made her more bitter. On that day, however, she acknowledged his success and clapped her hands to congratulate us, which made the shell bracelets on her beautiful arms jingle.

Pannoam had been right to persevere; the dogs proudly served humans. She conceded: "You've invented a sentinel with fleas."

When Pannoam praised his animals, stroking them and repeating to each of them, "Good dog!," she couldn't resist teasing him: "Poor Pannoam . . . If people only saw you . . ."

My father winked at me, which meant, "Your mother's so fond of me that she bristles the moment I pet an animal."

And a moment afterward, my mother winked at me goodnaturedly, which meant, "Your father loves it when I tease him."

On the evening of that fruitful day, I went to my own house. Mina, sitting cross-legged on a mat in front of the doorsill, was grinding grain. I divined, from the tears that she wiped away when I approached, that she was mourning our twins.

I saw her with new eyes. She didn't look like a woman, but instead a little girl who had grown up and put on weight. Her round face, spotted with freckles, betrayed a kind of sad astonishment; her soft lips, which were a little too thick, a little too pale, were half open, half closed, while her protruding eyes were fixed, painfully resigned.

I felt pity for her. A sweet pity. A tender pity. A caressing pity.

I squatted down and, without a word, took her in my arms. Relieved, she let herself go, showing that she'd been waiting for me to do so for a long time. A bizarre situation: though we were on the cusp of a torrid summer, we were protecting each other, curled into a ball, compact, as if the truth of the twilight was the cold, as if only the heat we generated would keep us from dying.

As I hugged Mina, I was thinking about Noura. What a contrast! The foreigner had made me tense, whereas Mina moved me. The foreigner had made me awkward; Mina made me powerful. The foreigner could do without me; Mina needed me.

For the first time, in being with my wife I felt I was where I should be. Up to this point, I'd been lending myself to our marriage; that evening, I gave myself to it. Mina was mourning her dead children, to be sure, but someday she would look at our living children and laugh for joy. I could get rid of her morbid melancholy all by myself.

I gave Mina's neck a gentle peck and then, moving her hand toward my penis, showed her that I wanted to take her.

She bowed her head. Crawling on the ground, she drew me inside our house, closed the door, then got on all fours again. There, in the half-light, we copulated slowly, silently, meticulously, without any passion, like convalescents . . . To my surprise, I found it pleasant.

*

"Excuse me?"

At the entrance to the village, where I welcomed her, Noura stared at me, taken aback.

Thinking she was joking, I remained standing there, smiling, in front of her. Without showing the slightest emotion, she opened her eyes wide. "Who are you?"

"Noura, we met two days ago!"

"We did?"

Had she forgotten the moment we'd become acquainted, near the Linden Tree of Justice? Suddenly I wasn't sure.

"Yes, we did! . . . You know . . . I'm the man who . . . that is, the man to whom . . ."

After all, I wasn't going to recite the sentence she'd addressed to me—"Don't look at me like that; I'll get pregnant." An embarrassing memory.

"To whom?" she repeated, encouraging me as if she were talking to a moron.

I took a deep breath and cried, "I'm Noam, son of Pannoam, the village chief."

Her face lit up.

"Noam! What a pleasure to see you again!"

Transformed, she seemed delighted, and slipping one arm

under my elbow, she continued on her way, leaning on my arm familiarly.

"What a relief that we're settling here! Everywhere else was all country bumpkins! Dreadful . . . down and out, ugly, lame. I didn't have to persuade Papa, who usually has such a hard time making up his mind; this time, he agreed with me. We really escaped the worst!"

She spoke enough for both of us in a monologue that was charming, effervescent, tumbling, as varied as a nightingale's song.

The way she'd received me had rendered me speechless. What? She didn't remember me, she only recalled the chief's son? My position seemed more enviable than ever before because now it allowed me to capture Noura's attention, to win her respect, to strut about with her on my arm. This contact, no matter how tenuous, made me tremble, especially when her fingers lightly touched my hair.

I assented to everything she said. Once again, she'd made me act like an idiot, but a happy idiot. Better yet: forgetting that I was walking through my own village, I felt privileged to be promenading through it in her company. A goddess had pulled me out of the mire and raised me to her level. Noura had the ability to invert positions.

"How soft your skin is . . ." she cried.

Stopping, she contemplated the violet-colored, dense, vigorous veins that snaked toward my wrist. With her index finger, she traced one of them. I shivered. Noura paralyzed me: no woman had ever behaved that way with me; I became a desirable piece of meat.

Aware that I was flustered, she waited a few seconds, then continued walking as if nothing had happened. As we moved past the potter, I stopped listening to her babble, trying to recover my composure by taking deep breaths.

I showed her the new house that my father was offering them. She was delighted by every detail—the proper fit of the stones, the weaving of the wicker ceiling, the attic that served as a granary, and the sophistication of the cob, which looked like a single smooth substance rather than the mixture of clay, straw, and horsehair it was.

When Tibor arrived, loaded with sacks and accompanied by a donkey collapsing under the weight of his bundles, Noura shouted, as if she were just discovering the situation, "Oh, Papa, let me help you."

With a peremptory gesture, she ordered me to seize two large bags that her father was carrying on his back, and then she grabbed a flask.

"There, that's better . . ."

Tibor's dark, ample cloak, which had multiple pockets, made it seem that he was hauling a stocky body around, but in reality, he was thin and wiry. With his majestic, ebony-colored beard and hair shot through with white, he had an emaciated face with a prominent forehead, structured around a sharp, hollowed, turned-up nose and, more dramatically, around gray, shadowed eyes that lavished a fervent consideration on their object. His hands attracted attention; large, slender, strong, and with clean nails, they were as intelligent as his face.

Like his daughter, Tibor was bubbling with contradictory forces, lively and weary, passionate and casual, curious and blasé. Unlike Noura, one mood was dominant: a morose nostalgia. One part of his mind lived in the past, ruminating on his loss; this could be discerned in his pupil, fixed on a distant point, or in a gesture he left incomplete or a sentence he didn't finish. Was this sadness part of his temperament, or did it derive from the recent tragedy, the death of his wife and sons?

I thought the numerous bundles contained the tools that Tibor used to care for people, but I discovered that what he had saved after the mudslide occupied only a single canvas bag, whereas the others were full of robes, scarves, and shoes.

"Did your clothing survive the mud?" I exclaimed in good faith.

"No," Tibor replied, "we lost everything. These are the new clothes I bought for Noura during our journey."

I looked surprised. He lowered his eyelids. At that time, an upper-class woman like Mama had five outfits, in accord with the seasons or occasions, no more and no less. Tibor seemed not only to tolerate his daughter's eccentricity, but even to promote it. Did it distract him from his grief?

He took a piece of black rock out of a pocket, went up to the house, studied the wall, felt it, then took a stone out of it with the help of a flint chisel; then he wedged his rock in the hole he'd made.

"What are you doing?" I asked.

"I'm inserting a thunder stone."

"A what?"

"A thunder stone. The thunder stone has been hit by lightning and captured its powers. Spirits live in it. It warms and protects, like fire. For example, when your back hurts, you apply it to your lower back, and the pain is alleviated. Here I'm embedding it in the wall to safeguard the house."

"How can you be sure that lightning has struck your stone?"

"I found it one day at the foot of a rocky needle that had been shattered by lightning during the night."

From that day on, I acquired the habit, as my father had commanded, of visiting Tibor and his daughter daily to ensure that they had everything they needed.

Noura displayed a different mood every day, and then changed again. When I crossed her threshold, I could never guess what would happen. Sometimes she ran toward me, radiant, proposing that we take a walk; sometimes she greeted me like an old homebody who wanted me to taste her cooking, or indeed stuff myself on it; sometimes, she made a face indicating that I was bothering her; sometimes, absent, prostrated, lost in her internal depths, she didn't even deign to look up.

She constantly changed her outfits—robes or tunics made of

fine nettle cloth, which proved to be softer and more flexible than hemp, either bleached or dyed red and decorated by their wearer with embroidery or even colored stones and shells—and I quickly understood that it was not enough to notice them, I had to talk to her about them. She took pleasure in my commentaries, which were always flattering, and then, a few seconds later, she said, a touch of pity in her tone: "Poor Noam, you don't know anything about it."

I looked at Tibor, seeking support. Once again, she added, "He doesn't know anything about it, either. Men don't know anything about it!"

She laughed. One morning, I dared to question her: "And women?"

"Women don't know, either. Have you met any elegant women in the village? Apart from your mother, of course."

She guffawed again. I frowned.

"Noura, explain to me: if you don't dress for either women or men, who do you do it for?"

"For myself!" she retorted, scandalized that I hadn't perceived that obvious fact.

Her line of argument unsettled me. In our community, no one acted for themselves alone. What planet did she come from?

Noura was often ill. Not seriously, not always with the same complaint, but often. Then she received me stretched out on cushions, spoke in a lackluster voice, and moved slowly, insinuating that I might be seeing her for the last time. How could someone who seemed to have such a perfect, healthy constitution accumulate all these symptoms? One day her temples were hot, another her stomach was sluggish, another her joints hurt, another she had a scratchy throat, another her ears were buzzing, another her eye was swollen, another her mouth was dry . . . I would never have imagined that a body could present so many problems, and still less that a single person could suffer from them all successively.

At that time, Tibor was prospecting the territory, looking

for medicinal plants, and he proposed that I accompany him. I agreed, eagerly, because I wanted to use these remedies to relieve Noura's discomfort.

While we were walking about, Tibor pointed out an unheard-of dimension of Nature that turned out to be much richer and more complex than I imagined. Before, I knew that the spirits reigned—the Spirit of the Lake, the Spirit of the Stream, the Spirit of the Wind, the Spirit of the Storm—but had not moved beyond an embryonic understanding. An eminent wise man, a subtle magician, and a skilled interpreter of spiritual powers, Tibor taught me that spirits were hidden in every tree, every stone, every plant, and that they would help us if we understood them. He taught me how to decipher the universe.

"Take this linden tree, Noam, the Linden Tree of Justice under which your father governs the village. Very active spirits live in its bark. Have you noticed that people grow calmer when they approach it? They feel the spirits' influence. The spirits that live in the hollow of the trunk let a little of their power escape into the air, of course, and more into the leaves and flowers. Look at this linden leaf: what shape does it have?"

"The shape of a heart."

"Precisely! That is why it calms. When you brew these leaves, you obtain a liquid that comforts you, even makes you sleepy, like a lullaby sung at bedtime. And now look at the flower. Can you spot the mark of the spirits? What do they inspire in you?"

"Uh . . ."

"To what would you compare this flower?"

"So tiny . . . you might say . . . no, it's stupid . . . you might say a tuft of hair . . . nose hair!"

Holding it up to my nose, I sneezed. Tibor's eyes sparkled. This austere man smiled at me as soon as I took an interest in the mysteries.

"Bravo! You've grasped the essential point! It looks like a ball of little hairs, like the ones in our nose. Just think that a brew of these flowers combats the flow of liquid that troubles us so much and irritates our nostrils in winter."

"No!"

"Yes. My grandfather and my father proved it. I will prove it to you by giving Noura an infusion."

I was amazed by the horizons he opened up to me.

"So the spirits not only have powers, but also provide clues?"

"You've figured it all out, Noam. A healer is a spiritual tracker. He sets out in search of prints, and his art is keen observation."

"With his eyes?"

"With his eyes, nose, taste buds, ears, fingers. With his imagination, too."

"His imagination?"

"Yes."

"Observe with his imagination?"

"The imagination is the language the spirits use to address us."

To initiate me into the necessary powers of the imagination, Tibor interrupted our peregrinations, had us sit in the shade of an oak tree, and forced me to daydream.

"Nothing is more productive than daydreaming if you want to understand the world. But be careful! Don't sleep—stay awake! Don't dream—daydream!"

"How?"

"Stop thinking about things in terms of their usefulness, forget what serves you, what you eat, what shelters you. Contemplate."

"Not so easy."

"Detach yourself from your needs, your desires, your expectations. Stop reasoning. Rid yourself of your relationship to the world. Breathe slowly, deeply. Let yourself in."

At first, I was so annoyed by my failures that he advised me to consult the intercessors.

"The intercessors?"

"Beings that will allow you to leave yourself behind, to enter the land of daydreams and join the spirits."

"For example?"

"Fire. Water."

One evening, he showed me that by staring at a flame that flickered, flared up, died down, became slimmer, fled toward the moon, returned to lick the log, wrapped the wood in its reddish curls, crackled with sparks, hid in the embers and then exploded in an impetuous wall of fire, I ended up, fascinated, becoming the flame's prey; I no longer thought by myself, I thought through it, or rather it made me think.

"There. The spirits express themselves."

The next day, he subjected me to the same experiment with water.

"Moving water is a liquid flame."

Fixing my eyes on a mountain stream, its foam, its constant shimmering, I was able to feel the energy of its source, to sense the dance of aerial spirits above its waters.

"Tibor . . . I'm losing control . . ."

"So long as you control things, you'll see only what you want to see, understand only what you say. On the other hand, if you let yourself go, open up to whatever comes, the spirits will appear."

Tibor used hypnosis through the elements—flickering fire, flowing water, the wind in the trees—to reach a state of day-dreaming; once he'd entered this territory, he embraced the true texture of the world, its organization, its connections, the poem the spirits have been writing since time immemorial and that we wretched humans do not perceive.

"We're blind to the world because we've blinded ourselves. We're deaf to the world because we've deafened ourselves. Daydreaming saves us by taking us back to the world."

"What am I going to find?"

"Truth is in the interstices. In what lacks clarity, sharpness, logic. In suggestion, images, discrepancies. It was by daydreaming that I unearthed the medicine I'm most proud of."

Tibor took a carved wooden box from one of his pockets, opened it, and showed me an off-white powder.

"It reduces fever, absorbs headaches, alleviates bodily pains, soothes joints. Remember, we gave some to Noura last week. She was disappointed to be cured so fast; she would have liked to take advantage of her condition all day."

I laughed; the distance Tibor took with regard to his daughter relieved me. I had no such distance.

As for the powder, I recalled it all the better because that evening I had taken it to my mother, who often had headaches and who had quickly recovered.

Tibor told me how he had discovered it.

"One day of golden sun, I was sitting idly on the lakeshore, leaning against a willow, that strange tree that grows alone, avoiding forests and choosing Nature's empty places, the stagnant arms of rivers, the shores of a marsh, damp embankments. I'd eaten too much. Receptively, I entered a daydream and the spirits called out to me. "We live under deep in the trunk, under the ash-colored bark, the only place where the willow doesn't weep." In fact, the branches were weeping; they were soft, drooping; the leaves wept delicate silvery tears; the willow was pouring its sorrow into the Lake, except for the trunk, which stood upright, strong, robust. The spirits went on: "Our powers reside there. The trunk does not suffer and keeps the tree from falling." I scraped off some willow bark, and when I got home, I made this powder, an extract of white willow. It's very bitter, but that doesn't matter: used in an appropriate quantity—I struggled to find it—it soothes supremely. The spirits had told me that within the weeping willow there was a substance that kept people from crying.*

---

* I have used and shared Tibor's powder for many thousands of years. During the Middle Ages, physicians stopped using it, probably because of the violent stomach aches that it sometimes caused. Finding myself in England around 1750, I suffered an unfortunate accident: the carriage that was taking me to Chipping Norton bogged down, and the travelers had to wait along the roadside. One of them, plump and afflicted with rosacea, told me about his problems. Fevers were spreading through

With Tibor, hiking trails, crossing fields, and plunging into forests became fascinating: I learned to experience Nature and to dream it, both with my eyes open and with my eyes closed. We discover as much outside the self as we do inside it; the spirits are in everything.

Thanks to our soakings, our extractions, and our brews, Noura recovered. Some days, she accompanied us. At first, I believed that she was developing an interest in her father's activities, but she focused on the soil, the flowers, the herbs, and the barks for a different reason: she was looking for smells, with the intention of making perfumes.

This disappointed Tibor, who would have preferred that she

---

the English countryside, laying low children, women, and even the heartiest men. This clergyman, who was both intelligent and experienced, as much a scientist as a practician, was passionately seeking to improve the lives of his contemporaries. He reasoned in accord with the theory of signatures, which teaches that the remedy of an illness is never far from its causes. Since he was telling me about his suffering, his failures, and his despair while we were on a road adjacent to a pond, I was tempted to help him, and pointed to the willow grove in front of us. "Since febrile affections thrive in damp or marshy places, the solution must be hidden there, Reverend. Which plant easily survives in these conditions?" He looked where I was pointing and contemplated the weeping willows. I led him to a specimen, inserted my finger into one of the tiny holes that perforated the trunk, and then sucked it. "Perhaps this bitter substance in the bark protects the tree from diseases it might catch from having its feet in cold water?" In turn, the clergyman slipped his little finger under the bark, tasted it, took some leaves and chewed them, grimacing: "Why not? The bitterness reminds me of the Jesuits' powder, that herb from Peru that alleviates swamp fevers. Here it can be procured only as contraband—the Jesuits and the Anglicans don't get along well . . . Thank you, my friend, I'm going to find out where this path leads." On 25 April 1763, Edward Stone presented to Count Macclesfield, the president of the Royal Society of Medicine, a report on his successful treatment of fevers with willow bark, dried in a bag set near a baker's oven, pulverized, and then administered to fifty patients. Later, an Italian pharmacist isolated the active principle contained in the bark, "salicin," and then a French pharmacist used it to produce soluble crystals he called "salicyline." Finally, in 1899, in Rhenish Prussia, Felix Hoffman, a chemist who wanted to treat his father, who suffered from rheumatism but could not digest this medicine, succeeded in synthesizing pure acetylsalicylic acid. Bayer, the dyestuffs laboratory where he worked, did not take out a patent—the French had already done that—but instead marketed the substance worldwide under a new trade name: aspirin. Bayer thus became a giant of the pharmaceutical industry; until 1919, it remained the world's only distributor of aspirin.

join him in finding the curative properties of plants. I pretended to share her interest, in order to create a complicity between us.

Alas, she asked my advice only to humiliate me. As on the topic of clothes, she declared that I knew nothing about the subject, and that I would take the smell of a polecat for honeysuckle. Although that was false, I didn't protest; if you tried to show Noura that she was mistaken, she flew into a devastating rage, fell ill, and, for a week, more closed in on herself than a hedgehog, showed nothing but cold indifference.

Nonetheless. The arrival of these two foreigners excited me. I'd never had so much fun as I had in their company, even if Noura often shunned me, even if Tibor sometimes disappeared right in front of me, melting, his eyes wild, his skin livid, chewing on a plant—a powerful intercessor—that he refused to share with me.

In the evening, I saw Mina, who was feeling better since we had begun making love again. Though she still wasn't pregnant, I sensed, by the way she looked at me, by the shiver with which she received me, that her whole body was hungry to be with child.

Every night, after dinner, we retired and shut the door. Once we had completed our copulation, she collapsed on her back, out of breath, and gazed at me with gratitude. I stretched out on my side, facing her, enjoying the animal pleasure of sharing our mat. Then Mina looked up at the ceiling and began mechanically twirling her hair around her fingers in a gesture dating from her childhood. I fell asleep wondering whether Noura, after sleeping with a man, would do something so girlish.

Certainly not . . .

*

"Why don't you ever smile?"

Noura radiated light and attracted people's eyes, but unlike other women, she never crinkled her eyes or opened her lips.

"I'd smile if I were ugly."

At first, I found her curt reply shocking, before I discovered, in the course of the following days, that she was right: some faces need a smile to shine—but the most beautiful ones do not. Mina smiled a lot to harmonize her features, to make them comely. Noura just had to appear.

My father, on the other hand, was becoming depressed. His battles with the pillaging Hunters were increasing in frequency and in animosity—three soldiers had been killed, an old man beaten up, women and children wounded, five granaries destroyed, an aurochs dismembered, sheep and goats stolen.

"These attacks will grow more intense this winter, when the Hunters run short of food. Our reputation does us a disservice: the plunderers come directly here, because they know we've stored up supplies."

My father's worries turned out to be proportional to our opulence. One morning, sitting under the Linden Tree of Justice, he let his anger show clearly. "The more we succeed, the more we're targets. I need to take a number of men out of the fields and train them to fight."

He smacked his head and looked at the Lake.

"And yet, if the problem could be reduced to that . . ."

He fell silent. I moved closer to him.

"What? What else is there?"

"Nothing."

I put my hand on his, and when our skin touched, I felt that he was tense, cold.

"Father, I don't understand: everything is going well, you're arming us against the impending dangers, and yet you seem anxious."

He stared at me, pensive.

"I hesitate to discuss it with you, Noam."

"Tell me."

"My role as chief requires me to take on our worries."

"Someday, your son will be the head of this village."

He relaxed.

"Get ready. We're going to travel. I want to see if my fear is justified before I tell you about it."

When I told Tibor that we would be taking a trip, he asked me if he could join the convoy: that would allow him to gather unknown herbs, flowers, and fruits. I interceded on his behalf with my father, who acquiesced.

During the days preceding our departure, Pannoam organized the expedition by going to see Dandar, his foster brother. Dandar had helped the village emerge by working as a potter, and he was now taking advantage of his success. Every year, he enlarged his workshop, invented new tools, and built additions to his house; flanked by three wives and fifteen children, he needed space and prosperity . . . His sons worked alongside him, one kneading clay, another supplying water, another making pieces of pottery, others attending to the fire, the wood, and the painting. They produced several terra cotta plates, pots, and amphoras every day.

In the past, Dandar had had to travel to find suitable clay, and this made him a well-informed man. He explained to my father how to reach Sculptors' Cliff, the place that interested him.

"Why there?" I asked Dandar one evening, when my father was talking with his sons.

"I haven't the faintest idea. Your father wants to go to Sculptors' Cliff but won't tell me anything else."

I liked to meet Pannoam at Dandar's house, because in addition to his customers, the potter's three wives and fifteen children were always passing through, talking from morning to evening and creating a constant hustle and bustle.

That evening, my father came out looking happy but tired. He raised his eyebrows and sighed: "I'd grow deaf if I had three wives!"

"Dandar doesn't seem unhappy."

"He isn't. He likes movement all around him, and he's got it!"

"Three wives . . ."

"Families with several wives rarely work smoothly. Here, the harmony comes from the fact that they're sisters. He married the eldest. The youngest married his brother, but when the latter died in a brawl with the Hunters, Dandar, out of loyalty to his brother and for the sake of his nephews' future, married her. Finally, when the third sister reached maturity, the other two advised her to marry the man. Rightly so."

"Don't they stab each other in the back out of jealousy?"

"Do you know any sisters who manage to escape jealousy?"

We burst out laughing, thinking about my sisters and their bickering. Pannoam scratched his ear.

"As they grew up, those three sisters were sheltered from rivalry, something your mother and I were incapable of doing . . . Dandar's three wives like their husband, and all three of them like each other. An exceptional case of harmony."

"Father, haven't you ever thought of taking a second wife?"

My father stopped, reflected, looked at the Lake, hesitated, and then turned to me with amusement in his eyes.

"Have you seen how your mother gives me hell when I pet a dog? Just imagine the cataclysm if I petted a woman . . ."

We chuckled for a long time.

The morning of our departure, I went to Tibor's house to pick him up. He'd doubled in volume by stuffing the pockets of his cloak. Noura, very pale, her lips mauve and her nostrils pinched, accompanied her father as far as the door, kissed him, and then approached me.

"Bring my papa back. I'm counting on you."

I was stunned that she showed me so much esteem.

"Trust me, Noura. I'll get myself killed before I let anyone touch Tibor."

"Thanks. And I'd prefer that you come back alive, too."

A tear welled up in her eyes. She hurried back into the house and, from a distance, waved good-bye to us.

Pannoam had gathered his pack of hounds, as well as a squadron of ten men—three porters, seven warriors. On the way, I asked my father why he had brought along such a crew. Growing somber, he replied: "I'm trying to compensate for the mistake we're making, Noam."

"What mistake?"

"Traveling together. The current chief and the future chief are traveling side by side, at the mercy of the Hunters. If we were killed in an attack, the village would lose its leaders."

At night, we slept outside, in places my father had chosen carefully, protective but open clearings with multiple escape routes, gaps where assailants could not corner us. The warriors took turns guarding our bivouac, and the dogs remained on alert.

For the moment, the only enemies we encountered were the mosquitos that buzzed near the Lake, in the curtain of reeds, but every night Tibor spread a plant around us that drove them away.

When I rubbed these crinkly little oval leaves, I noticed that they emitted a fresh, yellow smell.

"The fragrance repels mosquitos," Tibor told me.

"But it smells good."

"Not to a mosquito."

"How did you discover that?"

"Bees love it. If you rub it on a branch, you can even persuade them to establish their hive on it. One day when I was daydreaming, I heard the spirits' logic: 'What we intended for the bee, we didn't intend for the mosquito.' Since the spirits had reserved these leaves and these flowers for the honey-makers, it was plausible that they placed on them a repellent for blood-suckers. I just had to verify it."

In the morning, he and I collected the bee-herb* placed around our camp and put these precious leaves in a bag, so that we could take them out again in the evening. To the members of our group who were bitten despite these precautions, Tibor applied extracts of myrtle, which, by drying out the skin, relieved irritation.

After a week of traveling, we saw our goal before us: Sculptors' Cliff. As we approached it, Pannoam explained why this place was so unusual. There, it was all rock. The waters of the Lake washed gigantic brown rocks that extended far beyond it and allowed no flower, no grass, no tree to grow, for lack of humus. The mineral had won out. Stone had rejected life.

"Humans used to live here. They settled in caves, of which there remain a few traces along the path they carved out of the rock. That is why this place is called Sculptors' Cliff. But no one lives here now."

When we reached it, we saw that Pannoam's information was correct. Between the clefts, bluffs, and promontories, our ancestors had cut a path wide enough for a pilgrim and a donkey, bordered by precipices on one side and rock walls on the other. Terrified, I imagined the difficulty of the project. Even if the path followed the twists and turns of the rock, how many months or years had it taken? How many workers had broken the stones with other stones? Where had they found the various resources that the undertaking required, the stubbornness and the patience?

We stopped to eat along this arid shore. The air was so pure that it seemed to have disappeared, deprived of density to the point that I was astonished to see at the zenith a bird of prey spreading its wings in threatening flight. When the porters and warriors began a nap, I asked my father, "Have we walked a whole week for this?"

* Lemon balm or citronella, a kind of geranium

"Yes."

"What are you worrying about?"

I turned to Tibor, who gave me his approval with a doubtful look.

Pannoam stood up.

"I need confirmation. For the moment, I'm relying on travelers' stories whose elements I'm trying to connect, but either the travelers were mistaken or they were boasting."

He signaled that we should follow him. The path, paved with loose pebbles, forced us to watch where we put our feet; sometimes it went around projecting rocks, sometimes it slipped into narrow crevices. Finally, the stone masses became farther apart, and we reached the shore of the Lake.

"Did you note the place where the path meets the Lake?"

We bent over the crystalline water, which allowed us to see the continuation of the path.

"Look, it goes on."

Pannoam entered the water and gradually moved downward.

"Steps!"

The first steps remained visible, but the following ones disappeared in the obscurity of the Lake. Pannoam went as deep as he could, and when his head went under, we helped him get out.

"Isn't it strange that they dug stairs under water?"

"Completely stupid," I exclaimed. "Apart from the fact that they're useless, what a technical challenge!"

"I agree with you, Noam! Why did our ancestors undertake work that was so difficult and devoid of interest?"

"Morons . . ."

Pannoam looked at me without hiding his disappointment. "People who call those they don't understand morons are merely showing their own stupidity."

I tried not to take offense.

He pointed to the shore that we could see in the distance,

beyond the tranquil surface of the water, tinted pink by the setting sun.

"The next clue is located over there. It will take five days to reach it."

According to his information, we were on a finger of the Lake; if we continued to walk along its shore, we would end up on the other side.

I said I was sorry we weren't using dugout canoes.

"What difference would that make?" Tibor said. "Canoes stay close to the shore and don't move any faster than a walker."

"Canoes could take us straight over there."

"Absolutely not! The poles have to touch the bottom, so they become ineffective in the middle of the Lake. If the Lake could be crossed, intruders would land on our territory. No more safety! We'd have to monitor both the land and the water. Danger doesn't usually come from the water."

Pannoam looked at him at length, then sighed, echoing him: "Usually . . ."

Fear twisted his face. What was he thinking about?

After five boring days of walking—over rocks, brambles, dirt, then brambles again—we came to a hill that was completely without greenery and that rose up across from the one we'd gone over.

"Let's find the path."

"What path?"

"Not the one along the water, but the sculpted one that comes out of it."

Pannoam had hardly said that before Tibor cried, "There! There!"

We ran toward him. He had spotted the excavated path that descended from the heights above and ended at the Lake.

My father didn't hesitate. Despite the difficulty of reaching the water, he leaped into the dark blue liquid and then, proceeding carefully, sought to find steps cut into the rock.

"I feel them! Like a stairway!"

"Extraordinary!" Tibor murmured excitedly. "Just like the ones on the other side!"

"What?" I said. "Did other ancestors make these here? Why?"

Pannoam raised his head and looked at me.

"Above all, *how*? You can't cut stone under water, especially when you can't see what you're doing. The stairway continues below me—and I'm tall."

We helped him climb out of the water. He sank down on a little mound.

"What I feared is happening."

"Come now, Father! There's nothing to worry about. They were just as crazy on this side of the Lake as they were on the other side."

Pannoam looked down at the ground and said, his jaw clenched, "First of all, they weren't crazy. And secondly, they weren't different from the people on the other side: they were the same ones."

"Excuse me?"

"There were no shores."

"Excuse me?"

"There was no lake."

"Excuse me?"

Pannoam stood up and became grave. "The path cut in the rock started over there, at a distance of several days' walk, and ended here. A single trail had been cleared in the open air. People walked it on dry land. There was no lake, just a rocky valley. Water covered the passageway. The process that many of us deny and that we think began recently actually began a very long time ago . . . What we see is not its beginning, but its continuation."

"What, father?"

"The water is rising."

He blinked and tried to catch his breath. I was afraid he might collapse, but he remained standing, confronting the possibility of

a boundless lake. He murmured, "If the water doesn't stop rising, how far will it go?"

Suddenly, I shared my father's anxiety.

*

On our return, the villagers received us as heroes. Children
galloped toward us, women ululated, men beat out rhythms with
their tools. They all formed an honor guard and then stamped
their feet and bowed down before us all the way to Pannoam's
house.

What had we done that was so extraordinary? My father and I
had come back with an enigma, Tibor with three sacks of herbs:
nothing spectacular that might have immediate consequences . . .

The villagers had been attacked several times by Hunters,
both singly and in groups; weakened and fearful, they were glad
that seven soldiers were returning to their posts and that their
chief was resuming his position. Just seeing him reassured them.
Pannoam incarnated the success, courage, and solidity of our
community; his absence had greatly alarmed them. As I walked
behind my father at the head of our procession, I had to admit
that succeeding him some day would be a perilous challenge.

Mina welcomed me back with pleasure, hugged me, brought
me the refined dishes she had prepared, buns filled with hazelnuts cooked on a hot stone, a wild rose compote. I recounted a
few episodes from our trip to her, and she listened without saying a word; she nodded her head, hardly following, hoping that
we would crawl over to the mat to try, once again, to conceive
children. I agreed to this all the more willingly because I had
endured three weeks of involuntary chastity.

What a contrast with Noura the next day! She reacted to everything, demanded details, argued in a loud voice, peppered
me with questions, returned to one point, challenged another,
and even forced me to confide information that was supposed to

remain confidential! With Mina, my account of our trip had produced a brief, short-winded monologue punctuated by a hand that offered me more to drink or eat; with Noura, it unleashed an eruptive, passionate dialogue that lasted all day and left us, in the evening, delighted, our minds on fire.

Dare I admit it? I dragged my feet on the way home. I imagined what awaited me—Mina, her docility, her clay-colored eyes, her soft lethargy, the ritual that bored me to tears. If my expedition had already enlightened me regarding the dullness of our married life, our reunion only accentuated my unease.

I hurried off to tell my father that I needed to talk to him immediately.

"Here?"

"It doesn't matter, Father. Some place where there will only be you and me."

By reflex, he took me to the Linden Tree of Justice. All around, the hills, blackened by the night, seemed like animals lurking, ready to spring on us. A dark, vaporous blue covered the Lake, on which tortuous clouds weighed. Piercing the silence, an owl hooted in the distance.

I came straight to the point.

"Father, I want to take Tibor's daughter as a second wife."

He opened his eyes wide. Obsessed by the rising waters, he hadn't suspected that I would want to talk about domestic problems. He looked me up and down condescendingly, as if, like a parasite, I was distracting him from the essential point.

"Why do you want a second wife?"

"You know why, Father."

"I do?"

"Even if you avoid the subject."

"What subject?"

"Mina isn't giving me any children."

My father's hostility disappeared. His shoulders relaxed, he relaxed. I'd touched a sore point.

"You never reproach me for that, Father, and I'm grateful to you. But Mama doesn't show the same restraint. She detests Mina."

"I know."

"She has good reasons for holding her in contempt: Mina doesn't seem able to ensure the continuation of our family. What good will it do, Father, for me to learn from your experience if I don't transmit it in my turn? What is the point of ruling, you and I, as deserving chiefs if our family line dies out tomorrow? If it was a spirit, would our village approve of you?"

Pannoam retreated into himself. I suspected that my father had ruminated on these questions at length. After a long time, he ventured to ask, "Are you and Mina doing what you have to?"

"Every night."

"Well . . ."

"Mina gets pregnant; I do my duty. But her children aren't healthy."

I didn't regret saying "her children" instead of "our children," so convinced was I that their deficiency came from Mina. My father laid his hand on my knee.

"I feel guilty, Noam. I made a poor choice. I didn't go beyond the fact that her father was the head of the third village in the direction of the setting sun; I didn't check the vigor of their blood. I thought like a chief, and not enough like a father."

"Your reasoning remains excellent. I'm not proposing to repudiate Mina, only to marry a second wife, one who will perpetuate our family and offer you strong grandchildren."

"Why Tibor's daughter?"

I remained silent; I didn't know where to begin—Noura had countless admirable qualities. While ideas passed through my mind, my father continued: "Not a bad choice . . . A healer plays an important role in a community. Through this marriage, we would increase our chances of keeping him here. Tibor seems very attached to his daughter, doesn't he?"

"He adores her."

"Perfect."

Thinking that he approved of my desire, I stood up, my knees trembling.

"Do you agree, then?"

With an imperious gesture, Pannoam ordered me to sit down.

"I'll tell you in a few days, Noam."

"What?"

"I have to think about it."

"Think about what?"

"In Mina's case, I acted in haste. I won't make the same mistake this time."

"But . . ."

"And then, I dread households with several wives."

"Your foster brother . . ."

"Don't cite the example of Dandar to me; I consider him an exception. Rendering justice under the linden hasn't left me with a high opinion of households with several wives, far from it! Either the women wage war on the man, or the man mistreats them, or the women fight among themselves, or they fight through their children. A viper's nest seems more tranquil to me."

"But . . ."

"No! Don't exhaust your tongue, and don't fatigue my ears. In a few days, you'll have my decision."

He was ordering me to be silent. I obeyed. Feeling impatient, I tried to think of a way to accelerate his judgment.

"Do you want to meet her, Father?"

"Who?"

"Noura."

I was sure that when he got to know her, noticing her grace, her lively intelligence, her elegance, he would conclude that my proposition was a good one!

"Noura?"

"Tibor's daughter."

I shivered. I'd never suspected that he'd paid so little attention to the girl . . . What kind of man was he? Seeing Noura once was enough to remember her, and even to be crazy about her!

Standing up, he examined me with a touch of pity.

"No need. That doesn't enter into my consideration. I'll let you know my decision soon."

Without saying another word, he returned home.

That evening, lying on our conjugal mat, I succeeded in pushing Mina away, but visions of Noura in my new life prevented me from sleeping, arousing joy one moment and sadness the next, because I didn't know if I would benefit from them. Pleasure followed pain, pain followed pleasure; I was swarming with contradictory ideas.

It seemed that dawn would never come . . .

As soon as I got up, I fluctuated. On the one hand, I wanted to race off to Noura's house and tell her that I had asked permission to marry her; on the other, I controlled myself. First of all, I had to inform Tibor, since marriages were subject to the authority of parents. And if Pannoam refused, Noura, who was capable of being cruel, would see me as a fool; I'd seem ridiculous, a boy rather than a man, and I'd lose her respect. For the first time, paternal power hampered me, the loyal son who venerated his father.

Consequently, I avoided Noura, saying that I had work to do in the fields.

To make my deception more plausible, I went to our lands and made a show of splitting some firewood. When the sun started to go down, I caught sight of Tibor and his daughter walking on a nearby path. They waved to me. Without hesitating, I hurried toward them, axe in hand.

They greeted me warmly. Both eagerly displayed their harvest, Tibor bragging about a red fern he hadn't yet studied, Noura about yellow apples whose aroma she found intoxicating. She was radiant.

When Tibor moved about ten paces away to dig up a mushroom he'd spotted under an oak tree, I confided in Noura.

"I spoke to my father yesterday."

She laughed.

"How do you do that, usually? Do you whinny? Bark? Bleat?"

"Don't make fun of me, Noura. I spoke to him about you."

She stopped laughing.

"About me?"

"Yes."

She peered at me, tense and attentive.

"What did you say to him?"

"I . . ."

"Yes?"

I was on the point of telling her when a cry rang out, a heart-rending cry.

Someone was being attacked. Dogs started barking, furious, impetuous, violent. A fierce fight was taking place behind the curtain of trees.

I trembled. I'd guessed what was happening.

Brandishing my axe, I raced toward the noise.

When I burst into the clearing, I saw, in the distance, my father on the ground, surrounded by his dogs, who were defending him against five Hunters armed with clubs who had come to steal our sheep.

The Hunters were killing the dogs one by one and were about to finish off my father.

"Help!" I shouted. "Help!"

I ran toward the battle as fast as I could. Peasants rushed toward us, carrying digging sticks, hoes, and cudgels, but given the distance we still had to cover, none of us was going to get there in time.

Although I was running flat out, I saw every detail of the horrible scene.

The Hunters, leaping over the bodies of the dead dogs, were nearing my father, lying wounded and bloody on the ground and wielding a spear to protect himself. One of the Hunters raised his weapon to kill him.

"No!" I screamed.

The club was about to fall on my father when a figure suddenly appeared, shoved the Hunter aside and, with one blow of his axe, cut off his head. The four other Hunters spun around and saw a giant. By reflex, they positioned themselves to face him. But they had hardly budged before the colossus cut them down.

Five cadavers!

Five cadavers in five lightning blows . . .

The giant saw that we were climbing toward him and, without hesitation, strode rapidly away.

Out of breath, I was the first to get there and rushed to my father, who was lying in a pool of blood among his enemies and the motionless dogs, their heads crushed. His eyes were glassy, and he was holding his knee as he groaned with pain, panting, unable to speak, isolated in his suffering. I was bending over him when Mama, short of breath, horrified, her blouse gaping open, leapt to my side and threw herself on the ground.

"Pannoam!"

She looked down and screamed: the Hunter's blow, deflected by the giant, had smashed my father's foot and fractured his shinbone. The Hunters had dislocated his leg.

My father closed his eyes. His head rolled on the ground. He heaved a great sigh.

Mama shook him.

"He's dead . . ."

I thought I was going to faint. Only my bewilderment prevented me from staggering.

The villagers surrounded us, breathing heavily. Tibor crouched down, felt my father's wrist, sniffed, and plastered one ear against his chest.

"He's not dead."

Mama struggled to form words: "But he's going to die?"

"From his loss of blood, or from the infection of his wound."

Mama repeated, over and over, "Pannoam is going to die!"

Tibor grabbed her hand.

"Unless I operate on him."

"What?"

"Will you allow me to operate on him?"

"Yes."

Tibor turned to me.

"What about you, Noam?"

I answered as my mother had. Swiftly, Tibor tore off one of his large pockets, tied the fabric tightly around the edge of Pannoam's knee to stop the flow of blood, and then looked for Noura. Standing over the body, her face as pale as marble, she was staring at her father. He told her, "We're going to cut off his leg."

Raising my head, I seemed to glimpse, on the top of the hill, the giant's silhouette. Who was he? Who had saved my father? Why would a Hunter spare a Sedentary? By what aberration was this solitary giant avoiding everyone, both us and his fellows?

Did he sense my eyes on him? He disappeared.

*

We gently placed the wounded man on a stone table Tibor had installed at the rear of his house. My father was no longer reacting, but he was breathing.

Tibor turned to the villagers who had gathered in the house and around it.

"Pannoam has lost consciousness. As soon as I cut into his skin, the pain will wake him up. I want four men to control him in case he struggles."

My comrades stepped forward.

"Everyone else out!"

I had my sisters take our mother away. The room emptied. Tibor gave my comrades their orders: "Each of you will take one limb. The man holding the wounded leg will immobilize only the thigh, above the break."

They did as they were told.

Tibor took my wrist, led me to a wooden chest, knelt down, and whispered in my ear, "I have a special job for you, Noam. Try to make him drink something you've dissolved this powder in."

He showed me a vial that I recognized.

"The powder you take some evenings? The intercession?"

"Yes."

"The one you forbid me to take?"

"I do that for your own good."

"My own good? And you're asking me to administer it to my father!"

I had raised my voice a notch. He adjured me to whisper.

"Listen to me, Noam. The powder relieves pain, to be sure, but afterward you can no longer get along without it."

"Even with will power?"

"The powder erodes your will. It makes you need to take more of it. You claim to be its master, but in reality, you're entering its service. Don't fall into the trap I've been caught in for years."

"What about my father?"

"One dose, a single dose, won't create a habit. Moreover, I don't have a choice."

"What is it?"

"Hemp."*

He showed me a box containing a brown powder.

"And this is poppy. You put it on a damp cloth and as soon as your father groans, put it over his nose. Without suffocating him. Understood?"

Dripping with sweat, he hurried back to Noura.

"As for you, do you remember? Do the same as your two brothers . . . You hand me the instruments, you hold them in the air without putting them down when I'm not using them. Clear?"

Noura nodded, already concentrated on her task.

---

* Cannabis

I have few memories of the operation, because on many occasions, verging on passing out, I averted my eyes.

As soon as the stone instruments fashioned by Tibor reached flesh and bone, my father regained consciousness. He roared. It took the combined strength of my comrades to keep him pinned to the table. My poppy compresses gave him temporary relief, but Tibor spent so many hours cutting out tendons, severing muscles, polishing the ends of bones and suturing the wound, that my father repeatedly howled in hellish pain. Every time, Mama rushed into the room, panicked, convinced that my father was dying, and every time Noura intervened with her calm authority, calmed Mama down, and made her leave.

When the operation was over, Tibor used herbs and unguents on the skin to control the infection and close up the wounds.

"Finished! Leave him here with me. I can take the edge off his pain."

Exhausted, sweating, my comrades and I left the healer's house.

On the threshold, Noura, her face showing her fatigue but her posture unbent and resolute, brought us something to drink. When she served me, her eyes begged for the rest of my story: what had I said about her to my father?

Not feeling up to the task, I told her I would answer later. She did not insist and returned to help Tibor.

My father recovered consciousness, and Tibor used his pain relievers with moderation—in large doses, the willow bark tore the stomach lining and prevented blood from forming scabs, which hindered healing.

Pannoam lay in Tibor's house for a week. My mother, my sisters, and I visited him every day. Noura no longer left his bedside, showing a patience that dazzled me.

As my father gradually became my father again, tongues loosened. Though worry about their leader had at first left the villagers speechless, now they were talking about the strange giant who had saved him. They questioned one another. No one knew him. However, a few claimed to have already glimpsed him in the distance; elderly people said he had been hanging around in the area for years, or even decades. The mystery encouraged stories: some said that he was the god of the hills who had come to spare a courageous inhabitant; others that he was the spirit of the village, come to save his community; and according to my sisters he was the ghost of Kaddour, our preceding chief and my grandfather, who had come to preserve his family line. People wanted to identify him, but no one set out to track him down, not even me; we convinced ourselves that, being supernatural, he gave up his human appearance when he didn't need to mix with humans.

My father got to know Noura. His eyes sought her when he felt pain, thirst, or hunger, and thanked her as soon as she had met his needs.

"What a shame Noura isn't interested in plants!" Tibor sighed in my presence. "She behaves better with patients than I do. She has the composure, endurance, devotion, and kindness that ensure the medical treatment's success."

One day my father, having recovered from his fever but still in pain, got up.

"I recommend you get an aid," Tibor said.

"I have one already: your daughter."

Noura and I smiled.

"I was thinking of a different kind of aid," Tibor explained. "I've seen it used by a healer in the north. We can cut a stag's shinbone to the length of the half-leg that you lack and attach it to your thigh with leather straps, allowing you to lean on it. You will no longer run, and you won't walk well, but you'll be able to stand without fatigue. What do you think?"

"You've gained my trust, so I'll follow your advice. You saved me."

"Thank you. I'll consult the best stone-cutters for your half-leg. There's no material harder than a stag's shinbone."

My father returned to his house. Tibor suggested that Noura come to the house to change the bandages and clean the wound, and my parents enthusiastically agreed. Although Mama knew how to take care of children, she didn't have Noura's experience. The healer's daughter had been watching for years as her father treated the wounded, and she showed gentleness, constancy, and rigor. I saw with delight that she was winning over my family.

"Father, who was the giant?"

"What giant?"

"The one who killed the Hunters, the one who saved you."

"I'd lost consciousness."

I told him what had happened. He looked away, coldly. "Are you certain?"

"The whole village will confirm it."

"And what are people saying?"

"That it was the god of the hills. Or the spirit of the village."

"Yes, maybe . . ."

"Or Kaddour, your father."

"Why Kaddour?"

"I don't know. It's logical . . . His ghost came down to help you."

"Oh? Logical . . . Nothing else?"

"Uh, no . . ."

My father shrugged his shoulders. Every time I mentioned the giant, he withdrew into a hostile silence. Was it that his pride couldn't tolerate the idea that someone—even a god, a demon, or a spirit—had saved him? When I asked him about it, he replied, cutting, "It was Tibor who saved me."

Then, after a moment, he added, "And his daughter."

I was jubilant. Events had favored my cause. Now that my father was recuperating, my confidence in the future was increasing. When I asked him again if I could take Noura as my second wife, he would agree.

During his convalescence, I was often on the brink of embracing him and exclaiming, "And?" Out of respect, so as not to badger him, I refrained.

One morning, he received the sculpted stag's bone. Tibor strapped it on him below the knee, and he tried to walk on it. Noura patiently supported him, encouraged him, so delicate, so slender alongside him, so frail and yet capable of holding him up when he swayed, of helping him up if he collapsed. Noura bent but didn't break, like a reed in a storm. Seeing this, I felt overwhelmed: the most important woman in my life was helping the most important man in my life. Tears stung my eyes. What luck to know and love these two people! And what happiness that they were fond of each other! The future seemed bright.

As soon as they ended the session, I rejoined them. Noura was giving Pannoam something to drink.

"Father, we have to talk."

"About what?"

"Noura."

She looked up abruptly, as if she'd been stung by an insect.

Pannoam raised his eyes and looked at me calmly.

"You're right, it's time to talk about her. I have made my decision."

I shivered anticipating the wave of happiness that was about to break over me.

"I shall marry Noura," my father announced. "She will become my second wife."

2

The bear was staring at me.

Brown, powerful, massive, muscular, it stood on its hind feet in front of me, twice as tall, three times as broad, four times as heavy, five times smellier. Its shiny nose twitched to identify me. For the moment, it was wondering about me. What would it decide? Enemy? Friend? A single blow from one of its paws would knock me out.

Terrified, my throat on fire, my neck stiff, my back icy, I made myself as small as I could. If only I could have sunk into the ground! The bear's presence crushed me; I could sense its hot, hostile breath, its pulsating power restrained beneath its thick fur. Behind the long snout, its dark eyes held me motionless. Its ears, wideset on the top of its round face, quivered in an attempt to hear the sounds I was making.

Sweating, I held my breath; only the trembling of my limbs showed that I was alive. The bear opened its maw, which was an astonishingly delicate pink in color with hooked canines and powerful molars, and let out a cry that shot through me. Contrary to my expectations, this growl, which was neither ferocious nor threatening, was an expression of boredom; it even had a trace of disappointment.

Scornfully, the bear looked away, let itself drop easily onto all fours, and, as if I no longer existed, continued on its way with a swinging gait, nonchalant and relaxed. Just as it was leaving the clearing and moving beyond the brush, it stopped and looked at me as if asking, "Well, are you coming?"

Its flat, obtuse skull made it clear that there was no room for negotiation: you either obeyed or you died.

So I followed it at a respectful distance.

Now that it was sure I was coming, it pretended to have forgotten me.

When it reached the riverbank, it stopped to drink, wetted its humped neck, shook its nostrils, licked its chops, sneezed, spat, and then became absorbed in contemplating the running water. Suddenly its left paw shot out, penetrated the water, and came out holding in its claws a terrified salmon that wriggled about, its scales shimmering with all the colors of the rainbow. Who would have thought that such a lumbering brute was capable of moving so swiftly? The bear tossed the fish into the air, watched it wriggle, and then caught it in its gaping mouth. It crushed the salmon three times between its jaws and then gulped it down.

Tired, it left the river, followed the path marked by the moss along the bank, and climbed a pile of rocks, where it disappeared.

What to do? I hesitated. At that point, I could get away, taking advantage of the current and swimming as fast as I could.

Slowly, carefully, I climbed the rock pile, as well; when I reached the top, I saw a circular pit in the granite beneath me.

I couldn't believe my eyes . . . A naked woman, slim, trembling, fine-boned, with blond hair falling over her shoulders, back, and breasts, was curled up, held prisoner. The bear moved toward her. She changed. Looking into its eyes, she smiled at it, stretched out on the ground, spread her legs, lifted her arms to take the giant's head in her hands, and brought her lips to its muzzle. They kissed.

The kiss went on, lascivious, penetrated and penetrating, and then the bear, as if it had become weightless, covered the woman's slender limbs, something she not only tolerated but encouraged. They copulated.

As I turned away, disgusted by the sight of them copulating, I heard a dog howling on my right. I spun around to tell it to be quiet, slipped on a stone, lost my balance, and . . . woke up.

Around me was our house.

On my right, outside, a dog was whining.

Within reach, on my left, Mina was asleep.

It was dark everywhere.

I sat up. The bear? What was it teaching me?

Troubled, dumbfounded, I lay down again and thought about the scene, forgetting about sleep.

In those days, we attached great importance to dreams: they represented the hospitality that humans showed for the non-human. Gods, spirits, demons, and the dead appeared to us. If, during the daytime, an impenetrable wall separated them from us, night opened the doors through which spiritual entities slipped. The ears, mouth, eyelids, nostrils—those unguarded interstices opened up, and movement between the external and internal began. Each dream connected us to the world, to Nature, souls, forces. Dreams enlarged us. Where the sun limited us, darkness opened us up to immensity.

During our encounter, the bear had respected me, suggested that I follow it, and taught me what pleasures—the salmon, the girl—awaited it. What could I conclude from that?

At dawn, I gulped down the gruel Mina had prepared for me.

Her eyes sparkling, she was dancing about, clucking, singing to herself. For several days, she had been showing this girlish excitement, which I pretended not to notice. She continued regardless, trying to catch my eye, imploring me to look at her, eager for my attention. Didn't she realize that she was exasperating me? She belonged to my past, not my present. Since Noura had dazzled me, I'd been putting up with Mina, seeing nothing but her graceless appearance, the mediocrity of her flat features, the platitude of her conversation, the opacity of her mind. Now that, under duress, I was not being allowed to take a second wife, the first one irritated me.

The first and only . . .

I got up, crossed the threshold of the house, and strode away.

"Noam, I have to tell you something," Mina cried from the doorway.

"Later!"

Nothing interested me less than what Mina was thinking. Preoccupied with my dream, I decided to join Tibor on his daily quest for medicinal plants.

Placid, downy clouds, half pink, half bluish, were floating through the morning sky, contrasting with the dark green of the forest. Fragrances, light, birdsong, everything was awakening, a little reluctantly. Even the river's current balked at resuming its torrential flow.

Emerging from the brambles, draped in his voluminous cloak with its many pockets, the healer's face darkened when he saw me.

"I'm sorry, Noam. There's nothing I can do."

"What are you talking about?"

"Noura . . . It had seemed to me . . ."

"Excuse me?"

"I would have sworn that you and Noura, that you two, I mean . . . you . . ."

I stiffened, closed my fists, and mumbled, with my jaw clenched, "I don't know what you mean!"

"I thought you wanted to marry Noura."

"I already have a wife."

"So does your father, but that doesn't stop him."

"My father is my father. The chief is the chief."

Tibor examined me and then exclaimed. "I'm sorry, Noam. I always think I'm so smart . . . You're showing yourself to be far more sensible than I am."

Exasperated, I agreed. I wanted him to go into raptures over my submission; I wanted the people as a whole to praise my servility. Whatever my father demanded, I would obey. If I succeeded in making my bitterness appear to be a sublime abnegation, if I clothed it in morality, I would save face, continue to be the

Noam the villagers knew, and escape spite, humiliation, despair. Otherwise, how would I endure the unendurable?

Tibor pressed my wrist.

"You're showing great wisdom, Noam."

Great wisdom, exactly! I was intoxicated with my virtues, I delighted in my heroism, I adored myself as a sacrificial victim. Very great wisdom . . . .

Nevertheless, a part of me was struggling not to roar the opposite: I hated my father for marrying Noura, I hated Noura for accepting, I hated Tibor for acquiescing, I hated Mama for putting up with it, and I hated my allegiance, my loyalty, my cowardice, my defeat.

Wisdom . . . What wisdom? I detested nothing more than my wisdom. My wisdom drove me mad.

I walked alongside Tibor in silence, giving myself a chance to calm down. Then I told him my dream and asked him to interpret it.

"Was this the first time that the bear appeared to you in a dream?"

"No."

"Have you encountered bears in reality?"

"Often. At a distance. I didn't run away; I stood in awe of them . . . Bears fascinate me. It never occurred to me that they might attack me. When I was a child, Pannoam blamed my recklessness."

"I think the explanation's obvious. The bear is your animal; it's your totem."

"Wrong! Our family's totem is the wolf."

"Your father's totem, not yours."

"What? It's impossible that I could have a different totem!"

Tibor stopped and gripped my shoulder.

"Don't think of yourself exclusively as a son. Think of yourself as you."

"How?"

"Noam isn't Pannoam."

"Be clearer."

"Noam can't be reduced to a part of Pannoam. A fragment of Pannoam. Even just the way your father named you sets a trap."

"A trap?"

I was very far from understanding, or even beginning to understand what Tibor was suggesting. He sighed and, without explaining, redirected the conversation. "If the strong, solitary bear is your totem, you have its characteristics.* You have already proven

---

* We considered the bear the incontestable king of the animals. Neither a pack of hungry wolves nor a sounder of furious wild boars could overcome it. Not only could no predator dethrone this invincible giant, but its courage subdued us; its solitude astonished us. It reigned from afar, without meeting its subjects.

We were very proud of the few qualities we shared with it. Like the bear, we knew how to sit down, how to stand up, climb, dance, and swim; like it, we put the whole sole of our foot, including the heel, on the ground; like it, we ate meat as well as vegetables. Provided with fur, we would surely have resembled it! We claimed that our sperm had the same consistency, our flesh the same taste—although I didn't know anyone who tested this belief.

The bear did not suffer from the reputation it has now, that of being a gluttonous, stupid, clumsy, lazy plantigrade. These slanders derived from the Christian church, which sought methodically to erase the immense respect that the bear had enjoyed for millennia, a reverence that some tribes developed into a cult. The church set out to eliminate the pagan bear, both in the forests and in people's brains. Nothing was to compete with the one and only God.

How did the church set about this? First, it put another wild animal on the throne. A religion that emerged in the Middle East, Christianity, imported a Middle Eastern sovereign: the lion. The king of the South supplanted the king of the North. All kinds of qualities could be attributed to the lion because it was a literary animal, not a concrete animal—it was not found in Latin, Celtic, Germanic, Slavic, or Scandinavian Europe—except in the Balkans. To motivate this substitution, the clergy henceforth spoke only of the bear's vices: its blind strength, its slowness, the lumbering heaviness of its body and mind, its gluttony, its laziness. They even managed to convince people that it was fearful!

Next, the bear was eliminated by hunting it intensively, which reduced it to the status of big game.

Finally, it was ridiculed by domesticating it. From a solitary majesty, it was demoted to a public buffoon. As property owned by the vagabonds whom the church scorned, bears were exhibited, chained, and muzzled at fairs and markets, alongside tumblers, jugglers, and conjurors. These sad clowns earned their keep by performing, under duress, a few elementary tricks and a couple of awkward dance steps.

For a man of the Lake, witnessing such a decline was deeply upsetting. I was almost as humiliated as the bear. Trampling on its dignity amounted to denying my beliefs. In any case, someone who does not respect living beings ceases to respect me.

your strength; the whole village would testify to that. You run fast, you swim well, your aim is accurate, and your fighting is perfect."

"Yes, but what about solitude? Am I solitary?"

"That's the new element. The bear came to show you that last night, at the time when becoming aware of it will be useful to you."

I bent my head. In fact, the sorrow caused me by Noura's marriage to my father was isolating me.

I raised my eyes and looked at Tibor.

"Is it possible to suffer from loneliness amid one's friends and family?"

He trembled and murmured melancholically, "Such is the destiny of a man who thinks for himself."

From his downcast eyes, a certain something fragile that welled up in him, I understood that he was talking about himself as much as about me.

How different he was from my father! Pannoam was the sum of decisions, orders, acts, whereas Tibor vibrated with countless questions. At that moment, I felt close to him.

"Is the bear your animal, too, Tibor?"

He smiled at me.

"The owl is my animal, Noam."

"You're not nocturnal!"

"The owl participates in other worlds, in the invisible world, the world of the gods, the world of spirits and the dead. Like it, I seek out what is hidden from most people; I remove the veil of appearances."

"The owl is an excellent totem, isn't it? A totem that produces more happiness than the solitary bear . . ."

"Can we experience happiness when we no longer have any illusions?"

With those words, Tibor left me.

I went down toward the Lake. The sky was clearing. The village, which I couldn't yet see, existed through its sounds, cackling, bleating, and lowing, then through the sounds of stone-cutting, stakes being driven into the ground, flint being sharpened, barley ground, clay kneaded, the dull pounding of hides being beaten to soften them, and finally the instructions shouted by craftsmen, children's cries, and the women's gossip.

I reached the main street and headed for the place where my father dispensed justice. Sitting under the linden tree, facing two families, Pannoam was dealing with a case involving stolen game.

Watching him from a distance, I felt as if an axe were cutting me in two: on the one hand, I felt my usual love for him; on the other, a violent desire to strike him made my fists itch. Incoherently, I superimposed images, sometimes that of a fine, upstanding, merciful man, and sometimes that of a cripple with a hostile grimace. Where was the truth to be found? How could I rid myself of the bad father and keep only the good one?

Noura appeared, her head high, saw me, checked to be sure Pannoam was still busy with his case, and then rushed toward me. Her impatient eyes, the color of gilded emeralds, showed her joy.

"Congratulations, Noam!"

A viper's bite would not have caused me to jump higher.

"I beg your pardon?"

"Congratulations!"

She was smiling, luminous, sincere, delighted. Since I frowned, she added, "What good news for you and Mina!"

I was furious. What? Did she think her marriage to my father constituted good news? Oh, for Mina, no doubt . . . But for me?

I looked at her coldly.

"How dare you?"

"What?"

"Taunt me!"

She stammered, unused to being the object of my scorn. "But . . . Noam . . . any man . . . you've always claimed that . . ."

"Noura! The situation already makes me sick. There's no point in making it worse by mocking me. Even if you're having fun."

Her face paled and, pouting, she cried, "I'm not having fun and I'm not mocking you! I'm delighted that Mina is pregnant!"

I was speechless.

She explained, thinking that I hadn't heard her, "I'm delighted that you're expecting a child."

Seeing my stupefaction, she opened her eyes wide, snorted, and then burst into laughter, her hand over her mouth.

"No! You didn't know?"

She guffawed.

"Didn't you notice?"

I shook my head. She continued to laugh gaily, showing her teeth, looking around to find witnesses.

"Anybody can see that, Noam! Mina has been growing a little belly for three moons . . . You really don't look at your wife very carefully!"

"I don't look at her at all!"

My voice had resounded in the middle of the village. Providentially, no one was up and about yet; only my father, who was far off, looked up, but the distance prevented him from catching what I'd said.

I was overcome by shame, not for having said what I'd said, but for having failed to control myself.

Noura looked at me. The vehemence of my tone put an end to her banter. For a moment, we remained silent. Then she pointed to an oak stump.

"Let's sit down."

We sat side by side facing the Lake, which spread its tranquility to infinity, its blue merging with that of the azure sky. Ducks flew over us in a V, driven by some obscure need. Under the Linden Tree of Justice, my father was receiving farmers involved in a second case.

Noura gripped my hand. Moved by spite or anger, I tried to push her away, but the contact with her skin, so soft, so warm, disarmed my resistance. I surreptitiously contemplated her. My eyes caressed the outline of her cheek, rounded, smooth, downy, then lingered on her hair, thick, shining, and worn piled on top of her head, with a few loose locks brushing against her forehead, her temples, and her pretty ears, accentuating the purity of her complexion.

Noura breathed in the pristine morning air, lowered her long lashes over the panorama, and confided in me: "I played a role in the conception of your child. An important one. I'm proud of my contribution."

"Excuse me?"

"I helped you."

Helped us? Helped me? Did she know how cruel she was being? Was she intentionally choosing the most hurtful expressions, or was she unaware of what she was doing? Complacently, she added, "I advised Mina to pray to the mother goddess, the source of sources, and to offer her big-bellied figurines. And better, I brought her the best herbs, the ones that promote fertility. Mina did what I suggested."

"So it was you who prescribed the nettle tea for her?"

"Yes. Well . . . Tibor did it through me."

"She served me that tea every day!"

"It strengthens men, too. On the other hand, have you drunk clover tea?"

"No."

"Raspberry tea?"

"No."

"Perfect. Oh, I was forgetting. According to Tibor, Mina should now stop taking the raspberry tea. I don't know why, he told me that this morning. Please convey his message to Mina."

Her right hand tapped the back of mine. Her smooth, rosy pink arm contrasted so strongly with mine, which was brownish, veined, twisted.

"Are you happy?"

I was seething. How long was this conversation, which was sidestepping the real issue, going to last?

Exasperated, I decided to pour out my heart. "No, I'm not happy. Because I don't give a damn about what happens to Mina. Because Mina annoys me. Because Mina bores me. Because Mina isn't the wife I wanted, just the wife my father forced on me."

She cast a worried glance in Pannoam's direction, to be sure that he wasn't spying on us.

"Did he make a mistake?"

"He reasoned in his own way, as a chief."

Her lips trembled, her pupils darkened, and she asked again: "Did he make a mistake?"

"My father allied his family with the family of a neighboring chief. Who we were, Mina and I, what we hoped for, what pleased us, what we had in common or what opposed us to each other played no role for him. The villages were what was mattered; peace treaties and trade mattered, not individuals."

Looking me in the eye, she stubbornly repeated, "Did he make a mistake?"

"As a chief, no. As a father, yes."

"What's the difference?"

"A father wants his son to be happy. A chief wants his community to be happy."

"But your father is a chief. And you're the son of a chief."

"True . . ."

"So how can you allow yourself to criticize your father?"

I stood up, deeply hurt.

"Don't play games with me, Noura; let's stop beating around the bush. We're not talking about her, we're talking about you. I'm not condemning my father for having chosen Mina as my wife, I'm condemning him for having chosen you for himself."

Scarlet, she stiffened. Irritation sharpened her features, gluing them to her temples, to the bridge of her nose. Her face became as hard as it was feminine.

"How does that concern you?"

"Pannoam stole you!"

"Pardon me?"

"He stole you from me! He stole from me!"

"He stole from you? Because I belong to you?"

Disconcerted, I fell to my knees and, in a tumultuous flow of words without order or respite, alternating between ecstasy and suffering, I told her everything, the passion in my heart, my desire to marry her, how I had asked my father for permission to take her as my second wife, how I waited after he was attacked by the Hunters, my hopes during his convalescence, and then my distress, the preceding day, when I learned that he was ignoring my wishes and keeping Noura.

"Why didn't you say anything to me?" she whispered, pale, her nostrils quivering.

"According to the rule, a man is supposed to talk first with his own parents, and then with the parents of his intended."

"I'm still the first person concerned!"

"I tried to tell you, Noura. I was going to speak to you when we heard Pannoam crying out and the dogs barking. Remember, I stopped and ran to help."

"Yes, I remember. I also remember that that evening, after the operation on his leg, I suggested we finish our conversation."

"I'm sorry, I was dying of fatigue, and the amputation had upset me."

"And the following days?"

"You were caring for my father. I presumed that would help us."

"Us?"

"So he would consent."

Listening to my own explanations, I realized that without saying a word to her, I'd always acted as though Noura shared my thoughts, as if Noura approved of me, as if Noura wanted us to be together as much as I did.

She summed up my confusion by puckering her grumpy face, "You never told me that you dreamed of marrying me; you never admitted that you had feelings for me, or were even attracted to me. Do you confide only to silence?"

"Really, Noura, it's so obvious!"

"What is?"

"That every man who meets you falls in love with you."

A glow crossed her iris, and then she asked me to get up and take my seat on the stump again, relieved that Pannoam had not noticed our quarrel.

Sadly, I turned toward her.

"If I had told you, would that have changed anything?"

Her eyes filled with tears, and she ran away.

*

So it was my fault . . .

Because it had taken me months to perceive my adulation, and because I had then kept quiet about it, Noura and I would never wed.

This realization, even as it confounded me, revealed a truth I hadn't known: I had a certain power. Yes, I had the power to intervene in my life instead of merely undergoing it; at least I had learned that. I was discovering that I could be myself rather than someone else; for the first time, I had found a part of my life that was indeterminate, a crack, a gray area, a gap that I didn't know how to qualify and that philosophers would call, thousands of years later, "freedom." Unfortunately, I perceived this only after the fact; this awareness, far from alleviating my bitterness, aggravated it: I would not marry Noura.

In the world into which I was born, not only did freedom not have a name, but it wasn't even common. That is why Noura stood out, Noura the insolent, Noura the unusual, the person who overturned customs. At her age, she ought to have already been married! And a mother! Moreover, the beauty and education of the woman who was now to wed Pannoam had raised her to the status of an excellent match. Why had she been so slow? How had she escaped her destiny as a wife thus far? *Why* I didn't know. *How*, that I had understood: Noura had imposed her character on Tibor, who feared her moods, her furies, her tears, and who savored her joy. Mama said that Noura led him by the nose, but she led him mainly by the heart. He loved her. She had created a bond that went beyond paternal responsibility. Concerned not to contradict her or make her rebel, he handled her with care, observed her aspirations, and considered her his equal.

Noura had established a similar relationship with me. I talked with her, listened to her; we discussed men's and women's subjects; I cared about her opinions; I argued with her, admitted my mistakes, and never treated her harshly.

The villagers respected Noura. Having come from elsewhere, with an undetermined ancestry, dressing, speaking, and behaving in her own way, unpredictable, sometimes haughty, sometimes affable, cheerful at sunrise, melancholic at sundown, charming, devoted, selfish, vulnerable, sensitive, insensitive, she was surrounded by mystery. Had a man married her, the villagers would have known better what to make of her, but her status as a proud, intractable virgin added spice to her foreignness. Everyone saw her as a queen. An incontestable queen.

The incontestable queen of an unknown realm.

In reality, this realm was herself: Noura ruled herself; she conferred with herself and obeyed herself.

I, too, fell under the influence of Noura's proud independence . . . I ceased to adhere to my father's ideas and decisions. I detached myself from him. To be sure, I didn't go so far as to break with him, but I did start down the path that leads to rupture, the path of doubt. Was my father right to take a second wife when he had already founded a large family ready to succeed him? Was he right to ignore my desires, to give priority to his own appetites over mine? Was he right to lay waste to the harmony we shared?

Noura individuated us, Pannoam and me: her presence awakened in us vague urges that established our singularity, to the point of transgressing the rules. But by individuating us, she also set us at odds: she separated the father from the son and opposed the son to the father. Before her, one plus one equaled one. After her, one plus one equaled two.

I did not much like this libertarian contamination. Far from strengthening me, it distressed me. What was the good of deviating from the norm if it cost me my peace of mind?

That day, I returned home resolved to become the old Noam once again. Noura had muddied the pure, tranquil water of my existence. In the past, when I was splashing around, going nowhere, she had thrown me into floods, cataracts, tides, and torrents; whereas I was content with a puddle, she had doomed me to pounding waves. I was going back to my puddle. Farewell Noura, hello Mina. That was my life, wasn't it? What right did I have to demand more? I had a wife; I would soon receive an heir; I would replace my father as the head of the village.

Having crossed the threshold, I let Mina coo, strut, and prance, and then, as if I didn't know, I asked what had put her in such a good mood.

Mina pretended to hesitate, simpered, exulting in keeping her secret; finally, because I frowned at so much temporizing, she announced the arrival of a child. Below her low forehead, her puffy eyes, joyous and shy, awaited my reaction. With her little reddened hands deformed by work, she proudly stroked her belly, as if it had tripled in volume. I shook my head to drive away negative thoughts, repressed the feeling of having already experienced this scene, ignored the number of times that I had been excited in vain. Trying to convince myself that Mina was promising me a birth rather than a burial, I feigned ecstasy.

Blinded by her happiness, Mina suspected neither my wiliness nor my effort.

The day proceeded along the same lines. We had to officially announce what everyone except me had already guessed. Gripping my elbow, amorphous and purring, Mina savored the false exclamations of surprise, eagerly soaking up the conventional compliments, absorbing the good wishes we received, swollen with pride: one would have thought she had just invented pregnancy! Never had I looked on her with such disdain . . . she went around with a face that lacked ugliness as much as it did beauty, and awkwardly clothing a body without merit, she made remarks less valuable than her silence.

In the evening, sated, she curled up alongside me, lay her head on my chest, and quickly fell asleep. A smile escaped me, the only sincere one since that morning: Mina would no longer force me to inseminate her.

The night enclosed us.

In the course of the following weeks, life started up again. It appeared to be normal.

Although he limped on his stag-bone leg, Pannoam continued to walk the streets in my company. We conversed with the villagers, consulted the chiefs of neighboring villages, organized the consolidation of our reserves, expanded the group of warriors and dogs intended to protect us from the Hunters. More than ever, despite his discomfort and his infirmity, Pannoam was preparing me to replace him. Was this increased attention the result of remorse?

Mama had lost her gaiety but did not yet realize it; her eyes expressed an extreme astonishment. She, who had always lived in conjugal optimism, couldn't get used to the idea that her husband was, officially and without discussion, imposing a young rival on her. Disturbed, she began to see herself differently, to re-evaluate her body, which exuded nostalgia for her earlier perfection, and she was burdened with a new enemy whom she mistrusted and over whom she wouldn't triumph. Then she discovered that her remaining elegance had unconsciously masked a disaster, that she was piling on necklaces to hide her throat thickened by distended muscles, that she was wearing dresses with no belt at the waist. I pitied her. Her marks of age, the wrinkles that followed the arch of her eyelid at the extreme corner of the eye, no longer rose; they descended. Her face was growing heavier, and the glow of her cheeks no longer signaled her vitality, just her exhaustion.

When we found ourselves alone together, Pannoam and I spoke not a word. Except for public tasks, we no longer shared anything. Neither he nor I mentioned the point that divided us; every personal subject of conversation disappeared, including both Mina's pregnancy and the health of my mother, whose headaches Tibor the healer was treating. Chatting, joking, sympathizing—that spirited everyday exchange was becoming impossible.

As time went on, the silence grew heavier. Although at first it freed us, now it crushed us. Pannoam and I didn't have the strength to extricate ourselves from it. What I would never have imagined came to pass: I was bored in the company of my father.

This pained me.

It pained me to think of the past, which was lit by the innocent glow of affection; it pained me to think of the future, that morose plain on which I no longer aspired to advance.

Was Pannoam suffering, too? Alas, in his tortured face, fissured by constant pain, I couldn't discern what derived from the body and what from the soul.

Evil is division. Its blade had lacerated the pair that we formed, my father and I, but it had also split me down the middle. Two antagonistic beings struggled within me, a good son and a bad son, one submissive, the other rebellious. If I held my tongue, the rebel assailed the docile son. If I protested, the docile son gagged the rebellious one. Twofold and out of tune, I was engaged in constant war. There was no longer any impulse, any word, any phrase that I did not remember. The same tension operated in

the other direction: there was no longer any muzzling, any stifling, any bullying for which I failed to reproach myself. I was the
theater where a division was played out, I *was* the division, I was
the evil . . . and I suffered evilly.

That morning, Pannoam suggested that I sit with him under the
Linden Tree of Justice to deal with the plaintiffs. Ordinarily, he insisted that the hearings be confidential, maintaining that the presence of the public would affect the statements made by the parties.

"I want you to learn to judge, Noam."

Two villagers, one fat and one lean, appeared before them.
The fat one, whose name was Puror, complained that a dog had
killed five of his hens. The defendant, Fari, who sold ocher, retorted, "You just have to protect your hens better."

"I'm not going to enclose my hens to avoid your dog.
Otherwise, how would they get enough to eat? Kill your dog."

"Kill my dog?"

"Or tie it up."

"What good would a tied-up dog do me? He's supposed to
guard my house, scare off intruders, and eat foxes, rats, and
ferrets."

"Your dog massacred my hens. If you don't tie him up, I'm
going to put him down."

"If you touch one hair on my dog, I'll strangle you!"

Pannoam let them vent their rage. When they turned to him,
he said calmly to fat Puror, "Put your next hens in a pen high
enough so that dogs can't get into it. Then you will benefit from
your hens, and Fari will benefit from his dog. All the animals will
perform their work."

"That's a wise judgment," the thin Fari sighed.

"He should have to compensate me for the dead hens!" cried
the fat man. "Let him bring me five hens! Or let him bring me
eggs every day!"

Pannoam rebuked him. "Nothing at all. You should have
taken precautions."

"He's the one who destroyed everything, not me! Him and his dog!"

"I have spoken," Pannoam said as he stood up, his face severe. "You asked for justice, and you've received it. Now go home."

The two men went away, the thin one satisfied, the fat one cursing.

Pannoam leaned toward me.

"Would you have judged that way?"

I hesitated, then, seeing that he was waiting, I dared reply. "No. I would have required compensation for the hens. Puror came to complain about a loss resulting from the death of his animals. He's the victim. But he left guilty. Worse yet, he left worse off because now he'll have to construct a pen."

"That doesn't seem just to you?"

"No."

"Why did I make this judgment? Because to me it seems like the best option for our future. The number of dogs is growing in the village, and this kind of incident will happen again, unless we pen in the chickens."

"I approve of your establishing this rule. But it wasn't in force when this case occurred. It's unfair to punish someone who . . ."

"We have to frighten the people who raise chickens, not those who own dogs."

"Frighten? I thought you were concerned solely with the just and the unjust."

"Noam, such incidents will occur with our dogs."

"Ah, I see: you don't render justice, you render *your* justice."

He glared at me.

"Silence! Justice is what I decide under this tree."

"Oh? You decide? You don't render justice, you fabricate it."

"That's enough!"

He was scarlet-faced, choking with anger, wavering on his left leg. For the first time, I'd stood up to him, and this revolt had taken place viscerally, without my having even perceived it. I was left speechless, and he was outraged.

Silence returned. We hadn't exchanged so many sentences for weeks.

Pannoam sat down, rubbed his cheeks, his forehead stubborn, his eyes cold.

"Plan my marriage."

"Excuse me?"

"Organize the festivities: the ceremony, the flowers, the party. Your mother is ill."

Instead of admitting the truth—"Your mother is suffering" or "Your mother refuses to do it"—he claimed she was sick. I was increasingly unable to bear his smugness.

"Why me?"

"You're my son, my eldest child."

"You have other children; this is the time to remember that."

"Pardon me?"

"So far as planning your marriage is concerned, I think I'm going to be 'sick' like Mama."

"How dare you."

Without losing my composure, I brought my face close to his and said, with my teeth clenched and jaw set, "Aren't you sufficiently assured of my submission? Haven't you already trampled on me? Do you want to annihilate me, crush me?"

Confronted by my outburst, he shivered. I added, "Entrust this task to my sisters, not to me."

"And why should I do that?"

"Do you really need me to explain it to you?"

Shocked by my severity, he fell back on his seat and murmured, haggard, stammering, "I don't know. You say nothing. How am I supposed to guess?"

His sudden weakness did not arouse my pity.

"You are well aware that I hoped to marry Noura."

"Ah, so it's that old business . . ." he said with scorn.

At that moment, I perceived the distance that separated us. Once he had refused me Noura's hand and kept her for himself, he'd considered the episode over. I was annoying him by reminding him of an old, buried anecdote . . . Did my father know me so little? Did he think my ideas were so incoherent, my feelings so inconsistent? Did he believe that his directives changed the reality of minds and hearts? No doubt he was that naïve . . . that presumptuous . . . that egocentric . . .

He spoke to me as if I were a child. "That's life, Noam. It has pleasures in it, and women; sometimes we get access to them, and often we give them up. It's not a big deal."

"Not a big deal?"

"Not a big deal!"

"Giving up a woman is not a big deal?"

"No, Noam, it's not."

"Then give up Noura."

Stung, he withdrew his hand. His eyes sought new arguments around him, on the right, on the left, in the sky, on the ground, then settled on me. "I've devoted my life to you, Noam."

"No, you've devoted it to the village."

"I've never given my time to your sisters; I've never hunted or conversed with your sisters. I've given you priority."

"Why?"

"Because you're my double."

He went on. "You're my masterwork, my successor."

A cruel thought ran through my mind.

"It's yourself that you love in me, not me."

Pannoam frowned, perplexed, avoided gauging the acuteness of my remark, and continued in the indulgent tone he had adopted. "We're not going to quarrel over a girl."

"Precisely, father. Give up Noura."

This time, exasperation contracted his features. His lips trembled with indignation. He looked me up and down and shot back at me, "You already have a wife."

"So do you. An excellent wife."

"You're defending her because she's your mother!"

"Mama has given you eleven children, Father, eleven children in good health. Mina has given me none. Mama behaves like a chief's companion, always equal to her task, always at your side. Mina is proving incapable of that."

In a burst of violence, Pannoam opened his mouth to plead Mina's cause. But his intelligence reminded him that he would get bogged down if he tried. He rubbed his painful leg.

"I'm old, Noam."

"Exactly. Noura is too young for you."

Pannoam's eyes clouded over, and he exclaimed, with moving sincerity, "She makes me want to live."

He was telling the truth, and I knew it all the better because Noura produced the same effect in me. I affectionately gripped my father's arm and whispered, "When we're married, you'll see her every day; you'll get to hold our children. She will still make you want to live."

Pannoam bit his lip, his eyelids fluttered, and then he calmly freed his arm from my hand.

"I'm the chief. I do what is worthy of a chief."

"You're also my father."

"Yes."

"But you prefer being a chief?"

It was my turn to have tears in my eyes. I stepped back and waited for his reply. Impassive, he maintained his inflexible bearing. He looked at me without blinking and concluded in a steady voice. "Yes."

I turned my back on him to hide my sorrow, and before striding swiftly away, I shouted, "Today, the chief killed the father."

*

"Noam?"

I did not deign to react. With my eyes fixed on the Lake, sitting cross-legged inside our house across from the open door, I was harder to move than a mountain. Having arrived along with the clouds that veiled the horizon, my dark mood infected my words and actions, expressing itself in shrugs, a tendency to sigh, and a dense silence that precluded any questions. My surliness infected Mina. She had taken refuge in the half-light and didn't dare move or speak.

In the distance, there was rolling thunder. Arising from the willows, bitter and solitary, a bird's cry put a lump in my throat. A kind of latent despair weighed on the landscape, dulling its colors, paralyzing the reeds, immobilizing the water. Nature was holding its breath.

The growling thunder persisted, the daylight dimmed, and suddenly, like a horde of assailants, the rain pelted down on us. Lightning lacerated us, and raindrops fell like javelins, riddling the path, perforating the thatched roof, seeping down the walls.

Mina screamed. Panicked by the gods unleashing their fury, she slipped under the mat, her eyes closed and her hands covering her ears, while I, immobile, observed the water's assault.

My nostrils quivering, I enjoyed these convulsions, savoring their violence. The storm echoed my sorrow. In harmony with the lightning bolts, shivers ran through my limbs; my heart beat in time with the detonations; I inhaled the damp air to flood my lungs. Oh, how I wanted those sheets of water to crush us, the earth to open up under the armed tides of the heavens, torrents of mud to carry away humans, their homes, their goods, their families, their cares, their misfortunes! Ferociously, silently, I begged the gods to destroy us. What I wanted was the end of the world, nothing less!

Swept away by the apocalypse, I relished the storm's temporary darkness intensely, wishing that true night would swallow us up. Let everyone else join me in the fall! I had lost the essential. My father. Noura. Everything that mattered.

The rain stopped.

Silence.

An astonished silence.

A silence that seemed enormous. In proportion to the din that it had just ended.

Timidly, a few raindrops whispered, completing their fall to the ground. The roof groaned as if palpating its wounds. The sun came out again.

I blinked, buffeted by its chalky light. My state of mind changed. Having survived this tempest, was I going to let myself be dominated?

I stood up and walked away.

When I came to Tibor's house, I spotted Noura, who was taking a chilly little walk. Was she waiting for me? She ran toward me.

I held out my arms to her; she rushed into them, and we stood there, survivors trembling after glimpsing death, each of us huddling in the warmth of the other. I sniffed the hazelnut smell of her hair and caressed the soft flesh at the nape of her neck, moved to be holding her body against mine, her body that was so frail, her body that made such an impression on me when I came close to her and that, pressed against me, seemed tiny, fragile, precious.

I whispered in her ear, "Refuse, Noura, refuse."

She pulled away, looked at me, closed her eyes like a cat that fears it will be spattered as it laps, then stared at me.

"How can I refuse? No one has asked what I want."

"Refuse."

"They'll force me! I'm a woman, Noam; I have no power."

"You're a woman: destroy his desire to marry you. Be disagreeable, odious, indifferent. Deprive him of any desire for you."

She smiled sadly.

"You want me to become ugly?"

"You could never! Noura, drive him away, I beg you; make him sick of you!"

I took her in my arms again. At first, she melted into them, but then she broke free and jutted out her chin.

"Why would I do that?"

"For us."

"Us?"

"Us!"

Her features narrowed in annoyance.

"There has never been an 'us,' Noam. 'Us' never happened. You weren't capable of declaring yourself in time."

"Forgive me, I know, I realize that. I'm telling you now: I want to spend my life with you, Noura."

She pushed me away and took a step backward, pale.

"Is that right? Did you ever wonder if I would agree to be your second wife? Second wife! Don't I deserve better than that?"

Disconcerted, I stammered, "I . . . I . . . They chose Mina for me before we met . . . I didn't decide any of it . . . It's too late . . . I can't . . ."

"Kill her? No, but you could repudiate her."

"Repudiate her?"

I immediately felt compassion for Mina, her flaccid flesh, her languorous eyes, her discomfort, that of a little girl lost among women.

"She's pregnant, Noura."

"So?"

Hard, sharp, pointed, Noura was challenging me. Why should Mina be punished in such a way? If our children died, the gods . . . the demons . . . a spirit . . . I didn't know . . . In any case, no vice, no nastiness, no aggressiveness existed in clumsy, innocent Mina. I couldn't hurt her.

Noura's eyes sparkled, accusing me.

"Sometimes you have to strike and draw blood to get what you want. What do you want? What do you really want? Everything! That is, nothing. You have to choose."

"Noura, try to understand . . ."

"Me, a second wife? Never! I deserve better than that."

We looked at each other.

Feeling anger growing within me, I murmured between my teeth, "Don't be so proud, Noura. In a few moons, you'll become just that, a second wife."

"The first one is old!"

I was speechless. Had I heard her rightly? Not only was Noura scorning my feelings, trampling on my scruples, and stigmatizing Mina, but now she was insulting my mother. Mama, an old woman?

She seemed to be laughing at my stupefaction and nodded her head, resolved to bite.

"I'm young; she's old. I have my life in front of me; hers is behind her. With your father, I won't remain a second wife for long."

"What? You're waiting for my mother to die?"

"No, it's death that's waiting for her."

I slapped Noura.

She slapped me back.

We were trembling with rage. Fuming, as hotheaded as two boxers preparing for the next punch, we stood facing one another. She attacked again:

"In a few moons, I'll be married to Pannoam, not to you."

"Refuse to marry him, Noura, and wait."

"Why should I sacrifice a solid marriage to mere wind?"

"Please!"

"Assuming that I did what you ask, what would I gain? Out of spite or jealousy, Pannoam would oppose my marriage to you."

"He's suffering, he's wasting away, Noura. He will die soon."

"And will Mina be dead, too, at that time? My poor Noam, what an imagination you have! Is the future going to magically resolve all your problems?"

Trying to get a grip on myself, I repeated softly, "My father is not eternal."

"Which means?"

"Refuse and wait for me."

"Dream on! That might last a year, five years, ten years!"

"Pannoam is not eternal."

"Neither am I!"

Her fury exploded. "Why should I continually yield to what other people decree, to what men want? I did not come onto this earth to obey. I have always found a way to command. In a month, I'll be the chief's wife."

"You will obey him."

"We'll see about that!"

"What do you want, ultimately? The chief's place?"

"Why not?"

"At any price?"

"At my price: I'm giving myself to the chief. Clearly, both chief and future chief keep coming back for more . . ."

"You have no heart . . . All you have is ambition!"

"Tell yourself whatever you want, Noam."

"Who do you think you are, Noura?"

"Your father is the chief, and you, someday, will be the chief. Well, I'm the one who turns chiefs' heads."

She seized me by the throat and began to tighten her grip.

"Do you want me? Then let me tell you how it will go: I'll marry your father, and when he dies, I'll marry you. You're the one who's going to wait."

"Never!"

"Oh, yes! I'll be your father's wife first, and then I'll be yours."

"I won't come after him."

"What pride! Of course you'll come after him. And you'll be happy about it. And you'll thank me."

"You're insane!"

Her fingers stopped strangling me and caressed my cheek.

"I know you'll obey me, Noam. Like a goat, you'll come to eat from my hand as soon as I whistle for you!"

Beside myself, I pushed her away. She staggered, slipped in the mud, lost her balance, but with a furious effort, she managed to recover it. Back in control, she taunted me, hostile, proud, intense, as aggressive as she was magnificent. The violence between us redoubled in force. I no longer knew whether I was going to bite her or kiss her.

She saw my attraction. A sardonic smile lifted the corners of her lips, and she began to snigger.

The more she laughed at me, the more I was ashamed of myself, of my enchantment, of the control she exercised over my thoughts. Her disdain, her mockery, her teasing suddenly made me bristle.

I walked on down the path, resolved, and shouted, "Thank you, Noura. Thanks for your cruelty and selfishness. They'll help me stop loving you."

She broke off laughing.

"At your service, Noam!"

"You're even making me hate you."

"Come back whenever you like!"

Turning on her heel, she went back into her house. She'd barely made it in the door before she was cooing affectionately—remarks directed to Tibor, but loud enough for me to hear them. Through this profusion of endearments, she made it clear to me that our quarrel hadn't affected her, that she could get along perfectly fine without me—even that she felt true happiness without me.

*

Mina became my refuge. In her company, everything was simple; the slightest of my attentions delighted her, a mechanical caress, a bowl of water, an arm that supported her. Inexhaustible, she went into ecstasies over the fruit I harvested and considered the hare or otter I brought home from the hunt the best she had ever eaten. One word passed for a conversation, a smile for euphoria, a giggle for a belly laugh. Confronted by these reserves of enthusiasm, I played my role, and she rewarded me a hundredfold.

Contrary to all expectation, I felt at ease around her, at home in the home she had made over the years. Belatedly, I was discovering her domestic talents. Never did she let the embers on our hearth go out, unlike many scatter-brained wives who neglected the household fire and had to go ask others for a light. Round baskets of her own handiwork allowed her to store our food, clothes, and tools. When we ate sitting down, she spread colored mats on the floor that were always neat and clean. As for the walls, she'd used red ocher to adorn them, as the days passed, with geometric friezes—a series of waves, fish-bone motifs—based on patterns borrowed from Dandar's vases. Thanks to her obstinacy, our interior benefited from a warm, unique atmosphere, whereas our neighbors, who lived in an identical house, might as well have still been living in a cave.*

Mina practiced joy: she was amazed to be alive and went into raptures over what she had. Unlike Noura, she never wanted more. Her absence of ambition, her lack of perfectionism, and the mediocrity that I had formerly vilified, now seemed to me

---

* Each period has its color. Mine was red. All my memories are bathed in scarlet. From the earth, we had been able to extract ochers and learned how to prepare them. Even if their tints ranged from yellow to violet, red was dominant. Either nature offered us red ocher in raw form, or we obtained it by heating yellow ocher. Rare among flora and fauna, red distinguished us humans; it marked our superiority. We daubed weapons, tools, clothes, walls, and sometimes bodies with it, either overall or in part.

In the eighteenth century, a new interest in ancient times arose, probably because the Bible was losing its status as a scientific manual: scientists began to study prehistory. Lacking texts, they excavated humus, podzols, and silts. They continue to do so today. On the basis of these remnants, they reconstituted our world. Without elaborating here on their successes or mistakes, I will point out one constant: in their view, the Neolithic is brown. In films, book illustrations, and display cases in museums, brown is always dominant. Why? They find its vestiges in the earth—so do they believe that prehistory is earth-colored?

the pinnacle of intelligence. Why see the emptiness of life rather than its fullness? What advantage was there in that? What consequence other than frustration? To the emptiness of desire, Mina preferred the plenitude of pleasure.

I struggled to attain this satisfied wisdom: to remain in my role, that of the chief's son; to stick to my duty, obedience to the father; to pursue my responsibility to found a family; to remain with my wife . . . Shortly before, my life had displeased me because, as I saw it, all I had in that life were ingredients I rejected; now that I'd accepted them, it improved. I hadn't changed my life, only the way I saw it.

Out of prudence, I avoided Noura. I also avoided Mama, whose melancholy would have aroused my own. With regard to my father, I behaved as if no altercation had opposed us to one another. Noam and Pannoam had granted each other an amnesty—amnesia.

I made up my mind to organize the wedding ceremony.

Pannoam wanted an event that would eclipse in richness, splendor, and luxury all preceding ones, an event that would demonstrate, through its chief, the preponderance and prosperity of our community. Consequently, we would not limit ourselves to inviting the inhabitants; we would also receive the most influential clans in the lakeside villages. We expected no fewer than four hundred guests, which, at the time, represented a gigantic, unprecedented gathering.

We cut down trees to expand the clearing and polished their trunks to transform them into benches that we placed in a circle. In its center, people would dance. On its periphery, they would sing. Behind it, people would devour the victuals set out on planks. In the market, I recruited itinerant musicians, three flutists and four drummers, who recommended a horn player who emitted deep sounds that formed an ingenious counterpoint to the high tones of the reed pipes; I found him and hired him. For every detail—the flowers, the garlands, the outfits, the drinks, the dishes to be served—I consulted Mina, and her suggestions became my decisions. Finally, for several moons I commissioned gifts from the craftsmen of our village.

During wedding ceremonies, gifts were given, not to the married couple, but rather to the guests. The couple's prestige depended on them: the quality and quantity of the offerings either made or destroyed a reputation. Nothing was more expensive than a marriage, and many people skipped it, mounting each other without a rite, like animals.

The day of the wedding that had been so elaborately prepared came.

The sun was just shivering on the horizon when people began entering the clearing. Families were arriving from all over, as excited as they were intimidated. Our village's children were running among the guests, waving gourds. Blueberry wine was being passed around, and gullets were quickly being filled, but that didn't matter; we'd concocted drinks in abundance! Spirits rose along with the sun. Bodies and hearts grew warmer. The noise, voices, raucous laughter, congratulations, punches accompanied by jokes, everything indicated that people would get their fill of alcohol, cordiality, and dancing. Their voices became louder and louder; they became more excited, licked their lips, began singing tunes. Impatience grew. Cheeks glowed, glistening with sweat.

When the sun reached its zenith, the drums sounded.

Pannoam appeared at the end of a path. Noble, powerful, broad-shouldered, he was wearing a leather cloak decorated with shells sewn on it, a ceremonial outfit that made him seem taller and hid the fact that he was missing a leg. Everyone cheered.

Suddenly, from the other side of the clearing, the flutes struck up a melody, and people turned around: framed by a procession of women, Noura appeared in turn. An admiring murmur spread through the crowd. Dressed in a gown of pleated linen, almost transparent, Noura was splendid in her beauty, youth, and vigor.

In time with the music, lithely and gracefully, she walked down the path, looking slight alongside her corpulent bridesmaids. Her movements suggested a dance. A crown of immaculate lilies was woven through her braided hair, below which she wore a necklace and bracelets of fresh flowers. Delicate pigments had enlarged her emerald-colored eyes, outlined her eyebrows, reddened her lips.

Noura's complexion was incredibly luminous, lighter than that of any of the women around her. Our village women, who were kept busy washing clothes, picking fruit, hoeing, and gathering provisions, were exposed to heat waves, windburn, drizzle, and snow, so that after a few years skins that had not been chapped by the cold were tanned by the sun, but Noura had retained a child's complexion; by some miracle, the assaults of the climate and of labor had spared her.

The bride and groom met at the end of the path. He offered her his arm, she slipped her hand under it, and they moved toward the clearing. There, a masked sorcerer, half-wolf, half-owl and covered with furs and plumes, welcomed them with the ritual formulas.

Though at first I had followed the procession, I stopped at the edge of the forest. The festivities were proceeding as planned; my work was bearing fruit; I had foreseen everything except what happened to me: I was overcome by nausea.

Leaning on a walnut tree, I struggled not to collapse, tried to swallow, to breathe regularly, to slow my heartbeat, but something more powerful than my will rose up in my stomach. I vomited.

Once I had emptied my stomach, I was overwhelmed by lucidity. Up to that point, the countless details to be dealt with had concealed the ceremony's purpose, which now became blatantly obvious: Noura was marrying Pannoam!

In the center of the festivities, the sorcerer presented two earthenware pitchers to the bride and groom: Noura and Pannoam broke them, to signify that they were breaking with their former life. Then the sorcerer handed them a hemp cord; they tied it around their wrists, symbolizing the bond that they were accepting.

Tears welling up in my eyes, I turned my head away and saw Mama behind me, leaning against an oak tree, withered, pale, her face haggard.

We didn't have to speak. We were being crushed by the same helplessness.

I would have liked to distract her by telling her how beautiful she was, but contrary to her custom, Mama was nondescript. She, who was usually so pleasant and petulant, who ornamented her figure in such a flattering way, who wore jewelry with such flair, now looked like a caricature of herself, an overweight, worn, bitter matron whose beauty had vanished.

With a stiff gesture, she offered me a gourd.

"A little wine?"

Her slurred speech told me that she had already drunk more than a little.

I took the gourd and exclaimed, "Sure! Nothing better to do!"

"Nothing!" she replied, hiccupping.

I swallowed a mouthful. The blueberry wine gave me the warmth I was lacking. So I took another drink. She encouraged me. "Drink all you want. I've got lots more."

She sniggered, mumbled some indistinct words full of discontent, and concluded, "After all, I'm still the chief's first wife."

I drank another mouthful of wine and pointed to my father in the distance.

"Do you think Pannoam is waiting for us down there?"

"We can see very well from here, can't we? Don't you see him, the old man marrying the young woman?"

"I do!"

"On the other hand, from here it's hard to see that the infirm old man has lost a leg."

She took back the gourd and tipped the wine into her mouth.

"She's a strange one, that girl! Marrying a crippled old man . . . At her age, I'd have refused to do that."

I didn't point out the extravagance of what she'd just said: in accord with custom, Mama had been married without asking her consent.

She continued to spit out her resentment. "I wouldn't have accepted the status of second wife! Never! I didn't share. And by the way, I still don't share. I'm telling you, Noam, and too bad if it shocks you: if your father tries to get me to sleep with him, I'll send him packing!"

I looked at my haggard mother, thought of the splendid Noura, and even if such an eventuality seemed remote, I nodded my head. She appreciated my assent, and grumbled again, "Yes, but . . ."

Then she broke into tears. Beneath her coarsened face burned the indignation of an innocent, angry young woman. I hastened to take her in my arms. She howled, shaken by sobs, "What do you see in her, this Noura? What do you see in her?"

Should I answer such a question? I avoided it. "*You're* the love of his life, Mama. You're the woman Pannoam has loved for years; you're the one who's given him children. Noura is . . . a passing fancy!"

She clung to me. "Oh, that accident! That accident! It would have been better if the Hunters had killed him. I would have suffered, of course, but I would've mourned the man I knew. He's changed; he's a different person! A weak, infirm man who's falling apart. He no longer has his leg; he no longer has his head. Damned accident . . ."

Mama attributed all the recent upheavals to the attack on Pannoam; for her, Noura played no role in them. If my father's condition had not required attentive care, he wouldn't have noticed Noura. If he hadn't felt diminished by pain and his limp, he wouldn't have felt a pressing need for youth. Was Mama right? Or was she thinking like a woman seeking to belittle her rival?

"The healer," Mama grumbled.

"What about him?"

"He cast a spell on your father."

"Tibor saved him, Mama!"

She exploded, her eyes bulging and her hands beating the air, "Tibor neither saved him nor cured him, he prevented him from dying! Really, he went beyond his proper function. A healer doesn't act against Nature; he serves it. Nature wanted your father to die from the wounds he received. We mustn't thwart Nature!"

She bit her lip and stammered, "Oh, if he had died that day, I would have only marvelous memories! I would have mourned him with good tears, healthy tears, tears that would've flowed like so many testimonies of love for an exceptional husband. But instead . . ."

My mother didn't finish her sentence. Furious, she struck the tree's bark with her fists.

"Tibor plotted it all. He amputated Pannoam's leg to keep him at his house and bring him into contact with his daughter, and he gave him potions during his convalescence so that he would become infatuated with her. It was him, Noam; it was him!"

I didn't reply, having understood that Mama was in the grip of an obsession: she had to eliminate Noura from all this, erase her attractions. Mama refused to become the victim of a rival; she preferred to invent a fiendish healer.

In the clearing, the sorcerer began to sing in a nasal voice, and then his song was taken up by the audience. The drums beat the rhythm. The ceremony was coming to an end. Flower petals were thrown on the heads of the bride and groom as they walked, majestic, slow, and cordial, through the jubilant crowd.

Soon the dances and the festivities would begin. Later the married couple would withdraw to the house that we'd built behind the trees, near the river . . .

Mama looked up at me.

"How is Mina doing?"

"Fine."

"She'll succeed, this time?"

"I hope so."

"I've prayed to the spirits for her."

"Thank you."

"I know what you're feeling, my son. I know that Tibor has manipulated you, that he got you attached to his daughter and, at the last moment, married her to the chief rather than to the future chief. The damage is done. Jealousy is poisoning your heart, as it is mine, but I admire you because you're fighting! You respect your commitments; you respect your wife; you even respect your father. Just promise me one thing."

"What?"

"Don't respect your stepmother."

After a tense moment, she burst out laughing. I did, too. I hugged her for a long time. She wiped her nose on my shoulder, and then, with her hand, she pushed me toward the crowd.

"Go take care of Mina. When you get tired, come back and join me. There are several jars of wine in the house. We'll drink, you and I, and forget it all."

She went away, staggering and reeling, but not falling; her rage and her pride forbade her to fall.

Spotting Mina, who was looking for me, I went down into the clearing, crept up behind her, and put my arms around her.

"The most beautiful marriage I've ever seen," she whispered in ecstasy, leaning on me.

The musicians began playing lively tunes, and the guests soon entered the dance arena. Some of them struggled clumsily, encumbered by their bodies, while the best of them improvised variations on basic steps; I noticed an unsuspected relaxation and skill among men and women I knew in passing.

Around me, in a circle, many people were rocking in place, waiting for the trance to make them bold enough to sway their hips. The musicians played one song after another to keep the levels of enthusiasm at their height.

By keeping her eyes fixed on me, Mina begged me to dance with her. I was worried and pointed to her pregnant body. "Can you?"

"I want to."

We entered the crowd. Not being very used to dances, I tried to match my movements to the drumbeat, but I was always too late: the rhythm didn't enter into me, or my skin, or my blood; it remained beyond me. Mina, on the other hand, breathed the music. Astonishing! Despite her swollen belly, she moved with ease. When she spotted, in the corner of my eye, my sincere admiration for her, she became merrier than ever and, energized, danced to one song after another.

Exhausted, she gripped my arm.

"Let's go home."

I helped her make her way through the crowd and then, supporting her, to take the path to our house. She groaned. "That was stupid."

"No."

"I shook our baby."

"He loved it. Our baby, in your belly, has discovered that his mother dances well."

Mina blushed and calmed down. As soon as we got home, she threw herself on the mat.

"Mmm . . . sleep . . ."

"I'll keep you company."

"Go back to the party and then come back and tell me all about it."

I acquiesced, pretended to head for the clearing, and, as soon as I was out of Mina's sight, turned in another direction.

Alone in the house, lying down, Mama had drunk a great deal. From armpit to hip, the curve of her body was becoming less and less visible. Without a word, she suggested that I stretch out next to her and handed me a bowl of wine. I gulped it down.

In the distance, the orchestra was reduced to the feverish pulse of the night, a pulse that no longer beat in us.

As I lay down beside her, I whispered, "Sleep well."

She mumbled a reply, and, after drawing a few more breaths that mixed with the melodies and the laughter, her snoring rose to the ceiling.

In the middle of the night I awoke, my mouth furry, my tongue dry. Mama, wrapped in a lethargy that protected her from seeming ungrateful, didn't budge.

I stretched, and, my limbs exhausted and drained of strength, I made my way home with difficulty. Mina, half asleep, heard me come in.

"Did you dance?"

"A little. I'm sore all over."

"Are you proud?"

"Pardon?"

"You were the one who organized this party."

I grimaced, embarrassed, and she took my embarrassment for modesty. Getting up, she took my hand.

"Let's go for a walk, please."

The night was serene and cool, with a gentle breeze. The dark mountains, like recumbent dogs, seemed to be sleeping on the lakeshore. We decided to walk off-path, sheltered from the hubbub, under the shadowy, moss-covered columns of trees. We heard the silky rustle of our steps on the grass and smelled the sharp fragrance of the mint underfoot. Then the clamor attracted us, and we came out on a little hill from which we looked down on the clearing. At our feet, music, fire, song, and dance offered another night that was animated, turbulent, contrasting. The excitement of living was fully triumphant: meat was roasting over different crackling fires; some boys were fighting, others amusing themselves, sometimes both at once; and although most of the villagers were still on the dance floor, couples were beginning to leave.

I tried to see if Pannoam and Noura were still presiding over the banquet, but the distance made it impossible. The idea that they were already copulating made my blood run cold.

Mina laid her hand on mine, lifted it, and pressed it to her navel.

"Do you feel it? He's moving."

I discerned bumps moving under her warm skin.

She smiled at me, blissful. I replied with an identical smile. Ultimately, we ought to have been crowing. This marriage didn't matter . . . I almost savored the situation: down there, my father, a spouse older than I, was trying to seduce Noura, a spouse older than my wife, and yet we represented, Mina and I, the old couple, the solid couple, the one that had survived trials, the one that was observing all this fluff from the distance of maturity.

Mina cried out. "Look!"

She pointed to an owl sitting on a branch above us. Its mask was turned toward us; the pallor of its feathers caught the moonbeams, and its iris sparkled with the fires below.

"We have nothing to be afraid of, Mina; owls don't attack humans."

She shivered.

"Why is it staring at us like that?"

"I don't know."

Two downy disks made the bird's eyes look bigger, occupying the whole of its flat face. Its upper wings looked like a woman's shoulders, and its breast, which was a milky red speckled with dark brown, gave off an uncompromising sense of gravity. I recognized it as a barn owl, a hunter that flew on silent wings to catch voles, field mice, shrews, and even weasels and rabbits.

Mina muttered, "I hate animals that don't have shadows."

She stood up, walked forward a few steps, came back, started to go left, then turned right. The owl's head pivoted without its body moving. Mina exclaimed, aghast, "It's staring at me. I'm the one it's looking at."

After standing up and moving around, I had to admit that she was right. The owl, as if fascinated, kept its eyes riveted on Mina's movements. Amid a tuft of feathers, its eyes persisted, intense, unexpressive, bottomless.

Mina huddled against me to hide herself from the owl.

"What does it mean?" she whispered.

"The owl is a harbinger of change. It predicts metamorphoses."

"I'm scared."

The bird snapped its beak. Hard.

Mina trembled. I reassured her by rubbing her back, laughing. "Mina, think about it! We're going to become parents; a child is coming. That's the change it's announcing."

"I'm not convinced!"

Despite her meek optimism, Mina was capable of sinking into childish fears.

"Why would the owl be angry with you?"

"The gods and the spirits don't like me."

"Mina!"

"It's true! They've never allowed my children to survive. They curse me."

"Mina! I think it's simply that you're going to give birth soon, and it's worrying you. Everything will be all right."

I held her and covered her with kisses, and she calmed down— or at least gave me that impression.

When we were back in our house, on our mat, she cuddled up against my side, seeking contact with me. I held her tight. Two uneasy solitudes trying to forget themselves in animal warmth, that's what our love amounted to . . .

*

At dawn, to avoid meeting Noura and Pannoam, to avoid being subjected to their satisfied expressions, seeing their dark circles, swollen eyelids, blooming lips, the languor that accompanies a wedding night, I told Mina that I was going hunting and left without giving her a chance to be surprised or to groan.

A thin, translucid fog lay on the landscape and diminished its immensity. The Lake and the mountains had disappeared. Through the diffuse mist, the sun was reduced to a moon, and sounds were muffled. Only the hoarse cry of a jay penetrated the torpor.

I got lucky: with my sling, I bagged three hares in record time. The rest of the day was mine.

While the sky was clearing, I decided to visit the magical tree.

To these pages, I confide this: for millennia, I have encountered trees with which I have woven relationships—I'll say more when the opportunity occurs—but none of that would have happened if I hadn't met the Beech.

I discovered it one morning in my childhood, because a squirrel led me to it. I recall every detail of that day. We always remember the first time, the one that begins a cycle, the initiatory moment given new life by the ones that follow it in the course of existence.

Tracking a wild boar with my friends, I'd strayed from our group for some reason—did I feel a need to be alone?—and had ended up in a wild forest without any paths or landmarks. On a stump that was being eaten away by saffron-colored mushrooms sat a squirrel, its tail raised like an umbrella, nibbling on a nut it held in its forepaws. Sensing my presence, it had looked up, and, relieved to see me, with a brisk movement of its muzzle, it signaled that I should follow it. Nimble, red, supple, it moved in zigzags; too light to walk, it hopped and bounded rapidly, stopped for a moment, waited for me, caught my eye, and then, reassured, took off again. It wasn't running away from me; it was making sure I was right behind it.

Beyond the forest, the squirrel came to the isolated beech tree, where it halted, turned toward me, and climbed up the trunk. There again, it stopped halfway up, its head down, its eyes blazing, just to make certain that I was still there. I also shinnied up the tree, slowly, cautiously, with the awkwardness of a human being without pointed claws. My clumsiness amused it. When, out of breath, I reached the branches, the squirrel had disappeared.

The tree then entered into contact with me. By inspiring a feeling of well-being in me, by enchanting my nostrils with a sweet, yellow perfume, the Beech whispered to me: "Lie down." I stretched out, my legs and arms hanging down, my belly on a large branch whose smooth bark seemed to me no thicker or less soft than skin. The Beech insisted that I close my eyes. Obediently, I fell asleep and had sumptuous dreams sent by the tree: I soared through the air, becoming a bird, pollen, a cloud, wind, all the spirits that were associated with the Beech.

I descended from my perch calmed, enriched, ecstatic to have received the revelations of the Living One, of the Great Soul, the one that includes humans, animals, plants, waters, stones, the one that, through the mediation of the tree, had judged me worthy.

Delighted, I caught up with my comrades but told them nothing about what had happened to me. What could my rudimentary words have conveyed to them?

I returned to the Beech frequently. Its leaves swished when I appeared, its branches flared out, its trunk sheltered me. I coiled up in it for hours at a time.

When I was about eleven years old, the Beech initiated me into a mystery. To this book, I'll confide the innermost of my secrets.

Thrilled with the whiskers on my chin, proud of the down that covered my cheeks, I was filled with new vigor, with an energy that made me want to run, jump, swim, split wood, lift stones, fight. So much sap was surging through me that I was extremely active. But the more I did, the more my dissatisfaction gnawed at me.

One afternoon in the spring, the Beech received me when I was boiling over with it. It invited me to perch on it, and as I was moving from branch to branch, it gave me a gift: I felt a wave of delight well up and then spread between my thighs and my belly, a wave that grew, expanded, invaded my torso, deepened my breathing, accelerated my heart. Each time I thought the pleasure was going to fade, it grew. The intensity of this euphoria scared me—but overcame all resistance. My neck swelled, heated up. My lips were on fire. My ears burned. I was sliding along the main branch of the tree, my legs hanging down and, from one shiver to the next, from a tremor to a light touch, I made my way toward the unknown. I gradually lost control, wondering where the pleasure would reach its culmination. Suddenly, satisfaction made me stop breathing; something broke in me. A warm liquid shot forth, flooding my lower abdomen. I hardly had time to cry out before I fainted.

When I opened my eyes again, I awoke in a different world, a bigger universe that was captivating, troubling, and where such bodies devoted themselves to these vertiginous delights. I caressed the tree; I kissed it. The adult Noam had just been born. Here and there, in the hollow of my calves, on my thighs, along my sides, a few tremors still ran, like joyous memories that didn't want to die away. Glued to my navel, a trace of happiness remained, a chalky, dried patch that flaked off when I touched it. Embracing the Beech, I thanked it: never had I experienced such joy.

Blissful and ecstatic, I remained there for a long time, until I no longer felt anything other than fatigue. My limbs heavy, I returned to the earth.

Afterward, I often came back to rub against the trunk. The smells mattered, the odors of the leaves, of the wood with its seeping humidity, of the amadou that intoxicated me. At first, I visited this mystery without understanding it, sometimes without experiencing it again because the sensual convulsions were slow in coming, were interrupted, or even failed to appear, in which case I badgered the tree: what had I done to upset it?

Finally, I understood—the Beech taught me—how best to shape what happened between us, how my skin trembled against its tree skin, how the rocking motion I impressed on it had to remain delicate, how the caress of the bark made my penis swell, how the latter exploded, volcanically, releasing its semen.

What human beings call the "solitary pleasure" wasn't solitary for me: it was pleasure with the tree. The Beech had taught me sensual delight.

I hardly need to say that once I was married, I no longer enjoyed this delight in my copulation with Mina. Ever. Our intercourse always had a forced, laborious, utilitarian nature, to the point that its end relieved me of a cramp and a duty. To reach sensual ecstasy, I had wait until . . . But let's not get ahead of ourselves.

The day after the wedding, the day when I escaped my spouse, when I avoided Noura and Pannoam, I took refuge in the leafy heart of the beech tree and made do with daydreaming there. When the sun went down, I returned to the village.

The Beech had washed away my cares: in its silence, in its light, everything that revealed itself to be human, solely and excessively human—resentment, envy, a son's dissatisfaction, a lover's frustration—had melted away. The day on the tree had relieved me of my social denseness by returning me to a body, a simple body among bodies, a natural element at the heart of a munificent Nature. I'd sluffed off my importance, and thus lightened, I found full satisfaction merely in existing.

At the edge of the village, a boy was watching the path. As soon as he saw me, he ran toward me.

"Noam! Mina is giving birth!"

I stopped dead. Although Mina's belly was growing larger, I hadn't thought she was ready to give birth.

The boy persisted: "She's asking for you. So is your mother. The women are there."

This detail caught my attention. It was understandable that

Mama would be with Mina—she was supposed to help her give birth—but the fact that other women were present at an event that normally took place in darkness and privacy worried me.

I ran to the house, found the crowd and pushed through it, and saw Mina prostrate, her back on the ground and her thighs open amid soiled linens. Why was she lying there like that?

Among my people, women squatted to give birth. The pelvis forward, they adopted a posture that allowed for a rapid expulsion, the baby finding the way out by itself; the mothers let themselves be borne on a wave. To spare themselves effort, they held onto a low wooden beam or else relied on their partner, who, positioned behind them, supported them by the armpits. In addition, over the preceding months Mina had prepared herself for this effort by strengthening her knees, sitting on her heels every day and getting up slowly.

The birth had to be going badly for the mother to lie down on her back with her legs spread. Then there were screams, tears, panting, the matrons urging the unfortunate woman to push, and the whole affair taking a tragic turn.

Mina, pale, her eyes closed, almost unconscious, groaned among silent women.

"What's going on?"

When she heard my voice, she opened her eyes. A glow of hope passed through her red-ringed pupils.

"Noam!"

I knelt down to caress her ashen, damp forehead. Exhausted, she closed her eyes again, while her bluish lips formed a smile.

Mama came up to me.

"The contractions came early."

"Is that a good sign? A bad sign?" I cried, taken aback.

Mama told the village women to withdraw. Without a word, their heads down, they went away.

Mama put her hand on my shoulder and directed me to a

corner of the house. On the ground, she pointed to a dark mass crusted in blood, soiled linens twined around it.

"This is what came out. It was already dead in her belly."

I leaned against the wall. My head was dripping with sweat. Distraught, I stammered, "Mina was right. We're cursed."

Mama wiped my temples and spoke clearly: "*She* is cursed, my son. Not you."

"Yes, I am!"

"No! Do you want proof?"

Dumbstruck, I scrutinized my mother. With a jerk of her chin, she gestured toward Mina.

"She's losing blood. We've been trying for hours to clean her up, but she continues to empty herself out. A wound is oozing inside her."

"What?"

"She's dying, my son. She would already have drawn her last breath if she hadn't been waiting for you."

Without further reflection, I threw myself on the ground and clasped Mina's mottled cheeks between my palms.

She opened her eyes, broken, and stared at me with all the intensity of which she was still capable. Sadness and shame slipped into her pupils.

"Forgive me . . ."

"Forgive you for what, Mina? We'll try again; you can do it."

Her features settled into an ambiguous expression that meant, "I'm not fooled, but it's kind of you to lie."

She reached for my hand and gripped it with what little strength remained to her.

"Afraid . . ." she murmured.

I put my lips on her forehead, and, touching her cold skin, I understood our relationship: Mina was a little girl who'd been entrusted to me so that she might become a woman. Once she was married to me, she'd tried hard to accomplish her tasks, to unite herself with her husband, to get pregnant, to feed babies, and she did so awkwardly, with difficulty; it was never easy for her. Everywhere, she had failed, and she was spending her last moments weighing the extent of her failure.

I bent down and whispered in her ear, "You've made me very happy, Mina."

A new emotion surged up in her face, which was so close to mine: joy! Joy won out over remorse and fear. Joy shone with an unbearable brilliance.

I smiled at her, and my smile transported her to a summit.

A tremor shook her body. Her grip tightened.

"Mina!"

She exhaled.

"Mina!"

I shook her fingers to make them respond.

"Mina!"

Mama took me in her arms.

"She's begun her journey to the other world, Noam."

I contemplated the wide-open eyes that no longer saw me.

Mama whispered, "Her blue soul has left her breast, risen above us, and left the house. She's headed toward the Lake."

Stunned, I stretched out next to Mina's body. I could tell from her inertia and the coldness that was overtaking her limbs that she was no longer there, that she was now moving ahead alone, that she could no longer count on me; yet I needed to keep something of her, to clasp it to me, or at least to embrace her memory.

Dare I admit it? I wept. I wept for a long time.

My tears bore the color of the affection I'd lavished on Mina: the color of pity. In the emotions she had aroused, in the tenderness I'd shown her, there was nothing but compassion, that sympathy with regard to a person weaker than oneself, charity toward the destitute. I'd always felt sorry for Mina; sorry that she was fearful, awkward, graceless, a timid lover and an inadequate mother; sorry that she had to struggle to achieve her destiny; sorry for her defeats; now I was sorry for her final failure, dying in childbirth, dying so young . . . And this pity was—I understood this as I clung to her body—not only a complete acceptance of her, but also a kind of love. A bitter, excruciating, lucid, unhappy love, but still a love . . .

Contrary to custom, I didn't wait.

Tradition demanded that the body be publicly exposed for a day so everyone could pay their respects and then that it be buried. But I knew that no one would truly pay respects to Mina, this little girl lost in the world of adults. Because her family was dead, she didn't matter to anyone but me.

I told Mama that I would bury her that night. She exclaimed, "I'll inform your father."

"Why?"

"As head of the village, he . . ."

"I don't want to see him! Absolutely not! Not him, not Noura! Do you understand? Mama, do you understand?"

She said in a sad voice, "Who understands you better than I do?"

I wrapped Mina in a cloth, with her shell necklace around her neck, and did the same for the child. Then I plunged into the dark forest, carrying the two corpses on my shoulders. Mama followed me at a respectful distance, concerned that I not remain alone.

Using a hoe, I made a hole not far from a gnarled and mossy oak tree. Determined to protect my wife and child from hungry wild animals, refusing to let them be eaten by birds of prey, I dug deeply and long in the clay soil. When the grave was finished, I went to the clearing where the festival had been held, and with Mama's help, I picked bunches of flowers that I threw into the hole.

Mina loved lilies and was mad about their fragrance. These bouquets would accompany her on her way.

Finally, I arranged her like a sleeping child to get her ready for her next birth. This involved difficulties; already stiff, her limbs did not bend easily, but I persisted, forcing her knees to touch her chin. According to our beliefs, she could only be reborn in this way, in a fetal position, in the earth. Once I had succeeded in this, I laid the newborn against her belly.

Mama handed me the pot of ocher that she'd brought with her. I spread the red powder—the blood of the dead and of the resurrection—over the two bodies, then made a narrow line of ocher emerging from their nostrils to show breath the direction of life.

I filled in the hole and flattened the burial mound. How comforting physical effort was! Digging, filling in, leveling, those were tasks I could do, and their execution kept my sorrow at bay.

The grave covered up, I lay down alongside it and devoted the night to asking the spirits to welcome Mina and my baby. Behind me, Mama was also praying. Mentally, I sent farewell kisses to the little girl I had married, a child who had been little loved, even with all the love she had to offer.

Dawn was glowing on the horizon. Like the village, the Lake was still asleep. A pale sky was spreading its ashen reflection on it. My eyes scanned this placid expanse. The air, the water, the forests were abandoning themselves to the same silence.

A chickadee landed on the grave.

I examined it closely. In contrast to others of its kind, which were lively and energetic, it displayed a soft sluggishness. It kept its eyes fixed on me.

"Mina?"

The chickadee did not fly away, stubbornly staring at me. Was I dreaming? Had I slept so little that I was nodding off? It seemed to me that the bird resembled Mina in its minimal plumage, its commonness, its sweetness.

After a few moments, the chickadee flew off and perched on the oak. I turned to Mama.

"I'm leaving."

She jumped.

"Excuse me?"

"I'm going to leave the village."

"For how long?"

"Forever!"

Mama rushed to me and grabbed my arm.

"Noam, no! No one can survive outside the village."

"I'll live like a Hunter."

"Noam, everyone who has been banished has been found dead."

She was referring to the two men whom Pannoam, at an interval of several moons, had condemned to exile: each of them had been found dead under a tree, bearing no trace of combat or violence, as if they had, like a cut flower, rotted there.

"Don't mix things up, Mama. They were expelled against their wishes because they were being punished for their crimes. But I am leaving of my own free will. I want to leave; I need to leave."

"You're running away!"

"Maybe . . ."

Mama fell silent and looked at me for a long time, her eyes streaked with red.

She murmured, simply, "If I were young, I'd leave with you."

After that, she took me in her arms, pressed me to her breast, and, turning her head so that I couldn't see her tears, strode off toward the village.

Never had she addressed a hurtful word or gesture to me. Never had her attention failed. I had devoted my life to idolizing my father, but I now realized that my mother was more deserving of my love. Decidedly, I didn't understand women at all.

Did I understand men?

Or myself?

Mama having disappeared, I set out for home. There I stuffed some things into a bag and hung my bow on my shoulder.

Farewell to the clan! Farewell, Father! Farewell, Noura! I left the village without anyone noticing.

Crossing the forest, I passed close to Mina's grave. Sitting on its branch, the chickadee froze when it saw me.

Then, as I continued on my way, the bird spread its wings and followed me.

The gods and the spirits hated me. Despite the indignant denials of my mother, who directed all her hatred toward Mina, I no longer had any illusions: the gods and spirits would not allow me to carry on my line. Mina turned out to be not the object but the instrument of their vengeance; through her, I was their target. Why?

An hour's walk away from the village, I stopped, sat down under a tree, drank some water, and cracked a few nuts.

From there, I surveyed the whole landscape.

The Lake was calm, its surface untroubled by any current. The forest was reflected in it, pure, clear, immobile. Not a breath of wind. No lapping of waves. No honking of a bittern. A brown heron wearily beat its wings, but since its feathers slipped ineffectually through the air, it gave up trying to take off and froze, reduced to a branch stuck in the water.

I tried to determine why gods and spirits were reprimanding me. Had I offended a spring by bathing in it? Had I deprived the earth of one of its fruits—a root, a truffle, a turnip—without noticing? Had I inadvertently transgressed a sacred circle? Had I uttered impious words? Even when I rummaged through my thoughts, I found nothing. The wrath of the gods and spirits went back several years: the punishment had been inflicted as early as my marriage to Mina . . .

The beige chickadee fluttered, hesitated, then settled on a branch above me. Although it avoided my eyes, it didn't leave me. When I looked at it, it tilted its head, embarrassed, shy, like Mina. Its intriguing presence encouraged me: if Mina's soul lodged in this bird was escorting me, there was something I still had to do. I was going through a test instead of crouching in a hole. Maybe my misfortune's trajectory wouldn't be irreversible . . .

"Noam, I need to talk to you."

I saw Tibor, wearing his voluminous cloak, suddenly appear in front of me.

"The women told me about the misfortune that struck Mina, and then I noticed your departure, this morning, as I was beginning to gather my herbs. Forgive me for having spied on you. I wanted you to know that I feel your helplessness and that I'll do what I can to help you. You're irreplaceable, Noam."

This unexpected compliment, bursting forth at a time when I was wondering what I had done wrong, overwhelmed me. My blood froze; my lips trembled.

"I'm mediocre."

"Noam, you're intelligent, curious, considerate, benevolent. If I was told that you'd offended someone, I wouldn't believe it."

"The gods and the spirits don't share your opinion. They think I've offended them. For years, they've been punishing me by preventing me from founding a family."

Tibor sat down beside me. He spread his legs and rocked from right to left.

"You're drawing hasty conclusions, Noam. During these past years, Nature has shown you its wisdom."

"What?"

"Let me tell you a memory of mine. Like your father, I am fond of dogs. In my first village, before the mud buried it, I was raising a female dog. One night, she gave birth to five pups. When each of them popped out, she delicately caught the pouch of skin enveloping them, opened it with her little teeth, licked the newborn, and then nudged it toward her nipples so it could nurse. Suddenly, a sixth pup arrived. The mother dog looked at it, sighed, and left it on the ground. Shocked, I picked it up, tore open the sack, and showed the pup to the mother, who,

exhausted, granted it three licks of her tongue that she immediately regretted and turned away. At the time, her behavior revolted me. But two moons later, I could see her lucidity. Forced
to feed such a litter, she had used up her strength and started
to die, incapable of fulfilling her role. If I hadn't exercised my
powers as a healer, if I hadn't fed the puppies and treated the
mother with herbs that reinvigorate the blood, they would have
all succumbed."

"What are you insinuating?"

"Nature knows. When the mother rejected the sixth pup,
Nature foresaw that she would feed five, not six. Nature thought
it was better that one die so that the others and their mother
could survive. Nature anticipates, calculates, sees far. We, with
our noses glued to the present, remain blind to the future."

He gently massaged my shoulder.

"If your child perished before term, that means it had neither
the power nor the vocation to live. This spontaneous rejection
expresses Nature's wisdom."

"And what about Mina? Does her death also derive from
wisdom?"

Tibor continued in a calmer voice: "How many miscarriages
did she have?"

"Three."

"How many babies that did not live for more than a year?"

"Four. No, five."

"That shows that your wife could not carry out her destiny as
a woman."

I bowed my head, resistant to this argument and to criticism
or underestimation of Mina.

Tibor continued in a level tone, "We're wrong to be angry with
the gods and the spirits. Since we cannot divine their intentions,
we imagine that they must be absurd, violent, illogical, arbitrary,
wrathful, capricious, or vindictive. On the contrary, we should
consider them clear-sighted. They show neither malevolence nor

stupidity; they foresee. Don't doubt their intelligence; doubt ours, which quickly reaches its limits."

He laid his hand on mine again.

"If the gods and the spirits have taken away your wife and your children, it's because they aspire to something better. They will prove that to you someday."

The chickadee, busy cleaning its plumage, wasn't listening to us. I thought about Mina, about her furtive passage on earth, her short life full of suffering and disappointed hopes.

"Where do we find the strength to keep going?"

"All living beings are survivors, Noam. The living have survived birth, childhood illnesses, famines, storms, battles, cold, sorrow, separation, fatigue. The living already have the strength to go on."

"To go on for what purpose?"

"To live. Life is its own goal, Noam. Nature attests to that at every moment. As a healer, I don't resist Nature. When I heal someone, I imitate Nature."

"But you're fighting against death."

"I'm not fighting against death; I'm fighting for life."

"Do you accept death?"

"Nature needs death to perpetuate life. Look around you. This forest has existed forever and nourishes itself. Look carefully! No debris. Nothing useless. Excrement, cadavers, and rotting materials are all useful. Branches fall and enrich the earth. Trees fall, and their rotting fertilizes plants, mushrooms, worms. Animals die, and their flesh, their hides, their bones provide food for other animals. When you walk through brush that mixes heather with suckers, you're walking on countless preceding forests. Dead leaves give rise to living leaves, young shoots arise from decomposition. Every fallen creature produces a new one; each death enlarges being. There are no defeats. Nature knows neither a halt nor an end because it recycles by connecting with new forms. It is through death that life is reborn, perseveres, and develops."

"You fought to keep my father from dying after he was attacked."

"You're blaming me for that because it separated you from Noura. But I didn't eliminate his death. Pannoam will die some-day. I prolonged his life, using the life forces at his disposal and at mine."

Silence fell. In front of us, indifferent, the Lake stretched out under the springtime sun.

Tibor pointed to my bag.

"What are you going to do?"

"Live."

"So much the better."

"Far from the village."

"In another village?"

"In the forest."

He cleared his throat.

"Aren't you afraid of the Hunters?"

"I'll become one of them."

For a long time he remained silent. Then he stood up, dusting off his cloak.

"I would have loved to pass on my knowledge, to hand down to you those secrets of Nature that I've received or discovered. I saw you as my disciple."

He shook his head.

"To complete my teaching, my daughter would have had to . . ."

He blushed and fell silent, waiting for my confirmation. I nod-ded. Then, biting his lip, he murmured:

"Ah, Noura . . . Noura . . ."

When he realized what he was doing, he stopped, feeling guilty. Noura was proving fatal for him, for me, for my father, for my mother. He swallowed hard, looking into the distance. "You're the son I would have liked to have, Noam. Or the son-in-law. I will come here regularly. If someday you need me, you'll find me here."

Without looking at me, he left, following the path bordered by ferns that wound down the rocky slope. The tall, noble silhouette of the man I would have preferred as my father disappeared.

I rose, picked up my bag, and continued on my way.

After a few moments, the chickadee soared past me with frightened eyes, as if to say, "What an idea, heading out now! Did you forget about me?"

There was no longer any doubt: Mina was inhabiting the chickadee, because I had in fact forgotten her.

The following days brought me much-needed distraction. I rambled, hunted, gathered, cooked; every evening, I experimented with different sleeping places. The picturesque aspect of these activities kept me from getting tired of them.

I wanted my young body to belong to Nature, which was eternally young. Everything in it amazed me: the perfect dawn; the blazing sun; the light-saturated clouds; the vivid blue of the sky; the noisy torrents; the curtains of rain; the murmur of streams; the bitter, virile song of the wind; the sweetness of twilight; the questioning of the shadows; the comforting stars; the coquettish moon that took on the color of copper or silver. Since I'd been staying there, the splendor of the universe had been restored to me; I merged with it and celebrated a new wedding.

Curiously, I didn't encounter a single Hunter. While our village paid troops intended to protect us from pillaging and killing, I moved peacefully through forests and fields populated only by animals. At most, it seemed to me that I'd once spotted a worrisome shadow, that of an unusually large individual, which vanished; I decided that I'd dreamed it—especially since it seemed vaguely related to the giant who had rid Pannoam of his attackers.

A discovery astonished me: two hours were enough to provide for all my needs. In a few movements, I bathed in the same river where I'd rinsed my rags.* The thickets were so full of game, the streams so full of fish, and the trees so full of fruit that feeding myself demanded little effort. What a contrast with my work schedule in the village! No more fields to be cultivated, flocks to be guarded, dogs to be trained, objects to be traded, or house to be repaired—not to mention the imperatives connected with my father: discussing, advising, pacifying, meting out justice, and overseeing our militia. Now my days were my own.

At first, this was a relief: freed from constraints, I enjoyed this spare time. Later, it weighed on me. I came to find the emptiness of this respite oppressive, and I suspected people of having invented the division of labor and community life to dissipate their boredom.

Some mornings, I felt nostalgic. Under a pure sky, the prospect of a day without tasks depressed me, and I dreaded getting through it. In the village, I would have hesitated between several constraints: here, I had the choice among the useless, the gratuitous, and the superfluous. Generally speaking, I went to the magical tree, climbed up the long trunk, lay down on one of its

---

* People have always tried to keep clean. It's a human passion. Although I have encountered slovenly individuals, I've never known a dirty epoch, or a society that held griminess in high esteem.

The desire for cleanliness is unchanging. On the other hand, the definition of cleanliness has changed countless times. For instance, the reputation of water has varied, depending on the historical period. In my youth, we believed in the virtues of running water and bathed in rivers and streams, mistrusting stagnant water. The Greeks and Romans valued the immobile water of swimming pools, cold and then warm, whereas in the Middle Ages people were crazy about steam rooms. However, in the Renaissance, after so many plague epidemics, baths were accused of opening the pores and thus promoting the introduction of deleterious germs into the body. Accordingly, people took dry baths, using powders, leaves, alcohols, vinegars, and floral solutions. A strong body odor was considered a proof of excellent health, with the difference that aristocrats, even as they bragged about having B.O., masked it with perfumes. The custom that made these people dirty, as seen from a modern point of view, proved to be founded on a concern about hygiene. Finally, water came back . . . Presently, our knowledge regarding bacteria and viruses has expanded the territory of dirtiness and indicated new requirements.

Cleanliness persists; dirtiness evolves.

branches, and mixed my caresses with its own. These ecstasies, followed by naps, repeated two or three times in a row, provided me with delights, of course, but tired me out. The pleasure didn't wear out, but my body did. I got to the point where I forced myself to abstain from it.

Melancholy affected me more in the evening. The stars lit up, the moon had the place of honor in the sky, and wispy clouds mounted toward it, hastening to pay it homage: I saw myself as minuscule, miserable.

However, pride prevented me from going back. What? Retreat when I had not advanced more than a single step? Resume my status so soon after I had disengaged myself from it? Out of the question! To be sure, everyone would warmly welcome me back; no one would disapprove of my absence, and they might even celebrate my return. But I cherished only the Noam who had left the village, the one who had asserted his fortitude by daring to make this risky decision; he alone deserved my respect. On the other hand, I scorned the Noam who wanted to go home. A duel was taking place inside me between the savage and the village dweller, between the free man and the prisoner, between the Noam who had no father and the submissive Noam.

Preferring division to cowardice, I pursued my life at the heart of Nature.

One afternoon when the cherry trees were heavy with their abundant purple fruit, I was sitting on an embankment, maintaining my equipment. Since dawn, I had cut dead, dry branches to make arrows, sharpened flint points that I had attached to their tips, and strengthened my bowstring by making it thicker. Now I was stuffing maple leaves into the empty horn in which I stored my living embers.

Clouds had approached, gray, blackish, threatening; they formed a moving army that was advancing toward the Lake. Silent, disciplined despite their differing volumes, they obscured the sun and invaded the panorama. Their slowness was spreading something terrible and inexorable, the growing darkness making it all the more to be feared because it was a long time coming.

Massed, compact, the clouds were waiting. They held their breath. As they pressed against one another, they changed in consistency: no longer clouds, they became smoke, heavy smoke, thick and sooty . . .

A lightning bolt flashed to the left. A silence followed, the silence of soldiers who are concentrating, ready to attack.

The thunder resounded. A second lightning bolt ripped the horizon.

All at once, the clouds burst. Like blood spurting from a wound, a downpour began.

I picked up my bow, my quiver, my bag, and went to take refuge under a monumental oak.

A third lightning bolt flared.

The wind grew stronger, as if it were obeying the lightning. It divided itself into violent gusts that flattened the grasses, shook trees, and plunged into the forest. It howled. Its wildness made it incoherent, blowing in one direction, then in another, rising, calming, colliding with itself, whirling.*

---

* There is nothing more fugitive than wind. Anyone who wants to observe it is subjected to its whims: we have to wait for it to rise, determine its source, gauge its intensity, its temperature, its humidity, its violence. Whether wind blows or subsides, it escapes.

According to us, the Peoples of the Lake, there were six wind gods. These six were differentiated by their direction and their temperament. From the north descended two gods, one friendly and one hostile: Bor the cool and Kek the furious. From the east came another pair of twin gods: Zof the soft, who awoke with the evening star and brought us springtime, and Zef the mad, who destroyed everything. Finally, Meuro came from the west and Noto from the south. It seems to me that the Greeks, long afterward, perpetuated this observation when they explained that Aeolis, the god who directed the winds, had six children.

We didn't know whether these gods lived in the heavens or in the mountains. In spite of their intransigent character, and even if their brutality often seemed to us without purpose or reason, we tried to influence them by means of prayer and offerings. On the other hand, it didn't occur to us to make use of them. We lived near them; they dominated us. Certainly, from time to time we took advantage of the presence of one

I shivered. What terrifying anger! What did the gods and the spirits have against humans? What had the Peoples of the Lake done to deserve this escalation?

Curled up in a ball, I could no longer protect myself from either cold raindrops or gusts of wind.

The rumbling of thunder grew louder, lighting bolts grew more frequent, the chaos was at its height. I was in the midst of the storm; it was aimed at me.

I closed my eyes, hoping for invisibility.

But the rumbling swelled again, impetuous, ferocious, inflexible, to the point that for a moment I thought it was going to grind me up. I opened my eyes.

Something flashed and blinded me.

Lightning struck the oak.

The oak cracked like a person screaming, then split in two with a heartbreaking groan. It was falling on me.

I leaped away, avoided being crushed, and took off through the forest. Where could I find shelter? Was there any refuge?

Distraught, frightened, I ran. Several times, I slipped on the ground streaming with water. I was covered with mud. The cold, the wetness, and fear made me shiver. My teeth chattered. I was going this way and that, wandering about, without finding any escape. Would I spend the entire storm running for my life?

Thousands and thousands of relentless raindrops assailed me, while the wind beat down the waves of rain in transversal attacks. It sprayed, stung, diluted, soaked, slid, tore away, dripped, drowned.

of them to quickly dry our laundry, but we did it secretly. We feared them as much as we were ignorant of them.

When, later on, people made use of the winds, I was surprised, at first shocked and then enthusiastic. The way sailboats played with the winds to travel dazzled me, and then I understood why sailors, scientists, and merchants felt the need to know more about them. As for the mills that exploited winds' enormous muscles, I saw them appear for the first time, and I admired them for centuries. Their recent disappearance pained me; however, I note that today they're returning in the form of turbines intended to produce electricity, which delights me.

In an area where I suddenly emerged, I noticed rocks. I rushed toward them and spotted a dark opening. A cave!

I went into it. Thinking myself saved, I threw myself against the back wall and, on the way, tripped over something warm.

A groan rang out.

It turned into a hoarse cry, then a cavernous howl.

The bear! The bear was living in the cave. No doubt I'd awakened him.

I backed up.

The bear got up and looked around.

I'd surprised him so much that he'd just realized an intruder had stolen into his domain; in an instant, he would attack.

Panicked, I decamped and ran along the rocks, my chest tight, breathing with increasing difficulty.

A root sticking out of the soaked earth caught my foot, and I fell. There was no denying it: my final moment had come.

But when I turned around, I saw nothing but the raindrops, dense to the point of grayness. The bear wasn't chasing me. Because of the thunder and lightning? Was he perhaps trembling at the back of his cave?

I got to my feet and started moving along the cliff. I detected a crevice too narrow for the bear. I slowly slipped into it and waited until my eyes became accustomed to the darkness; when I was convinced that no animal was living there, I plunged into the opening and collapsed on the rock.

*

I stayed there two days and two nights.

Furtively, I went out only to drink or relieve myself. The rain persisted, insisted, heavy, continuous. In two days it rained more than it usually did in several moons. In the humid shadows of the cavern, its monotonous, dismaying hiss established a still, vast, depressing lassitude.

Leaving would have been imprudent. Not only did I not know where I was, but the downpour had made the ground treacherous, the landscape opaque. Everything was floating in indistinctness; the world was being liquefied. With a twinge of sorrow, I thought of my bow, my quiver, and especially my bag, which contained the tools I needed to survive, flint knives, ropes, hides, my fire-making kit. I was eager to get them back.

On the third day, the rain stopped.

Starving, I stuck my head outside, made sure the bear was not there, and then left my cave.

Where was I?

I tried to collect my memories of where I had run to determine which direction to take. Alas—was it a failure of memory or the result of my exhaustion?—I failed. Nothing reminded me of anything. Zigzagging during the storm, I had involuntarily entered into an unknown territory.

Worry made me feel weaker. If I didn't find my bag soon, I wouldn't survive.

Feverishly, I looked for something to eat. This part of the forest was composed solely of oaks, beeches, and maples, none of which bore fruit; as for game, without my bow and arrows, I wouldn't succeed in catching any.

The situation seemed hopeless.

By some instinctive tenacity, my legs still carried me forward. More intelligent than I, they followed the slope, that is, the path to the Lake. Was it a few steps away, or a day's walk?

Around noon, tremulous with hunger and rage, I sat down at the foot of a tree.

I couldn't believe my eyes.

In front of me, a hare was hanging. Caught in a snare attached to a bush, it had died, suffocated. Without wondering who had installed the trap, I detached the animal.

I was finally going to eat. Raw? Who cared? Once I'd skinned it, I would eat it!

On all fours, I searched the ground, looking for a sharp stone that would cut the hare's skin when I noticed that a shadow was covering me.

I turned around, raised my head: the giant!

The furious Hunter, holding his club over his head, was getting ready to smash me to bits.

I screamed, "No!

The giant began to bring his weapon down on me.

"Pannoam!"

The club veered away at the last moment and struck the moss, right next to my skull.

Stupefied, the giant looked at me with exasperation.

"Why did you shout 'Pannoam'?"

His question made me realize that I had called on my father to help me. The giant repeated, in a hostile tone, "Why Pannoam?"

I hung my head, too ashamed to admit it.

The colossus brandished his club again, his face red with anger. "You called him because he's your chief, you poor worm. Well, your chief isn't going to save you. You've stolen from me; you're going to die."

He gathered momentum and brought his club down again.

"He's my father!"

The club grazed my cheek and pulverized a big stone on the ground.

"What?" the colossus roared.

He dropped his weapon on the ground.

"What are you doing so far away from your village?"

"I've left it."

A cruel light shimmered in his pupils.

"Why?"

"I no longer want to be there."

He stared at me, and during this examination, I deduced that, sluggish and anemic, I would have the strength neither to run away nor to fight this mountain of hate-filled muscle. His wrist was twice the size of mine, and his arms were three times as large as my thighs. I prepared myself for my execution. He exclaimed, "My nephew!"

The giant lifted me up, clasped me to his solid torso, and hugged me vigorously.

"My nephew!"

While my feet were dangling in the void, my head was glued to his bushy hair, his hirsute beard, whiskers poking between my lips. Like his odor, his embrace proved so powerful that I didn't react, worried about being suffocated.

He put me down, took a step backward, studied me, his eye mischievous, a smile stretching his oxblood-colored mouth.

"A handsome fellow!"

And he clapped me on the back. I had to use all my strength to avoid falling.

There was no longer any doubt! I recognized him: in front of me stood the Hunter who had killed the men who attacked my father, the one who had put an end to five lives in an instant.

This giant had so impressed the villagers that he fed our dreams. His identities varied: the spirit of the village, the god of the hills, even the ghost of Kaddour, my grandfather and the previous chief. The elders claimed to have long seen him roaming around the Lake, whereas I had seen him only during the attack on my father. Now that I came closer to him, I realized that he was a man, certainly out of the ordinary, strong-limbed, muscular, rough-cut, disheveled, gigantic, but a man.

I murmured, "Who are you?"

"Barak, your uncle."

"My uncle?"

"Pannoam's brother."

My father had never mentioned having a brother; he had only mentioned his sisters, who were all married to chiefs of neighboring villages, aunts whom I had never met.

He chortled when he saw my pensive face, "Didn't that bastard ever tell you about me? Doesn't surprise me . . . Not only does he think he's superior, he thinks no one else exists. From time to time, I think he's sorry not to have been his own origin, to have depended on parents to be born, not to have given birth to himself. He's quite a guy, that Pannoam!"

He was talking about my father crudely, though a certain tenderness tinged his tone. He added, "I'm the second. That is, the second boy . . . Between him and me there were three sisters and two miscarriages. Yes, yes, don't laugh: I'm your father's little brother!"

The giant, beaming, thumped his breast. A powerful, muffled, hollow sound arose from it.

I peered at him.

"Are you the one who saved him from the five Hunters?"

He looked away, wanting to avoid the subject.

"Was that you?" I asked again.

He clicked his tongue and sighed.

"I should have intervened sooner. They really messed him up."

He looked me in the eye. "No?"

I nodded and told him how Tibor had saved Pannoam's life by amputating his leg and then sculpting a leg made from a stag's bone for him.

The colossus grimaced on hearing these details, as if anatomical manipulations were repellent to his sensitive soul. He spat.

"And you," he exclaimed, "what's your name?"

"Noam."

"You're his eldest son?"

"His only son."

"The one who will succeed him?"

"Yes."

"What are you doing here?"

I shook my head.

"It's a long story."

"I've got time."

My eyes were smarting and blurring my vision; standing up was torture for me; and as for my stomach, it was consumed with pain. Feeling the pressure of his curiosity, I admitted in a muffled voice, "I'm starving to death. It's been three days since I ate anything."

Delighted, he burst into laughter.

"Of course, my thief was hungry! Come on, boy. We're going to cook the hare you were getting ready to steal from me. In the meantime, you can take the edge off your appetite by nibbling on walnuts and hazelnuts."

Admitting my deprivation was humiliating, but faced with his affability, all embarrassment melted away.

He walked back up the forest path. I struggled to keep up with him. His strides, which were only a little faster than mine but longer, covered twice as much terrain; he was constantly getting ahead of me. As soon as he turned his back on me, I trotted after him with quick steps to catch up, looking ridiculous. Then, as soon as he turned around, I resumed a more dignified demeanor. Never since my childhood had I felt so minuscule.

We came to a wall of brambles. He went around it, crouching down to pass between thornless bushes, and pushed through the foliage. We came out in front of a hidden hut built using branches and animal hides.

"Welcome."

He grabbed a bag full of nuts.

"Enjoy."

Then without paying any more attention to me, he took up a flint knife to deal with the hare.

I went for the nuts.

"Chew slowly," he scolded me. "Otherwise, you're going to throw up."

As I was eating, he skinned the animal, lopped off its head, gutted it, and cut it up. Then he pressed each piece between two stones.

"It will cook faster this way."

Frustrated, he looked at me. "Making a fire after three days of storms won't be easy . . . Do you have any embers?"

I explained to him that I had lost my horn with embers—along with my bow and quiver—when lightning struck the tree.

"What? You'd taken refuge under a big oak?"

"Yes, an enormous oak! But that didn't prevent it from being struck by lightning."

"That was probably *why* it was struck! Lightning is attracted to prominent points."

"It is?"

"Yes. If, for example, the two of us were put in a field during a thunderstorm, I'd be hit by lightning, not you, little fellow. Farewell, Uncle Barak."

He clucked and then frowned.

"Didn't they teach you that in the village?"

Shrugging his huge shoulders, he examined the various bags that had piled up in the hut.

"Where did I put my lighter?"

He went through the bags one by one, got annoyed, swore, and took his fire-lighting kit out of the fifth one.

"Finally!"

I noted that this man who lived alone talked all the time. Was that because I was sharing his shelter? Had he developed the habit of talking to himself? The more I observed him, the more I leaned toward the latter interpretation, insofar as his commentaries and curses rarely called for a response.

Using pyrite—a metallic rock—he rubbed the flint. Sparks flashed out of it and landed on the tinder, a mixture of tow and amadou, that he had arranged under and around the meat. The fire still didn't take.

I watched him with amusement. His technique didn't teach me anything new; all of us in the village knew it, but we no longer made fire that way. If someone accidentally let the embers go out in their house, they borrowed some from their neighbor. We passed fire from one to another; no one wasted their time making it.

The spark became a flame: my uncle had succeeded! He seized a leather bag containing dry woodchips, and another with firewood.

"This escaped the deluge; it'll burn without smoking us out."

In the middle of the hut, he shaped a hearth, and the fire began to burn.

"How does my nephew want his food cooked? On a spit or a hot stone?"

"You choose."

"Hot stone!"

Once the fire was burning, he laid large, flat stones on it, and then, when their temperature rose, he spread the pieces of game on them.

"And now you enjoy the smell, hope, and practice patience. While we're waiting for the feast, tell me what brings you here."

I usually said little about my personal feelings, but I told him everything. My passionate love of my father. My marriage. The arrival of Tibor and his daughter. My distaste for Mina after Noura appeared on the scene. My desire to take Noura as a second wife. Pannoam's injury, his convalescence, and his decision to marry Noura.

At this point in my narrative, Barak could no longer contain himself.

"Ah, what a snake! What a nasty piece of work! The pervert! That's just like him. He pays no attention to anything or anyone, unless someone is pointed out to him who . . . He's doing it again!"

"Doing what again?"

My uncle froze, beside himself with rage.

"Nothing. Go on!"

I continued to relate my obedience, my return to Mina, my

efforts to accept the situation. I concluded with the death of Mina and our child.

"Nothing linked me to the village any longer. And most of all I don't want to see Pannoam and Noura and their happy faces. I'm not strong enough!"

My uncle's big hand crushed mine.

"I understand you, my boy."

Then he examined the ceiling of the hut, as if looking for something, hesitated, and then stammered, "Your mother isn't too sad?"

"She weeps, yes. She has so many reasons for despair. Everyone is abandoning her: my father, me."

"Ah?"

He seemed to be moved. I asked, "Do you know my mother?"

"No, I don't know your mother."

Sadly, as if defeated, he hung his head and didn't utter another word until the hare was ready.

Once the meal was finished, a need for rest overwhelmed me as quickly as a blow to the nape of the neck. For two days and three nights, huddled in the cave, I hadn't slept at all, suspicious, watching out for the bear, waiting for the hurricane to end. After a gut-wrenching yawn, I stretched out on Barak's mat, pushed away a few mouse turds, and fell asleep.

When I woke up, the half-light already surrounded us. Above me, I saw my uncle contemplating me.

"You talk in your sleep," he exclaimed.

"To whom?"

"You were talking to a bird . . . you were trying to catch it . . . begging it to come back."

I sat up. Mina! What had happened to Mina? Or rather to the chickadee into which her soul had migrated? I realized that I hadn't seen her since the storm started.

"What do birds do during a storm?" I asked my uncle.

"Like us, they protect themselves. Some succeed in doing so; some don't, and die."

I remembered Mina in the course of our life together, Mina frightened by the darkening of the zenith, the booming of the thunder, the lightning, the gusts of wind, Mina who holed up in our house, Mina who hid under a mat, Mina who was still trembling after a rainbow appeared. Had she survived this unleashing of Nature? Had she fled? Had she taken refuge in the oak tree? If so, had she been struck by the lightning? Burned along with the trunk?

I shivered. Assuming that she had survived, she had lost me during my flight through the woods. I imagined the frail bird either dead or forsaken, and tears tickled my eyes.

"Hey, you're hiding something from me," my uncle said.

I didn't answer.

Barak got up, unfolded his limbs, stretched. His joints cracked. Never had I met such a giant; it would take three men like me to make one of him.

"Come watch the sunset," he ordered me.

He went out, and I followed.

On the other side of the brambles that defended his home, he insisted that we walk at a distance from one another.

"Remember this, Noam," he explained as he stepped over ferns, "nothing must indicate where the hut is. Always come to my home by a different path, and don't step on the same grass, crush the same moss, or trample the same soil."

"Don't you get lost?"

"The way is marked."

"No."

"Yes!"

I looked at the leafy carpet of the forest floor. Not a trace of a path.

He laughed. "Look up!"

I scrutinized the branches that the twilight had made colorless.

"Don't you see?" he asked.

He pointed to a vine that was visible despite the declining daylight. Then another. And another.

"I didn't mark the way on the ground, I inscribed it on the sky. Not bad, huh?"

I applauded.

Water continued to drip from the canopy, infusing the vegetation with new vitality. The nettles grew to the height of my shoulders; clematises climbed the trunks. The forest was growing darker from moment to moment, and the slope we were climbing—which was sometimes slippery—was increasingly choked with underbrush.

I asked Barak, "Why so many precautions? With your strength, no one would take the risk of confronting you. Even a bear would hesitate."

"That's true! A bear attacked me one time, and it was sorry it did. I wasn't: it provided me with my best winter blanket."

"Why are you hiding?"

"When there are several of them, the Hunters are a danger."

"Oh . . . But you killed five of them at once."

He snorted, aware that he wasn't telling the truth. I persisted, "What are you afraid of, Uncle?"

"Get going!"

His eyebrows knitted, his eyes angry, he scolded me in a tone that brooked no argument.

We came to a grassy enclave, a clearing in the forest that opened up to the sky. Above us, the stars. Below us, the Lake. I was relieved to see it again, like a member of my family, and sighed with pleasure.

Barak understood, because he murmured, "Although I'm no longer part of the village, I'm still from the Lake. Aren't you?"

I nodded, bowing my head. We were experiencing the same peace of mind, the same indefinable union.

The sun had disappeared. The air was getting cooler. A wolf's howl greeted the descent of darkness. Its gloomy, interminable complaint emphasized Nature's immensity.

Above the flat, solidified, almost mineral lake, the moon seemed to be liquid. Waves of light streamed from it, reached the surface of the water, spread fluidly over it, covering the banks and adjoining forests, overlaying the landscape with a mysterious sheen.

I turned to my uncle.

"Why did you go up into the woods one day never to come back?"

He bit his lip, swallowed, rasped, "That was such a long time ago . . ."

I respected his reticence. Since the morning, this hermit had talked a great deal, more than he usually did in a year. I looked away for a moment and contemplated the stars.

Now the wolf's howl was coming from a great distance, from the farthest corners of the world, from the frontiers of the audible. But no matter how far away the carnivore's sepulchral voice might be, I didn't stop listening, uncertain whether I was still hearing it or dreaming it.

Barak suddenly broke the silence: "My first memory is of my brother Pannoam. A happy memory! I venerated my elder brother; I admired his self-assurance, his character, his knowledge, his intelligence. Walking alongside him filled me with pride. No matter where the images come from, yesterday or today, Pannoam is handsome. At each stage of his life—little boy, teenager, mature man—he proved that he could charm people. If the gods lend him health, he will one day show us what a magnificent old man looks like. As a child, I resembled a sickly branch, and I convinced myself that his splendor, by shining on me, would warm me, fortify me, even make me handsomer. Since I imitated him in everything—playing, self-expression, the way I behaved and ate—he drew me to him, that is upward, for which I mutely thanked him. I idolized him. I needed his presence as much as

I needed water to drink. The itinerary of my life seemed to me crystal clear: I would remain at the side of my big brother until the end of time. Unfortunately, I should have wondered . . ."

He paused as he cleaned his toenail. Fearing that he might lose the desire to talk about himself, I urged him to go on: "About what?"

"Whether Pannoam loved me."

He looked at me fixedly.

"I loved him with a sincere, complete love without reservations, but did he love me?"

I hung my head, so strong an echo did his question awaken in me; during our conflict regarding Noura, Pannoam's hardness had led me to doubt the reality of his affection.

My uncle continued. "Pannoam inspires so much love that one assumes he feels love himself. But his case turns out to be trickier than that."

"In what way?"

"Pannoam loves as it suits him, when it suits him."

I shivered at the accuracy of his remark.

"He cherished his brother so long as this bond pleased him. What better company could you have than a boy who reveres you, approves your remarks, your acts, your choices? However, in adolescence the younger sibling turned out to be less practical to love."

My uncle pointed to his enormous body.

"Just look at the monster that emerged from the snot-nosed kid I used to be! Nobody expected that, not him, not my parents, not me. From a twig, I was transformed into an oak. I grew everywhere. And it didn't stop. I'd been dazzled by my elder brother's strength, and now I was three times stronger than he was. Every day, I made him aware of his inferiority."

"Jealous?"

"Pannoam is one of those proud people whom jealousy doesn't affect. He's very fond of himself and doesn't desire to become anyone else. On the other hand, he abominates anyone who outshines him. As soon as I realized that I was surpassing him, I did all I could to stop growing and filling out: I fasted, avoided exercise, corseted my limbs, and prayed to the gods and spirits. I took care to rig our fraternal competitions: when we ran, I managed always to fall; when we dived into the Lake, I swallowed water in order to swim badly; when we hunted, I hid some of the animals I bagged—with my muscular arms and back, my arrows flew far and brought down big game . . . In short, I tried not to embarrass Pannoam. But, alas, Nature and the gods had decided differently . . ."

"Is that why you left?"

He coughed. My question had thrown him.

"I would never have left for that reason. First because I couldn't believe that my brother would cease to love me. And second because I adored him."

"Why, then?"

He fixed his eyes on the silvery moon and seemed to no longer see anything but it. The moon illuminated the scarred skin of his gigantic face.

I protested, "Barak, I've been truthful with you. Why won't you do the same with me?"

He cleared his throat, bade goodbye to the moon, looked back at me, heaved a sigh, and then, embarrassed, finally said, "Your mother."

"What about my mother? You've told me that you didn't know her."

He cleared his throat again.

"I . . ."

"Were you lying to me?"

"I wasn't lying to you. I was buying time . . ."

"Yes?"

"I said I didn't know her as your mother . . . I knew her . . . as Elena."

His face lit up as he pronounced those syllables.

I was dumbstruck. For years I hadn't heard anyone say my mother's first name. We—her sons and daughters—called her "Mama," my father called her "wife," and the villagers called her "the chief's wife." "Elena" disturbed me, showed her to me as different, alien, stripped bare; the name "Elena" endowed her with a hidden life, an unsuspected substance. The way Barak, blushing, pronounced this name implied not a girl, but a woman. For his full, deep red lips, whispering "Elena" was equivalent to giving a kiss.

He smiled, and, with his irises vague and his eyelids half-closed, planting his feet on the ground to support his reverie, he plunged into his past.

"I'd wandered far, very far away from the village to catch fish. Fishing served me as a pretext. With this monstrous body of mine and given the way Pannoam had begun to stiffen in my presence, new emotions were troubling me, making me want to be alone. I was trying to learn to live without following in the footsteps of my brother, modeling my words on his expressions, my thoughts on his. Detecting his annoyance, I was ashamed of my awkwardness, I blamed myself for being me, I fled. Every expedition took me farther away; I explored unknown territories, swam in unknown streams. On that day, I had followed herons that were having a field day among the reeds, a sign that they had found an abundance of trout or pike. As I advanced, crouching and inspecting the clay soil, I heard a song, then came upon a dazzling scene: Elena was washing her clothes. Her voice, as clear and fresh as the water, rose over the reeds and reached the sky. Moved, I hid among the plants. I held my breath. Her face, as full, fleshy, and pure as the timbre of her voice, fascinated me. The movement of her arms, her handsome white arms and her beautiful rounded shoulders, made my blood rise to my cheeks. In spite of myself, I sighed. She looked up. I stood, and instead of screaming in fear on seeing the giant who rose up out of the water, she smiled. An immense smile. A smile of pink lips and perfect teeth. No need to speak. It was love at first sight."

He lowered his voice, as if he was afraid of being spied on.

"We formed the habit of meeting at the water's edge, and these meetings quickly became indispensable to us. At that time, Pannoam's marriage was being planned, not mine. Kaddour had already selected Isa, the daughter of Mardor, the chief of a neighboring village. Pannoam was satisfied with his fiancée, a pretty girl who was clean, a little cold, had a large dowry, and descended from a rich family that ruled over a village of twenty houses. Pannoam talked to me about her with a pleasure that was tranquil, not feverish; he had already settled into the comfort of an advantageous marriage. But I was afraid my choice of a fiancée would break the rules. As a ruse, I took advantage of the festival of lights, the one that celebrated the longest day of the year, during which the Peoples of the Lake traditionally gathered on the Plain of the Horses where, in the past, the Battle of Ilode had taken place. This celebration provided an opportunity to drink, feast, dance, and especially to find a spouse. I managed to introduce Elena's family to our father. Elena was the daughter of a chief, oh, a little chief, or rather the chief of a little village. In Kaddour's view, Elena was not an advantageous bride for Pannoam, his eldest son and successor, but she was good enough for a younger son. People were amused to see us side by side, I the giant and she the ravishing girl of the Lake, and then—was it an effect of the wine, or the heat?—our fathers agreed on the spot. Our stratagem had succeeded, and we pretended to be discovering each other for the first time. On that evening, and subsequently on many more, Pannoam and Elena met. Their relations began in a cordial, polite manner. When he was conversing with Elena, I never detected in Pannoam's eye a glow that seemed to say, "She surpasses Isa; she pleases me more." He hadn't realized how special she was."

He scratched his head.

"That's when I did something foolish."

Smoothing his beard, his eyes saddened; he mumbled, "What an idiot!"

He struck his breast with his fist.

"Yes, in retrospect, I can see my error."

"What error?"

His face darkened.

"Little by little, I told Pannoam about my passion. I confessed my enchantment, my euphoria, my enthusiasm, the way seeing her made my heart race, the delight of our kisses—even if we hadn't yet slept together—my dreams magnified by Elena's image, and waking up with words of love addressed to her on my lips. On that basis, Pannoam confused . . ."

"Confused what?"

"His case and mine. Since he didn't feel for Isa what I felt for Elena, he concluded that that was Isa's fault, not his! He decided that Isa did not inspire love, whereas Elena did. Because he wanted to feel what I felt, he stole Elena from me."

I was speechless. Elena . . . Noura . . . Twenty-five years later, my father had acted in exactly the same way. I now understood Barak's furious exclamation while I was confiding in him: "He's doing it again!"

Swindling his brother . . . cheating his son . . . Pannoam didn't see a woman; he saw a man seeing a woman. He didn't choose or desire by himself; he needed the desire of someone close to him to see the chosen woman, and, by imitation, to become passionate.

Divining the thoughts that were agitating me, Barak let me ruminate. The longer I was around him, the more I realized that this ferocious fellow was endowed with an exquisite sensitivity, excitable, to be sure, but delicate in his feelings and careful not to wound others.

Sitting on a little hill, surrounded by a silence whose intensity was emphasized by the flight of a bird of prey, the slightest rustle of leaves, or an owl's ethereal hooting, we remembered, overwhelmed, past acts of violence.

The wolf howled. Shivers ran down our spines. It had come closer. Its hoarse song foreshadowed tracking, capture, killing, the prey's guts ripped from its abdomen by murderous fangs.

"How did my father steal . . . my mother from you?"

Barak stood up and turned around.

"At first, I didn't suspect his plan."

Stopping dead, he looked at me with care. "You're likely to find this displeasing, Noam."

He hesitated, held his breath, recovered his composure, and made up his mind. "Kaddour would never have changed his mind: Pannoam would marry Isa, Mardor's daughter, a union necessary for power, wealth, peace. Kaddour was inflexible where his succession was concerned. Whereas he allowed me my whims, he demanded complete obedience from Pannoam, a devotion in proportion to the task he would inherit. Pannoam was not to deviate from his destiny as chief."

"And?"

"The village that Mardor led collapsed. It was subjected to invasions, sacking, pillaging, rapes. The Hunters concentrated their attacks on it. In a few moons, it was running short of food reserves, flocks, orchards, fields—and soon men, because the hostilities spilled a great deal of blood. Mardor himself was slaughtered during a brawl—but in any case, by then he had nothing left to lose but his life."

"What about Isa?"

"Her death was unnecessary."

"Excuse me?"

"Scarlet with anger, Pannoam accused Kaddour of forcing him to marry an indigent orphan coming from a pulverized village. Kaddour apologized. Pannoam took advantage of this moment of weakness to ask him for Elena's hand. My father summoned me—I was returning from the hills, where I had killed a bear, my first—and, without giving me the time to brag about my exploit, he announced that the right of the eldest son required me to cede Elena to my brother."

"The gods and the spirits have always favored Pannoam!"

"The gods and the spirits had nothing to do with it."

"All the same . . . Mardor's village annihilated . . ."

"Don't evoke either the gods or chance, or circumstances. Pannoam organized the whole thing."

"Pardon me? Are you insinuating that my father . . ."

"I'm not insinuating; I have proof."

"What?"

"The Hunters' testimony."

"What Hunters?"

"The ones he paid to destroy, steal, kill."

"The Hunters live by themselves, and . . ."

"Some of them sell their services to the highest bidder. They wander the world in groups. Their hatred of the Sedentaries brushes aside their scruples. If they're told what to do, how to get in, what to take, who to target, they don't cost much. For a few sacks of wheat, they'll tear people apart. Back then, I was as naïve as you are now, and I would never have imagined such a maneuver. I thought I was just running up against an abusive order issued by my father. In my view, Pannoam remained totally innocent. Even a victim."

"How did you answer Kaddour?"

"I was petrified."

"You?"

"Muscles don't make you intelligent. My intelligence is very slow."

"Did you plead your case?"

"I was torn. On the one hand, I loved Elena, but on the other, I loved Pannoam. I wanted them to be happy. And I owed obedience to my father."

"So what did you do?"

"That night, without talking to anyone at all, I left."

"Without explaining to Pannoam? To Elena?"

"They got an explanation the next day: my death."

I stared at him, speechless.

"In a clearing near the village, I made it look like I'd fought. I put boar's blood on the ground, the stones, the tree trunks. Here and there I hung bits of clothing, as if a predator had torn them off me. Then I left signs of the path I'd taken to flee by abandoning my bag, my broken bow, and my splintered arrows, getting rid of the objects I was carrying as well as my ripped clothes. I ended up naked on the rocks that overlooked the Lake, the very place where, the day before, I'd stored the corpse of the bear, the recent conquest of which I was so proud. At dawn, when the shepherds appeared on the hills, I shouted as loudly as I could, and picking up the bear's body, I feigned a struggle with it. It struck me, crushed me, groaned and roared, as I imitated defeat and exhaustion. Finally, I let out a scream of distress and fell beyond the cliff, grappling with the animal. The current carried the bear and me away, because at that spot a torrential river meets the Lake, creating movement. A good swimmer, I pretended not to move and let myself be carried away by the water. In the distance, I saw the shepherds running about and pointing to the two cadavers drifting off . . . That's how people decided I'd been killed by a bear."

He struck his thighs with his fists. His story, years later, still flabbergasted him.

"That evening, I dumped the carcass in the middle of the Lake, swam, and landed here, naked, without any belongings. I've lived here ever since."

"Barak, why did you do that?"

"I wanted Elena to feel free to marry Pannoam. As long as I was alive, she would never accept him. If I was alive, Pannoam wouldn't be marrying her, but raping her. If I was alive, their marriage would become a torture. If I was alive, neither Elena nor Pannoam would ever be happy."

I examined the shadowy figure seated next to me, withdrawn, shrunken. Despite the obscurity, I could see that his eyelids were fluttering. Barak was fighting against emotion.

"I thought only of her, only of him. I disappeared."

He shook himself, sniffed, sighed, then contemplated the moon with tearful eyes.

"I even hoped that, as she mourned my death, Elena might find a kind of fidelity in marrying my brother."

*

Barak taught me how to live a life outside society. Though neither of us proposed it, we stayed together, sharing our hunting, our fishing, our meals, our naps, the sun, the rain, the cabin made of hides and bristling with brambles. Our association was, for us, obvious. We were linked by blood, to be sure, but our genuine familiarity stemmed from a common destiny: we were both Pannoam's victims.

Still, we didn't blame the man who had stolen our fiancées and doomed us to reclusion. Why?

"When you love, you never stop loving. Love is transformed; it doesn't disappear."

Barak told me that one day, and I agreed with him. Whatever we reproached Pannoam for, we didn't hate him. Rather than rancor, we felt disappointment, made more intense by sadness. In this outcome, we assumed our share of the responsibility: if Pannoam fell, it was because we had placed him too high. To sober up, you have to have been drunk first! Blinded by his charm, incapable of feeling a more nuanced affection for him, sensitive to his arrogance but unaware of his egoism, we had been lacking in judgment. For his part, by considering us insignificant, Pannoam hadn't changed; he'd revealed what he already was.

We changed. He didn't.

Disillusioned, we spent our convalescence going about our lives far from the social issues that Pannoam symbolized. Had men betrayed us? Had women escaped us? No matter! Nature became our partner, our source of amazement, our joy. My uncle and I resembled one another, I think: we were both seeking enchantment.

That's why Barak prattled. By venerating birds, taking delight in fruit, swimming, he was laying the foundations for his choice to be an exile. He justified his new world using the language of the old. Driven by an innate propensity for pleasure, he'd ended up thinking that he obtained the best option, going so far as to thank his past for having forced him to break with his former life.

"Don't we live better here than in the village, my boy? If I feel like snoozing, I snooze. If I want to run, I run. If I'm hungry, I hold out my hand."

He saw his solitude as a liberation, not a privation.

"Remember your days down there: they were all work, all the time. You had to toil away to provide your fellows with things to toil over. That's how it goes: work is divided up to lighten it, but the division makes it harder. Everyone ends up a prisoner of their duty; everyone forces their neighbors to do the same. They live to work instead of working to live! What have you gained by coming to the woods? Your whole day is at your disposal."

I agreed. Occasionally, I wondered if we weren't exaggerating—the dividing line between sincerity and boasting is sometimes quite thin—but it suited me to claim that I had chosen what I was undergoing.

Barak overwhelmed me with words. Never had I encountered anyone as voluble as this hermit! He yacked on and on from dawn to dusk, describing the panorama, the clouds, the state of the vegetation, his digestion, describing in detail everything he was doing or would do, opening conversations on countless different subjects. Was he compensating for so many years of silence? Was he making up for lost time by taking advantage of a companion? In any case, I noticed that despite his denials, nothing was as repugnant to his sociable temperament as separation.

A marriage of opposites, Barak was made up entirely of tensions: a recluse, he cherished company; lonely, he chattered; passionate, he melted with sweetness; violent, he radiated tenderness.

In the same way, he oscillated between modesty and immodesty. Good at hiding his feelings—and especially their delicacy—he exhibited his body. I saw him naked when we got up and when we went to bed. No physical function interrupted his chitchat; penis in hand, taking an enormous piss, he continued to converse with me; squatting, struggling red-faced to push out a stubborn turd, he was still talking.

His easy-going ways, though unsophisticated, had a healthy character that forced me to question our behavior. Why should we be ashamed of our bodies? Why, out of shame, should we conceal what is necessary? When he urinated or defecated in front of me, my uncle shocked me, but he didn't disgust me. His absence of embarrassment even emanated a kind of wisdom: "I am a natural being within Nature," it seemed to say. He taught me that modesty was an artificial convention. Did humans think they were human because they respected it? They didn't show that they were humans, only villagers. I learned to behave in a more relaxed way.

On the other hand, Barak's erotic frankness disturbed me. He went about with his penis not only hanging out, but standing up. How many mornings did I hear him comment, admiringly, on his erection?

"Well, look how healthy we are!," he said to his dick, laughing.

He stood up and expected me to witness his glorious member—"Well, my boy, look what happened to me during the night: I've gained in volume!"—and went out of the cabin to masturbate. He didn't go far away, because I could hear the agitations of his hand, his panting, then spasms, moans, and finally an incredible roar. In my uncle's case, everything was immoderate . . . When he came back, he might comment on the act, "You never get tired of it. Every time is a first time. What pleasure!"

Soon, after a few sessions, he asked me, "Don't you jerk off, my boy?"

He scrutinized me, jovial, encouraging, with a worried look on his face.

I got flustered; I should have admitted the inadmissible, the most private of the private, my embraces with the beech tree. I said nothing.

He shrugged.

"Give Nature a hand when she calls on you for help. It's excellent for you, for your moods, for your health."

I reacted in an odious fashion; instead of telling the truth, I put on a learned, severe mask, the kind an adult wears when scolding a kid, to explain to him that I'd been making love with a woman since I was thirteen and that I didn't scatter my seed in vain.

"Ah, you need a woman?" he replied calmly. "That's normal. I understand. I know . . . Do you want me to procure one for you?"

"One what?"

"A woman."

"It's like you're offering me an apple."

"You can only eat an apple once."

Before leaving the hut, he winked at me collusively, "We'll talk about it later, whenever you want . . ."

Barak taught me to give up my villager's point of view, my defensive way of seeing things.

He enjoyed storms, whereas the Sedentaries loathed them. Rather than condemnation, for him rain represented the gods' and spirits' leniency. "What's good for plants, trees, and animals is good for me." Together, we breathed in the bland spindrift that the raindrops vaporized. Barak helped me admire the lugubrious nobility with which the showers endowed the landscape, to prize the disappearance of the sky, the vanishing of shadows, the simplification of colors. Rain lengthened objects, whereas the sun crushed them; its delicate penumbra gave substance to tree trunks, branches, rocks, as if they were instantaneously rehydrated. Everything seemed full.

The storm past, we enjoyed its delayed effects, the perfume that rose from the earth, the dancing brook, the rise of sap, the grass that stood up again, the blossoming flowers, the lustrous leaves, the birds' petulance, the azure that exhaled a purified breath.

One morning, he announced that we were going to take a walk.

"Where are we going, Uncle?"

"What an idiotic question!"

He strode off with such long steps that I followed him without quibbling.

A little later, on a treeless hill from which we could contemplate the Lake to infinity, I asked my question again: "Where are we going?"

"We're walking. Haven't you noticed?"

And he plunged into the green labyrinth.

After an interminable descent, he pointed to an oak that had fallen. Its bark offered us a bench.

"Let's stop a moment."

In this smooth-columned bower, the sun's rays pierced the foliage, painting oblique fringes where insects danced. Millions of wings were beating in the daytime torpor. The forest, dense and alive, murmured with song, humming, crackling, stridulating, the sound of wings.

The clouds parted long enough to reveal a clearing behind the tree trunks. Long-legged, supple, elegant does grazed there, their eyes ringed as though with kohl, their hooves delicate and light. Their slow grace made it seem that time had stopped just so we could enjoy the spectacle.

Two males entered the clearing. There were tremblings in the herd. The adversaries positioned themselves for a fight, pointing their antlers at one another and threatening. Rivalry burned in their dark eyes; their nostrils quivered with rage. Which female were they fighting for?

Barak smiled at me.

"Humans, animals: the same concerns!"

The battle had still not started; they hadn't yet moved beyond intimidation. Their hooves marked the ground, imprinting the furor of wild blood.

One of the stags belled and stamped the earth, ready to charge. The other lowered his head, tilted it to the right, and then, in fits and starts, as if nothing was wrong, started to retreat to the side, toward the edge of the clearing. He was giving up. The first stag swelled his majestic breast and looked the females up and down, triumphant.

Barak stopped smiling. He had just identified himself with the stag that was giving up the fight. When he turned to me, I understood that he had recognized me, too, in the defeated stag.

A cracking sound emerged from the bushes, and suddenly, as a body of water is muddied, the does fled in a single movement. The clearing was empty. We could almost doubt that we had seen them, those silky animals; they seemed to be a well-guarded secret that the forest showed and then took away.

"Let's eat some nuts," Barak said.

Under the cover of the trees, we took advantage of this captivating haven. Everything there manifested life, the oak saplings, the slender suckers, the tufts of stems that grew on the stump of the fallen tree.

"How splendid!" I murmured. "You wanted to show me this place?"

"Not at all. I didn't know where we'd end up."

"What?"

He stood up, ready to leave. "I walk to figure out where I'm going."

As we wandered on, I realized that Barak wasn't kidding. He

didn't foresee where his feet would take him; he walked because he liked it, liked the pure physical exercise, the discovery.

"As soon as you decide you're going to a specific place, you stop seeing things. The journey becomes tedious."

He was asking me to let myself be surprised, to welcome whatever our ramble brought us.

"That's the crux of the matter, enjoyment. When you know where you're going, you're satisfied with just getting there."

Live in the moment. Put the goal in the background. Barak's educational program completely contradicted Pannoam's.

The daylight was fading.

"Let's go back, Uncle. Show me the path."

"No. It's up to you!"

"But . . ."

"If I show it to you, you might not get lost."

He asked me to lead the way. Embarrassed, not wanting to appear foolish or irresolute, I set out in an arbitrary direction.

Night was falling.

I stopped.

"I . . . I think I'm lost."

"No big deal," he replied.

He took things in hand, and in a short time we had lit a fire and eaten. He smoothed out the ground to form two sleeping places.

I was worried. "Will you be able to find our way back?"

"I absolutely don't remember it."

"What will we do?"

He threw his head back. "We'll raise our eyes."

He pointed to the black vault strewn with stars. "The gods of the heavens will help us." The stars provided reference points for those who observed them: the constellations of the Little Tadpole and the Big Tadpole, whose tail ends with its brightest star.*

"That one points to the upper part of the Lake."

---

* The Little Dipper, the Big Dipper, and the North Star

From this examination, he drew a conclusion: "Tomorrow, we'll go that way."

Barak was right. Doubly right.

First, his intuition took us home. Second, setting a destination deprived a journey of its interest—unlike the preceding day, my attention was concentrated on returning home, and I didn't take delight in the various places that we passed through.

We reached the hut at twilight. While I was putting a layer of fat on my burning, blistered feet, I watched Barak loafing around in the buff. Singing in a gravelly, powerful voice, he was rubbing his scarred flesh and massaging his balls.

A suspicion assailed me. Was it him? Was he the monster?

I remembered the words he'd used during our discussion, which kept nagging at me: "You need a woman? Want me to procure one for you?"

A rumor was making its way around the Lake: the bear was stealing young women. He was wild about having sex with them. It was said that he imprisoned them in his lair and possessed them. When they gave birth to a boy, he turned out to be half human, half bear, a biped completely covered with hair and endowed with exceptional strength.

Because of his coarse remark, I wondered whether Barak could be behind these disappearances. Might he not be the bear who was kidnapping young women during the night? From a distance, by moonlight, people might take his silhouette for that of a bear . . .

"Uncle, have you heard about the bear that's kidnapping women of the Lake?"

He mumbled, without looking at me, "Yes."

"What do you think about it?"

"What do I think about it?" He stopped scratching himself and stared at me. "People have been trotting out that nonsense since I was a child." Snorting, he added, "I'd like to meet the person who first saw the bear."

I didn't follow, so I persisted: "Why?"

"That fellow committed a crime and then tried to hide it by accusing a guilty party that terrified the villagers. Later, bastards like him repeated his lie. How many generations has that been going on?"

He cracked his knuckles.

"Male bears don't want our females; I've spied on them. Male bears copulate only with female bears, and even then not to excess, once every two years, and then they're done. There's no doubt about it: Sedentaries who kidnap and rape invented the story of the bear. Pitiful! They make me sick."

"Uncle, would you take a woman without her consent?"

"What?"

"If you feel desire . . ."

"Noam, if I feel desire, I service myself! And I do it alone! I thought you'd noticed that because when I leave and come back every morning, you look offended. Nature gave us hands, boy, and why do you think that is? And, actually, one is enough."

"If you felt desire . . . not in general . . . but for a particular woman . . ."

"Yes . . ."

"Would you take her by force if she refused you?"

"I've known it to happen."

"What?"

"Seeing horror in a woman's eyes. And it killed my desire."

"Ah . . ."

"Worse yet: it killed it for a long time! I shared her opinion: I find myself monstrous."

"Uncle, you . . . women might find you attractive."

He blinked, sniffed, coughed. He was trying to hide his emotion and failing.

"I know . . . Your mother found me attractive . . . For me, that would have been enough for my whole life."

Suddenly he stopped dreaming and pointed at me.

"Ah, I understand why you're asking me these questions . . . Because I offered to 'procure a woman' for you?"

I hung my head, embarrassed. He guffawed, slapping his thighs.

"Oh, my nephew, my nephew . . . I meant 'take you to see a woman,' a woman who would be interested in sleeping with you. I know where to look."

"Excuse me?"

"I know Huntresses who . . ."

I lurched backward, horrified. Had I heard him correctly? Was my uncle suggesting that I have sex with a Huntress?

He thought my wide-eyed look expressed desire.

"We'll go. But we'll have to sacrifice a doe, a boar, some significant gift, because . . ."

"Stop, Barak! A female Hunter isn't a woman!"

"She isn't? What is she then?"

"An animal!"

"You and I are animals, too."

"There are superior races and inferior races."

"Where did you get that idea, my boy? If I've learned anything these last years, it's that the Sedentaries' prejudices about Hunters are like children's stories. They serve certain people's interests. Whenever somebody sets out to enslave others with invisible chains, they resort to that kind of legend. Superior, inferior! Human, not human! Civilized, barbarian! What a bunch of bull . . . The charlatan passes for a wise man, and the gullible gratefully take the bait. If your father hadn't used the fear and scorn the Hunters inspired, would he have managed to . . ."

He stopped.

"No. I'd rather keep quiet."

"Bizarre . . . You're seldom quiet."

"I'm doing it for your own good. Or rather for the illusions you still have . . ."

In spite of his volubility, my uncle kept secrets. Faced with my stubbornness, he promised to tell me the story in the future.

"Why not now?"

"When you're capable of understanding it."

"Or when you're capable of telling it to me . . ."

He fell silent: I'd hit the mark.

I think I was crazy about the moons I spent with Barak. He'd chosen the luminous side of life. Because he was both melancholic and joyful, he gave priority to happiness. Active and lazy, he cultivated his idleness. This delightful companion, though fiery, never lacked a sense of humor. Although I made fun of his manias—beating off while looking at the Lake, taking a daily plunge into the cold water and belling like a stag, erasing every trace of access to his hut—he didn't take offense but instead retorted, "A little respect, my boy! Don't forget you're speaking to a dead man."

He, who was so clear-sighted, acted as if he were invisible. Even twenty-five years later, he did everything he could to give credence to the idea that he was dead.

"Why don't you settle farther away, Barak? Then you wouldn't have to hide out."

He sighed, annoyed by the question, but relieved that I had asked it. "I tried that . . ."

He told me about his attempt, two years after his exile, when he thought he'd finished mourning his love for Elena. Without counting them, he'd walked for several moons away from the North Star, beyond the horizons we could see from where we were.

"I stopped in a village. I was accepted. Curiously, I was treated better. My bearing impressed those people. They thought it was a wise tactical move to show off a giant. I didn't do anything there, just wandered among the houses to make it obvious I lived there. One day the chief announced that he was giving me his daughter. I declined."

"Out of fidelity to Elena?"

He stared at me, stupefied: he hadn't thought of that. Rejecting the idea, he repeated the explanation he'd always given himself.

"In the forest I'd left behind, I'd carried my village with me: the new one seemed to me inferior. When I left, I'd taken my fiancée with me: the new one was no match for her. Everything promised to be second-class. If I were to take a bride, I preferred Elena. If I had to live in a village, I preferred mine. This one resembled my old one too much and not enough. That made the present bitter. I concluded that I would only marry . . . life in the wild."

He let sand run through his big, scarred fingers.

"Noam, if I suggested that we leave, that we settle elsewhere, days and days from here, would you follow me?"

"I . . . I don't know."

"Right now, we're clearing out! Are you coming?"

In me, the answer had surged up. It perplexed me. I disappointed myself so much that I dug deeper to find a desire for the unknown. Alas, "no" kept coming up, stubbornly, imperiously, and I ended up admitting it. My uncle's shoulders sagged; he was not greatly surprised.

"You need to remain near them."

"Who?"

"What you flee, you don't leave. You just move farther away from it. That's all."

Barak was training me to gather and hunt food almost every day. Nothing displeased him more than foresight. "Provisions, what a horror! That's how Pannoam made the villagers dependent! Producing, piling up, preserving, guarding, distributing, planning, that's the path to slavery. They convince themselves that they possess things when the things possess them. Before, it wasn't like that."

"Before?"

"Pannoam is doing to us what he does to the sheep, goats,

aurochs, and dogs: he transforms us into a docile flock. At the same time as the domestic animal, he's inventing the domestic human. Submission is gaining ground. No one lives free anymore. Every child is born into the constraints of laws, rules, and obligations they have to find their place within. The only way out, Noam, is to leave, to erase everything he taught us. That's why I don't practice foresight, and I never will, as life in the wild demands."

"But when I met you, you were checking your traps, Barak."

"Setting traps is hunting!"

"Setting traps is foreseeing."

"The storm prevented me from going out; I had to . . ."

"You foresaw!"

"A little respect, my boy! Don't forget you're talking to a dead man."

Stubbornly, Barak opposed the world of yesterday to the world of today. The old world seemed to him natural; the present world was denatured, humans having become too important in it. Instead of freeing themselves from physical constraints that were ultimately easy to satisfy, they'd created supplementary constraints, numerous social, moral, and spiritual constraints that confined them in the village like a prison.[*]

---

[*] It was with Barak that I first discovered a conflict I would encounter constantly in the course of the millennia: the quarrel of the ancients and the moderns. The ancients wanted to *preserve*; the moderns wanted to *transform*. At least, that's what they said . . . but a more attentive examination reveals something else.

The ancients wanted to safeguard the world not as it is, but as it was. As they saw it, the present, already perverted, provoked indignation. Without hesitation, they pointed to the right model in a past they hadn't experienced. My uncle Barak, right in the middle of the Neolithic age, brandished a marvelous "before," a lost golden age in which humans did not live in society. Nostalgic, he tried, by himself, to resuscitate this mythical time. A melancholy utopia.

The moderns, giving priority to innovation, consider themselves rational, pragmatic, whereas they are actually playing with fire and tend to become arsonists. Not only do they destroy what exists, but they also establish elements whose future and harmfulness they do not suspect. My father Pannoam introduced us to agriculture, seeing an advance in it. He never imagined that for humanity, a life entirely concentrated on the soil might lead people to work more, settle permanently in one place,

One day, we pulled off a masterful hunt. Luck was with us, and we bagged more game than we'd foreseen, four large black boars, four boars whose tusks crisscrossed their ashy snouts, four boars that, even when tense, seemed ready to charge. Barak was jubilant.

"What a superb day, my boy! Good weather, good hunt, excellent food. We deserve a woman, don't you think?"

He'd been shooting this question at me more and more often. Each time, I pretended not to have heard him, and that greatly amused him.

"My nephew goes deaf as soon as anyone says the word 'woman.' What an odd malady . . . The problem is that it can only be treated with a woman."

That day, he teased me further: "Oh ho, it seems to me that your deafness is diminishing."

I grumbled. He laughed all the harder: "I don't expect an immediate answer, Noam. I'll ask you again later."

After a nap under a tree, he said as he stretched, "There's a stream near here. I'm going for a swim. How about you?"

I preferred to lie quietly on the moss, contemplating the endless processions of ants. He hummed as he walked away. The afternoon went on, peaceful, fragrant. Barak quickly returned, completely dry, and sat down beside me.

"Noam, I was almost spotted."

"By whom?"

"A man I've seen around the village."

"What?"

---

burn forests, destroy the diversity of flora and fauna, confront famines, impoverish food supplies, create raids and wars, and even overpopulate the earth. Progress is not only the history of knowledge; it proves to be just as much the history of ignorance: it operates blindly as far as consequences are concerned. A prospective utopia.

At first sight, it seems that in this duel, everything revolves around knowledge: the ancient clings to earlier knowledge; the modern invents new knowledge.

But in reality, the old fantasizes about what it believes it knows, while the modern fantasizes about what it will come to know. So I'm afraid that, in fact, everything revolves around ignorance.

"A man wearing a cloak, a vast black cloak."

"With ash-gray hair and an emaciated face? Searching the pits, the embankments?" I smacked my head and exclaimed, "It's Tibor, Noura's father."

Though I didn't understand why, Tibor's presence moved me.

Nodding his head, Barak registered the news and then, suspicious, spat out, "Why is he digging around in this area?"

"He's collecting medicinal plants."

"So far from the village?"

"It's surprising, but why not?"

I was lying. Normally, Tibor returned from his expeditions at dusk, which limited his field of investigation. An idea exploded in the depths of my mind: Tibor was looking for me. The idea displeased me, and I rejected it.

Barak concluded, "I got away from him. In any case, he wouldn't recognize me."

My uncle moved me when he showed his concern for keeping a low profile.

"Don't worry, Barak, your disappearance was successful. No one ever mentioned you to me. Apart from the fact that the subject makes both my father and my mother uncomfortable, they both believe you're dead."

He looked at me, unsure. To calm him, I insisted, "I alone know the truth."

He hesitated for a moment, then murmured, "Surely not."

"Pardon?"

"One person knows it: Pannoam."

Stunned, I scrutinized my uncle's rough face. He looked away.

"My brother exceeds his fellows in intelligence. What deceives them does not deceive him. The clues I left, my tracks, my cry at a time when the shepherds could see me, my fall at a place where no one could help me—it was all so clear, so well-conceived, so perfect that he must have been suspicious. It occurred at the opportune moment. I think he divined my stratagem and validated it by pretending to believe I was dead. He gained so much from doing so! A wife and happiness."

"Barak, you're imagining things!"

"Maybe. In any case, he knows it now."

"Well . . ."

"He saw me when I saved him from the five Hunters who were attacking him. The panic in his eyes changed colors. While he was defending himself against his aggressors, he expressed the anxiety of someone who's about to die. As soon as I intervened, he showed a different terror, that of encountering a ghost, a phantom from the past. He screamed in fright and fainted."

Each time I mentioned his savior, the mysterious giant, Pannoam had told me again that he'd lost consciousness; when I pressed him, he'd walled himself up in silence, curtly insisting that "Tibor saved me." Maybe this behavior hid the truth my uncle was declaring. The farther I advanced, the more I realized that my father was a patchwork of secrets, despicable secrets.

"What were you doing on the borders of the village that day?"

Barak almost replied, but then didn't. "That's another story . . ."

He stood up.

"Well, we've talked enough. What a marvelous day, Nephew! We deserve a woman, don't we?"

He grinned at me, his eyes crinkling around the edges, his hand urging me to follow him.

"Not yet . . ."

He broke out laughing. "Oh ho, 'not yet . . . ' We're making progress, my boy. Will you someday say yes to your uncle?"

"Maybe." Raising my head, I smiled back at him. "You go ahead. I could tell I was frustrating you. Go ahead, you don't need me. Do what you used to do."

"Are you sure?"

"You certainly deserve a woman!"

He liked my reaction. Full of a new vigor, he clapped his hands and grabbed a boar, the one with thick bristles.

"This is a perfect gift! All right, a quick dip and I'm out of here. One mustn't keep a Huntress waiting. Good night, Nephew. Don't wish me the same; mine's going to sparkle! See you tomorrow."

He went off, whistling and loose-limbed, his chest thrown out and his back arched, and I sensed that he was barely able to refrain from running.

Once he'd disappeared, I curled up, perturbed. Pannoam's lies . . . Tibor's presence . . . I tried to keep busy, to distract myself, to struggle against the past, but the village persisted within me, in my memories and in my imagination. Worse yet: like a worm in a piece of fruit, it gnawed on my thoughts and grew larger.

Tibor had something to confide in me. It had to be important for him to take so many risks by venturing this far.

But what could it be?

*

My uncle returned, exhausted and proud of himself, around noon the next day. His dilated nostrils and swollen lips and eyelids testified to his success. The blossoming of his senses had dried up his constant stream of words, a continual smile floated on his face, and no matter what I proposed, he acquiesced.

During our evening meal, I told him about the worry that had been preying on my mind since the preceding day, without mentioning Tibor.

"Uncle, I want to return to the village."

"What? Are you giving up on life in the wild?"

"No! I'll continue; I'm staying with you. But . . . it would please me to . . . to see it again . . . from a distance, of course . . . it . . ."

"I understand. Do as you wish."

I wasn't begging his permission; I didn't know how to get back to the village. During the storm that struck down the oak under which I'd taken shelter, I'd wandered around aimlessly for a long time, without retaining anything about my surroundings. So I was asking him for help.

He promised to help me: we would leave at the break of dawn. He murmured, "I'll take advantage of the opportunity to show you something edifying."

This time, I paid close attention to our route, memorizing everything that served as a landmark, rockslides, clearings, streams, slopes. Having to rely on Barak to guide me to the village limited my freedom, and even though I was fond of him, I rejected this dependency—which he wanted no more than I did.

We were moving swiftly—Barak usually covered this distance in one day. Although my strength and endurance had grown during my time with him, I managed this exploit only by gritting my teeth.

Worn out, saturated with information I'd begun gathering at dawn, I was no longer registering anything at all when we came out on a hill that looked familiar to me. I opened my eyes wide before the spectacle.

The isolated oak tree that had served me as a refuge at the beginning of the storm lay on the grass like a wounded man.

The giant axe of the lightning had passed through the trunk and split it down the middle. The bolt had gone down as far as ten feet from the base, making the fibers explode; then the two halves had given way under the weight of the branches and collapsed. Now the oak was reduced to a massive stake deprived of limbs or leaves, with a slender woody heart that had been laid bare. On the ground, the debris of its former splendor had either dried or rotted, offering a feast for the mushrooms and insects that were ravaging it.

"Don't go any closer, Noam. The damage has affected

the roots. The fire has burned everything inside, all the way down into the earth. What remains upright could collapse any moment."

I'd been very lucky to escape the catastrophe . . . Ever since my childhood, I'd come upon trees that had been struck by lightning. Most of them had survived, showing rolls of bark where the damage had healed, because the lightning bolt had only grazed the trunk, leaving a scar. Sometimes the lightning penetrated to the center of the trunk, burning it and leaving a hole without killing the tree, creating a cavity in which my friends and I hid our treasures. The whole tree rarely burned, because that could happen only if the rain stopped. Here, the lightning had done a maximum of damage.

"Let's sit down at the edge of the woods, eat and sleep a bit," Barak suggested. "You'll see the village tomorrow."

We set down our bags and stretched out on the dandelions. Behind us, the mauve shadow mounted, while in front of us the sky was turning amber.

A sudden beating of wings swept down on me, and I instinctively closed my eyes. When I opened them, I saw an agitated bird that was fluttering its feathers and, its beak open, chirping joyfully. It was a chickadee.

"Mina?"

Driven by a happiness that overcame it, the bird landed on a branch, greeted me, pirouetted, fell from its perch, caught itself, and then, after short flight, took up a position not far away.

Her beak pointed toward me, she chirped. Her eyes shone as she stared at me.

Emotion overwhelmed me. With this bird, my past was rolling over me, a past that gilded, like a subtle flame, the little, clumsy Mina, her persistent distress, her sorrowful resignation. Tears sprang to my eyes, uncontrollable. I crawled forward on my belly, and when I was as close as I could get to the perky little bird, I murmured, "I'm glad to see you, Mina."

A loud voice resounded, "So you talk to chickadees now?"

Frightened, the chickadee flew away and huddled in the crook of a tree branch. Barak had caught me weeping. I confessed, trembling, "I don't talk to chickadees, I talk to *one* chickadee. The one I lost."

With his mouth rounded sympathetically and his eyes opened wide, he nodded as if he understood, telling me in that way that he wanted to truly understand. So I told him about the feeling I'd had on the morning of the burial, as soon as this chickadee appeared over Mina's grave, and then how sad I was to have lost her, and finally my heart-rending joy upon finding her again.

Barak nodded and contemplated the horizon, where chickadees were chirping, whirling and swishing about in the twilit atmosphere.

"Chickadees live in groups. Yours doesn't. You're right, my boy."

He offered me some hazelnuts. "Will you still have a little energy after dinner?"

I sighed. "Not much, Barak. I'm not a colossus like you."

"I'll reveal one of your father's secrets to you."

"Does it have to be this evening?"

He persisted. "An evening when the moon is a crescent. It sheds almost no light. Let's take advantage of it. Maybe, if we're really lucky, we'll even . . . No! I won't tell you any more!"

He flattened out the young shoots and stems behind me.

"Rest a little while. I'll wake you up once the forest and the village have gone to sleep."

In the middle of the night, my uncle shook me and whispered that the moment was right.

We groped our way. The heavens and the earth had sunk into obscurity; only birds of prey, with their sharp cries, were haunting the shadows.

Barak had ordered me to keep quiet, to follow him closely,

taking care to place my footsteps in his. He knew exactly how to go.

We approached a rock wall located high above the village. No one went there because it was said that bears hibernated there. I was about to mention this to Barak when we heard voices. He stopped us behind a grove.

Below us, a group of shadowy figures were slowly climbing the rocky path. When the crescent moon briefly emerged from behind a cloud, I counted five men. We could hardly see them, but I immediately identified them as Hunters.

Climbing, they were panting, struggling, complaining. No doubt they were transporting sacks . . .

"Follow me!" my uncle whispered, once they had passed the bend where we were hiding.

Barak took my hand, and with an agility and lightness that I wouldn't have thought he possessed, led me to the top of the rock wall. There, we could crawl on all fours as far as the edge and look down on the group climbing toward us.

As soon as they were close to the wall, a shadow detached itself and placed itself in front of them. It was welcoming them.

"Put all that down."

I shivered. It seemed to me . . . No . . . impossible . . . .

"Now, let's count it all up!"

There was no doubt about it: I was hearing my father's voice. I turned to look at Barak, who silently nodded.

The Hunters set down their bundles of wheat, grains, chickpeas. My father counted them and then drew a dividing line on the ground.

"This is for you. This is for me."

Grumbling, the Hunters loaded up their share.

"I'll give a sack to the man who helps me store mine," Pannoam announced.

A short Hunter hurried toward him. Following Pannoam's instructions, he moved a rock. My position prevented me from seeing anything at all, but the scene seemed clear enough: they were putting the provisions in my father's hiding place.

When the task was completed, the short Hunter hastened to catch up with his group, which was disappearing. My father waited a moment. Despite his limp, he slowly, self-confidently began his descent.

In silence, in the crisp darkness, Barak and I returned to our sleeping place. I was disoriented, revolted. Too many new thoughts were disturbing my mind. This episode pulverized decades spent idolizing my father.

When we had stretched out, I drank, handed the gourd to Barak, and said, "My father . . . the Hunters . . . I don't understand."

"You've understood, Noam, but you won't accept the obvious. Like me, in the past . . . Pannoam maintains relations with the Hunters. Think: what does he base his domination on? His skills and the protection he provides. He developed his skills. To justify the protection, he has to maintain, among the villagers, a feeling of insecurity. As soon as your father noticed that the number of Hunters was diminishing, he decided, in full agreement with a few others, to organize regular pillaging, mainly on nights when the moon was a crescent. Marauding that didn't shed any blood, but nonetheless called for firm control . . ."

"People were wounded . . . There were even two deaths!"

"That adds to the credibility."

"Do you mean to say that my father plans attacks on his own villagers?"

"Attacks and thefts. Not all of them, because the Hunters, the real ones, do exist. He hires others."

"Monstrous!"

"Above all, intelligent. The uncontested chief is the one who chooses his enemies carefully and then promotes them as even more formidable than they are."

I scratched my head. I had always considered my father

decent and noble, and I was discovering that he was deceptive, cynical, manipulative.

One detail particularly scandalized me. "Why, by the way, does he keep part of the profits? He has no need of it. He's got enough."

"You're defining wealth: having more than you need. Your father has always dreamed of opulence."

"Absurd!"

"Destiny offers us three possibilities, my boy: rich, poor, or happy. The rich man has more than he needs, the poor man has less, and the happy man has enough for his needs. Listen to your uncle, who has observed his brother: Pannoam is wallowing in abundance, because this traffic has been going on for a very long time. Moreover, that's what allowed me to save him . . . I had spied on the conversations of the five Hunters he'd hired at the time. They were complaining about being cheated by your father, about not keeping enough of their booty even though they were taking the risks. Several times, they'd demanded that Pannoam give them a raise, but he rejected it scornfully: 'If that's not enough for you, I know other Hunters. Don't think you can't be replaced!' More than his refusal, it was his haughtiness that they resented. In their brutish view, not only was the arrogant Pannoam swindling them, but he also considered them less than nothing. They were boiling over with humiliation, and hatred was growing in them. Sensing that they would resort to violence, I started spying on them . . . I imagined that they would operate at night, but they were so afraid of failing that the day they spotted Pannoam alone with his flock of sheep, they didn't hesitate, despite his dogs, to attack him. The moment they pounced on him, I rushed in, too. Alas, they had a head start, and when I got there, I . . ."

"They were going to execute him. You saved him . . ."

"Yes, but . . ."

Stubbornly, Barak was reproaching himself for intervening so late. What he was revealing made my head spin . . . My father's treachery . . . Barak's loyalty . . .

I seized his big, rough hand. "Why did you save him? You're not your brother's keeper."

"Yes, I am. He was my keeper when I was too little. I became his keeper when I became too big."

My uncle's pure heart overwhelmed me.

"You love Pannoam in spite of everything, Barak?"

"Of course."

"He doesn't deserve it."

"That doesn't change anything. As a child, I had blind love; as an adult, I have clear-headed love—but it's still love."

"It's not fair."

"Love has nothing to do with fairness, Noam."

*

I slept late that morning and got up with the impression that I hadn't dreamed. On the other hand, the night's revelations, along with the aches, tormented me when I woke up; I felt heavy, stiff, worn.

Half-heartedly, I began my first day as a disillusioned son.

Pannoam's duplicity dumbfounded me. How did he manage to guide a people, render justice, incarnate righteousness, and impose virtue while behaving so badly in secret? Although I had always seen his appetite for power, I'd confused it with a taste for responsibility, an ideal of moderation. But this wickedness and hypocrisy, this rapacity . . .

I was that man's child . . .

And I had admired him . . .

I'd even loved him . . .

Perhaps I still loved him?

I thought of Tibor, who had ventured so far following me; gauging the distance between his behavior and that of my father revived my desire to see him again. For that matter, wasn't he the reason I'd undertaken this journey?

Lying at my side, voluminous in his animal hides, my uncle was snoring majestically. Seeing that he, too, felt tired after the preceding day's expedition reassured me. I leaned over and whispered in his ear, "Barak, I'll be back by midday."

The bundle of furs grumbled something, the equivalent of agreement.

I hoped that Tibor would also head for the place where, when we said farewell, he'd promised to meet me. My expectation was fulfilled. I spotted the big, black cloak. The healer was on his knees, examining a bush, his knife in his hand. I called him. He turned around. His face lit up.

We ran toward one another and exchanged a long and hearty embrace. With deep emotion, I clasped his bony body to mine.

He took a step backward to look at me. We smiled. I was pleased to find the same clear, precise features, sculpted into weather-beaten skin, his fine, powerful nose, the tousled curls of his gray hair. He murmured in his resonant, otherworldly voice, "You're doing well. I'm glad."

"And you, Tibor?"

His complexion changed in color; his gray eyes clouded over. "Oh, as for me . . . ."

That man had never talked to me about himself or about his feelings; we discussed plants, trees, anatomy, potions, poisons, healing. Despite days and days spent conversing, I knew nothing at all about his private life. Should I have kept asking?

Despite his elusive response, I tried to decipher the mask of his expression. As if he discerned that, he froze and stared at me.

"I thought you were dead, Noam. One day, I found your bag, your bow, and your arrows at the bottom of a flooded ravine. That worried me. I admit that I looked for you. A little."

"A little?"

"A lot."

I avoided confessing that I had suspected that Tibor had been looking for me when Barak spotted him so far from the village. Neither did I dare ask if he had investigated on his own or if his daughter had demanded that he do so, because I was loath to mention Noura. Taboos hindered our conversation. Tibor put his healing hand on my shoulder.

"There are things you and I don't wish to say, and others we don't wish to hear. Tell me what you want Noam, as you want to tell it."

Calmed, almost authorized to lie, I recounted my departure, my current life, life in the wild. But this account, which omitted the chickadee, Barak, my discoveries about my father, and my recent thoughts, proved to be very thin.

He listened to me attentively, and I suspected that he grasped what I was omitting underneath what I was saying. A silence followed.

He frowned.

"I've stored your bag and your bow and arrows carefully. Shall I bring them to you?

"No, thank you. I'm getting along without them."

The silence returned. Muzzled, our dialogue was struggling.

Tibor looked up at me, examining my face.

"Do you want to hear news of the village?"

"I don't know," I retorted, closing up.

"I understand," he admitted dully. "To leave is to decide not to know."

"Precisely!"

Silence fell. In our minds, countless sentences that we would not utter bounced around. We scrutinized each other, simultaneously victims and accomplices of what was tormenting us, reaffirming our solidarity with a look of disconsolate sympathy.

"In any case, I will always regret losing you as my assistant," Tibor exclaimed. "You showed a genuine gift for learning, remembering, and discovering the properties of medicinal herbs. I would have liked to transmit my knowledge to you; you would have embellished it, and it would have borne fruit. Shame! My knowledge will die with me."

"All is not lost," I objected.

"Pardon?"

"You'll communicate it to your grandchildren."

"My grandchildren?"

"Noura's children . . ."

I shivered. If I had succeeded in uttering her first name, saying "Noura and Pannoam's children" was beyond my strength.

Pensive, Tibor shook his head. I tried to discern something from his face, but he deliberately wore an evasive expression. What would the union of Noura and Pannoam produce? Was she already carrying a baby? Not yet? These questions twisted painfully in my head and did not cross the threshold of my lips.

Our silence was becoming unpleasant and all the more unbearable because we had so much to say to each other.

"Farewell, Tibor."

Cravenly, I turned on my heel and walked away, ashamed, disappointed, feeling constrained.

Tibor's voice rang out: "Noam! Noam!"

He hurried to catch up with me.

"Noam, may I ask you a favor?"

"I'm always at your service, Tibor."

I had finally formulated a sincere sentence. Nothing delighted me more than proving my affectionate respect to Tibor.

His forehead furrowed. He scratched the nape of his neck and shot a feverish look around him, as if an enemy was about to appear.

"The village is in extreme danger, but I will abstain from telling you more about it. Can you simply assure me that I can discuss it with you if events spin out of control?"

"Tibor, I've left the village. It no longer concerns me."

"For your mother, for your father, for Noura . . ."

"No!"

I'd shouted. Somewhat thrown off balance by my rebuff, Tibor grabbed my forearm.

"I'm a sensible man, Noam, you know me. Can you promise me that I'll find you here at the full moon?"

I stiffened and tried to pull away. He gripped me even harder, his face wrinkled, his eyes imploring.

"I'm begging you, Noam."

Reluctantly, irritated by this disagreeable scene, I replied by drawing a distinction: "I'm saying 'yes' to you, Tibor, not to the village."

When he heard my words, his features reorganized themselves. Tibor let go of me, relieved, sighing.

"Thank you, Noam. Let's meet on the morning of the full moon."

I promptly departed, without succeeding in calming my fury. I couldn't bear the promise he'd wrung out of me.

*

There's something worse than not knowing; it's imagining . . .

Since I'd refused to hear any details regarding the village, I imagined atrocious calamities; deprived of material to nourish my reflection, I ruminated, brooded, turned things over and over *ad nauseam*.

What were Tibor's silences concealing? What was his worry covering up? Despite numerous tragedies—the demise of his wife, the death of his sons, the disappearance of his village under a mudslide, the loss of his property—he'd retained his imposing presence, his altruistic energy, his winning curiosity, his desire to improve people's lives; he had never wandered from his path or stumbled. Unlike my father, he wasn't hiding any shadows inside him other than his private sufferings. And now this healer, so strong, so honest, had admitted to being afraid. To the point of begging me for help. What was going on?

The things we flee always catch up with us. The village and its inhabitants were now constantly on my mind.

The chickadee had also followed me. Remaining at a distance prudent for a bird, she escorted me stubbornly.

For his part, my uncle was overflowing with vitality. Was it because, having briefly been a deserter, I had returned to life in the wild? Was it because he'd relieved himself of his brother's horrible secrets? Was it because now he was bawdily braying that he'd "deserved a woman" without my raising an eyebrow?

He disappeared this way on several occasions, returning the next day triumphant and exhausted.

"Ah, my boy, how I envy animals! They only fuck when they're in rut. The rest of the time, they don't feel the itch, they go about their business, they sleep; their crotch leaves them in peace and quiet! Whereas we . . . we're in rut year-round, in heat in every season. What rotten luck! From time to time, I'd prefer to be a bear."

"Are you kidding?"

"Obviously, Nephew! I'm so thrilled my blood is boiling. I never get tired of it."

"What *could* you get bored of, Uncle?"

"Nothing that gives pleasure. Want to come along next time?"

"Maybe . . ."

This "maybe" delighted Barak. He figured he wouldn't have completely rehabilitated me until I accompanied him. My reluctance seemed to him to be morbid childishness.

The moon was waxing. I observed its growth with a mixture of anxiety and impatience. What would I learn from this rendezvous?

When I thought the moon had reached its maximum size, I told Barak that I would be gone for two days. He seemed to sense my destination because he didn't ask for any explanation.

I made the journey at his pace, the rapidity of a long-legged colossus, which tired me out less than it did before. In the evening, I slept not far from the stump of the tree that had been hit by lightning, and then, in the early morning, I walked as far as the hill where the healer and I were supposed to meet.

When I saw three silhouettes, my heart leapt in my breast.

On the promontory, Tibor, Mama, and Noura were waiting for me.

Mama hugged me tightly, without loosening her embrace. We formed a single unit. Like we used to do. Like before my birth. All-enveloping, she wept into my neck, discreetly, delicately, and, by contagion, my eyes filled with tears. Her warmth; her silky skin; her soft, rounded body; her sugary rose perfume—all these odors intoxicated me, obliterating the present moment to take me to a time apart, pure, sweet, luminous, incorruptible, a place where the affection of a mother and her son pulsated. How had I ever been able to leave her?

Caressing her back, I held her pressed against me. My eyes shut, my mouth closed, I tried to express to her through this contact that I loved her more than ever since I'd learned about her youth, her chaste love for Barak, her broken happiness, her mourning, and then the reconstruction of her life with my father, bravely, without complaint. In her heavier body, I could now discern the weight of her sorrows, of what she had given up, of her compromises and resolutions, and all this made it infinitely more moving to me.

She released me. We stared at each other. Mama looked human and feminine to me. For the first time, I no longer saw her through the eyes of a child, but those of a man.

"You've lost weight," she said, stroking my cheeks.

Noura approached us.

"Hello, Noam."

I shivered. Seeing Noura, who was intense and strung as tight as a bowstring, and hearing the velvety timbre of her voice, disturbed me. As was her habit, she refrained from smiling; her perfect features glowed naturally.

Tibor looked at me with embarrassment. "Excuse me for acting on my own initiative, Noam. I didn't want to betray your trust, but the crisis made it necessary."

The three of them looked at me seriously, signaling that the moment for celebrating our reunion was over.

"We need you," Mama cried.

"You're the only one who can save us," Noura added.

For the moment, I was more astonished than worried. The bond that I perceived between Noura and Mama disconcerted me: far from being rivals, they spoke with a single voice. Though there was no visible friendship between them, there wasn't any enmity, either; solidarity in the face of danger had pushed their disputes into the background.

"What's going on?"

Mama turned to Noura. "Explain the situation to him."

Noura nodded. "A certain Robur has been hanging around our village, along with a gag of stupid, stinking brutes. They're not Hunters, but they're not much better, lice off a dog's back that prosper at the expense of others. They would've left if they hadn't sensed there was juicy prey here: our village has been lavishly developed, and its chief . . ."

She hesitated a moment.

"Is infirm!" Mama interjected.

Noura blinked to confirm Mama's judgment. She went on, "When Pannoam ordered him and his gang to leave, Robur laughed."

"Worse," Mama added. "Robur announced that he would become the chief."

"By what right?" I exclaimed.

"The right of the stronger," Tibor replied. The healer was wringing his gnarled hands.

"Robur stood in front of Pannoam under the Linden Tree of Justice and challenged him publicly: 'If you want to protect your villagers, prove that you can.' They're going to fight."

During my childhood, intruders accompanied by looters had contested my father's legitimacy and tried to take control of the village; Pannoam had fought these impudent wretches and killed them. Blood settled such cases.

"Should this Robur be feared?"

Mama stepped toward me. "A few years ago, your father would have had him for lunch. Now he's lost a leg, grown old, and no longer keeps himself in shape, and his reflexes are slowing. I'm afraid he's no longer capable of defending us."

"He's completely incapable!" Noura asserted coldly.

Outraged, Mama shot her an incendiary look; now as before, she couldn't put up with people criticizing Pannoam. But she decided to ignore Noura's insolence; the state of emergency required it.

"The fight will end badly," she murmured.

"Does Pannoam realize that?"

A silence followed my question. No one dared offer an opinion. Mama looked at Noura, who looked at Tibor. All three of them sighed.

Mama broke the hesitant silence. "If he doesn't realize it, we do. And so does Robur! He'll win the duel; he'll kill your father."

"And he'll rule the village," Noura concluded.

I tried to take a little distance on the problem.

"How will the villagers react?"

A disdainful grimace twisted Noura's little face.

"The villagers are governed only by fear. Which scares them more: Pannoam's decrepitude or Robur's violence? They hesitate. Don't count on those passive animals intervening on Pannoam's behalf. When I think that Pannoam could die for them . . .!"

Mama confirmed this with a snort of exasperation.

Inwardly, I corrected her assertion: Pannoam wouldn't be fighting for them, but for himself. Out of pride, self-love, a taste for power. In my heart of hearts, I didn't believe my father would act out of altruism.

Far from discerning my thoughts, Mama, Noura, and Tibor implored me with their eyes. What were they expecting? What solution was I supposed to provide? The purpose of their mute request escaped me.

I cleared up any ambiguity. "I've left the village."

"It's your village!" Mama said, indignantly.

"I no longer live there."

Her face turned red with rage as she looked at me. "You think you can erase years in just a few moons? You no longer care what happens to those close to you? You no longer have a family? Am I no longer your mother? Are you no longer my son?"

I hung my head. "What can I do?" I muttered.

Mama planted herself in front of me, lifted my chin, looked me up and down, and ordered me, "Go back to the village and tell Robur that Noam, the chief's son, will not allow his heritage to be stolen from him."

Noura ardently agreed. "That moron didn't invent embers, but he will immediately understand that he risks more in attacking you. Robur calculates quickly."

"Take back your rank, my son," Mama demanded, laying her hands on my shoulders.

I was no longer capable of reasoning, having been reduced to a clearing open to the winds and ravaged by gusts from opposite directions. What should I do? Help Mama, or return to life in the wild? Satisfy Noura, or return to Barak? Save the village, or save myself *from* the village? I was a mess of conflicting desires. Once again, events were fragmenting me. Who was I? Which Noam would respond?

The presence of three people I cherished, their anxiety, their supplicating insistence, the hope that lay in their hearts won out.

"Okay."

Their faces lit up. Dismayed, I was already reprimanding myself: I hadn't chosen, I'd given in.

"When is the duel?"

"This morning!" Tibor said.

And without further delay, the healer, Noura, and Mama led me to the village.

All along the way, one question tormented me. How should I behave with regard to Pannoam? Now that Barak had revealed his cynicism, I was going to meet my real father, not the one I had naïvely imagined for years. I sensed that my disdain would be transformed into aversion.

Once in the village, we didn't go to the building constructed at the time of the wedding, destined to house the love between Noura and Pannoam, but rather to the old family home, the one where I had lived until I married.

When I entered the main room, Pannoam, busy getting ready, was sharpening the flint of his sword. Bent over, half-naked, his eyes narrowed, he didn't hear me come in, and I had a moment to take in the extent to which he'd changed. His muscles had atrophied; the skin on his arms hung loose under his diminished biceps; the bones protruded at his shoulders and elbows; and his loins had broadened around a sagging belly. Having simultaneously grown both fatter and thinner, his body had lost its coherence.

Sensing my consternation, Mama whispered, "Marrying a young woman didn't bring back his youth."

Her cruel remark was spot on. Pannoam no longer had the bulging, victorious chest and broad frame that all by themselves guaranteed his stature as chief. His back was hunched. White hair mixed with black on his temples and on the middle of his head, making his mop of hair look dirty, neglected. In addition to his wrinkled features, his jaundiced skin testified to his confinement, his lack of exercise in the open air, and his boredom.

On the night I'd seen him trafficking in merchandise, I'd identified him by his voice, which was intact, but I hadn't perceived his physical deterioration, whereas in broad daylight his decline overwhelmed me. An unexpected emotion deluged me: pity. This father whom I had fetishized as long as I remained at his side, this father against whom I'd been railing ever since I fled—now I felt sorry for him. Devastated by seeing the ravages of old age and amputation, I wanted to console him.

He looked up.

A genuine joy spread over his face.

"Noam!" he cried.

Without thinking, he opened his arms to me, and I threw myself into them.

"My son," he repeated, holding me close.

How feelings disconcert us . . . They live their own life, apart from ours, as if they had an existence independent of any context. Leaving the present, I was suddenly seven, twelve, twenty years old, and I was no longer the hard, disillusioned Noam who had discovered the devious dishonesty of his father; I was the eternal child, the steadfast son, devoted and affectionate, like it was my first day in the role.

He looked at me with love and whispered, "I forgive you."

In a second, my enthusiasm melted away.

He forgave me!

Euphoric, his eyes shone with clemency as he contemplated me. He forgave me . . . For having left? For having lived without him? For having committed the crime of lèse-Pannoam? From his point of view, I was repenting of my sin by returning, and proving that it was impossible to survive without him.

He forgave me . . . for having escaped his egoism, his authoritarianism, his betrayals?

He forgave me . . . On hearing that word, I understood that, capable of everything, the worst or the best, he always considered himself to be in the right. Whatever he did, he saw it as just, legitimate; above and beyond his actions, he judged himself to be good. His strength flowed from his high degree of self-esteem.

He forgave me . . . Did he have any idea that I had more to forgive *him* for? Obviously not.

His face radiated generosity. Was there anything more intolerable than that generosity? One might have thought he loved me; in reality, he loved loving me. Rather, he loved himself for loving me.

I glanced behind me. Mama, Noura, and Tibor, pleased by the welcome my father gave me, gestured for me to push forward and resolve the situation. I decided to give the speech we'd prepared in advance.

"Father, I have come to resume my place."

I added, bowing my head, "If you'll have me."

Pannoam ruffled my hair.

"Welcome, Son."

I got straight to the point. "Who is this Robur?"

My father, invigorated, drew himself up. In an excellent mood, he struck his chest with his hand, picked up his sword, and showed me its sharpened edge.

"The man I'm going to kill today."

Cheerful, triumphant, full of himself, he tried to walk evenly across the room, despite his prosthesis, enlarging his strides and his gestures. He boasted. He explained to me—and the rest of his audience—that the little runt had provoked him and that he would inflict on him the same fate that awaited toads of his size: he would cut his throat. Lyrically, he referred to his multiple victories, convinced that he would add to the list.

"Always victorious, Noam, never defeated!"

Was I going to whisper to him that, in his condition, he would immediately pass from undefeated victor to undefeated cadaver? Voluble, talking too much and too loudly, Pannoam was getting high on his legend, on his past exploits and his exploits to come; he was playing a role, that of the hero, overcompensating with feigned energy for what he lacked in real energy. Everything seemed forced. Sensing that, he overdid it, exasperated.

Once again, pity swept over me, but this time it was a pity without tenderness, a disapproving pity: it seemed pathetic that a former great chief should caricature himself out of vanity.

I interrupted his monologue: "I'll let you warm up, Father. Let's not disturb our champion before the duel. We'll celebrate your success together."

He stopped in the middle of his sentence, the words on the tip of his tongue, and looked at me with embarrassment, disconcerted to have convinced me.

Then the flash of lucidity faded, and Pannoam resumed his act where he had left off, swaggering and looking for the appropriate weapon.

We left. As soon as we were outside, Mama, Noura, and Tibor attacked me.

"You were supposed to propose that *you* talk to Robur!"

"In his place?" I replied.

"Yes! And suggest that you challenge Robur!"

"In his place? Don't be as delusional as he is. You've seen as well as I have that he thinks he's in perfect shape. You've noticed as well as I have that he'd rather die than back down. Particularly in front of us. He no longer lives in this world; he lives in a past world where a young and vigorous Pannoam dominated everything."

I took Tibor's arm. "He has to be the one to decree that I'll replace him. He, and he alone. For that, I need your help."

"My help?"

"Do you have any buckthorn?"

Tibor studied me. His eyes shimmered, amused.

"I thought you were my best pupil, but here, the pupil surpasses the master."

He broke into laughter. I joined in.

Mama and Noura didn't appreciate this complicity that excluded them. "Might we know what you're laughing about?" Noura shouted, her nostrils flaring.

Tibor turned to her and, for once, put her in her place. "I've often shown you that bush, my daughter, but as usual, you neither listened nor remembered what I said. Its little red fruits, which roe deer love, increase pugnacity; its bark, dried and served in a tea, fights constipation."

"So?" she retorted, little disposed to recognize her error.

"Our friend Noam wants to have a drink with his father."

"Precisely!" I confirmed.

"A bowl of strong wine, highly spiced, because the buckthorn powder we're going to put in it emits an unpleasant odor. To intensify the effect, I'll add a few flax seeds."

I concluded, for the benefit of Mama and Noura, "With his guts in an uproar, Pannoam will be forced to give in. He'll make a decision."

Mama spontaneously kissed me and whispered in my ear, her voice weary, "I just hope it's the right one."

Pannoam did not spot the ruse. He drank with me, continuing to strike flattering poses. Little by little, in the course of his preparations, I saw that contractions in his abdomen were making him uncomfortable and that painful spasms were shaking his gaunt cheeks. His will fought against the threats made by his bowels; he even increased his boasting and swaggering. Suddenly, his face paled and he slipped away.

He returned a little later, pallid, but pretended to have recovered until further, violent spasms obliged him to run off again.

This time he was gone longer. He returned feverish, sticky with sweat, and shivering.

"Noam, I'm not going to be able to fight."

"Postpone the duel, Father."

He glanced at me with fury.

"If I ask for a delay, I'll be confirming Robur's claims. I would be giving him the victory without a fight. He would take over the village."

He wiped his forehead. "I have an idea."

He held out the spectacular necklace of pearly shells that he wore as the insignia of power.

"I'm making you chief. After all, I've spent my life training you, and now you're ready. *You* will confront Robur. He'll eat dust."

"Father, I don't know . . ."

"I have spoken! For me, it's over."

He laid his hand on my shoulder, even as he leaned against the wall, shaking and overwhelmed.

"I'm putting you in charge. I'm proud of you, my son, and I love you."

*

When I went out of the house, transfigured, wearing the insignia of power and entrusted with a weapon, Mama, Noura, and Tibor immediately divined what had just happened. In silence, so that Pannoam would continue to be unaware of our conspiracy, Mama embraced me, Tibor congratulated me, and Noura smiled at me.

A murmur was spreading.

Rhythmically, blows and cries rose among the houses. People were striking the ground with sticks and chanting ritual formulas, women were ululating, men were clicking their tongues. This hubbub oozed a call for murder, a desire for bloodshed.

Tibor hurried to the source of the tumult.

"Quick! Robur has been waiting in the square for a little while now. He's getting impatient. The villagers have gathered there, and this bastard is winning them over to his side by insulting your father and mocking his tardiness."

I followed him and burst into view near the Linden Tree of Justice.

Shouting and percussion ceased.

An awed murmur ran through the crowd. I had not been seen for moons, and people were even less expecting to see me appear wearing a sword and the famous necklace.

I planted myself in front of Robur. No need to verify his identity. Heavy-set, as broad as he was high, hung with all sorts of amulets, wearing a pendant made of animals' teeth, and decked out with a wolf's head on his skull, he displayed all the signs of someone who wants to be a frightening warrior. Even the dirtiness of his beard and his thick hair said "Fear me."

He seemed grotesque to me, not because he lacked physical arguments—a massive veined neck like that of an ox; swelling muscles; heavy, compact fists; shortish legs that made him both quick and sure on his feet—but because his narrow forehead with its two deep lines, his bloodshot eyes, quivering nostrils, and testy bearing all indicated the stupidity and narrow-minded obstinacy of a man who takes his aggression for bravery and his pretentions for real stature.

Noting my necklace and my sword, he addressed me. "Who are you?"

"Noam, son of Pannoam."

He growled, "Pannoam doesn't have a son."

"You are misinformed."

I turned to the villagers. "Am I Noam, son of Pannoam?"

They screamed "Yes," which displeased Robur; he sensed that the wind was turning in my favor.

He stamped his foot on the ground, imperiously, drooling slightly.

"Where is Pannoam?"

"At home."

"He's refusing to fight!"

"With whom?"

My reaction made Robur choke with indignation.

"With me, of course!"

"Why?"

"Because I challenged him. If he wins, he remains chief. If he loses, I become chief."

Our conversation annoyed him in the highest degree even as

it plunged him into insecurity. Whereas he had foreseen an easy victory, his plan wasn't working out as expected. I continued calmly, knowing that my tranquility would completely destabilize him. "I think you're mistaken, Robur. You claim to be fighting the chief of the village? I am the chief of this village."

"Since when?" he shouted.

The brute's vehemence proved to me that he was either an idiot or that he feared defeat.

"For twenty-five years and a few instants. My father has just given me my due."

I pointed to the necklace, which he had been ogling since the beginning of our confrontation. Then, to establish my authority, I asked him: "And you, who the hell are you?"

"Robur!"

"Well, Robur, I advise you to go on your way."

The villagers applauded noisily. In their eyes, I incarnated the legitimate chief—or, rather, to follow Noura's reasoning, they thought the power to protect them was on my side.

Robur wavered. Part of him wanted to get out of there, but another part would find it hard to endure the public humiliation. When he turned to his henchmen to consult them, these men, who were bitter, testy, let him know by their growling and acrimonious gestures that he had to take me out. Since they weren't taking the risk of fighting, they allowed themselves to be overtaken by resentment, boiling with hatred and spurred on by the desire to massacre. Robur's temporizing exasperated them.

Robur, finding himself cornered, was shivering. On all sides, danger loomed. If he didn't confront me, he'd have to confront his men.

Tibor approached me and whispered in my ear, "Get ready to fight, Noam."

"Robur is playing for time . . ."

"Not for long. Who made him chief? These animals. He's their prisoner."

In fact, Robur no longer dared address his gang, so much were they shouting him down, threatening, tense, hostile, vindictive. He turned and looked me up and down. "Ready to fight, you runty little son of a cripple?"

His brigands cheered him on.

"Ready!" I said, gripping the hilt of my sword.

Robur lifted his axe over his head.

"You son of a yellowbelly, offspring of a turd, I'm going to cut you in pieces and make you eat your balls. If you have any . . . Maybe your father, who lost them along with his leg, didn't think to give you any! You wimpy eunuch, I'm going to bury my axe in your ugly mug so you can give it a good lick before you die!"

These insults, far from troubling me, elated me. If Robur was the type of warrior who kept his morale high by ranting and raving, he must lack true self-assurance and real courage.

I raised my sword. To my own astonishment, I was delighted by what was about to happen. How satisfying! The anger that had been brewing in me since that morning, indeed for many moons, could explode. This short-legged moron was offering me relief.

I proclaimed, trying not to let my impatience show, "That's enough, Robur: you leave or you die! Now!"

Brandishing his axe, he charged me, fire in his eyes and a roar on his lips.

I evaded his first attack. He spun around and tried again. I nimbly slipped aside. He persevered, beginning to think I was a coward, and imagined he was in control of the situation. I let him rush me several times and struck no counter-blow so that he would grow bolder, tire himself out, and lose his balance.

The eighth time he charged, I did not avoid him; I countered his attack, sent his axe flying, and, without the slightest hesitation, thrust my sword into his belly.

He stared at me, his eyes wide, his mouth open, dazed, and fell to his knees. Bellowing with pain, he tried to pull out the blade. With a cruel pleasure, I drove it in further, twisting it, so as to rip his bowels apart. He wailed.

Finally, when I decided it was time, I suddenly withdrew my weapon.

Robur collapsed. Blood pooled beneath him. He howled briefly, shuddered, yelped, and then the rigidity of death pinned him to the ground.

I shouted to his pillagers, "Get out, and take that with you! Otherwise, it's your turn next."

The villagers began a long ovation that included cheers and ululations. To judge by their ardor and animosity, one might think they were the ones who'd fought . . .

On the sidelines, Mama and Noura were contemplating me, admiringly.

In everyone's eyes, I was now the village chief.

*

After the feast, I spent the night in my old house, the one where I had lived with Mina.

I didn't sleep. The rapid sequence of events was overwhelming me. Destiny, after my escapade in the wild, was eagerly making up for lost time.

To celebrate my accession to power, the villagers had improvised a feast, some of them procuring meat, others putting it on spits, lighting a fire, bringing fruit, or pouring out liberal amounts of wine. At the banquet, Tibor sat on my right, Mama on my left. Splendid, she was once again the chief's woman, the chief's only woman. Not only had my wife died, but Mama's position as mother could be claimed or taken away by no one else. To my great delight, she had adored shining at my side, as proud as she was satisfied, radiant, imperial.

Busy emptying his intestines, Pannoam had not appeared at

the feast. Noura, out of decency, had also abstained. However, I remembered the look she had given me when, over the smoking cadaver, I had washed my arms of Robur's blood. More than admiration, I had discerned a wild fascination based on a turmoil that was intensely physical; her face and neck had turned a violent scarlet. In spite of herself, she had emerged from her reserve. Had she, for the first time, seen me as a strong man, not the submissive son of Pannoam? Seeing myself in her eyes, I saw myself as handsome. For a moment.

Killing had not revolted me. It had seemed to me an excellent solution. After game, both furred and feathered, I was taking the life of a human. Unlike animals, Robur had attacked me; unlike animals, Robur had wanted to harm me. All things considered, I'd found it easier to slaughter this guy than an animal: I'd eliminated a danger and put an end to the stupidity, envy, and bile I'd detected in him.

I was idly stretched out on the mat where Mina and I had tried to make children. My memories of us didn't sour my mood; they tired me. With distance, I remembered only Mina's sweetness, her awkward devotion, her desire to do good, forgetting the boredom, the annoyance and impatience I'd experienced. Mina was becoming an episode in my life that I cherished, well suited to produce an agreeable melancholy.

I was also touched by my father's decision to keep the house intact, unoccupied. Ordinarily, no building remained empty, the chief immediately assigning it to a family. For me, Pannoam had deferred the reappropriation. Had he hoped I would return?

My opinion was changing. The fact that he had transferred power to me calmed my doubts. By abdicating the day before, he had shown an acute sense of his responsibilities. Faithful to his duties and wanting the best for his village and for his son, he had proven his coherence. His career as chief and father completed, after so many battles, so many worries, he was finally going to rest.

At dawn, I disapproved of my judgment, which lacked nuance.

What a clod! Either I admired him or I scorned him. Couldn't I acquire a view of him that was pertinent and balanced? Admit his complexity? Pannoam had both the most dizzying defects and the most sublime qualities. True, his virtues were accompanied by vices that were proportional—that is, enormous—but did the perfections work without the imperfections? Perhaps you have to love power too much to put up with it at all . . . Is it possible to devote oneself to others in spite of them, and sometimes against them, without ever thinking a selfish thought? If Pannoam had kept fear alive, he did it to ensure the peace and cohesion of the village. When he skimmed off his share of the Hunters' pillaging, he was showing them that he was still chief. Without question, he was swindling his subjects, but didn't the latter prove ungrateful at the first opportunity, as I had seen facing Robur's threats? They stopped supporting a weakened Pannoam; they preferred him dead. In the end, wasn't it understandable that he retained a portion of the spoils to guarantee his subsistence, to improve his old age, to counter reversals of fortune? Reigning doesn't prevent anxiety, and assuring security doesn't keep anyone from feeling insecure.

Yes, Pannoam's behavior masked his faults. But didn't hypocrisy serve the common good? If Pannoam delivered only the illusion of justice, if he presented only a simulacrum of decency, these appearances were what counted most. Despite his falseness, he provided a model for the people, embodied the necessary merits that everyone had to mirror. Ultimately, it mattered little that in the darkness of the night he revealed himself to be different, because no one knew! In his case, even hiding his secrets was part of good governance.

How lacking in subtlety I'd been! I'd never stopped seeing him as either all white or all black. From now on, I would accept him with all his facets.

As I walked to his house, I decided to include my father in my initial actions as chief and to consult him when making most of my resolutions in an effort to treat him considerately and make it easier for him to retire.

When I got there, he welcomed me with a burst of laughter.

"Ah, Noam, I'm feeling much better."

"So much the better, Father."

He offered me a drink.

"Noura described your battle with Robur. Your hand didn't tremble. I'm proud of you."

"I had to do it."

"And you did. Congratulations."

Pannoam pointed to the necklace. "You can give it back to me."

I froze.

Sure of himself, he came toward me and, not expecting the slightest resistance on my part, took the necklace off my breast and laid it on his own.

When he saw my distraught face, the left corner of his mouth rose in a spasm that looked like a smile.

"What? You took that seriously?"

"But . . ."

"Noam! You played the game superbly well, thank you. Now that I've recovered from that temporary indisposition, everything goes back to normal."

"You . . ."

He stopped his banter, stood still, and said to me in a peremptory tone, "An upset stomach doesn't mean that I no longer hold power. Or that I have ceded it to you. Don't be ridiculous."

I stood up, cold, tense.

"Father, you're going back on what you did."

"Yesterday, I did what yesterday's chief had to do. Today, I'm doing what today's chief has to do. Noam, I couldn't fight, but the village had to be defended: I acted as chief by sending you to kill that lout. This morning, I have recovered my health: I continue to act as chief by resuming power."

"Do you consider me incapable of exercising it?"

"I trained you for that. But I'm still here, my boy; you'll have to wait until I'm dead."

He laughed, making fun of my dismay, treating me like a child. His concern and joviality struck me like so many daggers. He gently repeated, "Yes, Noam: wait. I waited with my father, Kaddour."

"That's not the same."

"It isn't? Why?"

"Kaddour abruptly collapsed one day while out walking in the sun. The spirits and the gods received him when he was in the prime of life. Whereas you . . ."

"I what?"

"Your bowels are no longer bothering you, Father. But will you be able to fight on one leg? Without any training? Could you have defeated Robur? Aren't you subject, yourself, to moods that you later inflict on those close to you? You're not well, Father. You'll feel better as soon as you retire."

Pannoam fell silent. He was reviewing countless ideas without finding one he could use to oppose me with. I expected that without arguments, he would recover his lucidity.

He drew himself up and turned his angry eyes on me: "Never!"

He fulminated so much that he was shaking. When he realized it, he shook even more.

Eager to put an end to this demeaning scene, I went to him and started to tear the necklace off. Holding onto it, he grumbled angrily: "Did you really think I'd given you power, you poor imbecile?"

I stopped trying to wrench away the necklace and replied with the same hostility: "I should have known, given how often you steal what belongs to others."

"What?"

"It's a hobby of yours . . . Taking Elena away from Barak. Taking Noura away from me. And now, taking power back from me."

Barak's name staggered my father. He shuddered. His eyes opened wide. He didn't understand how I'd learned about that. I took advantage of the situation to strike the death blow. "Not to mention, of course, your treasure . . . Yes, your treasure! Or should I say your booty? What you steal from the villagers with the help of the Hunters. Come now, don't pretend to be surprised! Those sacks you've been storing in Bears' Cliff for ages. I wonder, moreover, if a single bear ever hung out around there . . . You've been lying about everything to everyone for a very long time."

Pannoam clung to the wall to prevent himself from falling. Plunged into helpless disarray, he didn't dare look at me.

Then he set his jaw. Rage invaded his features. Detaching himself from the wall, he grabbed two weapons and handed me one of them.

"Fight."

"Excuse me?"

"If you want power, take it. Fight."

I took a step backward.

"Never."

"Why?"

"You want me to fight against my father?"

"Fight."

He pointed his sword in my direction. I didn't react. He waved his sword to begin the battle. I remained frozen. Furious, he leaped forward and, with one blow, cut my arm with his blade.

With my free hand, I pressed on my wound to keep my blood from flowing.

"Fight!" he bellowed.

I looked hard at him. Pronouncing each syllable slowly, I retorted, "I will not fight you."

"Why? Why?" he bawled, waving his weapon.

"Because I would win!"

I threw my sword at his feet and left at a run.

Before leaving the room, I saw him on the floor, screaming with anger, a mass of pure hatred, suffering, and resentment.

As I climbed straight through the hills, I felt the intoxication of freedom rising in me. I wasn't fleeing the village, I was going back to life in the wild, the life I had chosen. Each step gave me more strength; my muscles were vibrating, my legs boiling, and I could hardly resist running.

No more! Farewell to intrigues, rivalries, betrayals! I was finished with society, that net that traps, wounds, suffocates, and I was leaving a father who had brought me up for his own sake, not mine. When Pannoam claimed to have prepared me to rule, he was lying. If the exercise of power demanded fraud and rapine, he should have informed me of that, and then trained me for it. He'd preferred to keep me in the dark because he liked to use me as a flattering mirror. For him, shining in front of me, draping himself in honesty, and strutting heroically were more important. Vainglory corrupted my father's good qualities.

I'd left him on the floor, humiliated, wailing. He knew that, disillusioned, I was now aware of his perfidy, and he cursed me. What good news! Let him detest me, yes, let him thoroughly detest me! His hatred would free me from him.

I walked for a long time, which gradually calmed me. Even though the sun had continued to shine these past weeks, every day was more bitterly and mordantly cold than the last. Winter was coming on.

Night fell just as I rejoined Barak at his hut.

He welcomed me with joy, but calmly, far from imagining what had happened.*

---

* As I write these lines, a memory rises up.

Paris, 1749. I'd been thrown in prison for a debt I had not repaid. The limestone fortress, which was damp, cold, and redolent of saltpeter, would have seemed sinister to me had a certain young man not been held there. He was voluble, passionate, lively, charming, and his conversation delighted even the guards. He had been nicknamed Golden Mouth. His atheism had led him to be put in prison, but his high connections

"Let's go eat outside, my boy; we won't be able to do that much longer."

We sat down on a rock platform that looked out on the lusterless moon. The stars gave off a diffuse light, as if they were behind a veil that dampened the shadows.

and the intellectual reputation he enjoyed had made it possible to temper his incarceration in Vincennes. Not only were books, paper, and ink made available to him, but he also received his friends. One of them visited every week. He was about the same age and emitted less external brilliance, more internal light. He was nicknamed the Musician because he either sang or threw himself toward the harpsichord that Golden Mouth had procured. I loved to spend time with them. One sunny Sunday, perhaps because we had drunk and eaten too much, I told them a little about my youth. Prudently, I told them my story not as a part of my life, but rather as the memory of an Italian tale I'd read, the author of which I'd forgotten. Golden Mouth and the Musician listened to me fervently. So I mentioned Barak, his spontaneous kindness, his joy, his compassion, his life far from the village. "He's man in the state of nature," exclaimed the Musician, "man before society has corrupted him!" Then I described, still as though recounting a novel, my father Pannoam, his desire to possess, his simultaneously manifest and hidden enrichment, and the authoritarian power he wielded to keep his goods. The Musician murmured: "My friend, you have illuminated me!" Golden Mouth looked at him and said, "I see! You're going to answer the Academy of Dijon's question about the origin of inequality, and you'll side with nobody!" The Musician laughed. "Then Nobody must be monsieur's identity. What is your name?" Just to play along with the joke, I replied, "My name is usually Ulysses, but it's Nobody when the creditors come calling." Golden Mouth soon left the prison; I never saw him again, any more than I did the Musician. On the other hand, I read the latter's book a few years later. He painted a portrait of the noble savage in the state of nature, in which I recognized my uncle Barak. And the second part began this way: "The first man, who, after enclosing a piece of ground, took it into his head to say, *This is mine*, and found people simple enough to believe him, was the true founder of civil society. How many crimes, how many wars, how many murders, how many misfortunes and horrors, would that man have saved the human species, who pulling up the stakes or filling up the ditches should have cried to his fellows: Be sure not to listen to this imposter; you are lost, if you forget that the fruits of the earth belong equally to us all, and the earth itself to nobody!" Afterward, the Musician, in dazzling pages, distinguished between natural inequality, whose origin we do not need to seek, and social inequality, which proceeds from humans. The institution of property establishes an inequality of patrimony unrelated to physical inequality. Later on, it generates oppression, social classes, and conflicts.

What a surprise it was to discover that my naïve narrative had produced philosophy! I often reread the Musician's discourse, as well as his other essays. I also like to peruse the works of Golden Mouth, which may be less fundamental but are stimulating through their joyful freedom, which reminds me of the fascinating whimsy of his conversation. Ah, one detail: Golden Mouth's name was really Denis Diderot, and the Musician's was Jean-Jacques Rousseau.

"My right knee's throbbing," Barak muttered. "That means that snow's coming."

While he lit a fire, I told him about my expedition. He listened to me, alarmed, without any commentary except for his open mouth.

As soon as I had narrated the final scene, the one in which I condemned my father by talking to him about Barak, Elena, and his nocturnal trafficking, his eyes sparkled, and I knew that my words avenged him.

After I'd finished my story, he cried, "You didn't say farewell to your mother or Noura?"

"No."

"Perfect! Saying farewell makes it impossible to leave, or at least to leave well."

A rush of aggression toward them shook me. "In any case, they got what they wanted!"

"Pardon?"

"They didn't want me to come back; they just hoped to save Pannoam and the village."

Stung by an additional jab of pain, I added, "And to keep their position: wives of the chief. They used me. Like Pannoam."

I was aware that I was denigrating them excessively, but was I really slandering them? Noura clearly wanted to retain her privileges, and Mama, though she loved me, had enjoyed playing the role of the chief's mother. These ambitious women shared Pannoam's taste for power. Would they put up with Pannoam if they didn't? Besides, what did they love in him?

My role suddenly appeared less glorious. Whereas I believed I had acted in accord with my own will, I had simply done what Pannoam, Noura, Mama, and even Tibor were counting on; I'd been reduced to a tool that they manipulated. What a moron!

Barak leaned toward me.

"I almost lost you, then?"

He understood that I could have not returned and reproached

himself for having waited for me so nonchalantly. I examined him: this mass of muscles, the flesh gleaming with health, this shining hair and thick beard sheltered a tender heart. In his disappointed lips, his imploring eyes, in the wrinkles on his forehead, my uncle's sincerity seemed to me so patent, so unlike my father's cunning, that I wanted to hug him.

He saw that. He enveloped me in an embrace as brusque as it was enthusiastic. Clasped to his powerful torso, hardly able to breathe, I didn't push him away; I let myself be infected by the warm affection he radiated. Why couldn't I have been given Barak as my father?

"Uncle, I have only one thing to say."

"Yes, Nephew?"

"We deserve a woman, don't we?"

And we broke into laughter.

*

The cold took us by surprise.

At dawn, we saw dark, slow-moving clouds coming in, carrying snow in their flanks. Sluggishly, they occupied the sky to the point of making it disappear, then dimmed the light. The first flakes fluttered down indecisively, hesitantly, like incompetent scouts reconnoitering the terrain; they vanished as soon as they touched the ground. Finally, battalions of flakes streamed in, falling ever more densely, loading the atmosphere with a milky opacity.

The snow continued to fall for several days and nights. To counter the cold snap, we'd put on our furs—cloaks, booties, mittens—and kept the embers constantly alive in the cabin. For food, we drew on the small stocks we kept under a layer of pebbles.

Every meteorological event brought us together, my uncle and me. Imbued with a deep reverence, we contemplated the spectacle offered by Nature, the gods, and the spirits. Barak was never worried: he admired. Had he been faced with the worst of hurricanes, he would have been delighted.

Since his childhood, he often told me, the lands around the Lake had grown ever warmer, both in winter and in summer. More and more clement temperatures prevailed.

"In the olden days, the Lake stayed frozen for five moons, where now it only freezes for one or two. Pannoam and I had so much fun sliding on the ice! It was thick and solid, not at all dangerous. Sometimes we traveled long distances. One winter, we even tried to cross the Lake; fortunately, hunger brought us home after six days."

Barak was so fond of recalling this enchanted period when he and his brother ran around exploring the universe together that I wasn't sure how much of what he told me was exaggerated or true.

"Our ancestors dealt with a harsher climate than today's. For some reason, the gods and the spirits treat us better. We're no longer obliged, the way our forebears were, to live in caves year-round."

One morning, when I opened my eyes, I awoke somewhere else. Time had been suspended, the air had become denser, and I was crushed by the silence.

On emerging from the hut, I discovered that the snow had stopped falling.

A bright light filled the forest, cast by the blue sky, rising from the immaculate ground that refracted the azure.

This silence testified to another world. It expanded space to dizzying proportions, absorbing everything. I no longer heard anything but myself, my heartbeat, the breath whistling through my nose. When I took a few steps, it seemed to me that the crunching sound produced by my feet disturbed the whole forest. Uneasy, I stopped and listened. The slightest creaking of a branch, wings flapping in the distance, the tiniest paws of a squirrel running up a tree trunk, each sound broke the peace. In the summer, noises melt into the silence to become part of it; in winter, noises become foreign to silence.

Barak approached, moved.

"Just look at what the spirits and the gods have concocted for us over these three days. Wonderful work."

The trees, muffled in white, no longer trembled. The snow had decided to foreground the pale, scaly bark of the silver birches, transforming the oaks and poplars into simple, graceless dark trunks.

"Let's move somewhere else, Noam. The hut doesn't protect us from the cold."

"What if we caulked the cracks? And added moss?"

"That wouldn't be enough. Anyway, when we returned to the hut, our footprints in the snow would be easy to follow. The packed snow would show the way."

"Barak, who are we hiding from?"

He didn't answer me. Finally, I asked the question, "Where are we going?"

"To a cave I know. Not far from the Huntresses' Cavern."

"You mean . . ."

"Yes, yes, my nephew, those famous Huntresses we're visiting because, as you put it the other evening, we deserve a woman."

We emptied the hut of the things we couldn't get along without and then walked toward our shelter. Our progress was slowed by the snow. How did the light, fine, powdery snow become so much heavier as soon as our legs sank into it? Between being burned by exercise and being burned by the cold, I was subjected to two fires: in my lower body, the effort inflamed my quads and calves; in my upper body, the frost stung my hands, stiffened my arms, scorched the skin on my face. Lagging behind my colossus of an uncle, I was forced to breathe more deeply to keep up with him.

"Are you sure you know where you're going, Barak?"

He growled. Although the snow had covered up all our landmarks, it revealed others that didn't escape his sharp eyes. I just blinked, dazzled by the intensified light.

We were passing through a landscape that the snow had

softened, undulated, and wrinkled here and there, where the foothills began.

Barak pointed to a pile of rocks partially buried under snowdrifts.

"Here's our new residence."

"There's not a bear living here?"

"I've closed up the entrance."

Illustrating his words, he moved an enormous rock, then a second, then a third, which cleared the access to the orifice.

"Don't ask me to do that every day, Barak."

Rolling away even one of them was beyond my abilities. The giant replied, "I'll take care of these little pebbles, my boy. Nature has conceived us perfectly: you can slip into things; I can lift them. We all have our strengths."

And we lived in this cave for several moons.

*

"My boy, we have to make ourselves handsome for the Huntresses! That won't be easy . . . given the weather."

Deprived of water by the frost, Barak was fretting. Anyone who imagined that solitude had made him dirty would have been committing a serious error. Although he rarely trimmed his beard or his rebellious shock of hair, Barak had a strict regime when it came to hygiene. He scrubbed himself with ashes before washing and took either a full bath in a river, or a shower under a waterfall. Equipped with a small, porous rock, he regularly scraped away the calluses that armored his heels. After meals, he brushed his marvelous white teeth with the help of bamboo sticks and then rinsed his mouth with a decoction of mint.*

---

* Today, humanity represents its ancestors—such as my uncle in the Neolithic—as having serious dental problems, their teeth either rotting or missing altogether. This is a great mistake; I can testify to that. Contrary to popular belief, prehistoric men and women had very healthy teeth. Why? Because they had no cavities. They escaped this plague because their diet consisted mainly of meat and

On the evenings when he had prepared himself for a visit to the Huntresses, I detected a trace of vanity in him: he smeared his body with honey, let it sink in for a moment, and then went off to swim and came back with smooth, shiny skin. Just before he left me, he put his hair in order by means of animal fat, and then rubbed his wrists, neck, and ankles with tansy flowers that he kept in a pot, that yellow plant that most people called "smell-good" because of its powerful camphor-like fragrance. During our rambles, Tibor had noted that tansy kept ticks away from us and lice away from plants; from this, he had concluded that since it repelled little bugs, it would probably also expel little humans by promoting contractions in women about to give birth.

During the winter, Barak had turned our cave into a washroom. Every day, he packed snow into hollowed-out tree trunks; when it melted, the trunks were transformed into water storage tanks, some of which were used for drinking water, others for cooking or washing. Even if it was limited to ablutions, Barak did not give up his ideal of cleanliness.

"Are you ready, my boy?"

We had prepared gifts. Although wild game animals did not go out much—most of them were hibernating—they left clear tracks in the powdery snow as soon as they took the risk. Less quick-moving, sluggish, hares, shrews, and otters fell under our slings' projectiles. It was pointless to use bows. The bodies steamed for a moment on the snow, and then the cold stiffened them and they turned brownish, after which we preserved them

---

wild vegetables. Cavities appeared just after the time I'm telling you about, when cultivated grains, pureed or boiled, began to constitute an important part of what we ate. Not only did these grains contain more sugar, but the process of transforming the plant into flour added abrasive elements to it: the millstone, as it ground the grains, left crystals in it that wore down our enamel. Finally, the second wave of cavities resulted from the nineteenth-century industrial revolution, which led to a diet that was even more refined and sugary. The history of food may reflect an advance—because people got taller—but it also reflects a decadence, that of our palates.

in ice outside our shelter, with such success that a morning's hunting provided sufficient food for several days.

My uncle had killed a roe deer to give to the Huntresses. When he proudly loaded it onto his shoulders, I guessed he had a reputation as a gentle giant to maintain.

We made our way, keeping close to the crest of the hills. Nature displayed all the shades of white—gray, iridescent, bluish, and greenish. Despite the multiple layers of clothing I'd put on, the cold cut through me, and though I hid it from my uncle, I shivered, and my teeth chattered. However, Barak kept up a steady pace that eventually warmed me.

We reached the bottom of a short cliff. Barak let out a modulated ululation, three times in a row—a code. The stone trembled, and what I'd taken to be bushes in front of a brown rock turned out to be branches protecting a leather curtain.

A female Hunter appeared. She recognized Barak. Their eyes shone. She raised the leather door and invited us to enter.

The cavern proved to be spacious, lit here and there with oil lamps. Countless odors filled my nostrils—smoked boar, grilled mutton, saltpeter, vegetable soups, rotting fruit, dung. Horses dozed near the entrance, stocky, muscular bays that whinnied half-heartedly as we passed. During our journey, Barak had told me that the Hunter women cultivated the gift of taming these wild quadrupeds, making them dependent, and then riding them.

"Ah, my nephew, seeing a Huntress clinging to the mane, their legs around the animal's flanks . . ."

He'd explained to me that these female Hunters, the Huntresses of the Cavern, lived without men. When they wished, they allowed men to approach them, but they never shared their space with them. They refused to be old-fashioned women just as much as they refused to be like today's new-fangled women. Among traditional Hunters, the female belonged to the group; she tracked animals, lay in wait for them, killed them; her activities were always the same except when she was bringing a child into the world.

228 · ERIC·EMMANUEL SCHMITT

She didn't do that often—every five years, at most—but she did it
long-term, breast-feeding her offspring for several years. Among
Sedentaries, everything had changed: women stayed home, devoting themselves to cleaning and tidying up, and produced a child
every year. The Huntresses of the Cavern disdained that status, in
which women counted for little, males ruled them, and their lives
were reduced to being wives, mothers, and domestic slaves.

"I don't understand, Uncle. Are they women or Hunters?"

"The difference exists only in your head, Nephew! Let me repeat that whether they're Sedentaries or Hunters, they belong to
the same race: ours. You'll be able to verify that."

An imposing Huntress came and stood in front of us.
Monumental, with arms as broad as my thighs and legs like tree
trunks, she displayed, beneath a harness of hides, breasts that
bounced sensually in rhythm with her steps. Her hips, though
implausibly cumbersome, swayed smoothly as she walked. To the
right . . . to the left . . . she looked like she was dancing. Her face
was dominated by her cheeks; only two minuscule chestnut-col-
ored eyes pierced it, along with a small, upturned nose.

My uncle lit up when he saw her.

"Malatantra, my beauty!"

The matron's smile revealed a row of very pretty teeth. Barak
laid the deer at her feet. She let out a shrill laugh.

"This is my nephew, Noam."

She looked me up and down like a piece of meat that was being offered to her. The inspection must have led to a favorable
conclusion: she clapped her hands and spoke several strange-
sounding names.

Huntresses gathered who were younger and more impatient.

My uncle outlined the evening's program for me: "We'll drink
dandelion wine, we'll eat a few stalks of celery,* and then you'll
choose the woman you like best, hoping she'll approve of you."

* Wild celery, which is tender, crunchy, and juicy, was found along the damp
banks of streams and was reputed to be an aphrodisiac. Tibor had described it for

We moved further into the cavern, which had distinct zones: beyond the initial stables, the zone where cooking was done, the one where tools were made, the one where the women slept—near the fires—and the one where waste was stored.

The conversation was going well; it was pleasant, thanks to Barak, who amused the group, but also laborious, because we shared few words. I don't know what language the Huntresses used—they spoke an idiom composed of borrowings from various others, like souvenirs from their travel.

Malatantra, the voluminous matron, remained lying next to Barak, and I suspected he had come for her.

One Huntress held my attention. Her somber, irresistible face had a high-colored complexion and the robustness that comes from living in the open air. Tall, with sinewy legs, sculpted shoulders, and long hands, she radiated something feminine and wild, an untamed power. Even though we were relaxing around the fire, vigor never slept for long in her body; her sudden, decisive impulses led her to rise, find some wine, pour it, offer us walnuts. In spite of myself, my eyes kept returning to her. Once, when she turned around, her furs whirled, and I glimpsed the outlines of her arched ribs beneath her skin. I immediately got a hard-on.

Barak noticed my excitement. Without taking his eyes off me, he leaned toward Malatantra and whispered something in her ear. She looked at me, examined the Huntress, then summoned her.

The Huntress crouched in front of Malatantra and, in response to what she said, replied with vehement gestures. I was worried.

Noting that I had paled, Barak spoke to me, "She's mute, Nephew. Does that bother you?"

So that was why she was so expressive! Since her mouth didn't speak, her whole body spoke. I contemplated her, vibrant, intense, talking with the matron, and the blood went to my head with such a violent surge that I could no longer think. Was she

me as a "vegetable penis." Today, chemistry shows that celery produces hormonal balance and works to prevent male impotence, thus justifying the healer's description.

accepting me or rejecting me? My attention was completely focused on that question alone.

The Huntress stood up and looked intently at me. Her eyes
clearly showed that she desired me. With an urgent command,
her hand told me to come with her. Marvelous: I was the one asking for something, and yet she was acting as if she were dominant.

She walked away toward a corner of the cave, lifted a kidskin
flap, and pointed to her bed of furs inside the cavity behind it.

I lay down in it; she lowered the curtain, and slowly stretched
out on top of me. She imposed her rhythm, her way, on me. Her
eyes looked deep into mine; she pressed her lips against mine. I
melted. Had I ever experienced this before? Our fluids merged,
mixed, and enriched one another.

She slipped over to lie beside me, her back on the ground, and
signaled that I could take her. My fingers stroked her warm legs,
reached her firm belly, and then, under her clothes, tried to caress
her breasts. She extricated herself from my embrace and leaped
to her feet. I feared I had offended her, such fury did I see in her
reaction, but she tore off her rags and stood before me naked.
I was thunderstruck. Unlike Mina's, her body bore no sign of
stretch marks; tight, clear, pure, it seemed to have been created
that same day.

Satisfied with my admiration, she lay down again at my side,
smiled, and, closing her eyes, offered herself up to my fingers.
What a pleasure to smell a woman's odor, to caress her flesh, to
cause that golden skin to shiver, to move back up to her high,
small breasts, whose nipples hardened when my hand brushed
against them!

I jumped: she'd taken my penis in her hand. Her eyes showed
her delight at my hardness, urged me to penetrate her.

Sill lying on her back, she spread her thighs and lifted her pelvis slightly to allow me to enter her. Nothing was easier, nothing
was warmer, nothing more intoxicating than to sink into her wet
depths.

As I moved, she gradually gave herself up to my movements, savored her sensations. Everything in her body responded to my rocking motion. Her hips moved in rhythm with mine, or inversely, because, subtly, she was in control. My solid member, enveloped by her burning, intimate flesh obeyed her demands. I wasn't making love for myself, but for her: her reactions excited me as much, if not more, than my own impressions; I became the instrument of an immense, magical event that was happening to her.

She began to moan. The slightest hoarse growl enraptured me and at the same time taught me what to do or not to do. I served her with passion, initiating myself into an unknown phenomenon: the pleasure of giving pleasure.

Suddenly, she shivered, and I perceived in her an incredible, frenetic liberation. I came, as well.

I pulled out of her, rolled to one side, and held her in my arms. Our hearts still pounding, we both fell asleep.

*

I loved that winter. Whereas the earth, shrouded, seemed as rigid as a cadaver, I felt more alive than ever. My uncle and I went regularly to the Huntresses' Cavern; we presented our big game as an offering and then spent the evening with our chosen partners. While Barak and Malatantra wriggled around in their little cavity, roaring joyfully, I holed up with my mute Huntress, and we squandered our passionate youth.

Every night, my penis stood to attention several times. After a nap, the Huntress urged me to do it again, but her mysterious odor, powerful, imperious, overflowing, inexhaustible, was sufficient incentive in itself. I couldn't say what this organic perfume consisted of; I couldn't name even one of its ingredients or connect them with smells I knew. A primitive intuition, below the level of my consciousness, was intoxicated by my wild woman, made my blood rush to my sex and led me to lodge it in hers.

Today, on writing these lines, a memory that escapes all language summons its aroma and warms my groin.

My Huntress's name was Tita. Or, rather, that is what her comrades called her, shouting, because she was hard of hearing. Solid, well-built, tough, she had won the group's esteem; far from behaving as if she were disabled, she showed more energy than the others and was not put off by any effort: I saw her transporting deer carcasses before skinning them, breaking recalcitrant horses, moving rocks, dragging sacks of snow, reinforcing the supports for beams, and carrying branches for use as firewood. Doing the work of four Huntresses during the day, she still proved able to make love like four Huntresses during the night.

She had chosen me. Malatantra told me that up to this point, Tita had rejected almost all the visitors.

"Since you appeared, you're the only one who counts," the matron added, shooting me an admiring glance.

Tita turned out to be the complete opposite of Mina, dynamic, disinclined to complain, more dominant than dominated, and sensual to the point of madness. When I set them side by side, the comparison left me with the illusion of a certain fidelity to Mina: I wasn't cheating on her, not even posthumously, because I was keeping company with her opposite.

Tita also represented Noura's inverse. As athletic as Noura was refined, Tita did not say a word, whereas Tibor's daughter, a magician with language, kept everyone caught in the nets of her talk, her wit, her conversation. I had decided not to think about Noura any longer; for me she was dead or, at least, belonged to a dead world, a universe to which I would never return.

Had I really forgotten her, insofar as I was trying to erase her with her opposite? It was a hard winter, and it went on and on. From time to time, a break in the cold weather gave hope to animals who poked their snouts outdoors; implacably, however, the frigid whirlwinds resumed their crazy gyrations, and the snowflakes turned into icy needles.

A terrible and interminable storm forced us to stay in the cave with the Huntresses as long as the piercing, violent wind prevented us from going outside, whipping to death anyone who ventured to do so.

The cavern oozed sex. Its geography had masculine places—rocky projections, vertical reliefs, hard walls—and feminine places—crevices, funnel-shaped holes, cramped cells, damp hollows. Paintings accentuated this eroticization of space, offering countless vulvas and a few phalluses drawn by the Huntresses themselves, some of whom excelled at preparing the wall, smoothing it, perfecting the engraving, handling the etching, and distributing the colors.

Despite the pleasure of staying with Malatantra or Tita, we didn't much like this forced hibernation, any more than did the horses, panicked by the sonorous panting, or the Huntresses themselves, who rejected the continuous presence of men.

Through this confinement, I understood how Malatantra had obtained her sumptuous physique: she fed almost exclusively on marrow, pure marrow, fatty and unctuous. For her, the Huntresses broke open animals' long bones, thigh bones or tibia, soaked them for a day and a night in cold water to get rid of the blood, and grilled them. When Malatantra allowed me to taste it, I found this melting substance delicious, with a flavor like that of hazelnuts. Suddenly, every time I looked at her, I naïvely imagined Malatantra to be composed of this adipose, tasty, caramelized texture, and I envied my uncle.

One morning, the gusts of wind diminished, the air grew more clement, and snowfalls became less frequent. Around noon, the last snowflakes fluttered down, light, wriggling, like late-arriving dancers not meant for the ground, but the air.

Barak and I got on our way.

Heavy precipitation had so covered the landscape that it seemed more pallid than white. Nature had simplified itself: pale, humid, mineral.

"This way!"

Barak, fortunately, was able to orient himself in this modified panorama. Due to my shorter strides, we walked at an increasing distance from one another.

"Are you all right, Nephew?"

"I'm all right!"

Our voices, muted by the snow, found no echo. As usual, we were following the lakeshore, one of the few landmarks that remained reliable.

"What in the world is that?" Barak suddenly shouted.

His exclamation, rebounding off the ice on the Lake, was lost in the distance but reverberated from the neighboring valleys.

Barak drew my attention to a human form in the distance, near the shore. It was covered with rags and a small amount of snow.

"It's a body. Some careless person who got lost."

He went down the slope and approached the cadaver.

"A woman."

He bent over.

"The poor woman! She must have frozen to death. A true suicide, going out in weather like that!"

Trying to catch up with him, I stumbled several times because the snow clung to my shoes, and then I sank painfully into three different holes. When, exhausted, I finally reached Barak, he was turning the corpse over.

"How sad!" he lamented. "A pretty girl, too."

I bent over in turn: Noura lay in the middle of the icy snowdrifts.

*

After my uncle had gently carried the body to our cave, I rushed to her, pressed my ear to her breast and cried, "She's alive!"

I heard Noura's heart beating, very fast, too fast. Then, placing my finger under her nostrils, I noted that she was breathing in short, rapid breaths, though her thorax remained motionless. Noura wasn't dead, but she was dying.

"She must have fainted just before we spotted her."

"Noam, do you want me to give her a good rub to revive her?"

"Certainly not!"

I had refused by reflex, fearing my uncle's rustic crudeness, without imagining that centuries later medicine would provide a scientific foundation for my refusal: if, through energetic contact, heat is applied to the skin, there is a risk of sending cold, peripheral blood to the body's interior, which can cause cardiac arrest. My spontaneous wariness regarding the giant had prevented a heart attack.

On the other hand, I venerated Noura so much that I realized I'd be unable to undress her.

"Barak, take off her wet garments. If we don't do that, she'll continue to freeze. I'll give you all the furs we have."

While he was stripping her, I looked the other way and took out the embers I'd transported in my horn, using them to light the several fires we'd prepared in the cave.

"Finished!" my uncle shouted.

I turned around. Noura, pale, her temples bluish, her eyes closed, her features pinched, was disappearing under a pile of covers. Kneeling at her side, Barak, his hands on his necklaces, was fingering his amulets and chanting the ritual formulas. I joined in, closed my eyes, and prayed to the gods and spirits so hard that I felt dizzy.

My uncle rose, heated water in an oaken bowl, added some honey to it, and cajoled Noura, "Here, my dear, drink this."

There was no way to know if she heard us. Barak carefully placed her in a sitting position, opened her lips, and slowly, drop by drop, poured the infusion into her.

"Give me your cap, now that her hair is dry!"

I handed him my hare's skin cap, and he settled it snugly on Noura's head.

I didn't take my eyes off her: it seemed to me that her skin was recovering its color, that her nostrils were relaxing, that her respiration was growing deeper, but as soon as I convinced myself that this was true, I doubted it, powerless to gauge how much was based on reality and how much on hope.

Toward dusk, Noura opened her eyes. Her dilated pupils didn't recognize me.

"I'm here, Noura; don't be afraid."

She faltered out, "Papa . . ."

She was racked by shivers. Her eyes moved in all directions. She uttered inarticulate cries.

Barak whispered in my ear, "She's delirious."

"What can I do?"

"Nothing."

Lukewarm, sugared water gave her some peace; once she had drunk it, she fell asleep.

Grabbing Barak by the arm, I led him to the back of the cavern, as far as possible from the dying woman.

"I'm going to find her father, Tibor, the great healer. He'll know how to treat her."

Barak scratched his head, grimacing.

"With snow like this, it will take you two days to reach the village. You'll spend two more days coming back with the healer. That's if there isn't another storm . . . Bold and pointless. Her fate will be decided here. Either she warms up, or she leaves us."

"I want to do something!"

"Do, do, do . . . do something stupid, yes!"

"What, then?"

"Keep watch and pray. The gods and spirits decide. Let's keep a good temperature in the cave."

Noura spent the night and following day between life and death, sometimes eaten up with shivering, opening her expressionless eyes wide, uttering long strings of words, then sinking into a sleep so deep that it caused us to panic. Finally, she sat up, looked around her, saw me, and smiled.

"Noam!"

I approached her, overwhelmed.

"Noura! Are you feeling better?"

Embarrassed, she lowered her eyes.

"I'm hungry."

A cry of victory resounded at the back of the cave.

"We won!"

Noura trembled when she heard Barak bawl. She turned around and saw him. He crouched down near her.

"Happy to meet you. My name is Barak; I'm Noam's uncle."

She stammered.

I explained. "Barak saw you in the snow, carried you here, and took care of you. He saved you, Noura."

Barak broke into laughter and roared in his coarsely timbered voice, "I had an interest in saving you, little one, because otherwise my nephew would have pulled out my hair. He cares about you, this fellow!"

And he gave her a wink—Barak behaved familiarly with everyone he didn't know. Noura shivered, realized that she had few clothes on under the covers, blushed all the way down to her shoulders, tried to hide her embarrassment, and batted her eyelashes in his direction.

"Thank you."

Her lips had murmured this word with such sweet grace that Barak melted with pleasure, bewitched.

Noura looked at me. "How long have I been here?"

"Two days."

She nodded, reflecting. Taking her hands from under the furs, she contemplated them, noticed cracks in the skin, frowned, and asked, in an urgent tone, "Might you have some grease?"

"Sorry?"

"For my skin."

Before I could react, Barak handed her the pot he used to tame his hair before visiting the Huntresses.

Noura smiled at him, weakly, and started smearing grease on her fingers, palms, and wrists. Everything was going back to normal. Moved to pity, attracted, I felt the moment coming when the capricious and authoritarian Noura was going to dictate our schedule.

I asked her the question that had been obsessing me since the preceding day: "Why were you walking along the lakeshore?"

She stared at me, shocked that I hadn't guessed, and retorted, with a crystalline timbre, "I was coming to join you."

I immediately sensed that she was again going to ask me to intervene in village affairs to deal with some situation. Hostile, and firmly resolved to refuse, I pulled back: "You were coming to get me, you mean?"

She shrugged, put down the pot, wiped the surplus grease that stuck to her fingers on her dried-out lips, pursed them, bit them, clicked her tongue, and looked back at me.

"No, to join you. I don't want to stay with Pannoam. I'm coming to live with you."

After this declaration, Noura chewed some walnuts, hazelnuts, and dried fruit, then went back to sleep.

All day long, my uncle watched me out of the corner of his eye, wanting to question me. He didn't dare. I was aware that he was mutely imploring me, but, turning away, finding new tasks to be done, I walled myself up in silence.

In the evening, Noura hardly moved; she swallowed, half asleep, the bowl of soup we'd prepared for her and, exhausted, remained stretched out in bed, her eyes closed.

Barak took me outside, into a pale darkness.

All around us, as far as the eye could see, there had been a battle, between the snow and the night. Snow had won. It reigned. The whiteness of its mantle shimmered, blue-shaded, through the bare branches. We were walking under starlight as much as under moonlight.

Barak put his hand on my shoulder.

"Are you happy, Nephew?"

"What should I be happy about?" I protested, in a sulky tone I had no control over.

"Noura, the woman you desire, is joining you and proving her love for you."

I hung my head, defeated, in pain, without being able to savor the situation.

He was indignant. "If Elena had joined me back then, I wouldn't have made a face like that!"

"Barak, would you have forced my mother to live a life in the wild? She was born in a village, and village life is all she's ever known. Would you have taken her to live in a cave in the winter and in the woods in the summer?"

"I . . ."

"You and I like it because we're men, but women . . ."

"They're not so different, are they?"

His big, innocent face sincerely asked the question and feared just as sincerely the response.

"They're different, Barak. When she came to live with us, Noura had about thirty dresses—even after the mudslides had swept away all her possessions! Noura loves clothes, jewelry, shoes, objects, perfumes, unguents. She belongs to the world of the village."

"She can change."

"Why would she do that?"

"For love. We've certainly changed, haven't we?"

"We've changed because our love was unrequited! In an effort to escape our failures and misfortunes."

Barak kicked a snowdrift and sighed. Suddenly clasping my face in his hands, he whispered, "Listen to what she's telling you. Listen to her better. Don't make the same mistake I did, Noam; don't spoil your life."

And he returned with a resolute stride toward the cave.

I stood there with my mouth agape. In my view, Barak hadn't spoiled his life. Why did he say that? Did he think it?

"Listen to what she's telling you. Listen to her better." These words resounded in my head. He was probably right . . . Listen to Noura better. Or just listen to her.

Noura did not speak for two days, as if her suffering had gauged the time it would take me to analyze our conversation. I was languishing.

The first rain of the springtime fell that night. It woke me up, and I heard the countless lukewarm drops beating on the remains of the snow, tapping on the branches and trunks, gurgling down the sides of stones. At dawn, I ventured outside and contemplated the landscape that was being enriched by forms, dressing itself again in vegetable and mineral colors. To be sure, these colors continued to show a faint moderation—yellowish greens, grayish browns—but they alluded to a convalescence, one in harmony with Noura's, and this deeply moved me.

I went to her and offered her a drink.

"Tell me what happened after I left."

"Everything deteriorated, Noam. I don't know what your last conversation consisted of, but Pannoam hasn't gotten over his anger. He swears, he complains; in his view, everything is wrong. Before, he was prudent; now he's mistrustful. He fears everything: strangers who pass through the village, visitors on market days, and the villagers all the time. When things go well, he suspects that a truth, always an unpleasant one, is being kept from him. Behind every sentence, he sees a desire to harm him, the leading edge of a betrayal. To hear him tell it, he no longer speaks with anyone but corrupt people with bad intentions. He thinks the village is becoming a cauldron of conflicts that are brewing, poisoning him, and preparing for his death."

She concluded simply. "I'm not happy."

By instinct, I tried to resist the affection she was provoking in me.

"Did you want that?"

"What?"

"To be happy?"

Her forehead contracted, creases forming between her perfectly shaped eyebrows.

I insisted. "You wanted to be a chief's wife, not happy."

She drew a deep breath, giving herself time to fully absorb my comment, then turned to me. "True. I wanted to be a chief's wife. But not that chief's wife."

Her eyes shone. They stirred me.

"What does that mean?"

"The wife of a great chief, not of a declining, infirm one who is chief only in name. Every day less vigorous, every day more bad-tempered, your father is crushing us. He gives absurd, contradictory orders so that our obedience will reassure him he's still in control. He's oppressing the village; he heaps abuse on your mother; he persecutes me. He only spares Tibor, whom he needs. What did you say to him before you left?"

"Nothing."

My reaction surprised me. Why, once again, should I save my father, hide his dark nature from others? Did I still love him? Or was I keeping silent out of vanity, outraged to be the descendent of such a wicked creature? If pride incited me to protect my father, then I was just as devoured by it. As much as he was. I'd inherited his flaw . . .

"You didn't say anything to him?" Noura repeated.

"Nothing unusual."

She grimaced, skeptical. I reproached myself for lacking in sincerity, but revealing the truth humiliated me.

"In any case, becoming more lucid about his decline has made him despicable. Instead of attacking himself, he attacks others.

Aware that he's falling apart, he's trying to strengthen himself by weakening us. It's a sorry move!"

"So you fled . . ."

"No, I didn't flee: I came to find you."

Why couldn't I believe her? Why was I mistrusting what could enchant me? Was I like Pannoam, cantankerous, on the defensive?

Noura hooked her arm through mine, and as always, her contact gave me goose bumps.

"I went astray, Noam. I followed my reason rather than my heart. When your father became infatuated with me, I became the chief's wife. That reassured me, flattered me. What stupidity! If I'd followed my heart, I would have . . ."

"Yes?"

"I would have acted as you suggested: made Pannoam lose interest in me and dissuaded him from marrying me. But reason advised me to be ambitious . . . whereas my heart . . ."

"Your heart?"

She smiled at me, calmed, blossoming.

"I'm here, Noam. I risked my life for you."

She seized my hands, pressed them, and brought them to her mouth to kiss them. I felt so much emotion that I kept silent. We looked at each other with passion. A thought crossed my mind. Letting go of Noura, I got up and walked around her bed.

"What?" she cried, astonished by my brusqueness.

I had to articulate the question that was tormenting me. I caught my breath and spat it out, sharply: "Aren't you pregnant?"

Her eyes opened wide, and she clenched her fists, her mouth twisting into a grimace.

"How could I be?"

"Excuse me?"

She glared at me. "How could I be pregnant . . .? The marriage wasn't consummated."

Once again, I struggled to believe her. Our conversation was torturing me. I fell on my knees beside her.

"Pannoam desires you!"

Her face closed off.

"Yes. He showered me with presents, but . . ."

She hesitated, scratched a bit of the blanket with her index finger, sighed, sought encouragement on the surrounding walls, then blurted out, "A leg wasn't all he lost when he almost died under the Hunters' blows."

"What? Are you insinuating that my father . . .? That they . . . That he's lacking . . .?"

"No, he kept everything. But . . . it no longer works."

She bit her lip in frustration.

"That discovery is gnawing away at him. Marrying me let him imagine he was young and vigorous, but when he failed to perform his conjugal duties, he realized he was just a worm-eaten invalid. The infusions of savory my father prepared for him haven't had any effect. He can't stand himself anymore. He hates himself."

I retreated.

"Noura, are you really telling me the truth?"

"How do we recognize the truth, Noam? By the fact that it humiliates us. I've confided in you a truth that humiliates me."

She seemed sincere. I nodded several times.

She went on, "Our marriage, your departure . . . Pannoam is still too intelligent not to understand that he's made a lot of mistakes. But out of stubborn vanity, he won't admit it and prefers to be angry at the whole universe rather than himself."

She cried, suddenly bubbly and light-hearted, "Will you have me?"

"Here?"

"Yes."

"Noura . . . living in this cave . . . it's no life for you . . . worthy of you . . . I can't . . ."

She caught my head in her hands and pressed her mouth against mine. My heart beat fast and hard. We were finally having that most perfect of encounters, the one that says everything without any words. Something powerful, sovereign was coming over us. Through the portal of our lips, we were moving from one universe to another, from the sinister world in which we had not kissed to the luminous one in which we had. I immediately felt we had been bonded forever.

She gently disengaged herself, traced a circle around my mouth with her finger, planted a quick kiss here, another there, then a wetter, fresher one on each corner, and then exclaimed, her eyes wide with joy, "Oh, how sleepy I am!"

Lying down gracefully on her side, she closed her eyes and went to sleep, blissfully happy.

*

In the distance, the ice on the Lake was cracking with deep, ponderous explosions that sent startled birds flying.

Noura was recuperating in sync with the rhythm of the earth.

Spring was late in coming. Freed of snow, the earth swept along in mudflows that testified to its fatigue, its erosion. Although the sun was shining, it was not very warming, and the sky, though less pale than in winter, wasn't emblazoned with a strong blue. Colors were brightening without reaching their full intensity.

Noura resumed eating, getting up, walking.

Our kiss had lavished peace on us. Without going any further, or even reproducing it, we savored its gigantic effect: the certainty of our union.

One evening when, too caressed by her voice, I brought my lips near hers, Noura stopped me with a serious air.

"I'm your father's wife, Noam. We can't go on so long as . . ."

"So long as what? We're living here."

"Papa must be terribly worried. And Pannoam doesn't know that I've left him. I don't want him to think I've been eaten by a bear!"

Chuckling, she implicitly alluded to Barak's fantastic disappearance. Those two were thicker than thieves and spent their afternoons in gossip competitions.

Twice, at night, Barak told us he would leave us to ourselves and went off to see the Huntresses of the Cavern; embarrassed by what Noura would learn if we talked about that, I preferred that lies and silence surround his escapades.

On the morning after Barak's second absence, when he and I were preparing to go hunting, Barak told me that Tita was sad I was no longer visiting her.

"What pretext did you give?"

"That you were taking care of our animals! I chose the bait she could take."

"And did she take it?"

"Yes. Remember that we're raising three magnificent horses and that you've tamed a couple of wolves. No less! Even if that doesn't equal what Noura has done."

He laughed. But the comedy of the situation escaped me.

"Is Tita expecting me?"

Barak nodded. I felt helpless. When I'd slept with the Huntress, I'd done it out of desire, to be sure, but also out of anger. In conflict with my father, separated from the village, I'd proved to myself that I wasn't doomed to solitude, that pleasure accompanied and gave spice to my life. If, later on, I had loyally returned to visit Tita, it was because I believed I'd never see Noura again. Thinking about my wild woman, that combination of vigor and honesty, I saw myself as unfaithful.

"It would be better not to be attached to anything or anyone," I sighed.

"You just have to be attached to your freedom."

Hares were running around everywhere, leaping, tumbling, pirouetting, executing an excited dance to roam the meadows and undergrowth that springtime had returned to them. Barak, who was never blasé, laughed to see their little asses popping up here and there. Although most of them ran, yielding to the pure pleasure of moving, some were voraciously grazing, hypnotized by the tender grasses that they'd been waiting for so long; others rubbed the tips of each other's noses, their ears laid back, absorbed in a confab that would soon result in a litter of little hares.

By common agreement, we decided to gather rather than hunt, if only to respect this animal joy.

"Look, Malatantra's rivals!"

I didn't understand my uncle, who was pointing to some bearded vultures. I watched them for a moment and then understood better. Making high-pitched trills, the birds of prey were sharing the body of a doe; every so often, one of them took a heavy bone in its talons, flew away, and, soaring high and calm, dropped it. Because the bird aimed for the edge of a cliff or a pointed stone, the bone broke when it hit the ground. At the sharp crack, the scavenger flew back down, landed, grabbed a fragment, and enjoyed the newly exposed marrow.

"These are bone-breaking vultures. They do the same thing with tortoises: they drop them from high in the air to break open their shells."*

Barak led me to a spot where purslane grew. We gathered the leafy stems that crept over the soil, and then he pointed to an area full of turnips that we could easily uproot. The pinkish bulbs piled up in our bag.

Abruptly, Barak asked, "When are you leaving for the village?"

I stopped, scandalized.

---

* For a long time, vultures lived near villages, and then near cities, not because they liked humans but because they took advantage of our carrion. It therefore sometimes happened that an individual would get hit on the head by a bone, especially when he was careless enough to stand so still that he looked like part of the landscape. One day, in Greece, an old bald man was taking a nap, sitting with his back to a stone wall. A vulture flew by and dropped a tortoise. I don't know if it broke the tortoise's shell, but it broke the skull of the man it had taken for a stone. That is how one of the greatest playwrights, the author of tragedies that are still staged today, twenty-five hundred years later, lost his life. His name was Aeschylus, and I will have more to say about him later.

"Why do you ask that?"

"It will happen."

I was shaken by exasperation. I was oppressed by an identical feeling, and every morning I wondered how many days we were going to hold out, worried about the ineluctable prospect of our return.

"Noam, women are different. Noura lives with us: she doesn't have a choice, she's recuperating, and she satisfies you. But I know, and you know, that her stay here can't last. Hasn't she already explained that she wants to clarify the situation there? Let her father know she's still alive? If her feet don't lead you back to the village, her talk will."

Two hares with shining fur, their backs arched, their long ears folded back, were rubbing and tickling each other with their mustaches. Barak contemplated them with a grave tenderness.

"My boy, I've remained here because your mother, convinced that I'm dead, has never come looking for me. Had she turned up, I would have gone back to the village and claimed my due."

"Your due?"

"A life with her. A normal, happy life. Not that of a fugitive. I've become a phantom, Noam. The villagers think I'm a god, a spirit, an apparition from the past. I don't exist for anyone; I exist only for myself."

"What about Malatantra?"

"Malatantra, my perpetual sun. Have you noticed that at the end of summer she's like a female bear, very plump, ready to hibernate, but she goes into spring this way? Always in shape, our Malatantra!"

Cheered by the mention of the intoxicating matron, Barak clapped his hands with appetite. A desperate whining ripped through the air. The hares fled. A famished fox had one of them in its jaws and, feverish, starving, and violent, kept shaking it until the hare's final convulsions ceased. Then, relieved, it went away, still holding its prey in its teeth, and entered the shade of the woods.

"You, on the other hand, matter for someone," Barak insisted, ruminating. "You have duties."

"But . . ."

"Let's be clear: do you love Noura?"

"I love her."

"You want her to be happy?"

"Yes."

"Then you know what you have to do."

*

We left at daybreak. The air was warming up, but a dewy freshness persisted in it.

We crossed valleys, constantly climbing and descending. Nature had recovered its grandiose savagery. The mountains, still showing patches of snow on their crests, were vigorously green. A small, lone, wandering, lost cloud was reflected in the indigo waters of the Lake. It had been a long time since I'd heard so many birds; the multiplicity of their songs—whistling, squawking, cooing, peeping, chirping, crowing—suggested distinct plumages, offering us a multicolored concert.

Noura traveled on Barak's shoulders. They chattered like magpies, never parsimonious with exclamations, and their silhouette, which advanced before me, cheered me up: by virtue of the contrast, the athlete became more monumental, the young woman more petite, and I had the impression that I was following a giant who had kidnapped a child.

I was enjoying this hike through the virgin countryside, sensing that an episode—my joyful, carefree life with my uncle—was coming to an end. I didn't know what would happen next, but I understood that I was done with my innocent life in the wild.

In the evening, we approached the village. The trees, slender and straight, were beginning to fill out and seemed to be sentinels guarding the Lake, where swallows with lustrous blue-black wings fluttered about, squawking.

"A good night's rest, and tomorrow, my beauty, you'll return to your village," Barak announced as he set Noura down.

*

My father was dispensing his judgments under the Linden Tree of Justice.

We walked toward him silently.

When he spotted me, his face fell, and then, when he recognized Noura holding my hand, his eyes flamed. His mouth tense, the veins in his neck protruding, tics contracting his temples, he watched us come toward him as if a volcano's incandescent lava were about to wash over him.

I stopped a few paces from him.

"You're not welcome here," he growled.

"Hello, Father."

Resolved not to play his game of provocation, I remained inflexibly calm.

He pointed to Noura.

"That woman no longer enters this village. She must leave immediately."

We didn't budge.

He hissed at Noura, "I thought you were dead, and I was glad."

Without flinching, she replied, "I, too, thought I was dead, and I was glad. Thanks to Noam, I discovered I'm alive, and that makes me even gladder."

"Shut up."

"I feel sorry for you, Pannoam. By trying to be everything, you've ended up being nothing at all."

Scarlet, he screamed, "Shut up, you serpent!"

She moved toward him, stubbornly, and flattened her forehead against his.

"I'll shut up when you've repudiated me."

"Disappear!"

"Repudiate me publicly! Repudiate me! Give me back my life, and take back your own."

The villagers, who had told one another what was going on, were gathering on the square. My mother appeared.

Pannoam mumbled between his teeth, "I'll never do anything that will please you, you viper."

Noura laughed in his face and then spoke to me. "That's a fine declaration for a husband to make, don't you think, Noam?"

Beside himself, Pannoam took her by the neck. She shivered, stiffened, but instead of resisting or defending herself, she looked him in the eye with scorn. "Go ahead! Kill me! You can no longer kill a boar or a man. But a woman? Perhaps you could still manage it . . ."

My father, mad with rage, tightened his grip. Noura's face was turning purple. I intervened.

"Let her go!"

Devastated by a fury that he no longer controlled, Pannoam pushed me away and continued to strangle Noura. I threw myself at him, struck him in the face, the torso, the arms, and sent him rolling onto the ground.

Noura, her face on fire, was attempting to catch her breath.

Pannoam tried to get back up without success. He looked like a woolly sheep that has fallen on its back and, incapable of righting itself, ends up dying of suffocation.

I held out my hand to him. Reflexively, he almost took it, but then pulled back and spat in my face.

"Never!"

My mother rushed toward Pannoam, ordered me not to react, and helped him stand up. During this time, Noura was panting and massaging her neck. Once on his feet, Pannoam dusted himself off, turning several times to recover his dignity. He was suffering as much mentally as he was physically. I pitied him. Down deep, I couldn't bear seeing my father lose his hero status.

I approached and spoke to him in a low voice, so that he alone could hear me. "I'm back, Father, and I'll ensure your succession. You're exhausted. Let me take the burden off you. Let yourself rest, finally . . . The leadership of our community needs more than you can currently give it. You hold all the power, Father—including the power to pass it on. It's time. I'm your son, and you brought me up with that in mind. As a child, I thought I could never be as great a chief as you are, and I doubt it even now, but we can't hesitate any longer. Trust yourself. Trust me. I'm going to try."

I suspected that this speech, which I had rehearsed on the way, would prove useless; as I gave it, I noticed that it moved my father, whose fragility I'd underestimated. Weariness, harassment, and an awareness of his limits were blazing a path in him that my proposal could follow.

He staggered. He hesitated. In his heart of hearts, fatigue was contending with pride.

He jerked his head toward Noura.

"And her?"

"She'll marry me if you repudiate her."

He acquiesced, considering both the extent of his losses and that of his relief. An ironic smile appeared beneath his sad eyes.

"So, you're taking everything away from me, my son?"

Peace swept over him. Although he wasn't yet ready to say so, he accepted my proposal. Both of us knew it.

An enraged voice shouted, "He's not taking anything away from you, Pannoam. It's you who took everything away from him!"

Noura, who had caught her breath, was railing against Pannoam.

Does a spark light a fire? Noura's remark ignited my father's fury. In an instant, he exploded, scorched her with his eyes, and lurched toward me.

"Fight."

I murmured, wearily, "Father, don't start that again."

He screamed, if only just to show me that we had to stop whispering: "Fight!"

He threw out his breast and grabbed the sword that he wore during judicial sessions. He strutted. He struck poses. He was performing an act for the benefit of the villagers, incorrigibly infatuated with himself.

"Find a weapon and fight."

"I will never fight against you."

He bellowed, "This is the chief who would be inflicted on you, my friends, were I to retire: can't be bothered to fight!"

I continued to speak quietly, even as I felt serenity leaving me: "I exterminated Robur; you have a short memory."

"You do, too: have you forgotten how to fight?"

Descending from the heights of the village, a roaring voice resounded among the houses: "Pannoam, if you fight, you fight against me!"

The whole assembly turned to look: Barak, the giant, was coming down the path, splendid, broad-shouldered, his muscles bulging, his torso broad, his legs imperious, his hair swept back, giving him a thick, curly mane. His appearance terrified the villagers, who began to mumble prayers, caressing their amulets.

Mama started to step forward, stunned, unable to breathe. What? The fiancé of her youth was still alive? She thought her mind was betraying her. Her hand flew to her forehead, she bit her fist, and then, seeing that Barak was still advancing, at the peak of his virile beauty, she turned toward me, panicked.

With an encouraging smile, I said to her, "Yes, it's Barak."

Mutely, her lips repeated the word, "Barak," and she pressed her hands to her breast. I feared that her heart might not be able to stand the shock and ran to support her.

Barak, for his part, tried to avoid meeting her eyes, no doubt fearing emotions—Mama's, his own—and continued to move, his bearing haughty, with a sovereign ease, straight toward Pannoam.

The latter had grasped everything: his brother's return, Mama's turmoil, their unaltered affection. His jaws clenched, his eyes hard, he put all his energy into remaining steady, upright.

Barak stopped in front of him.

"You fight against me."

My father shivered and reflexively grasped his chief's necklace. A snort from Barak showed him how ridiculous he found him.

Barak addressed the crowd. "The son doesn't want to wound his father? That's to his credit! But brother will confront brother without scruples."

He displayed his axe.

"I'm ready."

And he added with a sly smile: "Finally!"

The incongruity of the situation paralyzed my father. I knew him too well not to guess that, obsessed by the idea of retaining his rank and not losing face, he was going to attack.

Leaving Mama, I raced to my uncle.

"Barak, don't provoke my father! The fight won't be equal; you'll kill him!"

He grimaced as he examined the stag's bone leg that supported Pannoam and roared, "What is my dear nephew telling me? That Pannoam has only one leg and I have two?"

He broke into laughter and went up to Tibor, who, having just arrived, was holding Noura in his arms.

"I imagine that it was you, the healer, who amputated his leg and made him another one?"

"Correct."

Barak shook his head and then returned to the center of the square, facing Pannoam. He called upon the assembly to be his witness, "What Tibor has done once, he can do again."

Barak swung his axe over his head and, roaring, sank it into his right leg.

The crowd screamed, and Mama fainted.

On the ground, deathly pale, his features drawn, Barak was beginning to pass out as he gripped his thigh to make a tourniquet. But his hands could no longer hold back the flow of blood, and he shouted to Pannoam, "Now we're equal, Brother. As soon as the healer has cut off my leg, we'll fight."

*

The period that followed remains foggy in my mind. Probably because confusion reigned among us.

After his amputation, I took my uncle to my house. We had hardly gotten there before Mama appeared at my door, a bundle of clothing at her feet.

"I'm moving in with you, Noam."

"I'd be glad to have you. Is Pannoam . . ."

"I don't care about Pannoam! I'm staying here and looking after Barak. When your father tried to stop me, I told him to go jump in the Lake!"

She approached Barak, who was sleeping, drugged. Her hands smoothed his hair, caressed his face, pulled the blanket up to his neck, crossed his arms on his chest. She cared for him with the delicate attention given to a newborn, except that a giant replaced the baby. Barak's sleep allowed my mother to re-establish contact with him, to keep her eyes fixed on him, to dare to make gestures and touch him in ways she would otherwise have repressed. Mama seemed to me like a young girl.

"He's as handsome as he was before."

She contemplated him, madly in love. Suddenly, embarrassed, she shivered and asked me, "Has he told you our story?"

"Yes."

She blushed, proud of her emotional turmoil. I put my arms around her shoulders and caressed her.

"He still loves you, Mama. His whole life, he's never loved anyone but you."

As tears ran down her cheeks, she protested, "I thought he was dead!"

"He wanted you to think that . . ."

She looked down, devastated, intrigued.

"You know more about it than I do . . ."

I smiled.

"You have a lot of catching up to do. Move in and arrange the house however you like."

At that moment, a shadow appeared in the doorway. Leaning against the frame, Noura announced that she'd brought bandages and the potions Tibor recommended. This situation reminded me of her arrival at Pannoam's house during his convalescence, the calamitous event that had triggered these tragedies. I feared a scene: Mama would attack her, and, given the two women's characters, the confrontation was likely to be formidable.

Mama looked at Noura, invited her to come in, and said in a level voice, "Show me how to care for him, Noura. I'll do it."

Noura nodded. Kindly, patiently, with devotion, she told Mama what to do.

"If it would reassure you, I could come by often."

"Thank you, Noura, but you will please keep your distance. We can't have a repeat of that nasty trick from last time."

Noura couldn't help chuckling. "There's no risk of that! As soon as I met Barak, he annoyed me, he talked so much about you."

Mama received that remark like a true young woman, at once overwhelmed and doubtful. Did she still inspire affection in Barak? Noura and I assured her that she did, but he hadn't yet told her so because, for the moment, they hadn't exchanged a word.

"Papa wants to talk with you," Noura whispered to me.

I followed her to Tibor's house, where she had resumed her habits, abandoning Pannoam.

As soon as we arrived, Tibor, a bowl of wine in his hand, told me about the operation. Sawing through such a bone, cutting such tendons, slicing through such muscles had exhausted him. He had never carried out such a difficult surgical task, especially because, as soon as Barak woke up, it took ten stout men and incredible amounts of sedatives to control him.

He proposed that I accompany him on a walk. The look he gave me suggested that he wanted to talk out of earshot of Noura.

"Of course, Tibor. I'd be delighted to hear what new plants you've discovered."

Noura raised her eyes to the ceiling and declared that she would remain at home. For a reason that escaped me, she found her father's research without interest.

We walked down toward the Lake, whose smooth and tranquil water mirrored the cloudless, brilliant blue sky. On its shores, the dark reflection of the forest gave the surface a mysterious depth.

Driven by an impatient joy, I felt that the long-awaited dialogue between father-in-law and future son-in-law was about to take place. While Tibor was discoursing on the virtues of thistles, I made the first move.

"Do you want to talk about Noura?"

"No."

I showed my surprise. He was amused by it.

"My daughter has never allowed me to have any power over her. That's probably why I like her so much."

He looked at me intently.

"Here's what's going to happen: Barak will defeat Pannoam, you will become chief, and you will marry Noura. Right?"

"We hope so."

He dismissed this reality as if it already belonged to the past and was no longer worth discussing. He admitted that he'd never been worried about Noura, not even during her recent disappearance. He knew that she was endowed with uncommon energy, intelligence, and determination.

"Even if everyone else dies, she'll survive. I don't know anyone with a stronger appetite for life. She's practically a monster, really!"

"Tibor!"

"Why should I blush to have sired an exceptional daughter? I'm proud of it. I'm proud of the fact that she doesn't need me."

"Still! When she was freezing and delirious, she called for you."

"Pardon?"

"She called for 'Papa . . .'"

Tibor cleared his throat, looked up to scrutinize the azure sky, his eyelids fluttering. My anecdote astonished him. A bird's laugh ricocheted off the water, again and again until it disappeared at the limits of the audible. Below us, svelte adolescents were purifying themselves by bathing.

"I wanted to talk to you about a dream, Noam. A dream that recurs constantly. It scares me."

"Yes?"

"We are on this shore, and we are swallowed up by the water."

"'We?'"

"You, me, Noura, your mother, the village. All the villages of the Lake. And the animals, and the forests. Nothing remains. A catastrophe."

I had infinite respect for Tibor, but being aware of his tendency to abuse certain mind-altering substances, I tried to bring him back to everyday reality. He interrupted me.

"I'm afraid."

"Come now, Tibor, not all our dreams predict the future."

"But they do! They emerge from it. They tell us about it. Sleep is still the only gateway the future passes through to reveal itself to us."

"I've had dreams that weren't realized."

"You haven't lived long enough yet. All my dreams have come true. That's why Noura's absence didn't torment me: my dreams had shown me her return."

The sun was climbing and getting hotter. Even without moving, we were dripping with sweat.

"I saw water submerge our world."

These words cast a pall over the peaceful countryside and the radiant silence. I couldn't take Tibor's statement seriously.

"We're far from that. Especially today. It hasn't rained for more than half a moon."

"In my dream, the water doesn't fall from the sky; it comes from the ground."

"How on earth does it do that?" I exclaimed, mocking.

"Don't play the fool, Noam. Rainwater forms puddles, not lakes. The water spread out before us here comes from the soil by means of springs; springs feed streams; streams feed rivers; and rivers flow into the Lake."

"Yes, but . . ."

"In my dream, the Lake gets angry. It grows. It spits. It belches."

"That's already happened. The water rises, and then it falls."

"In my dream, it doesn't calm down. It dies."

"The Lake dies?"

Within our universe at that time, no sentence could seem more absurd or sillier than that one. The Lake was life, the origin of life, an untouchable divinity forever superior to others. How could Tibor imagine that . . .?

"If that happens, we will die. Unless . . ."

He turned toward me.

"As soon as you become our chief, protect us."

I remained stupefied. He saw that and frowned.

"Have I ever spouted nonsense at you, Noam?"

I reflected and said, fervently, "Not at all, Tibor. Either you know something, or you keep your mouth shut. Your words speak with the same integrity as your silence. You never rave."

"In the name of that, believe me," he begged, tense and anxious.

I replied, more out of a desire to calm him than out of conviction, "I'll take your warning into account, Tibor. Keep your premonition secret, please, and don't tell people I'm privy to it."

Tibor agreed to these conditions and squinted in the direction of the rising sun.

"A family, three days' travel from here, makes boats. The biggest ones around the Lake. Meet with these people and ask them to work for us."

I scratched my head. Would I inaugurate my reign with this incongruous demand?

"Noam, do you believe me?"

I examined his noble face with its protuberant eyes and cheeks furrowed by long wrinkles.

"You're the only person I'm inclined to believe, Tibor."

Barak had recovered consciousness, his wound was healing, and he was recuperating. The first time he was alone with me, Mama and Noura having gone away, he beseeched me, in a desperate voice, "Nephew, save me!"

I moved closer to reassure him, but he didn't let me get a word in edge-wise.

"Get my bag, quickly. And take out the statuette."

I plunged my hand into his bag, rooted around, and found the object that was worrying him: a sculpture in bone representing a woman with large, upright breasts, enormous buttocks and thighs, and a rounded mons pubis that scarcely covered a prominent vulva with big, open lips. The head was missing, as if the artist had retained only the characteristics of great sexual value, allowing the viewer to imagine whatever face he wanted.

"Get rid of that, please! If Elena saw it . . ."

I laughed at his panic. Shame rarely visited my uncle.

"Mama suspects that during all those years, you must have . . ."

"Shut up. No allusion to Malatantra or the Huntresses."

"I swear."

"I don't want her to think that's all I desire . . . that kind of woman . . . when she's the one I love. Throw it in the Lake. Carefully, as an offering, and with the relevant formulas, you know what I mean."

I hid the statue in my bag.

"I'll keep it for myself."

Relieved, Barak laughed and gave me an affectionate thump on the back that almost knocked me over.[*]

Whereas I was counting on a rapid convalescence, in proportion to the life force that circulated in this Hercules, I noticed that he was recuperating slowly.

When, one day, I mentioned this to Tibor, he smiled. "Your uncle is doing better than he lets on, Noam. He's enjoying being an invalid so much that he wants to make it last."

Observing him, I could see how pertinent Tibor's reply was. Barak was enjoying being the sole center of Mama's interest and savoring the care that she lavished on him.

"Why," he asked me, "did I wait? If I'd known what to do earlier . . . It's well worth a leg!"

He'd set up a game: the game of true-false memories. Mama or he would describe the life they would have shared had they not been separated. To continue the story, the speaker had to obtain

---

[*] I was amused, thousands of years afterward, to note that statues like my uncle's, which were quite common in his time, led to interpretive quarrels among the historians who unearthed them. They saw in them "fertility icons," "homages to mother goddesses," just as they saw in sculpted phalluses "staffs of authority" or "spear straighteners." So much candor, and such an excess of prudery surprised me until I noticed that nineteenth-century researchers belonged to the Christian clergy, while those of the twentieth century belonged to the academic milieu, two different worlds in which, clearly, people didn't want to think about sexuality. Later, in reaction, more unrestrained intellectuals talked about "pornography," which seems to me an inappropriate way to define an erotic object full of health.

the confirmation "True"; otherwise, the listener would continue telling it where they'd left off. How did this criterion operate, given that they were improvising an imaginary life? The plausible became the true; the implausible became the false. Thus, when Mama claimed that on many occasions Barak had gone hunting for half a moon, Barak objected, "False! I could never be away from you, not for a single night." Then when Barak mentioned their ten children, Mama sharply pointed out that she'd given birth to fifteen infants, and seeing how robust their parents were and the enthusiasm with which they were conceived, they had all survived! On the other hand, each of them, blissfully happy, let the other imagine summer evenings, canoe trips, splendid feasts, and voluptuous mornings in bed, wrapped in their lovers' warmth.

Touched, I listened to these adults making up for lost time through a game and affording themselves the passion Pannoam had deprived them of. At the end, Barak invariably concluded, "It was well worth a leg!"

One day, I pointed to the stump that Mama was meticulously bandaging after having washed it.

"Seriously, Barak, why did you do that?"

"What?"

"Mutilate yourself."

"Do you want the nice explanation or the nasty one?"

"Sorry?"

"The nice explanation is that I'm clearing the way for you; not only am I purging the village of an incompetent chief who is clinging to power, but I'm saving my dear nephew from a thoughtless, deceitful father. The nasty explanation is that I'm taking my revenge! I'll gladly demolish the greedy devil who appropriated Elena and reduced me to living like a Hunter."

He laughed.

"Don't choose between the two explanations; they're complementary."

Mama was hypersensitive and vibrated with constant emotion. Barak's return made her as happy as it did unhappy; although she finally had him, she was aware of how much she'd missed. Often, as she left the house when we went down to the market, she shed tears, mixed, contradictory tears, some of joy, some of pain.

"You've never been so beautiful, Mama!" I exclaimed one day.

"Be quiet," she retorted. "Pannoam disfigured me."

"Not at all, I swear . . ."

"My soul is hideous. And it's his fault! My whole life I've tried to love Pannoam, and I think I finally managed to. I admired him, I found him strong, intelligent, loyal, subtle, powerful. Convinced, I had children with him. But your father managed to destroy that love that I so patiently constructed. I know now that he dishonestly rid himself of his earlier fiancée, that he stole me from his brother, and that he drove him away. Then he married Noura, which relegated me to a corner as a relic of the past, and in doing so, he betrayed my son. Soon, he'll fight against the only man I adore. Do you know the worst part? He's forcing me to become sicker than he is; he's compelling me to detest him; he's making me entertain foul passions: hatred, disdain, a thirst for vengeance. At this very moment, I hope with all my heart that he'll be defeated. Can you imagine that, Noam? I want Pannoam to die! Did I deserve that? Did I deserve to be filled with so many horrors? Your father has made me ugly, and continues to make me ugly."

The weather was taking a strange turn. Whereas the winter had been abnormally hard, spring was reaching new heights of warmth. Hardly had the buds bloomed into flowers or leaves before the sun undertook to exhaust them by drying them out, burning them up. Nothing fell from the sky, but brooks, streams, and rivers were high, and the surface of the Lake was rising. To be sure, it rose every year, but it usually waited until summer. What was causing these high waters? And how high would they get?

Most of the villagers welcomed this hot weather with joy because, living on the shores of the Lake, we lacked neither drinking water nor water to irrigate our fields. But it worried me . . . I couldn't forget either the expedition during which my father had revealed that the Lake was constantly encroaching on the land or Tibor's dream about the murderous rising water.

The time for the duel was approaching.

My father, abandoned by his family and friends, including Dandar the potter, his foster brother whom he had disgusted, practiced his sword skills every day with the soldiers who guarded the village. Although I no longer frequented him, I did glimpse him, from time to time, in the middle of the clearing, relentless, out of breath, stiff, sweating, trying to forge a new warrior out of his truncated body.

As for Barak, he could stand and was getting used to the prosthesis Tibor had made for him, but not practicing fighting.

When I reproached him for this one morning, he replied indignantly, "Come on, you don't want me to prepare to kill my brother!"

"That doesn't bother him."

"We all have our strengths. He has rage; I have muscle."

Then he added, concerned, "At least, I hope I do . . ."

Several times, I caught him doubting himself. Two distinct self-images inhabited Barak: that of the man, and that of the little runt. In front of the villagers, Mama, or Noura, he behaved like a colossus; in the presence of his big brother, he shrank. An old body image slipped in between reality and his person.

Let's hope my father doesn't know about this weakness, I thought with dread. Or he'll take advantage of it.

*

The sun was beating down.

Sweat was dripping from our foreheads onto our eyelids and

making them sting; our armpits were sticky; the smalls of our backs and our thighs were wet even when we stood still. Just breathing the dry air was enough to exhaust us and burn our lungs; the weather was excessive, portending the scene that was about to take place.

The combatants appeared and sized one another up. Which effort would cost them more, advancing or standing still? When they walked, it was clear that their balance depended on the sequence of movements and that they were continually in danger of falling, but standing still seemed to require all their energy. The two heroes inspired pity.

The village men and women had gathered to witness the confrontation that would decide their fate. Mama and Noura stood side by side behind me, trembling with anxiety.

What could I think except that I should have done all I could to prevent this duel? Two men I loved, or had loved, the two men who had taught me most, the two men who, each in his own way, had ardently wished my happiness, were about to fight. Their blood was going to be shed.

My father was the first to attack, holding his sword in front of him. Barak parried his blows without responding in kind. He had assured me that the fight wouldn't be long, so repugnant did he find it to put on a show or to pointlessly tire my father; however, he had told me that he would let Pannoam make a few attacks so as not to humiliate him—ordinarily, Barak crushed his adversary with a single stroke of his axe.

I saw that he was respecting his promise, allowing his elder brother to take the initiative several times.

Too nervous, and guided by fury rather than by his muscles, Pannoam fell after making an unsuccessful lunge. Normally, a fall like that would be fatal. Motionless, as if he had noticed nothing, Barak gave him time and the opportunity to get back on his feet.

Exasperated, my father assailed him again and again. Barak

forestalled his attacks, trying to counter him frontally to prevent him from collapsing.

When my father fell to the ground again, Barak said, "Shall we leave it there, Pannoam?"

"What? I haven't lost."

"That's because I'm letting you get up. For the second time."

"Coward!" cried my father. "You can't fight, and you're dressing up your pitiful excuse for a duel as nobility."

Barak didn't react to the insult. Pannoam added to it as he rose to his feet with difficulty, his limbs not obeying his commands, "On top of that, you're delusional! You're not so strong, Barak! I've been in control from the start."

Barak held his tongue, but his dark eyes and his frown showed that his brother's attitude annoyed him. He was getting ready to put an end to Pannoam's bragging.

His self-confidence restored by the idea of his superiority, Pannoam, in a surge of fierceness, threw himself at Barak. His sword sliced across his brother's muscular arm, a superficial wound that introduced blood into the battle.

Delighted, triumphant, Pannoam seemed drunk with malevolence.

"So, still the best, Barak?"

The giant sighed, resolved to put an end to the fight.

When he lifted his axe, he did so with more pity than aggression. When he brought his weapon down on Pannoam, the action said, "Stop disappointing me." When the blade broke the bones of his brother's thorax, the sadness in his eyes ordered his brother, "Stop being this ridiculous Pannoam and, in death, become the glorious Pannoam you once were."

Mama screamed in horror. Noura turned away.

My father lay on the hard-packed earth. Beneath him, a brownish liquid was slowly spreading, mixing with the dust.

The crowd cheered Barak.

He looked on them with scorn. For him, the scene was not

something to be celebrated. However, he restrained his contempt and silenced the crowd with a gesture.

"I'm transferring the power I have just won to my nephew, Noam. He will exercise it wisely."

He pointed at me.

The crowd applauded us. Ululations, clapping hands, and stamping feet reverberated as far as the Lake.

Our eyes, Barak's and mine, showed the same consternation. What? All that for this? All that for them? For these loudmouths? Our suffering, our wounds, Pannoam's death for morons who were constantly braying with fear or pleasure, but who limited themselves to braying?

I approached my father, knelt down, and leaned over him. He was still breathing. I turned his agonized face toward me. When he saw me, a glimmer of joy shone in his eyes.

"Noam . . ."

"Father . . ."

"I kept her intact for you . . ."

The grimace he was trying to transform into a smile told me that he was confiding in me a secret he was proud of.

"Father, what are you talking about?

A cloud passed over his face. The light began to go out of his eyes, and he murmured, "Noura . . . intact . . ."

And life left him.

*

With Noura at my side, I was contemplating the Lake.

Nothing on the water caught the eye, other than a dark boat and a flock of ducks. The day's heat had killed any noise. Everything was stagnant.

After the duel ended, Noura had tried to get me to talk, but I remained mute. My father's last words had cast me into an abyss. "Noura . . . intact . . ." He'd left this world revealing to me that he had safeguarded Noura for me; thanks to him, she'd escaped other men, all the predators, to come to our marriage pure; that was his last gift on earth, a present for his son.

I found the idea revolting! I could move beyond Pannoam's death only if I abhorred him. On the other hand, if he turned out to have been a good father, devoted and protective, I might collapse.

Who was he? A monster or a hero?

The temperature was falling, becoming almost pleasant. With my feet among the reeds, I perceived an indefinable, immense presence around me. The Lake, although apparently motionless, was boiling with a latent energy, swarming with everything that fed it, the brooks, streams, and rivers that, having wound through the dense forest, emptied into it.

Tibor ran toward us, agog.

"Barak fainted. His body is being shaken by spasms. He's sweating."

I leaped to my feet.

"That's impossible; all he has is a scratch."

Noura suggested a reasonable hypothesis: "He's suffering from having executed his brother. It's the emotion. Maybe he feels guilty? No one is more sensitive than Barak."

Tibor rubbed his bony chin, hesitating.

"No—I'm afraid it's . . ."

"What?"

"No, that would be too horrible . . ."

He withdrew into himself, his eyes riveted on the ground. He knew something, I could tell, that he didn't dare confide in us.

"Tibor, tell us!" I yelled. "We can take it."

He lifted his eyes and looked straight into mine.

"Where is Pannoam's sword?"

"I picked it up and took it to his house. I plan to bury it with him tomorrow. That way he will rest in a chief's tomb."

"I want to examine it first."

We went to the family home. Tibor walked past the body without looking at it, picked up the sword and, using rags, inspected it carefully, sniffed it, and then put a watery solution on its blade. He exclaimed, "It's just as I thought: he smeared poison on his blade!"

"What?"

"Pannoam knew he would lose. But he made sure his brother would, too, because he wouldn't survive him!"

I leaned against the wall for support, staggered by this news. Barak was dying? My father . . . toxic and destructive till the end?

I was receiving the answer to my question concerning his last words, "Noura . . . intact . . ."; that was the second poison, the poison he meant for me.

Noura and Tibor went to my house, where Mama, in a panic, was watching over Barak, who was delirious with fever.

Discouraged, my shoulders drooping and my feet heavy, I returned to the Lake and sat down on its shore.

Soon, I would be alone, without an older confidant, at the head of the village. I was witnessing the end of a world.

I didn't know how right I was . . .

Twilight came, soft and amber. Its honeyed light gave the horizon a copper color, while in the opposite direction the atmosphere was tinged with green, unveiling the first stars. Even the peeping of the birds did not disturb the serenity of the moment. A peace proceeding from the depths of the sky was descending on everything. From one moment to the next, the forest, by darkening, was bringing the shores closer.

I should have imprinted every image, every sound, every odor on my memory. This majestic Lake that we venerated, to which we prayed, and to which we made constant sacrifices, this Lake that seemed to us to be the God of gods, the supreme power, the beginning and end of our universe, would disappear. It would lap these shores under the sun's fire for only a few more days.

I was seeing it for the last time.

Very rapidly, like everything around it, it would be engulfed.

People, animals, and plants would perish in hellish suffering. Only a few individuals would come through it . . .

And not necessarily the best ones.

Thinking about Pannoam, about Barak, I believed it was the end of *a* world. I didn't know I was about to face the end of *the* world . . .

PART TWO
THE FLOOD

L et's have dinner together. I'll pay."
Noam recoils from the dashing, smiling forty-year-old
he's talking to.

Become friends? What's the point . . .

The fellow-feeling that germinates in him when he meets a human being always receives a wake-up call that brings him to his senses: "Don't get attached; you'll cause him to suffer, and that will make you suffer." Frankness is forbidden to Noam. He can't tell people who he is or talk about his memories, and still less reveal his particularity: either his interlocutor rejects his admissions and suspects him of being crazy or they believe him and, after a period of fascination, become jealous, rebellious, resentful. Invariably, the friendship disintegrates. And women? Noam sighs. If men are a field that he roams through, women are a forest where he gets lost. He has never understood women's reactions. Though perhaps he doesn't know how he reacts to women . . .

"The Triton seems like the best spot. Do you like fish?"

Watch out, there's a trap: if he responds to the culinary question with a yes, he's accepting the invitation and taking the first steps toward a relationship.

"Perfect!" he replies.

The best way to escape an embarrassing request is often to grant it. Is that a trick or cowardice? It doesn't matter.

The two chatterboxes leave the Mar Mikhaël bar where they have spent the twilight hours and climb into the sporty red convertible. They drive through Beirut. Hassan talks, turns the steering wheel, changes gears, waves to a friend as they pass, makes a U-turn, honks the horn, thanks him, and does all this with skill and dispatch, his frame relaxed, his gestures sweeping, displaying a supreme casualness. He emits the jovial charm, equal parts relaxation and macho self-confidence, peculiar to Middle Eastern men. His loquacity borders on pretension but does not fall into it.

They met in the café two weeks earlier. Since he started writing his story in the room he rents from the Widow Ghubril, Noam hasn't needed either solitude or formal habits to blacken paper. He writes everywhere. He leaves his room without leaving his book; he carries it in him, or rather he moves within it. Although at first he voluntarily sat down at the desk the way a fisherman goes to sea, now he no longer seeks his story; his story comes to find him. Hardly has he awakened before that day's page calls to him; he bends over the paper, and the lines come tumbling out, one after the other.

On that Monday, Hassan came and stood in front of him. His eyes on his notebook, Noam didn't initially see anything but the rather broad pelvis poured into dark-colored jeans, the top-quality leather belt, and the immaculate shirt made striking by an undershirt beneath it.

"Are you a writer?"

Noam lifted his eyes and saw Hassan's joyful, tanned, animated face.

"No."

"But you write all day long."

Noam blushed, as if he'd been caught engaging in an intimate activity. His concentration on the past has prevented him from remembering that he's still visible in the present.

"I'm not a writer. I'm . . ."

Seeing that Hassan was expecting an answer, Noam said, at random, "A historian."

"Awesome! What period?"

"The Neolithic."

Noam supposed that the dialogue would end there because he had noticed, through the millennia, that prehistory didn't much interest people, who, like nouveaux riches hiding away their impoverished relatives, fear any investigation into their origins.

"Fantastic!" Hassan cried, taking a seat. "I need an article on prehistory."

Since then, Hassan and Noam have met every day; after he gets off work, the Lebanese man spends an hour in the bar and devotes it to their discussions.

Hassan edits *Happy Few*, a trendy magazine with thick, glossy pages that offer both luxurious photos and bilingual texts written by the stars of the moment, the whole thing chock full of ads for the big international brands of cosmetics, watches, and clothes. Like his periodical, Hassan is interested in countless subjects. Agile, his conversation moves from politics to cinema, exploring fashion, decoration, sports, cooking, literature. Everything fascinates Hassan, but superficially—from his good quality flows his defect. Although he deploys an encyclopedic curiosity, going deeply into things bores him. Making superficiality a value, he considers it crude to confine oneself to monothematic conversation. Sticking to the topic revolts him; academic seriousness offends his taste for elegance; exhaustiveness puts him to sleep. This prancing talker gives Noam an accelerated account of the century he has landed in—he couldn't have asked for a more effective guide.

As they pass through wide streets crowded with cars and narrow streets crowded with pedestrians and hawkers, Hassan thanks Noam for his article on the Neolithic diet.

"A bombshell!"

That first day, to make his claim of being a historian more credible, Noam, subjected to an interrogation regarding the period on which he claims to be a specialist, resorted to his memory, not to learning acquired in a library, and confidently told Hassan about Neolithic habits and customs. The sole area where he came up short was quarrels among experts. Since the latter had no written evidence, only mute objects, the role played by interpretation proved to be boundless, opening a broad avenue for speculation, imagination, intellectual brilliance, and polemics. When Hassan asked him which camp he adhered to, Noam paled: although he knew his time, he didn't know the scholarship on it. Listening the Hassan, Noam learned that the history of prehistory is related to a history of the various prehistories constructed by historians.

That afternoon, Noam gave him four generously remunerated pages that were intended to shake up Lebanon's affluent youth by inciting them to reform their bad nutritional habits and return to the practices of the Neolithic.

"I propose a title: 'Our Future is in the Past: Eat Paleo!'," Hassan cries.

Writing this article captivated and disconcerted Noam: never had the Earth borne so many obese people! The fabulous rarity represented by Malatantra, the great lady of the Huntresses, that buxom female with gigantic curves before whom Uncle Barak had salivated, now constitutes an everyday phenomenon that no longer inspires either respect or seduction. If through her size, Malatantra reigned as Earth-Mother, Nature-Woman, Womb-Woman, her modern-day equivalents no longer have her status and are stigmatized, mocked. Plumpness, which used to be considered splendid and exceptional, has now become common and pathological. Of course, in his article, Noam didn't allow himself to comment on the magnificence of opulent women and abstained from pointing out that most eras have valued fleshy Venuses whose curves proved their personal blossoming and their economic success; he limited himself to stressing, in light of the past, today's innovations.

Does all change generate progress? Describing Neolithic life, in which people moved about only on foot, where they hunted or gathered, and where they made their own weapons and tools,

Noam realized that modern humans are a sedentary people who live inside, like a potted plant that never sees the open air or the sun: not only do we no longer move our limbs, but our bodies are transported by cars, trains, and airplanes. We eat very different kinds of fare: first we salted our food—Noam and his family didn't know that salt existed, and seasoned their food only with herbs, peppers, or spices. Then we sugared it—Noam used only honey, a precious substance that was difficult to obtain, given the height of the hives and the aggressiveness of the bees. Moderns use butter and oils, fats that were unknown to prehistoric peoples. Later on, people started eating grains—wheat, oats, rice—which appeared thanks to agriculture. Finally, modern people cook little or not at all, instead buying processed foods—bread, pasta, cookies, sausage meats, and prepared dishes. To that orgy of avatars, Noam's article opposed the Neolithic diet: fruit, nuts, wild vegetables, game, fish. People remained trim because the flesh of hares, deer, boars, and birds contains very little fat, unlike the meat provided by cattle and domestic swine. Although Pannoam, his father, had flocks of wild sheep—the ancestors of modern domestic sheep—and aurochs—the ancestors of modern cattle—his animals ate grass, not grains. Hypertension, diabetes, and even cancer didn't prosper in earlier times.

One detail causes Hassan to raise an eyebrow: "But unlike the American physicians who have promoted the Paleolithic diet, you reject the use of eggs and milk."

"I believe in fact that our ancestors seldom ate eggs, only in the spring, and only if they were taken from the nests, which they avoided doing out of deference to Nature. Not until hens were domesticated did eggs become part of the human diet."

"Starting when?"

"It's difficult to say exactly," Noam says pompously, masking his ignorance. "As for milk, butter, and cheese, they require complete sedentarization. Moreover, it took our ancestors a long time to be able to digest them."

"So how do you explain the fact that even though they were in such good health, they died before the age of forty?"

The blunt question saddens Noam, who immediately sees the beloved faces of the dead pass before his mind's eye, Mina and Pannoam in the lead.

"It was a healthy period, but it was violent. People didn't have time to reach an advanced age. Conflicts were resolved by duels. People hunted and fought wars. Cold weather and storms killed them. Dangerous animals were rampant. People ran, fell, cut themselves, broke bones, got injured. There were no remedies for infections. Few illnesses were treated, and no one knew the importance of hygiene. Giving birth and being born led to more deaths than births. In that young, strong world, there was room only for youth and strength, none for old age . . ."

"It's funny," Hassan says with astonishment, "you talk about it like someone who experienced it . . ."

Noam bursts out laughing—better for Hassan to think he's amusing, not perceptive.

The car stops in front of a tall house encrusted with balustrades differing in style and depth, depending on the story. Leaping from the porch, a young man rushes to the car door. Without saying a word or even looking at him, Hassan gets out, lets his keys fall into the valet's palm, and walks toward the entrance. A normal person would worry about entrusting such an expensive car to a stranger and would at least say a few words to him to create a contact, to be sure of his job, to establish loyalty, but Hassan wants to show that he's the opposite of a coward: the chic bourgeois who makes it clear that he disdains the inferior he hands his property to.

They enter a vast room hung with orientalizing embroideries with large motifs, traditional in their refinement, modern in their simplicity. Young ladies in gold lamé dash about between the tables, as silent as they are graceful. The rest is all silk ottomans, crushed-velvet benches, inlaid chairs, Venetian chandeliers, glasses in cut crystal, and dishes rimmed in gold. In the distance, a harpist who looks like a harpist—blond, diaphanous—is playing her instrument near the lamplit terrace, decorated with varnished urns. The guests examine the newcomers. Noam feels embarrassed to be dressed so simply, unaware that his radiance, his svelte frame, and the clear-cut beauty of his features constitute a passport much more powerful than a trendy suit.

Sitting down, Hassan, who makes it a point of honor to always be doing two things at once, consults his telephone.

"No, no, no . . . my cousin is joining us!"

"What? Don't you like him?"

"Yes, yes, I do! I've been around him since I was baptized. We were more or less brought up together in my grandmother's home. It's just that . . ."

"Yes?"

"He's a survivalist."

"Excuse me?"

"A survivalist."

"Sorry, that didn't exist in the Neolithic."

Hassan guffaws on seeing Noam's discomfited expression.

"Hey look, here he is!"

A beanpole appears at the entrance, spots Hassan, and walks in his direction. The tall, thin body, weary of its height, comes toward them bent over, its neck dragged down under the weight of the skull. The hunched back and hollowed chest, the belly consumed by the pelvis, the bent legs, this skeleton powerless to fully occupy its own volume walks slowly, as if the air presented as much resistance as water; at each step, his spindly thighs seem to be lifting leaden shoes. Blandness obscures the appearance of this man, who lacks color as much as he lacks depth: his clothes, his skin, his hair, his eyebrows, his beard all have a dull tone, a sort of anemic beige; his lips, almost bloodless, remain eggshell in color.

"Is he ill?" Noam whispers to Hassan as the emaciated man crosses the room.

"No, James carries the weight of the world on his shoulders. It's heavy!"

James reaches their table, greets them half-heartedly, and collapses on a chair. Worldly, voluble, peremptory, Hassan takes the situation in hand, orders drinks and dishes with a wave of his index finger, which, like a magnet, controls the movements of the waitresses.

Hassan is delivering a soliloquy. No dialogue is established between Noam and James. The former observes the latter, who is wallowing in a doleful indifference. Why did he come? Noam wonders. If you're bored everywhere, why bother to move?

Suddenly, a detail changes the atmosphere: Hassan has just praised Noam's erudition regarding prehistory. James's face lights up; he looks with attention at the guest he has been snubbing.

"Are you well-acquainted with prehistoric technologies?"

"Yes, I think so."

Eager to emphasize Noam's importance, Hassan summarizes the article that his friend has just given him on the Paleolithic diet. James listens carefully, won over, while at the same time scrutinizing Noam. Gradually, he becomes animated; from blasé, unruffled, phlegmatic, he becomes energetic and passionate. As soon as his cousin finishes his summary, he exclaims, "I'm very interested in our ancestors' science. They knew how to survive."

Noam smiles and corrects him, "You mean they knew how to live."

"Very true!" James replies. "It's we who are in error. They have so much to teach us."

Courteously, Noam hides the fact that he thinks the contrary. He, who has traversed millennia, witnessing technological, biological, and medical progress, does not idealize the ancients' teaching and harbors no nostalgia.

James leans toward him, his long torso covering almost half the table.

"You could be useful to us."

"How?"

"By preparing us."

"For what?"

James lets his body fall back on the chair and wearily reproaches his cousin. "You didn't tell him?"

"Didn't have the opportunity . . ." Hassan grumbles.

James looks Noam in the eye and says to him in a stronger voice, "I belong to the Doomsday Clock."

Noam nods, his lips pursed, his forehead pensive, weighing the importance of this revelation. The Doomsday Clock . . . He calls up vague memories, going back to the 1950s, a period when scientists had proposed a conceptual clock to warn of the risks humanity was taking. Symbolically, midnight marked the end of the world, and, every year, they determined whether the needle was approaching the fateful moment. This countdown alerted people to the extent of the danger. At the time, the sudden appearance of nuclear weapons and the Cold War between Russia and the United States particularly frightened people, so greatly did they fear the final conflict.

"Is it still at Chicago?" Noam asks, remembering the *Bulletin of the Atomic Scientists*.

"Yes!" Hassan says, approvingly, without noticing that Noam is working with information relating to the preceding century, not the present one. "James has joined the group that estimates the risks. He works with the best scientists and . . . how many Nobel Prize winners again? Fifteen?"

"Eighteen."

"Congratulations," Noam murmurs.

James leans toward him again, "We are one minute and twenty seconds from the end of the world."

A dense silence follows. The waitresses brings the mezze, a

profusion of small dishes containing tabbouleh, broad beans, fattoush, hummus, baba ghanoush, stuffed grape leaves, and spiced potato salad for the diners to nibble on. When the waitresses leave, James adds, "We've never been so close . . . The disaster will occur in eighty seconds."

James enumerates the reasons for concern. If, in every period, people feared physical phenomena—collision with a giant meteorite, volcanic eruptions, the propagation of a lethal virus—we currently fear damage done by humans. Not only would the use of atomic weapons unleash a cataclysm in the form of a third World War, but criminal or accidental manipulations could also lead not only to a devastating pandemic but also to a massive computer crash and, through a domino effect, the failure of banking structures and security systems. Ineluctable and uncontrollable, overpopulation will bring with it famine, and climate change will provoke collapse.

"Humanity is doomed to be destroyed, without a doubt. We're living through an unprecedented moment, a major turning point in history. We will soon enter post-history. At least some of us will, those who anticipate it and prepare . . . The rest will die."

"Are you referring to the survivalists?" Noam interjects.

James, scarlet-faced, loses his composure. "Along with a few friends, I'm constructing a refuge. We're stocking it with goods. But that's just a short-term plan. It would be better if we relearned how to behave like hunter-gatherers, like our forefathers, to face life after the apocalypse."

Hassan shoots Noam a glance sparkling with mockery: his cousin is straddling the boundaries of extravagance to such an extent that he has decided to laugh about it rather than weep over it.

Consequently, Hassan is transfixed by surprise when Noam declares, "Can I join you? In return, I'll give you prehistoric knowledge about fire, tracking game, fishing, weaving, pottery, and the hunter-gatherers' diet."

James extends his hand to Noam.
"Put her there, comrade!"

*

An air-conditioned limousine driven by a young Syrian chauffeur is taking Noam to the summit of Mt. Lebanon. It took an
hour to get out of Beirut with its burnt-carbon breath, its noise,
its traffic jams, and its baking-hot asphalt. Freed, the car is flying
down the road.

Noam contemplates the landscape and remembers. He knew this
land when it was virgin, in its natural nudity, with inexhaustible wa-
terfalls and a flora and fauna that belonged to life in the wild. Then
he saw the immense forests of conifers, Lebanon's wealth, become
sparser, cut up into wood for making furniture. Now, everywhere
he looks, he sees the traces left by humans who have converted a
mountain of sterile minerals into a fertile plain. Over the centuries,
the Lebanese collected scattered rocks and pebbles to build retaining walls that created terraces where the humus recuperated from
riverbeds became flat and arable. These stone walls still cover the
slopes, tiered from the coast to the eternal snow, although today the
grape vines and the mulberry trees planted for silkworms are rarer,
having been replaced by orchards and olive groves. The cramped
embankments made of dry stones, built without mortar, have been
supplanted by vast sloping ledges plowed by bulldozers and constructed with concrete that can bear the comings and goings of
heavy machinery or serve as sites for market garden greenhouses.
Among the age-old villages, secondary residences are multiplying,
bordering here and there on the quarries from which the construction materials were taken. Agriculture and urban sprawl have
tamed Nature, which, enslaved, rationalized, reified, is reduced to
items subject to the ups and downs of the market.

The chauffeur stops to get fuel. Noam gets out of the car, wanting to stretch his legs. The heat wave immediately takes him in its

grip, like a strangling hand, and forces him to breathe carefully. Despite his sunglasses, he blinks his eyes before this white sky devoured by the sun. A few meters from the pumps, a chain-link fence delimits an area where individuals are working, stressed, shouting orders to each other from a distance.

Noam approaches the workers and sees below them concrete basins bristling with pipes that plunge into them and poke out of them. He recognizes a fresh-water fish farm fed by the nearby river, whose flow has been diverted. The tranquility peculiar to this kind of place does not reign here. Using large nets, employees are removing the trout from the reservoirs and piling them on the ground. They do not flop around. Noam notices that they are lying motionless, belly-up, already dead, on the surface of the water. Looking at the brook, he quickly understands what has happened: the flow, very weak, is failing to renew the content of the fish tanks every day, and the temperature of the water is higher than the trout can stand: in water over twenty degrees Celsius, they die from lack of oxygen.

What are they going to do with these millions of cadavers? Ground up, reduced to powder, they will probably be used as feed for trout ... Noam feels a vague disgust, sighs, and gets back in the car.

A scene comes back to him. During a sumptuous summer, Barak and he were fishing along a river whose flow was brisk, fresh, abundant. Away from the main current, in a dormant part of the river where the water was idle and midges flew about, Barak suddenly appeared, lifting over his head an enormous pike with a pale belly and a yellowish back that was struggling with all its strength. Barak finished it off by swinging it against a stone. Once he'd laid it on the ground, he affectionately contemplated the fish with its pointed snout and red gills.

"Do you realize, Noam? He's old, strong, a victor: he defeated all the ambushes, all the enemies, all the fishermen. I'm the only one who's beat him. Look at his teeth! His adversaries couldn't dislodge a single one! We have to show ourselves worthy of him."

"What do you mean?"

"We have to prepare him in a way that's on par with his value, find the best herbs, accompany him with subtle vegetables, savor every mouthful. He deserves no less."

Barak had a real veneration for the fish he'd just killed, and in homage to his prey, he sought, on that evening and the following ones, to attain gastronomic excellence.

The motor starts up again.

That's what has been lost, Noam thinks. When James the survivalist longs for a Neolithic skill set that's disappeared, he's on the wrong track: it's wisdom that's been lost, the wisdom that placed humans in Nature as one of its elements. Barak thought he was stronger than the animal he'd defeated, not superior, and still less that he differed from it in essence. He respected the animal he was hunting. He considered himself its brother; not only would he never have locked up wild animals in the prison of a breeding farm, but he would've also refused to eat prisoners: rabbits raised in batteries, chickens that don't run, salmon that haven't encountered algae, all those distorted animals. "Master and possessor of Nature?" Barak would have laughed at modern humans' presumption of this Cartesian notion, that they'd been plucked out of Nature to dominate, constrain, and exploit it.

The driver tries to start a conversation. His efforts are sabotaged by Noam's curt replies.

Noam has kept quiet for two days. Holed up in his room, avoiding Hassan, he has waited for the car that James had promised him. He's thinking too much; his ideas are tripping over each other. How many ends of the world has he already escaped? Is extinction really coming, or do contemporary humans just enjoy scaring themselves?

The end of the world is an endless story. Usually, Noam refuses to listen to predictions of catastrophes, maintaining a deafness with roots in experience: over the past two millennia, he has often heard that annihilation was imminent. Monotheistic religions, basing themselves on the Book of Revelation, the last book of the New Testament, have regularly sown panic among whole populations. Catholicism, the first of these, did so wholeheartedly. According to the bishop Martin of Tours, the Antichrist was a radical impostor who would pulverize the planet around 400 A.D. Beatus of Liébana warned that a second coming of Christ and the final moments of time would occur on April 6, 793—what precision! The year 1000 triggered fears, first of all those of Pope Sylvester II, which echoed through Christendom. In the Middle Ages, Joachim of Fiore, an expert on plagues, predicted that the world would be obliterated in the thirteenth century, and then, because it didn't happen—there's nothing less obedient than calamities!—his disciples postponed it several times. British astrologers also got involved, causing the evacuation of London—which had twenty thousand inhabitants—on February 1, 1524, because a rise of the Thames was supposed to begin the Flood; when the latter failed to appear, they postponed it to the following century. The Protestants succeeded them so well that terrorizing predictions shook the sixteenth and seventeenth centuries, from Thomas Munzer to Martin Luther by way of Michael Stifel, Jan Matthijs, and Michel Servet. The epidemic spread to England, crossed the Atlantic, and prospered in the United States. Noam forgot neither the contribution made by Muslims through Sabbatai Zevi, nor, in the twentieth century, by the Jehovah's Witnesses, who constantly programmed and reprogrammed Armageddon.

One feature has transformed this worn-out skepticism that prophesied violence: it is no longer the All-Powerful that is punishing humans; it is humans who are exterminating Nature. From now on, God is excluded from the Apocalypse. Humans are enough. They can manage all by themselves.

Through its genius, humanity has dramatically weakened its destiny: the proliferation of nuclear weapons, the reign of machines that will one day do away with their creators, the exhaustion of sources of energy, the pollution that's altering the climate—all these dangers are growing. The ingredients for disaster are piling up. As Noam sees it, the terror James the survivalist feels is more rational than that of the religious, the devout, and the sectarians he has encountered over the centuries.

The limousine pulls up in front of a gray metal gate that is the same height as the walls and conceals the property. After a meticulous examination of their papers, a guard pats down the two men, searches the trunk, runs an explosive detector underneath the chassis, communicates by telephone with the interior, and finally opens the gate and authorizes them to enter.

Inside the gate, there is no paved road, only a gravel path that the vehicle follows carefully. As they crush the gravel, the tires sound like popcorn exploding in a pan. The automobile passes through a pine forest obstructed by brush that becomes less dense and surrounds a long rhomboidal building, as vast as it is low, extending its fifty meters on a single level. The roof is covered with solar panels.

James meets his guests on the steps of the mansion.

"Welcome to the Ark."

He congratulates Noam on having all his affairs in a shoulder bag and congratulates him again when he asks him to deposit his phone at the caretaker's lodge—the use of telephones is forbidden at the refuge—and discovers that Noam doesn't have one. The extreme simplicity of the prehistorian's way of life fascinates James, the scion of a rich family and a collector of electronic gadgets.

They begin with a tour of the refuge. On the ground floor, the rooms look like those in an ordinary vacation retreat, alternating common areas with spartan bedchambers. The basement, however, indicates the concern with survival. Having passed through the steel double doors, they walk among fabulous stocks of provisions. Canned goods, boxes of pasta, sacks of rice, and bottles of water fill the shelves above freezers in which meat, fish, and vegetables are piled up, and these freezers are connected to a generator in case of a power outage—something that happens often in Lebanon, where every citizen compensates for the short-comings of public services by subscribing to a private energy pro-vider. Large numbers of wool and mylar blankets are stored in one room, as well as first aid supplies and masks, ranging from simple cloth shields that prevent people nearby from being con-taminated to massive respiratory models with filters and goggles that protect against gas. One dressing room holds shoes, a second various outfits that protect against flooding, fire, and radiation.

"We have six months of autarky," James announces.

"Bravo."

"Six months isn't much. That's why you're joining us. How do we make a fire? What fruit, herbs, and mushrooms should we gather? How can we trap game? All those ancestral skills . . ."

"You can rely on me. By the way, do you have weapons?"

"No. Teach us to hunt and fight without weapons, or else how to make them in Nature."

After the provisions of sugar and salt, the tour continues, un-veiling heaps of bars of soap, toothpaste, brushes, detergents, disinfectants. This labyrinth ends in front of a security door that James avoids by turning around and returning the way they came.

"What's in there?" Noam asks, pointing to the thick slab of metal.

"Nothing, just the furnace . . ." James says, suggesting they go back upstairs.

*

That weekend, the Ark opens to members of the survivalist group and a few interested outsiders. About twenty trainees have an unprecedented experience: spending three days in the forest without resorting to the benefits of modernity.

Marmoud, a military veteran with highly defined muscles, is leading the expedition, seconded by Charlie, a former policeman of average height, lean, without any notable characteristics other than a taste for dark tobacco cigarettes. Along with Claude, a zoologist, Noam acts as an advisor.

The participants vary in age and profile: thirty-year-old bankers and engineers; militant environmentalist retirees; and middle-aged couples working as schoolteachers.

Marmoud establishes rules: they have to find their food in the woods, sleep there, build shelters to protect themselves from bad weather, and find their way around without being guided by GPS or compasses. Accidents are simulated through role-playing: an injured walker, an attack by robbers.

Little by little, Noam becomes aware of the extent to which anxiety structures the program. All shoulders, biceps, and triceps, Marmoud and Charlie teach the recruits how to fight hand to hand with sticks, how to camouflage themselves under branches, how to erase their tracks to prevent dogs from following their scent, and finally how to carry out commando operations that are at first dissuasive, then aggressive.

Three of them who understood these activities as a kind of athletic recreation are getting worried about them. Scratching the nape of his neck, Marmoud defends himself, "If something serious happens, some people will be organized; others won't. Starving, capable of anything, they'll roam the country, alone or in groups, and will become looters. Neither policemen nor soldiers will stop them. As we see it, surviving comes down to confronting anarchy, chaos, violence. That's what we also have to prepare for. Lucidly. Efficiently."

Within the team, a few people grind their teeth. Claude the zoologist's classes on how to capture, clean, and cook insects calms the trainees, and then, after feasting on grilled grasshoppers, Noam has clear success teaching them how to kindle a fire, select plants, and make Neolithic glue, birch pitch—heat the bark, then chew on it to keep it soft during the cooling that hardens it. Those suffering from toothaches now experience relief, just as their ancestors did.

As the hours pass by, the group becomes fragmented, loses its cohesion. Various motives have led these individuals to undertake survival training. The young city-dwellers are trying to regain contact with the trees, the land, the rivers, and want to forget the urban concrete. The wealthiest of them are hoping to cure themselves of that contemporary disease, consumerism; this training allows them to distinguish the essential from the superfluous, and thus to free themselves from objects. Some want to gain a little autonomy; in this fragmented society where everyone depends on work done by others, becoming capable again of building a cabin without help, of making a fire, a bow, or a spear is liberating. A few seek to spice up their everyday life, which is why Marie, a retired woman with environmentalist convictions, admits that when she goes home after these three days, she will appreciate basic services like running water, a gas stove that produces flame on demand, and a refrigerator that works. "I'm going to live in the apartment of miracles!" In reality, most of the participants do grow wiser thanks to survivalism, but few of them adopt it as a goal.

Noam identifies the inner core: Marmoud, Charlie, James, and Hugo, a twenty-year-old computer engineer. They're actively preparing for the world of tomorrow, the post-catastrophe period with its political, economic, social, and financial consequences, when structures—the government, police, army, internet, energy resources—will have collapsed. Far from engaging in a Boy Scout adventure, they are practicing with the conviction that the fateful moment is approaching.

The last afternoon, as soon as the group returns to the Ark, dissension arises between the radical survivalists and Marie. Explaining drily that the only real adversaries she encountered were squadrons of midges, snipers in the shape of horseflies, and ticks waiting in ambush, she indignantly objects to the military turn taken by the training.

"I don't understand your obsession with fighting . . . If something bad happens, I'm not going to become other people's enemy; on the contrary, I'm going to help them."

"You can't help everybody!" Marmoud retorts, slapping a mosquito on his temple.

"We have to try."

"You're dreaming! Just a naïve optimist! It's better to save twenty people than to let everyone die! Without the government, the police, the army, we'll be plunged into a war of each against all."

"You don't believe in human solidarity?"

"No!"

"Only the strong survive," Charlie adds.

"I don't agree with your ideas at all," Marie says. "To be an environmentalist, you have to want to save people, animals, the planet."

"I'm not an environmentalist," Marmoud replies heatedly. "I'm a survivalist!"

"We're fighting for our survival," Charlie stresses.

"When Noah built his ark to escape the Flood," Marie reminds them, "he wanted to protect all living beings."

"Oh, yeah?" Charlie replies cheekily. "And yet he didn't take anyone with him except his family. We're taking care of our family, too—other survivalists—even if our bond isn't based on blood."

"So everyone else becomes your enemies?" Marie exclaims.

"There are the elect, who prepare themselves, and the lost, who don't give a damn. I won't let the elect be plundered by the lost. The lost will lose. The elect will win."

Marie remains silent; Charlie focuses on lighting a cigarette; and Marmoud scratches his neck, where his nails leave reddening furrows. James diplomatically changes the subject, helped along by Claude, the insectivore.

They say goodbye, kiss each other's cheeks in parting, wave, and set out for home.

When the property has emptied out, Noam notices that James has absent-mindedly left his fatigues jacket on a tree stump and picks it up to return it to him at the villa; on the way, he feels a pocket that contains a heavy set of keys, the ones that open the cellars. He takes them and then, his crime perpetrated, hangs the safari jacket on the coat rack in the caretaker's lodge.

That evening, only the leaders stay at the Ark: Marmoud, Charlie, James, and Hugo, whose snack Noam shares. After three days of exercise, open air, and short naps under the stars, exhaustion no doubt excuses the limpness of the conversation around the table. Except for James, the men express themselves briefly, hasten the end of the meal, and never look at Noam.

He feels that he bothers them.

He has aroused their suspicion from the outset, despite the enthusiasm shown by James. His nationality annoys them: Noam introduced himself as a Greek. Pretending to be Lebanese would have been inept because the moment he mentioned a family name, he would immediately have been interrogated about his cousins here, his aunts there, his great-uncle in the mountains— that's the extent to which it seems that Lebanon, despite its millions of inhabitants, is still just an aggregation of families that all remain in contact with each other. Choosing a Greek identity affords Noam a certain safety: in addition to the fact that Greece is generally liked, he speaks Greek perfectly, though he is careful not to sprinkle his sentences with archaisms from the period in which he learned the language, the century of Sophocles and Plato, who spoke a pure Attic, greatly modified today. Now that he knows Marmoud, Charlie, and Hugo better, he notices that they systematically mistrust foreigners, immigrants, and migrants.

Noam leaves them early, on the pretext that he is tired. Taking refuge in his room, he waits.

At 11 P.M., the household falls asleep. Noam listens to James snoring on the other side of the wall.

Cautiously, silently, he goes down to the basement and, using the stolen keys, slips into the storerooms. Careful, he closes the doors behind him and does not turn on the ceiling lamps, using a flashlight instead. Having crossed the food storerooms, he reaches the metal security door in front of which James had asked him to turn back.

He turns the key.

He comes upon what he expected: an arsenal. Three tables display a myriad of bladed weapons, some that cut, others that perforate or are blunt. On the first table, machetes, scythes, scimitars, daggers, swords, sabers, axes; on the second, spears, lances, fishing spears, pikes, hooks, tridents, halberds, bows, crossbows, and blowguns with their supply of arrows, bolts, and darts; on the third, truncheons, clubs, sledges, hammers, whips, scourges, and sacks of steel balls. Against the walls, firearms proliferate, carbines, hunting rifles, assault rifles, submachine guns, sniper rifles. Farther on, there are shelves filled with handguns, pistols, and revolvers. Machine guns are lined up on the floor, and boxes of ammunition fill the adjacent recess. Noam's intuition is confirmed: the Ark is not a shelter but a bunker.

Noam enters another magazine, that of explosives, where he is looking at grenades and mines when he hears an altercation and footsteps.

Hurriedly, he switches off his flashlight and slips into a corner. Marmoud, Charlie, and Hugo enter, wearing tank tops and combat pants. They sit down around a small, empty desk, and put a computer on it. Hugo seems like an agglutination of two incompatible parts, a child's blond head screwed onto the body of a stocky athlete.

Hidden in the shadows of the arsenal, Noam holds his breath.

"At precisely 23:30, we will receive the communication with D.R.," says Hugo, as he connects the computer.

The others sigh.

"It's a pain in the ass not to be able to smoke," Charlie grumbles.

"You idiot! You should have stopped smoking a long time ago. You'll be able to survive a blackout, but not lung cancer."

"Don't piss me off!"

"I'm right."

"You're pissing me off *because* you're right!"

Satisfied, Marmoud condescends to keep quiet, belches, spits, and starts scratching himself in the depths of his pants. Noam notices that they behave differently in the absence of James; they're more relaxed, more vulgar.

Hugo stops fiddling with the computer and sits down, delighted.

"D.R. online!"

These initials emit such an aura that the three shady characters sit up straight, suddenly correct.

An image comes up on the screen that Noam can't see, and then a voice bursts forth, deformed by a filter: "Hello, Beirut. Where are you with your preparations?"

"Six months of autonomy, D.R.," Charlie replies.

"And regarding survival techniques?"

"Almost done."

"Excuse me?"

Marmoud butts in, plants himself in front of the camera, and proclaims, shooting Charlie a lethal glance: "It's done, D.R.!"

The silence grows longer. They worry. The voice finally continues, monotone, computerized, "We're going to launch Operation Horsemen of the Apocalypse."

They tremble.

"When?"

"Immediately."

"Where?"

"We'll begin in the United States. The Zachariah cell has

completed its preparation. It will be divided up and attack five nuclear power plants."

"Which ones?"

"You already know too much. Europe will carry on, followed by Russia and China. And you, what about the Chabrouh Dam?"

"The plan is perfect, and the equipment's in place. We're waiting for your order to send out the commando and set off the explosion."

"It's a matter of weeks. Be ready."

A whistle marks the end of the communication.

Ecstatic, the three warriors shout with joy, dance, exult, clap their hands.

"The big day's at hand, boys!"

"There'll be explosions everywhere."

"A new era will be able to start!"

"Hugo, go get us some beer!"

Noam understands that these men are acting without the knowledge of James, who is naïvely bankrolling them, and—more importantly—that their ambition goes far beyond survivalism. These militants aren't preparing for the end of the world; they're preparing to end it themselves.

I' d been contemplating it since dawn . . .

The Lake is an idea that dreams. No path, no details. Nothing persists; everything evaporates. As vast as it was immobile, it betrayed its breathing through impalpable iridescence, a gentle lapping of water. Delicate rippling motions came and went across its surface without any pattern; logic was diluted in its silent depths. Oscillating, undulating, palpitating, the Lake drowsed endlessly. Furtive, mute creatures were active in its dormant waters; sometimes their backs or their fins could be seen. What were they doing? Why didn't they ever come out in the daylight? They intertwined, grazed each other, wound around, murmured. Both alien and familiar, the Lake kept its secrets, and, though open to the world, it contained more that was unknown than known.

Looking out at this pensive setting, I was meditating.

How could danger suddenly emerge from such a nurturing place?

The Peoples of the Lake didn't fear the Lake. We venerated its peaceful surface. To be sure, it swallowed up the unskilled swimmer; the reckless canoeist; the impatient person who leapt in on a too-hot day; and the hunter walking on its ice, careless of the cracking sounds, but inevitably, humans were to blame. Its waters didn't attack us. If they rose, they did so little by little. No aggressiveness. No deception. A majestic slowness . . .

Other waters scared me: the waters from the sky, whose relentless, excessive buffeting we endured; the running waters, those of the nymphs that, at this time, were gushing in torrents, widening brooks, leaping out of their beds, driven by an incomprehensible wrath. The Lake, in contrast, and despite its rise, displayed only its eternal calm.

Tibor sat down at my side.

"Barak is recovering."

I was overjoyed.

"Have you put together an antidote?"

"No, Barak found it himself. His health dazzles me. He's recovered from his amputation, and now he's eliminating a mortal poison."

"That's Barak for you!" I exclaimed happily.

"That's Elena!" he replied. "She isn't just helping him live; she's also providing him with a reason to live."

"True . . . " I said, gravely.

Elena's and Barak's felicity left me feeling conflicted. Whereas I was terribly fond of both of them and wished them happiness, the sexual tension that enflamed them disconcerted me. Seeing Mama no longer as a mother but as a woman upset my whole way of situating myself in the world. Her curves, which were formerly so reassuring, harmless, and domestic, acquired an erotic aura; the heaviness that I'd imagined due to her age took on a lascivious consistency. Having sloughed off her layer of respectability, Mama was radiant, a provocative goddess of love, igniting desire in Barak's eyes and, by reflection, in her own. As a couple, they reeked of sensuality; their flesh vibrated with a perpetual appetite to join themselves together. In their presence, I had the impression that I was hampering, curbing their drives, limiting them to looks, caresses, furtive kisses, sensing that as soon as they were alone, they would pounce on each other. Barak's handicap, his convalescence, nothing reduced the sensuality that bound them together, and I had often, in the course of the night, heard hoarse cries, both enthusiastic and pleasure-filled, hers as loud as his. From my noble mother emerged a heretofore unsuspected figure, that of an unbridled lover, free, imperious, and uninhibited.

"Your mother is younger than you are, Noam."

Tibor tossed that remark my way as if he'd heard my thoughts. He went on. "She dares to do what you don't."

"I don't understand," I stammered, trying to check the conversation.

"Your mother has the courage of her feelings. You don't."

I turned toward him. He urged me on, "Ask me."

"For what?" I sighed.

"My daughter's hand."

I closed my eyes, overwhelmed. Since Pannoam's death, I had thought up one reason after another for putting off my marriage to her. Organizing the burial, caring for my uncle, consoling my mother, ensuring that justice was done, governing the life of the village—it had all justified my not marrying Noura.

"Watch out, Noam, she's going to get worried."

"She's supported me in my work so far, without a single reproving word or look."

"She's proving to you what an excellent chief's wife she is. But she has to become *your* wife."

I hung my head and confessed, "It's not so easy when you're used to having some self-respect . . . For a long time, I was forced to treat her as my stepmother."

"Man up."

I tried to sidestep the issue. "I . . . I'm a little scared."

"Of what?"

"Of her."

"Wrong! You're afraid of yourself. Afraid of not seeming up to the task, of not doing as well as you'd like."

"Rightly, no?"

"That fear merely gives rise to further fears. Replace it with confidence. Trust your love, your desire. You need each another, you and Noura."

"You make a funny father-in-law, Tibor."

"First of all, I make a funny father."

He smiled, he who was usually so gruff.

"And actually, I've inherited a funny daughter!"

He seized my hand and pressed it between his dry, angular fingers. "Don't make Noura impatient; she's not good at waiting, and she'll resent you for it. If you wait too long, you'll be dealing with an angry woman."

"You know her well . . ."

"No one knows Noura!"

Tibor, suddenly voluble, told me about his helplessness. How could he, a single father, successfully bring up a young woman? This challenge had been beyond him. As a widower, Tibor had not been able to rely on his wife or his own sisters, who had died in the mudslide. He had contemplated Noura, that mysterious creature, simultaneously obstinate and expressive, affectionate and closed-off; he had no idea toward which realms her dreams took flight. What did she hope for in life? What designs was she forming? She'd constantly escaped him; as a child, she was cold, she was hot, but above all she was never lukewarm. One day tender, another hard as nails, saying little, saying too much, bursting into laughter whenever she pleased, finding ordinary jokes humorless but guffawing at trifles that she alone had noticed. Fond of dramas, enigmas, and shot through with infatuations, called to undertake tasks that she kept secret, passing from fragility to arrogance, from naivety to cynicism, she rejected any command, any influence. Tibor trembled before this woman who feared nothing and no one. She recognized only one guide: herself; one model: herself; one logic: herself. He had seen from the start that she set out on opposing paths with the same self-confidence. At times, she withheld her thoughts, though not as a result of weakness, timorousness, or politeness: she found self-effacement fitting and the strategy opportune. At other times, she was frank, rude, and cutting, scornful of any decorum, simply because her words came to her like that. Was Noura uncompromising or cunning? Was she sincere or calculating? Both . . . Her nature in the morning was nothing like her nature in the evening. She went to bed one person and woke up a different one.

"There's not one Noura; there's an infinity of them. An innocent. A torturer. A cheerful girl. An unsatisfied one. A frail being. A brute. Supreme refinement. Savagery. When I got married, I wanted to raise several daughters. The gods granted my wish: they gave me a hundred and one. But I didn't raise her; she grew up alongside me."

"You're exaggerating: she listens to you as a father."

"She endows me with the status of father when she wants a father; at other times, she converts me into a brother, a son, a companion, a resigned ghost. My role can often be summed up as that of a favorite servant."

While I laughed at his unexpected eloquence, he persisted: "Tell her how you feel! Seduce her . . . Noura might be unpredictable, but one thing is still certain: with her, you can always fear the worst."

"Thanks, Tibor. I promise you I'll act. And I promise that to myself, too . . . Now let's talk about your prophetic dreams."

Tibor paled.

"I received another vision last night. Terrifying! Nothing remained of our world."

"What do you advise me to do? Build our homes in the trees?"

"The trees won't be spared. Everything will be underwater."

"What, then?"

He rubbed his temples.

"Water can only be avoided by water."

"What are you suggesting? That we build floating houses?"

Thrown off balance, he stared at me as he thought. "What an excellent idea! I think you've found the solution."

He stood up and extended his arm toward the horizon. "Ten days on foot from here lives a clan that makes canoes. The best.

People have told me about them. Their village is called the Gap of the Gods."

"The Gap of the Gods?"

"It seems that the gods regularly pass through their village. I didn't learn any more about it . . . But in any case, they're marvelous woodworkers, and they've perfected techniques for chiseling, shaping, and connecting the parts, then making them water-tight to make a boat, to increase its surface area. Go see them."

He interrupted himself, concerned. "I'm sorry, Noam! I'm issuing orders. Excuse me. You're the chief, not me."

"You're the chief's adviser, Tibor. I admire you. No one has contributed more to our community."*

I said goodbye to Tibor and went up to the market, which was full of people. At this point early in my reign, I paraded about a good deal. My presence lent credit to my seizure of power, the villagers confided their cares to me, and visitors returned home talking about the young chief.

---

* Readers may be surprised that I should rely on the advice of a healer in defining village policies. To understand this, you have to remember that rain and the pure azure of the sky came from the gods; the weather brought the gods' word directly. For thousands of years, people thought like that, no matter whether they practiced animism, polytheism, or monotheism. Meteorology belonged not to physics, but to theology. Rain showers, sunshine, winds, thunder, lightning, and hurricanes were parts of the divine theater. The sky provided a stage on which God, the gods, or the spirits resolved their disputes with humans, punishing here, rewarding there. It would never have occurred to me, for example, that the storms that brewed on the Lake came from somewhere else: in my closed world, limits didn't exist, I had no notion of the World or the universe. Neither would I have ever suspected that condensation and pressure caused the presence of clouds, their density, or their bursting. Only in the fourth century B.C., Aristotle's time, did people begin to give natural rather than supernatural explanations of meteorological events. In his *Meteorology*, Aristotle accounted for atmospheric phenomena by reference to the sun and the exhalations it produced. However, Aristotle's triumph was not total, and until the eighteenth century people combined scientific observation with the fear of God, who was the ultimate master, or even the Devil, who persecuted human beings. Storms, typhoons, heat waves, and droughts continued to be dramatized, full of meaning.

For me, the warnings given by Tibor, the one among us who best saw and understood the gods, nymphs, and spirits, were therefore indisputably legitimate. That's why I acted in accord with his advice.

After making a few trades, Noura joined me, staying close to my side during my conversations with major suppliers, the way a wife accompanies her husband. Her behavior was nearly perfect.

Sometimes, however, a fleeting smile appeared on her bored lips; the series of interlocutors, interrupting our time together periodically caused her to frown. Like her, I was increasingly annoyed. Something was being eroded in us. Although we enjoyed a friendly complicity, at this rate frustration would end up irritating us and putting us in conflict.

Between one tedious interlocutor and the next, I whispered in her ear, "Can I visit you this evening?"

She shivered and nimbly turned toward me. "Of course."

Once the pain in the neck had bored us to death, she added, "Papa won't be there. He has to collect herbs that can only be gathered by moonlight."

I was delighted by her lie; it confirmed for me to what point she cared for me and corroborated what Tibor had said that morning—that she was manipulating her father for her own ends. When she left me, I guessed that she was going to convince him to leave their home for the night, and that he would allow himself to be persuaded.

The day passed very quickly and very slowly. On the one hand, I was in a hurry for it to be over; on the other, I was so anxious about the evening that I devoted myself to a hundred governmental trivialities. Although torn, I felt a profound tranquility— I had made the right decision—and a terrified eagerness—how would I act?

Before night fell, I went off alone, upstream from the village, to the place where I usually performed my ablutions, and prepared myself for our encounter. My heart was racing; shivers shook my body. No one intimidated me as much as Noura.

Washed, perfumed, my hair clean and combed, and wearing fresh clothing, I presented myself at her home with a knock on the doorjamb.

Noura, superb, with milky skin and dark hair, dressed in a vaporous, almost transparent gown, remained in repose on the rug and stared at me without blinking.

"It's you?"

What a strange thing for her to say! We'd spent the day together, I'd told her I was coming, and that's the question she greeted me with?

"It's me!"

My answer sounded strange, as stupid as it was useless. It didn't mean anything . . . or rather, it did . . . it echoed the dialogue of innuendoes implicit in our banalities, an exchange that could have been reformulated like this: "Is it really you, the man who loves me?" "Yes, it's really me, and I've come to make love to you."

Noura didn't reply. I felt the tension of this silence. Still I hesitated. "Am I disturbing you?"

"You never disturb me," she whispered, in a tone that proclaimed the opposite.

How could I liberate the imprisoned tenderness in me that wanted to rush toward her?

Sitting with her legs folded under her, she decided to ignore me. An irresistible impulse caused her to gather her hair, as if she had nothing more crucial to do, revealing the white nape of her neck, as pale and fragile as a flower that had grown in the shade. She yawned, showing her pink mouth with its small, pearly teeth, and stifled a sigh.

I was on pins and needles.

She didn't look at me, but her eyes kept watch behind their sleepy lids and the fringe of her curved lashes.

I took a step toward her, hesitant.

She turned around, looked at me without flinching, with a flattering boldness. She was waiting. She accepted my advance. Her inertia called for my initiative. With a feigned cravenness, she started to smile.

Throwing dignity to the wind, I knelt in front of her and took her hands, moved to tears to find them so small, so warm, so soft, so fair. I kissed her delicate wrists, ten times, a hundred times, dying to make her see how I adored her, that I was throwing myself at her feet, that all I wanted was her happiness.

Impishly, she lifted my chin, brought my face closer to hers and, like a child, presented her velvety cheek to be kissed. Seeing through her artfulness, I ignored the proffered cheek and placed my mouth on hers. Our lips met instantly. Powerful. Vibrant. Noura sighed with relief, then with pleasure. Our tongues explored, rubbed against each another, cool, ardent, lively, thirsty for each other.

Noura stretched out on her back, pressing me against her. I was afraid I would crush her, but she held onto me, tenacious. Her eyes implored me. Her languor was throbbing with impatience. She wanted me to give her pleasure.

I slid inside her.

Once again, it was obvious: my sex was made to go inside hers. She gasped with astonishment, satisfaction, a desire for more. Our eyes remained locked. They asked a stream of questions: "What if I move like this? Do you feel that?" And, deep in our throats, the response: cries, growls, breath catching, roars.

Over and over, I kept myself from coming.

Suddenly, Noura froze, stiffened, and looked at me, her eyelids open wide, her eyes damp, their pupils dark. It seemed to me that she was looking for someone else in my eyes, not the man who had slipped inside her, that attentive, tender, vigorous Noam, but a Noam beyond kindness, an authoritarian, vanquishing lover, a conqueror who would wrench control away from her.

I thrust hard, penetrating her with all my strength.

Satisfied, Noura relaxed again.

I slammed against her, crashed into her. The shivers that ran across her features showed that she was developing an intense curiosity about what was happening to her, what was going to happen to her. She trembled beneath me, lucid but with abandon. Her ears reddened; her neck turned scarlet; her breast became mottled. She was panting.

Noura cried out. So did I. What I was losing in gentleness, finesse, and sensuality, I was gaining in arousal. Something was transcending us. My passion ceased to belong to me: it transfixed me, I endured it, I obeyed it. Noura and I were sharing a kind of madness.

She moaned, her toes curled, and her fists closed, her head swinging from right to left, left to right. I stopped, worried. She protested virulently: "Don't stop!"

I kept going. She struck my chest, scratched me, slapped me, these gestures of refusal allowing her to do the opposite, to fully accept the intrusion of my body into hers.

She trembled, screamed, and we came together.

The miracle had happened.

Afterward, we were exhausted.

Everything had become simple, simultaneously intense and banal. We no longer waited or expected: we had, we were.

She nestled in my arms, suddenly frail and little, which moved me. What bliss to be together without tension, frustration, or forced chatter, without desire or regret, fused, united, drained, listening to life beating in our chests! We savored the present, nourished by our vigor, our youth.

When I jumped to my feet to pour her a drink, Noura examined me with eyes that were confused and moist. They rendered me male, terrifying, magnificent.

She contemplated me, and that transformed me. For the first time in my life, I wondered if I wasn't handsome.

*

Are impediments the condition of happiness?

I'd hardly tasted ecstasy in Noura's arms before duty tore me away from it. The Lake was rising; the streams were overflowing; sodden, the fields rejected seeds, while the dampness rotted the remaining vegetables. Countless details justified Tibor's anxiety.

At first, I looked away, too dazzled by Noura, who was initiating me into unsuspected pleasures: lazing on our bed all morning, silent, our bodies intertwined; endlessly kissing this body that she was no longer saving; letting her style my hair for an entire afternoon to obtain results that were "cute," "frightful," or "ridiculous." Who could've guessed that I would love being transformed into a doll? Who could've guessed I would melt when she made fun of me? It was impossible to be bored with Noura, who embodied two, ten, twenty, thirty different women, one after the other! In fact, she was infinite women, one day submissive, another tyrannical, lascivious, morose, excited. In bed, she was full of surprises: flexible and drowsy, imperious and tense, quick and febrile, slow and languid, enticing and lustful, provocative and determined, seduced and passive, open and nonchalant, ticklish and untouchable, enterprising and voracious.

Just as she represented all sorts of women, I personified all sorts of men: the lover, the beloved, the friend, the enemy, the egoist, the benefactor, the dissolute, the blasé, the salacious, the tormentor. From sunrise to sunset, I wanted to hug her, strangle her, weep, laugh, run away from her, show her off, hide her, sacrifice myself.

Unfortunately, however, I was obliged to leave her: I had to meet with the canoe builders. A few experienced villagers would go with me. Ten days' walk to reach our destination, the time spent there, and ten days for the walk back: I would be gone for a good moon.

The morning of our departure, Noura fell ill. Pale, she had a headache and dull eyes; wilted, she offered me her hand without rising from our bed. I kissed her hot little hand, a slender object whose limpness told me that I couldn't make use of it at the moment.

"Go on, Noam. Do the best you can. I'll try to recover."

She was operating on two levels: while she approved of the chief and encouraged him to conduct this expedition, she disapproved of the husband, who was guilty of abandoning his wife sick in bed.

I was crossing the threshold of our house when I was stopped by Mama, her face scarlet.

"If you agree to this, you're no longer my son!"

Standing, her legs wide apart, she barred my way. Wide-eyed, her mouth ferocious, her complexion heated, she was trembling with rage, which added to her beauty.

"Pardon?" I said.

"You're going to do me the pleasure of sending him packing."

"Who are you talking about?"

"Barak. He wants to go with you."

My uncle hadn't proposed anything of the sort to me, at least not yet. Did he really expect to strengthen our group?

Mama screamed, "Tell him no! Otherwise . . ."

She shook a finger that threatened me with some terrible punishment and concluded, her eyebrows wrathful, "I will have warned you!"

I stepped toward her, wanting to calm her. She misunderstood, thinking that I was trying to win her over, and rebelled. "Walking, traveling, hunting, fighting: he's in no condition for that. It's out of the question."

I repressed a smile: to judge by the cries I heard during the night, my uncle was fit as a fiddle. I struggled against the desire to explain to Mama that she was the one who was in no condition . . . to do without him.

She saw that I was amused. She immediately changed register, veering toward the sentimental, "You understand, Noam, I've been waiting for him all my life. He comes back, I take care of him, and now he's taking off at the first opportunity, hopping along on one leg!"

A voice resounded behind her: "I'm not leaving, Elena; I'm protecting my nephew."

She frowned on hearing the grave, powerful, cavernous timbre of Barak's voice. Hearing it sufficed to move her. Turning to face the colossus who had joined us, she forced herself to maintain her hostile demeanor.

"Noam is perfectly capable of defending himself!"

"I'm perfectly capable of defending him, too, aren't I, Nephew?"

His complexion bright, his eyes shining, in splendid shape, Barak had dressed for the mission. Covered with skins and bags, he stood so straight, with so many muscles and so much eagerness, that it wasn't immediately obvious that he was missing a leg and wearing a stag's-bone prosthesis in its place.

He put his broad hand on Elena's neck, drew her to him, and pecked her shoulder with his lips.

"Elena, my love, allow me to love Noam. I'm not just fond of your son; I cherish him as my own."

"As our own?" Elena suggested, enamored.

They embraced greedily, incapable of restraining their ardor in public.

Elena and Barak had spoken aloud something I had perceived vaguely for some time: by representing the child they might've dreamed of bringing into the world, I had become their son. They had erased Pannoam's paternity.

When their embrace was over, I congratulated Barak.

"Thank you for escorting me, Uncle."

Mama stopped griping and, though languorous, looked at Barak with a reproachful expression on her face.

"So I have no influence on your decisions?"

"You influence my actions: I'll hurry to come back to you."

She giggled with pride, masking her joy behind a feigned muttering, then turned to me.

"Protect him, Noam. He's not a young man anymore."

"You hussy, would you prefer a boy?" Barak asked, patting her back.

She didn't reply, thirsty for his caresses.

"Mama, take care of Noura, please. She's ill," I said.

"Of course," Mama exclaimed.

"Of course what? Of course you'll take care of her? Or of course she's ill?"

Mama snorted.

"In order: of course she's ill; of course I'll take care of her. That's the difference between a young woman and a mature woman, my boy: the young woman falls ill, the mature one has a tantrum—she saves her energy . . . As the years go on, we learn to protest without putting our health in danger."

*

We were walking along the lakeshore.

The rudimentary path, used by merchants, craftsman, and even livestock raisers going to our market, had been inundated and washed out here and there. We had to make detours on several occasions when the water had advanced far into the plain, but the steep, stony parts had suffered less from the flooding.

Even far from the shore, the land, wet, dense, and shining, made walking difficult: we slipped, sinking into the mud up to our calves. Sometimes, so much mud adhered to our shoes that we could no longer bear their weight and devastating sogginess.

Vaguely oppressed, with a heavy heart and raw throat, I didn't feel the traveler's joy, the call of the unknown that reinvigorates us, fills our lungs, and lavishes on us a happiness that eases our efforts; I was dragging an indolent, demoralized body without appetite.

Barak tapped me on the shoulder. He looked glum, too.

"Leaving the village is heart-wrenching now."

"I feel as though I've been given a thorough beating."

"Our life is down there now, with them."

Barak was right. Our world had changed. It had a center—Elena for him, Noura for me—and its dull periphery depressed us. Leaving it produced the overpowering sorrow of exile.

"You stop being free when you're in love," Barak sighed. "Which is more valuable, love or freedom?"

He smiled again as he answered himself, "Love, without hesitation! I've used and abused freedom for years, and I've had enough of it! Freedom to do anything, but for what? Freedom is a sign of failure, a recluse's disease, a loser's handicap! Now all I dream of is running toward Elena, making her happy, enjoying her presence and her joy."

"I resent Pannoam more by the day. When he stole Elena and Noura from us, he stole our happiness. How could I have been so stupid as to tolerate it?"

"What about me," Barak roared. "My brother had only one superiority: that of persuading me of his. I swallowed the idea that he was better than I was, that he deserved better than me."

"So did I."

"That's normal; the son naturally attributes everything good to his father. But me . . .? Even after I discovered his tricks and betrayals, I saw his duplicity as an unbeatable advantage, a kind of complexity that a poor oaf like me didn't have the benefit of. You reacted in time."

"Thanks to you . . ."

"And to Noura. She risked her life to come find you."

Reflecting on this episode, I shivered and wished I could go back and press Noura to my heart. My uncle checked the impulse.

"What is the Lake going to do?"

"Tibor has received dreams. The Lake is swelling and covering the shores without warning."

"Why?"

"Tibor just gleaned some images and sounds, no explanation."

"Too bad! If we learned what it's up to, we would intervene with the Lake."

"Tibor doubts the efficacy of offerings and prayers, Uncle. Actually, I do, too."

"Mmm . . ."

By reflex, Barak squeezed his amulets.

The expedition took place without incident, despite the difficulty of walking on the slippery, muddy soil. Gradually, the enchantment of walking did away with the pain, the cares, the feeling of being uprooted. Now that I had consented to this temporary banishment, I savored the beauties of our modified landscape. Sometimes the Lake spread out broadly, creating, at the level of the sedges, a swampy fringe; ducks, treating the grass like reeds, quacked and shook themselves before flying away with their feet dangling. At other times, the Lake assailed the rocky shores, and wild goats, capering from rocks to little hills, looked like sentinels guarding their ramparts.

In the evening, we made a fire to cook our meat and discourage predators, and we went to sleep at the same hour as the sun.

On the second day, after crossing a stream that sprang up in the woods, Barak slowed down.

"Your leg?" I murmured, concerned.

He reassured me by shaking his head.

"My boy, go on without me."

"What?"

Embarrassed, Barak scratched his elbows, and this movement made his enormous muscles swell—I was often amazed that with such biceps, he was still able to bend his arms.

"This stream leads to the Cavern of the Huntresses. I'm going there."

I stared at him, wide-eyed. He added, "That's also why I accompanied you."

I screamed with horror: "Barak!"

The colossus stepped back, made indignant by my indignation. "You louse! What are you assuming?"

"I'm not assuming, I know!"

"Excuse me?"

"I know what they get up to at the Cavern of the Huntresses."

Barak clapped his hand to his forehead, stifled an explosion, and then looked me up and down, his eyes enveloping me in scorn.

"What a petty, abominable little fellow you are! I'm not going to the Cavern of the Huntresses to fornicate, you dirty-minded weasel, I'm going there to bid them farewell!"

"Farewell?" I grumbled skeptically.

"Yes, farewell! I have spent some splendid moments there, and I want to thank the Huntresses."

"Mmm . . . Especially Malatantra."

"Malatantra first of all, obviously."

I continued to frown. Barak blew his stack: "Malatantra sells her charms to men, it's true, but that sensitive person will be happy to learn that I'm alive and that I've found the love of my youth."

"Are you certain, Barak, that you can resist being seduced by Malatantra?"

He consulted the clouds, pensively.

"No."

He looked back at me and smiled as he added, "In light of the risk, I've taken precautions."

"What would those be? Did you leave your balls in the village?"

He burst into laughter.

"Excellent idea! That would please our spouses . . . Imagine it, Nephew: a pot to seal our balls up in when we leave home."

He laughed again, shaking his shock of hair.

"I've taken my precautions regarding Malatantra: I not bringing her anything. No boar, no doe, no rabbit. Not even a little mouse. She's proud; she'll understand."

I smiled in turn.

"I'm sorry, Barak, excuse my mistrust."

"What a disgrace! One would have thought he was hearing your father talk."

I absorbed the criticism and signaled to the group, which, far ahead, wondered why we were dawdling.

At the moment when Barak turned off toward his new destination, he whispered in my ear, "Any message you want me to transmit?"

"Me? No."

"Not to anyone?"

"No . . ."

Annoyed, he stared at me. "Noam, once again, you remind me of your father: he forgot everything that embarrassed him."

"What does that have to do with me?"

"Tita."

This name startled me, and I was crushed by shame. The wild, superb Tita, the Huntress of my torrid nights, had left my mind completely. Suddenly, memories poured in, like a river in flood.

"Tita . . ." I breathed, echoing Barak.

Noura's arrival in my life had eliminated Tita. Faced with my uncle, I became aware that she had lived, was still living, and that my amnesia and indifference insulted her. I had disdained her for so many months . . .

Barak proved that I was related to Pannoam by revealing this defect: using people and then getting rid of them.

I stammered. "Tell her . . . tell her . . ."

"Yes?"

"That I've returned to the village and gotten married. That I was obliged."

"To get married? You're exaggerating . . . Authorize me to improvise a bit on the spot."

"I trust you, Barak. I don't know any brute more delicate than you."

He hugged me to him. As he was going away, I called after him: "How shall we proceed, Barak? I'll pick you up in twenty days?"

He jumped, frightened.

"You're out of your mind! After making a brief detour to the Cavern, I'll catch up with you at the Gap of the Gods. Staying longer would be dangerous! If I lingered there for several days and nights, I'd be capable of hunting for Malatantra again."

And he plunged into the shaggy depths of the forest.

As we approached the Gap of the Gods, we saw canoes and canoeists. They were fishing on the peaceful mirror, pure and full of sky.

Birds were calling, their echoes ricocheting, more undulant and more fluid than the water.

The hollowed-out trunks didn't limit themselves to moving along the shore; they dared to go as far as the center of the Lake. Their boldness stunned me. Up to that time, I'd only seen boats propelled along by a pole that the fisherman thrust to the bottom of the water, and on which he then pushed or pulled. Now I discovered paddles: poles that were flattened on one end and pushed against the surface alone, making it possible to venture into deep waters. This innovation made me dizzy. I sensed that thanks to this progress, the limits on travel had been had breached.*

Finally, we caught sight of the village, which was preceded by many openings where the inhabitants had cut down trees to carve dugout skiffs. We greeted groups who were cutting the limbs off conifers, and, when a bald worker asked what we were looking for, I told him that, as the chief of a major village ten days' walk away, I needed their expertise.

---

* Previously, dugout canoes stayed close to the shore and were used only for fishing. They were seen as a comfortable way of remaining in areas with a lot of fish while simultaneously keeping dry and having a place to temporarily store the catch. No one considered them a means of transportation. It didn't occur to anyone that boats might be useful for traveling or exploring. The possibility of using them for trade or war was even less envisioned. Sea travel by boat did not exist.

The bald man took us to their leader, Vlaam, a solidly built man about thirty years old, with red hair, a golden beard, and a low forehead. He received us in a workshop where he and his sons were hollowing out fir trees. Amid a warm, bitter, pungent, resinous odor, some of them were using flint tools to carve logs that others completed by burning them out with embers. On the ground, puppies were frolicking in the blond wood chips.[†]

After we were introduced, I explained our visit. "We want floating houses."

Vlaam stared at me, incredulous.

"Floating houses? I've never heard of such a thing . . . Why?"

"In case the Lake rises."

"Build your shelters farther from the shore."

"And if the Lake rises again?"

My reply, purely logical, disconcerted him. He tapped his temples, examined the shoreline, and returned his attention to me.

"Why would the Lake attack us?"

"No one can guess what the Lake wants."

"True . . ."

"At the moment, it's spreading," I concluded. Tibor had forbidden me to recount his dreams.

Vlaam turned to his sons.

"Floating houses! Do you know how to make those?"

They burst out laughing.

---

† The Stone Age? The Wood Age, rather! We saw wood as our friend. Thanks to its softness and its flexibility or rigidity, we used it for everything. Millennia later, this fact escaped archeologists because wood didn't last and had disappeared organically from the excavation sites. The appearance in the nineteenth century of three ages—stone, bronze, and iron—amused me greatly. To organize the collections of the museum in Copenhagen, Christian Jürgensen Thomsen, a Danish specialist in prehistory, distinguished successive periods: the Stone Age, the Bronze Age, and the Iron Age. He was right to establish that chronology because as soon as bronze was invented, stone was no longer used for tools; nor was bronze once iron was discovered. One material had driven the other out. But I would have liked to whisper to him that the constant was wood.

I persisted, unfazed, "Around the Lake, everyone says that you practice the best techniques. If someone were to succeed in making the first floating house, it would be you."

Vlaam accepted the compliment with pleasure. I suspected, judging by their manners, their accent, and their elementary sentences, that these rough artisans had merely developed a skill, carpentry, which constituted all their pride.

Vlaam walked among his sons and repeated, pensively, "A floating house . . ."

"A raft with walls," exclaimed the eldest son.

"A raft as the basis, of course. But trunks attached to one another have no stability. We would need outriggers.

"Goatskins!" the son called out.

"Amphoras!" a second son suggested.

Vlaam nodded. He continued to think aloud. "A barrier would have to prevent the water from coming in when it's rough."

"Planks?"

"Too heavy."

"A fence?"

"Sewn edges," Vlaam recommended. "Light."

As I listened to these ideas surging up, I could see that this clan had earned its reputation.

"Congratulations, Vlaam, you've already resolved the problems. Is it a deal?"

Vlaam almost shook the hand I extended to him, but thought better of it. He took the time to sit down, drink, wipe his mouth and beard, and then ask, "What are you proposing?"

"Our village has the biggest market on the Lake. For your boats, I will trade food, animals, grain, leather, fabric, and pottery."

Vlaam's eyes flashed, interested, and then grew troubled.

"If your village is ten days away from us, how would we proceed?"

"I'll supply you every week. In advance."

"No, you misunderstand me, Noam. How would you get your floating houses?"

I was dumbstruck, not having thought of that.

"You . . . You won't deliver them to me?"

"No!"

"I'll send my own men."

"You're joking! What I can't do, your men wouldn't be able to do, either. The floating houses would be too heavy to transport. Imagine the number of trunks . . ."

"Ah. Yes . . ."

"They can't travel by water, either. Even slowly."

"Why?"

"It would be impossible to give them the shape of a canoe, with a pointed prow that splits the waves. In any case, the paddles wouldn't be strong enough. The floating houses would drift off course . . ."

I reacted immediately and firmly: "Well, then, come build them in our village, Vlaam!"

Vlaam and his sons stared at me, stunned.

"Leave here?"

"Long enough to complete the construction."

Vlaam shrugged.

"Never!"

Turning on his heel, he considered the discussion closed and went back to polishing the boat that he was finishing. One of his sons approached him and said, "Father, remember what Derek said."

Vlaam shot him a venomous look.

"Excuse me?"

"Derek said that soon we . . ."

"Hold your tongue!"

"Father, Derek's prophecies . . ."

"Enough talk! Everybody back to work."

To me, he said, "You and your people can sleep in the raspberry clearing tonight. Take some logs for a fire. Our women will bring you something to drink. Tomorrow, you'll leave."

I went back to my companions but didn't tell them I had failed. In reality, I still hoped I'd have another chance to succeed. Even though the conversation had not gone well, I had glimpsed a weak spot in Vlaam when his son mentioned Derek.

Questioning the women who brought us water, I learned that two individuals reigned: Vlaam, a descendant of Azrial, the preceding chief, and Derek, his half-brother. The former governed the village officially, but the latter governed it unofficially. Vlaam held the legitimate authority, power, and knowledge; Derek influenced minds.

The more I learned about this Derek, the more he intrigued me. Despite his bastard status—his mother, the wife of the hereditary chief, had conceived Derek with an unknown person—he had succeeded in making a place for himself alongside his half-brother Vlaam, as well as within the community. He was called *Derek the Man with Mystery Hands* because he always wore mittens. His mother had covered his hands while she was still nursing him and had never permitted him to be seen otherwise. Today, he wore a variety of different mittens—in leather, fur, fabric—but was never without them. However, this oddity remained anecdotal in view of his principal characteristic: Derek conversed with the gods. His grip on the villagers proceeded from this exceptional gift. Inspired and inspiring, he guided the souls in this place.

Since I expressed a strong desire to meet him, the women informed me that for the past moon he had been up in the mountains questioning the gods.

They revealed to me why the place was called the Gap of the Gods. Several times a year, the gods who occupied the snowy heights descended along the river to go to the Lake.

"What do they do in the Lake?"

"They disappear into it."

For generations, the gods had been passing through this area. The villagers, favored and honored, were proud of their visits.

"Do you speak to them?"

"We prostrate ourselves before them. And they pass by."

"They pass without a word?"

"Without a word. It's very moving."

At that moment, an auroch's horn resounded in the distance. Another shepherd's horn, closer, carried the hollow noise farther.

The two women shivered. They looked at each other, amazed, then turned joyously toward me.

"A god is coming!"

"You'll get to see him!"

They got excited. Around them, men, women, and children were jumping about outside their homes, their workshops.

The women urged me to follow them. All the villagers headed for a meadow bordered by a rapidly flowing stream and knelt down in the grass. I imitated them.

Bowing down, respectfully motionless, people looked up just enough to see what was happening in front of them.

Suddenly, a high-pitched horn trumpeted a triumphal hymn. They sighed, fingered their talismans, their amulets, their totems.

"Here comes the god," one of the women whispered.

I kept my eyes fixed on the river.

A huge vessel moved along it. It shone with brilliant colors, yellow, ocher, vermilion, red, and was filled with strange flowers woven to make garlands or crowns, white, violet, mauve. The apparition, superb and majestic, was stupefying.

We could not discern the god, but we saw that he was lying on his back in the boat, his head toward the rear. Silent, serene, he let himself float along on the impetuous torrent.

The villagers recited prayers.

The exotic craft passed through the woods and reached the Lake. There, oddly, it did not slow down but continued rapidly toward the horizon.

The villagers chanted enthusiastic songs. Their voices filled the landscape, sincere, happy, grateful, strengthened by faith.

As soon as the rejoicing was over, I asked the women, "Do you approach the gods?"

"They do not tolerate that. They move so quickly. Did you notice the flowers? As beautiful as they are unknown. They're flowers from the City of the Gods."

"Have the gods risen up to look at you, to greet you?"

They giggled, considering me silly. "Do you think we're that important?"

I approved of their reaction. One question still bothered me: "Has anyone already gone up there? To the City of the Gods?"

"No one before Derek."

"Oh?"

"He goes there. He comes back carrying messages. Thanks to him, we prosper in peace."

There was no longer any doubt about it: I had to meet this man.

I envied this village its privilege of receiving visits from the gods, and I fell asleep speculating on these unattainable spaces: the City of the Gods, the Middle of the Lake. Were these two territories connected by secret networks? Did an underground tunnel allow the gods to regain the summit of the mountain? The Kingdom Below had to communicate with the Kingdom Above.

The next day, determined to wait for Derek, I claimed to have sore legs to delay our departure. Since Derek was consulting the gods, maybe he knew what the Lake was up to? Would he bring me information that would complement Tibor's dreams? If so, he would adopt an opinion different from his brother's . . .

In the late morning, I returned to the river, pretending to calm the pain in my legs by bathing them in its waters.

Nature is never silent. The river was roaring, tree branches were creaking above the trembling tall grasses, and the larks sang, the jays cackled at the edge of the forest, and pigeons flapped their wings as they landed. In short, everything was murmuring, squeaking, swaying, chattering. Sitting on the shore, I dipped my feet in the icy water.

Then I heard a fantastic bird. From dark foliage emerged a luminous sound, enticing, fleshy, whose roulades and cooing sketched sinuous curls against the sky. Sometimes, the song became shrill, golden, tenuous, thinning until it was a whistling; at other times, it descended, grew meatier, took on different colors, always in a subtle, charming way. To my ears, no animal had ever manifested so continuous a breath, and these cascading notes, rich and inventive, transcended in variety those of a nightingale.

Wanting to find out what this rare bird with its incredible trilling looked like, I tore myself away from the stream. Careful not to scare the bird away, I entered the stand of firs.

The sunlight was diffracted into oblique rays in which thousands of gnats were fluttering.

The song continued, elated, impatient, intoxicated with itself. It cast a spell over me. Its sweetness, like its brightness, touched me at the deepest level. As I advanced among the tree trunks, I kept an eye on the needle-covered branches so as to identify it. Alas, the bird remained invisible.

It receded into the distance. I followed it. In this valley, the vegetation was different, composed of mad, rough, dense bushes in which hawthorn attacked my thighs and bit into my shinbones. Even though I had a hard time keeping quiet—in addition to the thorns, the stones were flaying my bare feet—I approached the mysterious bird, at the height of my infatuation. Close now, my eyes scanned the branches. In vain!

I looked down and glimpsed a human form leaning against a rock.

The gentle warbling was coming from it.

I didn't dare believe it. The voice seemed to me neither a man's nor a woman's, and yet this immense body covered with multiple furs, with thin, soft hair, was emitting the chant that had enthralled me.

The person spotted me. He stopped singing and stood up, looking worried.

Embarrassed, I reassured him, "Hello. My name is Noam, and I'm the chief of a neighboring village. I'm sorry to have bothered you—I took your song for that of a bird."

He shrugged. "What are you doing here?" he asked me, suspicious.

"I have a job for the carpenters."

"Oh? What job?"

"Building floating houses."

He looked at me coldly, doubting that he had correctly understood.

"Floating . . ."

"Floating houses."

He was grumbling when the two village women showed up. They exclaimed, "Derek! We heard your voice. How are you? Are you back with a message from the gods?"

He nodded gravely. They received this response solemnly, then pointed to me. "Let us introduce you to Noam, the son of the prestigious Pannoam."

When he heard that, Derek shivered. He paid me a different kind of attention, more welcoming, more intrigued.

"Did you know my father?" I cried.

He looked me in the eye.

"That name is not unknown to me."

Aware of Pannoam's glorious reputation among the Peoples of the Lake, I was not at all astonished by this. Surreptitiously, while the gossips chirped, I examined his hands, which were covered by otter-skin mittens. Derek the Man with Mystery Hands . . . Why this precaution? Did he suffer from a defect? Was he concealing scabs, stains, or deformations that would have disgusted us?

I noted that at that instant, he was looking intently at my fingers.

He pulled himself together and became almost cordial. "Let's head back to the village together. You can explain what it is you want."

Escorted by the chatterboxes, we crossed the wood, the river, and the prairie. On the way, he limited himself to conducting an ordinary conversation; obviously, he was putting up with the chirping of the two babblers, a necessary evil that had to be endured before we could be alone.

I took advantage of this to observe him more closely.

Very tall, Derek left above all the impression of being lanky. Not very muscular, his torso perched on bony legs, endowed with narrow shoulders and projecting elbows, he had grown in height rather than in breadth, as if he'd been stretched. He surprised people. The part of his calves, arms, and chest that could be seen remained hairless; above a vast, prominent forehead, his brown hair, abundant and thick but without vigor, tumbled loosely over his fine, pink, satin-smooth, but withered, skin. Although there was a jaunty nobility in his emaciated appearance, his face betrayed a certain pettiness. Small brown eyes, too close-set, focused on the bridge of his nose before opening up to the world, while his mouth, dry, with retracted lips, reflected frustration. The absence of whiskers on his chin and cheeks prevented me from determining his age, and this exceptional hairlessness created a mask that hid more than a thick beard would have. On the other hand, his voice had, even when he spoke, a superb power that was mellow, smooth, and sonorous, enriched by a fruity resonance. Anything he said attracted people, suspended time, and enchanted. Unfortunately, it was Derek's only pleasing characteristic.

He made me uneasy. Because he himself felt uneasy? He seemed uncomfortable with himself, even ashamed . . .

As we walked, I inferred, from the seamstresses and embroiderers who looked up as we passed by, that women found Derek's singularity charming. They showed for him such respect, marked by fear and admiration, that I could sense the fascination he elicited in the very air we passed through.

In his home, we each sat on a three-legged stool. Derek poured me a succulent raspberry wine, then heard me out. I told him about my recent ascension to power, the wealth of our village, and the threats received in dreams by Tibor, our healer, who thought we were running a risk by living on the lakeshore.

"Why don't you simply move farther inland?"

"We're a People of the Lake; we don't know anything about those other places. Moreover, Tibor swears that moving wouldn't be enough to ensure our safety."

He indicated his approval, narrowing his eyes. I concluded my remarks by mentioning my idea of floating houses, my sudden appearance in his village, and Vlaam's refusal. Once I had finished my account, Derek rose and bowed to me.

"I salute the man that the gods foretold."

"Sorry?"

"Up there, they warned me that grave catastrophes would take place."

"Where?"

"All around the Lake."

"Oh? They told you that?"

"They've been telling me that for years. This time we won't be able to ward off the danger by making offerings. The calamity no longer depends on the gods: the Lake is overflowing with rage!"

His declaration struck me like a punch in the stomach. His information and Tibor's matched up. Derek went on, "They promised me that a man would come: he would save the village by moving it. You are that man, Noam."

He bowed again.

"We welcome the gods' messenger."

The turn the discussion had taken disconcerted me.

"Me, the gods' messenger? No! I guarantee you that none of them, either in dreams or in waking . . ."

"Didn't the gods contact Tibor? And didn't Tibor then send you here?"

"Well, yes . . ."

"Didn't the gods inform me?"

"Certainly, but the gods have never contacted me personally . . ."

"That doesn't matter! Don't judge the way the gods intervene in our affairs. They have also given me a role to play: to persuade the villagers to support your proposal. By obeying the gods' stratagems, we will fulfill our destiny."

"But . . ."

"My destiny is to save my village. Yours is to save mankind."

Derek's statements staggered me. His severe forehead, his hard eyes radiated such conviction that I remained silent. The idea that the gods thought of me, counted on me, was beyond my limited understanding.

*

Derek evinced a prodigious energy. Who, in our village, would have dared to attempt what he was undertaking? Over a period of a few days, he tried to persuade families to abandon the territory they'd been living on for generations and migrate to ours.

He didn't spare himself or anyone else: for those who resisted, he predicted disaster, and he assured those who hoped the move would prove temporary that the contrary was true. He bellowed, "The Gap of the Gods has been closed. Soon, the gods will come no longer."

"Why? What harm have we done?"

"None, to the gods. That's why they're trying to protect you, and through me as their intermediary, they advise you to flee. We have to follow Noam."

"Why?"

"Because this place is going to disappear. The Lake has grown angry. It will rise and submerge us."

Derek's way of operating was the complete opposite of mine.

Instead of comforting people, he made them worry. Worse, he terrified them. The irises of his eyes blazing red, his lips agitated, he belched forth apocalyptic descriptions of the future. Every detail of his predictions was shattering: giant waves, drowned babies, children carried away by the water like walnut shells, mothers hammered by the furious waters, people taking refuge on rooftops or treetops until the muddy whirlpool engulfs them in their turn, frothing eddies, bodies of water full of the cadavers of animals and humans, dead ancestors torn out of their tombs, odors, pestilence, thunderstorms, shadows, death.

As he spoke, Derek trembled, sweated, turned yellow, babbled, screamed, and hiccupped, shaken by the violence of the tragic scenes that his vaticination evoked. His prophecies were laden with authenticity, and the hypnotic powers of his voice left his audience in a state of terrified dizziness.

Tibor, with his noble features, reserve, and reflective discernment, would never have penetrated hearts and minds to this extent. Nor would I; I chose to absorb the anxiety rather than to spread it.

When Barak rejoined us, he attended Derek's harangues. They were complete opposites, one so very virile, the other saddled with feminine characteristics, but the orator enchanted my uncle.

"I love it!" Barak said at the end of Derek's sermons, while the panicked audience wept.

"Barak!" I said, indignantly. "He believes what he's saying; I believe it; the people believe it!"

"So do I, Nephew, so do I . . . I savor it! Delightful! What a show!"

Barak had returned calmed by his short stay at the Cavern of the Huntresses. With great elegance, Malatantra had wished him happiness with Elena.

"She didn't even turn me on. It was fantastic! I didn't even have to fight against temptation."

"In any case, you hadn't brought her anything."

He blushed violently. "I killed a doe on the way there."

"Barak!"

"Habit! I don't like to arrive at a lady's home empty-handed."

"Malatantra is hardly a lady."

"Oh, yes, she is, Nephew, she's a lady, a real lady . . . That much I remember perfectly!"

Derek was converting people to our objective every day now.

He inspired mixed feelings in me. Although I admired his efficiency, his language, the magic of his voice, certain points disturbed me: the ease with which he recovered from his predictive trances, how quickly he became jovial again in my company, drinking wine that was more than sufficient to slake his thirst. At those moments, I was no longer frequenting an alarmed public official, a serious clairvoyant, a prophet devoured by anxiety, but rather an impulsive, self-satisfied *bon vivant*. I sometimes suspected that he took pleasure in shocking, frightening, forcing consent, and even that he enjoyed manipulating the village.

His absence of scruples scared me as much as his sinister announcements: he changed the gods' initial message to suit his current interlocutors; without restraint, he transformed their sentences and altered his report depending on who was listening to him, thus delivering personalized predictions.

When I drew his attention to this, he retorted with disdain, "The gods commanded me to persuade. Would you prefer that I fail?"

"When you quote the gods, you're taking responsibility for representing them . . ."

"I don't lie."

"But . . ."

"I don't lie! I convey the truth."

There was no denying that he only misrepresented his memories to serve a good cause . . . I made up my mind to accept the fact that he established truth by telling lies.

*

At the start of the new moon, Vlaam summoned me to his house one evening.

"Our community is ready, Noam. We've spent the day packing up our equipment, filling our bags, and stuffing the essential tools and materials into our trunks. Do you assure me that you'll receive us well?"

"I swear it."

"Derek has brought everyone around to the idea."

"I see that. I admire you, Vlaam, for leading the village with another man at your side; that kind of sharing generally creates more problems than it solves."

"Do I have a choice?" he said wearily, rubbing his thighs, which were worn out by the preparations for the move.

He poured us drinks, then collapsed on a stool, his legs spread wide and his back against a beam. He heaved a great sigh.

"I may hold the power, but Derek has the authority. He influences the people."

"You're lucky he's your brother."

"My half-brother."

"You show indulgence toward a bastard."

Vlaam paled, hesitated, and searched the surrounding shadows, then murmured, "Careful, never utter that word."

"Bastard?"

He panicked. "Quiet! Everyone who has called Derek that has regretted it. That is, if they had the time . . . My father first of all!"

"Pardon?"

"One day, when Derek was about fifteen years old, my father Azrial, who actually got along well with him, made fun of his voice in front of my mother: 'Who did you make this bastard with? A cuckoo?' He died the following week. Fevers, tremors, difficulty breathing. The gods punished him. Then the same thing happened to an old woman in the village who had insulted

Derek. Then a boy who had created a malicious song using that term. Three dead! From that time on, we stopped using the word. Derek enjoys the gods' protection: they don't limit themselves to speaking to him; they also defend him."

Vlaam took a drink and let his feelings pour out, "I'm going away with my village, but I'm not leading it, I'm following it."

"What? You're not leaving because you've been convinced?"

"I'm leaving because I'm the last one who isn't convinced. Sometimes, the chief obeys those whom he claims to rule. I've made up my mind to accompany my sons on the path to exile."

The next morning, thirty men, women, and children, carrying their bundles in their hands or on their backs, left the land where they were born, prepared never to return. Many of them wept.

Barak came up to me and whispered, "I'm glad to be going home. I miss Elena so much I'm sick with it."

"I feel the same way about Noura!"

Barak laughed, then narrowed his eyes. "Aren't you going to ask me about her?"

Barak was raising the question I'd avoided ever since he returned. I swallowed and replied in a cavalier fashion: "Yes, of course. How is Tita?"

I'd asked the question automatically, only to please Barak. He answered in a measured tone: "She's pregnant."

"Tita?"

"With your baby."

Ahead of us, at Vlaam's command, the group began to move.

*

The youngest and the oldest grumbled; the weight of the routine weighed more heavily on them than on the mature adults hoping to rebuild their lives. Elderly men and women moved forward reluctantly; complaining and moaning, they sighed, wept, terrified by a slope to be climbed, discouraged by the idea of having to go around a mass of fallen rocks. The children, influenced by the solemn faces of their parents and prey to the worries that curdled the atmosphere, sensed the tragedy of the situation more than they understood it; they whined continually.

Our cohort did not resemble the groups that roamed through Nature. When the Hunters, having exhausted the resources of a territory, moved to a different location, they did it with a conquering joy; lively, determined, drawn to the new destination, they rushed eagerly toward a better place. They didn't abandon; they rejoined.

Around me, on the contrary, I saw nothing but grimaces and nostalgia. None of these villagers had wanted to go elsewhere; they were all moving under duress. The migrant is someone who doesn't want to leave.*

In the villagers, the desire to stop won out over the desire to move forward. Despite Derek's talent, the danger remained

---

* Over the centuries, I have encountered many columns of migrants. Not only have they never ceased to exist, but they have grown. Their frequency has increased, and so has the number of people composing them, rising from this group of about thirty to several hundred, several thousand, several million. For those who doubt whether humanity has improved, I point out this incontestable progress. Today, on screens, I see haggard families fleeing the abuse of tyranny or climate disasters; when I walk around Beirut, I meet Syrians trying to get away from the terrorists who are oppressing them, the bombing that's destroying their towns, away from famine, poverty, injustice, and chaos. Exodus is part of the human condition.

But those who are not fleeing reject this reality. Temporarily sheltered, anchored in their territory as an oak is anchored in its soil, taking their feet for roots, they think this space belongs to them and see the migrant as an inferior and a nuisance. What blind stupidity! If only the spirit of their ancestors would circulate in them to remind them of the distances they've travelled, their endless transhumance with fear in their bellies, uncertainty, and hunger. Why, in the depths of their bodies, do they not still carry memories of their forebears who survived danger, hostility, poverty, and wars? The remembrance of these courageous acts or the sacrifices to which they owed their lives would make them less insipid. If they knew and recognized their history, their essential fragility, and the volatility of their identity, they would shed the illusion that they're superior. There's no human with a legitimate claim to live in this place or that. The migrant is not the Other; the migrant is me yesterday, or me tomorrow. Through our ancestors or through our descendants, we all bear countless migrants within us.

abstract: imperceptible to the senses, it was merely a prediction. Had they been fleeing a real and present disaster, they would have run. But they were fleeing a future disaster. All this to say that they were dawdling.

I realized that it would take us twice as long to reach my village than expected.

Barak and Derek became friendly. Whereas many men evinced a spontaneous mistrust of this protégé of the gods, Barak loved to converse, joke, and sometimes even sing with him as they walked, inserting his cheeky voice below the ethereal arabesques that the enchanting throat delivered. In the evenings, Barak made a fire separate from the others and invited Derek and me to join him. He took out wine flasks he had acquired in trading with the Huntresses and, followed by Derek, indulged his taste for drink.

On one occasion, after several swigs, he leaned toward Derek and shouted, "Women like you!"

"Me?" Derek murmured, half-heartedly.

"Several of them, of all ages, would gladly take a tumble in the bushes with you. Aren't you thinking of getting married?"

"I prefer not to."

Barak, stunned, considered that response for a moment. Then he repeated, "You prefer not to?"

With a sovereign tranquility bordering on indifference, Derek said again, "I prefer not to."

Barak gave me a distressed look that meant, "I don't understand. Do you?" With an evasive pout, I admitted that I was confused.

The more we were around Derek, the less we understood him. My initial impression was confirmed: Derek with the Mystery Hands was not an ordinary mortal. With his unusual physical appearance, part male, part female, part bird, he didn't seek to behave according to the norm, either. A wife, a home, a family? Not things he dreamed about. An occupation? Even less. He was content to exist, alien, different, unique. Hardly surprising that the gods had chosen him.

"I prefer not to." Could his mystery be better summed up? "I prefer" revealed an inclination while "not" reduced it to nothing. Instead of unmasking its speaker, this sentence concealed him.

As for me, I slept badly at night, and my days were spent turning painful thoughts over and over. Tita was expecting a baby we'd made during our sexual escapades . . . Another man would have boasted about obtaining a child from such a sculptural, powerful, valiant woman whose blood, mixed with mine, would produce robust, healthy offspring. I would have crowed about this a few moons earlier. But Noura, who had come back into my life, was now my wife, and I adored her.

One evening, taking advantage of the absence of Derek, who was busy cheering up the village elders, Barak fed the flames with dry branches and examined me with a mocking smile. "Have you forgotten what I told you, Nephew? Have you already destroyed that annoying memory? Have you rid your past of everything that arouses remorse or regret, oh thou son of Pannoam?"

I guessed that his jesting was meant to refer to Tita. I didn't try to evade the subject. "No, I can't stop thinking about it. Tita . . . Noura . . . the baby . . . What do you think I should do?"

He snorted. "Me? Are you asking my advice?"

"You're the man I love most in the world, Barak."

He blushed with pride and choked out, embarrassed, "I love you, too, Nephew!"

He cleared his throat and added, "You're asking the advice of a dimwit who has wrecked his love life."

"Until recently!"

"I've made up for it at the last moment, I admit."

"What do you suggest?"

He slapped my thigh. "Stay with Noura. She will be the mother of your children."

"And Tita?"

"She will be the mother of her child."

He stood up, took three steps, and, with a stream of urine, irrigated the shadows that surrounded the fire. Groaning, sighing, he pissed at length, drunk with joy, as if he were feeling an essential pleasure. When he was done, he put his member away, perplexed, and returned to the fireside.

"Tita doesn't want your company. The Huntresses of the Cavern refuse to live with men. Lovers without husbands, they give birth to children without fathers and raise them alone—girls or boys, it doesn't matter. As strong as she-bears, those Huntresses! They tolerate us only when we prove indispensable. Otherwise, they want nothing to do with us."

He rubbed his arms vigorously.

"What a lesson in modesty, when you think about it! Knowing that we're of so little use should make us keep our mouths shut."

He looked at me intently.

"Tita doesn't understand why you're avoiding her. Or why her child will never meet its father."

"Because . . . because . . ."

"Don't you want that?"

"Yes, but . . . Noura!"

He scratched his beard and muttered, "Noura . . ."

I exclaimed, "Did you explain to Tita that I'd married Noura?"

"Of course. That had no effect on her. Like all the Huntresses, she's not jealous; they often exchange men. Tita can't imagine that Noura would prevent you from seeing her or your child."

"Noura would leave me if she found out!"

Surprised, Barak turned toward me.

"Leave you? You're optimistic, my boy: she'd kill you. At the very least."

He revived the fire by blowing on the sides where embers still glowed.

"In the end, the question for you isn't 'With whom shall I live?' It becomes 'To whom am I going to lie?'"

One morning, two days from the village, as we were getting ready to break camp, Vlaam, upset, said to me, "Noam, the old people are collapsing, they're aching, they're wasting away. Let them rest, even if we're approaching our destination . . ."

I immediately interrupted him, "We'll stop here. As long as necessary. Let them recuperate."

The news was received with more relief than joy. Apart from the fact that they were grudgingly walking toward the unknown, the old people had lost the habit of moving to a new home. During rest stops, they showed their feet ravaged by blisters in various stages, whitish ones just forming, pink ones that had broken, bleeding ones that had exploded, and yellow ones full of scaly skin.

Recalling Tibor's teachings, I asked Barak to help me gather plants that would relieve the sufferers.

"What are we looking for, Nephew?"

"Oats and sage."

"How do you remember that? I mix everything up when it comes to herbs: I forget their names, and I can never remember what problems they treat. You could've become a healer."

"Tibor wanted me to."

"Ah, my good fellow, you went for his daughter rather than his knowledge!"

"Actually, I took both of them!" I responded, laughing.

Barak was right: the details concerning plants and their powers arranged themselves spontaneously in my mind and composed a body of knowledge in spite of me. My rapturous curiosity about natural resources pushed me in this direction, and so did my conviction that I was living in a beneficial, generous world. Nature was not my enemy, but my mother. I didn't distinguish myself from it: I came from it, I depended on it, and I would return to it. Knowing Nature was tantamount to knowing myself. Tibor had strengthened this feeling of unity. Discovering, analyzing, inventorying, classifying, testing—all the behaviors that were later described as "scientific"—were connected with my religion, like a sort of prayer. Developing my attention to the universe expressed the respect I owed the gods, the love I had for them, and the gratitude that I addressed to them. Indifference would have been stupid. Worse yet: a betrayal. Wonder was part of my spirituality.

Barak found sage, which was easy to identify by its velvety, feather-like leaves, and I found wild oats.

Back at our makeshift camp, I told the old people to make compresses with the sage and apply them to their blisters. In the meantime, I soaked the oats in cold water, brought it to a boil, and then let it cool before offering each of the sufferers a footbath.

I taught the young boys to cut up mint and parsley, as well, and then asked them to apply the combination to the blisters as a poultice to dry them out.

"Next, you rinse. You apply. You rinse. That will keep you busy until evening."

Rubbing his beard, Barak observed with admiration the chain of solidarity I'd built.

"Don't tell me you haven't thought about it!"

He winked. I played the idiot. "Thought of what?"

"It's right nearby."

I knew he was referring to the Cavern of the Huntresses. That morning, in my eagerness to accept this makeshift camp, the image had crossed my mind.

Barak shook his head.

"A sign of fate, no?"

I smiled.

"You're making fate speak, Barak."

"No need to, it's very talkative. But, then again, humans are deaf."

The light was growing dim. The sun was slipping toward the horizon and covering the land with a gentle glow. Between the shores bordered with dark forests, the Lake was gleaming, bronzed by the setting sun that would soon give way to the mystery of night and yield to the cold of darkness.

After making multiple trips back and forth to bring branches to feed the fire, Barak and I had disappeared into the edge of the forest and begun our journey. We thought we'd been discreet, but after a few hundred paces, we heard Derek's voice: "Where are you going?"

I was about to reply that it was none of his business when my uncle said, "Follow us, Derek!"

Stupefied, I stared at Barak: how dare he make that decision without consulting me? Too late! Derek was at our side, delighted to join us for an additional adventure.

"Where are we going?"

"A gift!" Barak retorted, slapping him on the back. "You won't be disappointed."

Barak's initiative troubled me. Unlike him, I was tormented by a mistrust of Derek that was as instinctual as it was unfounded. If I had nothing precise to reproach him for, I blamed him for remaining opaque to me. Although he had supported me in everything I did from the outset, I found it hard to believe in his devotion. What was his ultimate goal?

To be sure, when I saw the artless smiles he and Barak exchanged, when I overheard their cheerful conversations, when they got drunk and fell asleep in each others' arms, I was ashamed of my mistrust, suspecting it of being fueled by jealousy, and I swore to be less frosty in Derek's presence. Alas, as soon as the sun came up, my reservations reappeared.

An enormous, amber-colored moon was touching the treetops. Owls swooped about in search of their prey, making their presence known by the clacking of their wings and their cries, the former drawn-out, the latter tremulous. Why were they hooting? Was it to signal our intrusion?

Near the cliff, Barak stopped and clapped his hand to his forehead.

"We forgot the game!"

"Barak, don't start that again!"

"I'm not going to show up at the Cavern of the Huntresses without a gift!"

"We don't want anything from the Huntresses! No trading tonight."

"Not for me, of course! Or for you. But for Derek?"

The latter was looking at us without grasping a word of our discussion. Barak made up his mind to explain to him where we were going, the Cavern's customs, and the Huntresses's very special brand of hospitality. He concluded, "If one of them pleases you—and one of them surely will—you'll have an incredible night."

"I will?"

"You deserve a woman, my boy!" Barak exclaimed, trumpeting his favorite expression.

"I prefer not to."

Derek repeated once again his enigmatic formula, and it stopped Barak in his tracks.

"What? You don't want pleasure? You don't want to get off? Show a little juice, my boy!"

Derek repeated, his face inert, looking elsewhere, "I prefer not to."

No reply could be more disconcerting for Barak, who froze, speechless. I took advantage of this to take him aside and tell him what I thought: I refused to allow Derek to enter the cavern and learn my secrets—Tita's existence, the child she was bearing. How could we be sure that Derek would keep them when he met Noura? Barak agreed, at first mechanically, then with conviction.

"You go on alone. We'll sleep here, Derek and I; I'll make a fire, fix something to eat. I brought along a hare, just in case . . . And wine, a whole skin full. At least I won't have to wrestle with temptation if I don't see Malatantra. Will you wake us when you come back?"

"Promise!"

"Do you want to take my little hare, for Tita?"

"I prefer not to."

We chortled. The joke gave us the illusion that if we didn't understand Derek, we could at least dominate him by mocking him.*

In the Cavern, preceded by the majestic Malatantra, who had become even more magnificently round, I was petrified when I saw Tita again. She seemed to me more beautiful than I remembered her; she still had her mahogany-colored skin, her clear-cut features, her sculptural figure, and her warrior's thighs, but now she also radiated a certain sweetness. Maternity was lending her a different kind of femininity. Her skin had gained a kind of

---

* Centuries later, around 1830 in New York, I met a man whose life had been ruined by a sentence like that one. Maddox Mayer was a lawyer and notary hunting down property titles and writing abstruse documents. In his flourishing offices on Wall Street, he had recruited copyists—at that time, there were no photocopiers to reproduce texts. Among them there was a puny clerk, smooth, conscientious, rigid, pale, who ate nothing but ginger cookies. One morning, when Mayer ordered him to copy a contract, he replied, "I prefer not to." This was outrageous, since he had been hired for that very task! Over the following days, the same exchange recurred. To every normal request made by his boss, he replied, "I prefer not to." For Mayer, this was the beginning of a torment. "His marvelous mildness not only disarmed me, it emasculated me. To allow your employee to command you is to be emasculated." The individual in question did not revolt, did not rebel, did not oppose him directly. Neither offensive nor insolent, he limited himself to repeating, "I prefer not to." Mayer was unable to reach him; what worked with other employees—complaints, threats, cajolery—slid off him, leaving him inert. Despite his irritation, Mayer, shaken, finally stopped asking him to do anything. The individual became totally idle, never left the offices, slept there at night, and spent his days looking at a wall. Haunted by a desire to murder him, Mayer realized that his employee was putting his mental balance in danger. So it was he, Mayer, who moved out. He tried to sell his agency. But each time, the potential buyer refused to sign the sales contract when he understood that he would also acquire "Mr. I-Prefer-Not-To." Mayer, bankrupted, hanged himself.

One evening, in New York, I bought a drink for an old, penniless sailor. The author of novels about seafaring, he was getting drunk because the last one, like its predecessors, had had no success. As we drank, I told him the story of my friend the lawyer. How surprised I was, decades later, to discover that he had written a story about him, renaming the individual "Bartleby"! The drunk was Herman Melville, and, in the meantime, his novel *Moby Dick* had finally found a readership.

fleshiness, her pupils glistened more, her breasts had grown larger, and so had her hips. Foreign and familiar, she overwhelmed me. Words failed me.

She was simple, didn't expect overblown language—which she wouldn't have understood—and cared little about decorum: she came up to me, took my right hand, and laid it on her swollen belly. The energy that emanated from it pulsed through me. Invigorated, I smiled, slowly, deeply, and then, putting my arm around her shoulder, I guided her toward the alcove.

There, I stripped and undressed her. We lay down alongside one another, suddenly shy, and I gazed at her, exploring her with my eyes and my fingers. Our encounter felt as if it were the first. She let me do what I wanted. Nothing sexual polluted our intertwining, though I got an erection by reflex; affection, deference, wonder prevailed.

We spent the night embracing one another, but I did not penetrate her. Copulating would have deprived the moment of its sacredness. Erotic embraces have a story, with a beginning, a middle, and an end, the orgasm signaling the time for separation. On the contrary, we wanted our contact to last forever. We were looking for a kind of pleasure other than the one that distances after having united; we cultivated a slow delight, without spasms, without apexes or nadirs. To the "little death" that follows genital pleasure, we preferred the long, throbbing life of caresses.

Gaiety and sadness absorbed me, overlapping one another. Jubilant to be examining this healthy, living body, full of vigor, I realized that at dawn I would leave it. Despair gave a bitter piquancy to my happiest kisses.

Objectively, paternity wasn't new to me. Mina had conceived eight children, five of whom were born. But when Mina announced that she was pregnant, it was something that had happened to her: she got pregnant; I didn't. The event transformed her organism without affecting me; gestation seemed to me, if not an illness, at least a purely feminine reality. With Tita, I felt the contrary; I was affected, touched, concerned. Although, unlike Mina, she would keep the infant for herself and get along without me, the marvelous life that was prospering in her belly owed me its spark. If I was not a father, I felt like a progenitor.

With Mina, I had been neither a progenitor nor a father. Before the birth, I was living with a pregnant woman; afterward, I was living with a harassed woman who was nursing a baby, changing its linens, washing it, while I observed from a distance. Burial put an end to the episode, and then another began. I remained detached from what was the basis for Mina's joys and sorrows.

Never had my heart beaten this way. This child existed because it was moving in her abdomen. This child existed because I dreamed of it. From Tita's body and mine, I made images; at first, I imagined a little girl just like Tita, a little boy just like me, but I gradually managed to combine our characteristics and took delight in the new being that was going to emerge, impatient to discover what the mixture of our bloods, of our substances, of our ardors, would produce. Were these caprices of intuition? Premonitions? With Mina, I'd always been overcome by a feeling of precariousness, sensing that her frail offspring would be taken away from us; here, I sensed the opposite. This descendent, whether a girl or a boy, would, thanks to the robust vitality of its mother, win out over childhood illnesses and become a tough woman or man.

At dawn, Tita fell asleep, tired out by so much intensity, and I contemplated her face without the constant tension inflicted on it by her deaf person's eyes. It emanated nobility, balance. Why didn't I come to live indefinitely with her? Why leave? I compared her honest rigor with Noura's feline graces and wiliness. Why did I adore Noura? Tita deserved my adoration every bit as much.

Love isn't fair.

At dawn, I slipped away, too cowardly to say farewell to my Huntress, to admit to her that I would not come back or see our baby.

I wept as I left the Cavern. I wept with disgust, disappointed in myself, saddened by my behavior.

The more I appreciated Tita, the more I detested myself.

While the sky struggled to clear, I rejoined Barak and Derek, who had fallen asleep head-to-tail next to still-warm embers. I couldn't help smiling as I saw the union of these two magical beings, apparently incompatible, whose friendship seemed as extravagant as that of a bear and a heron. Though they were the same height, they differed in every other respect. Barak was voluminous, Derek long. Barak muscular, Derek scrawny. Barak had tanned skin; Derek was pallid. Whereas Barak's good health rippled in his locks, beard, and body hair, Derek's glabrous anemia left onlookers afraid a ray of sun might burn him.

I shook my uncle. He groaned, yawned, roared, stretched his limbs, flexed his biceps, and cracked his joints. When he opened his puffy eyes and recognized me, he examined the surrounding area, realized where he was, and then, seeing Derek on the ground, cried, "Two emergencies, Nephew!"

He jumped to his feet.

"First, take a piss. Second, tell you what happened."

He carried out the first of these as he was accustomed to do, accompanying his act with gurgling noises and ecstatic sighs. Then he grabbed my arm.

"Come with me; I don't want him to hear me," he whispered, pointing to Derek. "Even if he's so plastered that it'll take him all day to revive. What a drinker! The soothsayer guzzled all my wine!"

We went off where Derek couldn't hear us and sat down on the trunk of a tree that had been uprooted by the wind.

"You have to know that Derek really sucked on the wineskin last night. Drunk, incapable of controlling himself, he vomited up quite a few secrets."

"What secrets?"

"You'll never guess!"

Barak was trying to excite my curiosity, and he was succeeding. In addition to the fact that I had a ferocious desire to think about something else, I was hoping to undo the knots of the inextricable Derek.

In a hoarse voice, Barak hit me with it: "The City of the Gods doesn't exist."

"Excuse me?"

"The people of the Gap of the Gods think the gods live on the snowy peaks of the mountains, several days' journey upriver from them. Derek went there, not without difficulty, and he discovered that there are no gods up there. It's a village, an ordinary village, except that ice and snow cover it for half the year. People live there."

"What about the flowered boat that I saw passing on the river, with the god lying in it?"

"It was a sarcophagus. The villagers of the mountains don't bury their dead. Probably because they can't dig in the frozen soil . . . According to them, the dead are not reborn on earth but travel to the Land of the Dead. The living wash the body, adorn it, and place it in a roomy canoe that they close up with a cover on which they paint the features of the deceased, and then they bedeck it with flowers and let it drift away, carried along by the current."

He turned toward me.

"That's what you saw."

He contemplated the Lake before us. Nature was reawakening, with quivering branches, movements in the thickets, insects buzzing, birds chirping.

"The people of the white mountain don't know where the river goes . . . They think it's the threshold of the beyond."

He scratched his chin.

"They're not wrong, since the river flows into the Lake. And the Middle of the Lake, as is well-known, is the Land of the Beyond."

We sat there, thinking. A blackbird, piercing the foliage with its song, exulted in a powerful, limpid voice. In Barak's narrative, rather than the naïve credulity of the two villages, one of them situating the Beyond in the river, the other seeing the gods in floating coffins, I discerned above all Derek's dishonesty; he had told us nothing of this.

"If Derek knows that, why didn't he tell his people?"

Barak looked at me as if I'd lost my mind.

"You're joking! No one would believe him. Just speaking is not enough, you have to be understood."

"Derek should have forced them to pay attention to him."

"You're crazy, Nephew . . . For generations, these villagers have thought the gods paraded in front of them. They named their place the Gap of the Gods! Their pride, their singularity, you aren't going to destroy that, I hope?"

"But the truth . . ."

"What if the truth is humiliating? Do you really want to explain to them that they aren't the elect of the gods, but rather imbeciles? And their ancestors? And the ancestors of their ancestors? Are you going to tell them that they belong to a dynasty of assholes?"

"No . . ."

"Well, then, why should Derek do that?"

I bowed my head, defeated. Because I had an imperious need to incriminate Derek, I opted to take another angle.

"Derek deceived me by assuring me that the gods foresaw the Lake's fury and that a man—me—would save us by taking us somewhere else."

Barak sighed, this time with embarrassment.

"That's true."

"He was laughing at me!"

Barak raised his voice, "Noam, what's gotten into you? Derek isn't mocking you; he has backed you and supported you from the outset."

"By lying!"

"Without him, you'd never have gotten the best canoeists on the Lake to leave their village and go to yours. He didn't just help you; he made it all possible."

"By lying," I repeated, faintly.

"Yes, by lying! Because do you really imagine that the truth would move a village?"

His angry shout disconcerted me. I wouldn't have taken that from just anyone, but the fact that Barak, the most honest, frankest person I knew, accepted such scheming confused me. I suddenly feared that I was wallowing in immaturity.

"You may be right, Barak; I'll think about it."

"What really matters to you? That the Gap of the Gods' carpenters work in our village or that they find out that their ancestors were stupid fools?"

"Put that way, of course . . ."

"Then put it that way! And stop finding fault with Derek!"

We went back to the fire, which had since gone out, and Barak prepared something for us to eat while we waited for Derek to wake up. Dawn was breaking; a few storm clouds were dissipating and unveiling the sun. Gnats were dancing in the light.

"Barak, should I tell Derek that you've revealed all this to me?"

"Would that be useful?"

I reflected for a moment.

"Ultimately, Barak, you give utility priority over truth."

"When I listen to you two, Derek and you, I ask myself only one question: why? Why lie? Why reveal a lie? For the same reason, actually: the common good. That's what matters! The true . . . the false . . . I don't give a damn about truth; if it bites us and gives us rabies, let it die in its corner! I couldn't care less about lies, either; let them strut all they want, so long as they help us! Stop fooling yourself, Noam. Are you going to tell Noura that you saw Tita again at the Cavern of the Huntresses, that she is even more beautiful than before, and that she will give birth to a splendid child?"

I shivered with emotion.

"You thought so, too, Barak?"

"What?"

"That Tita is even more beautiful than before?"

"Obviously!"

"And that the child will be magnificent?"

"May my balls be chopped off if it isn't."

I gasped; tears filled my eyes; my hands trembled. Barak grabbed me by the nape of my neck and hugged my head to his chest. His male odor, like camphor or burned wood, relaxed me, calmed me, and allowed me to weep. He encouraged me, "Oh, my boy, rid yourself of simple ideas. I'm in love with Elena? Then I'll deceive her by never mentioning Malatantra. You're in love with Noura? You'll keep on bullshitting her, not only for your own good, but also for the good of both of you."

Lulled by his cavernous voice resounding in his huge thoracic cage, to which I'd pressed my ear, I let myself be consoled, even though Barak was exhorting me to grow up.

"What's true of power is also true of love. Since you're bearing the responsibility of leading people, you'll deceive them for the common good. You won't tell anyone that with Derek's help, you scared the hell out of the carpenters. You'll claim that you're only obeying the gods."

"I believed it, Barak! I believed it! I really thought I was obeying the gods."

"That's still true."

"Derek made it all up."

"In making it up, he made it real."

"The gods didn't send me!"

"Who knows? Do you trust Tibor? Do you consider him honest?"

"Yes!"

"Derek and Tibor say the same thing, one of them by making it up, the other by testifying to it. We reach the truth as much via sincerity as via mendacity."

*

The carpenters settled in with a disconcerting fluidity. Rather than lodging them among us or adding new houses to our own, I chose to place them above the village, at a decent distance. In this way, our view of the Lake and our surroundings wasn't affected, and the members of the Gap of the Gods group reconstituted an autonomous community. I imposed this location on Vlaam by pointing out the proximity of a brook and a fir forest that would provide the materials for their work.

Our villagers seldom saw the carpenters, except when the latter went down to the market or the Lake. They liked this influx, which was good for trade. Among themselves, they laughed about my choice—making boats far from the water!—but they didn't mock me. Doing so overtly might encourage strangers to invade their cherished shore.

In my view, the proximity of the shore was of no interest. We were constructing houses, not canoes. These floating dwellings would not go to the Lake; they would be useful if the Lake came to them.

After our journey, Noura's embrace almost overshadowed my duties as leader. We were so hungry for each other . . . Neither she nor I had ever suspected what we discovered: that happiness consisted in being side by side. Chatting, keeping quiet, laughing, resting, eating, sleeping, climaxing—we found everything fulfilling only if we shared it. As a result, during the day, Noura often accompanied me to see the carpenters and praise their progress.

Vlaam devoted himself assiduously to our project, to justify this cruel exile, in his eyes as well as in those of his men. At first, he drew figures in the sand; then, assisted by his men, he made models; finally, thinking that he had resolved all the problems, he put all his craftsmen to work and set about constructing the floating houses.

He and his men lived in large tents. The warm weather made this possible. He advised those who were impatient to recover a certain degree of comfort to accelerate their work so as to obtain a shelter. Authoritarian, rigorous, fair, he proved to be a magisterial leader of men; he didn't need Derek at his side to govern a community. This struck me all the more because I saw in Vlaam a profound and instinctive reticence with regard to Derek, equal to my own. When I was around him, I felt like a mistrustful brother—without suspecting the extent to which the future would prove me right . . .

For his part, Derek moved back and forth between the carpenters' village and our own. Although he was motivated by his friendship with Barak, he also tried to enter into contact with our villagers, and succeeded in doing so, despite his startling appearance—or thanks to it. Women were delighted by the silky voice that emanated from this interminable, bony body, and some men, like Barak, were determined to protect him. Quite rapidly, he won their confidence and showed himself to be beneficial, benevolent, and warm. Why would I mistrust him?

I counted on Tibor to understand him better—or to better understand me? One day, when we were collecting herbs, I asked him, "Tibor, what do you think of Derek?"

He pursed his lips.

"Lots of things," he replied.

"Derek says he communicates with the gods, and he's duping us."

"I suspect that might be true," Tibor muttered.

"Why?"

"He avoids me. A seer doesn't avoid another seer. On the contrary, we ought to exchange all our information. But he slips away. By fleeing me, he's fleeing his own imposture."

"Imposture? Would you go that far?" I exclaimed, surprised by his severity.

"What about you? How do you know that he's deceiving us?"

I told him about Barak's indiscretions, the chimerical City of the Gods, the gods' illusory prophecy regarding a savior, me.

"Did you discuss it with him?" Tibor asked.

"With Derek? No. He disturbs me."

Tibor reflected as he went on cutting nettles. "That's normal."

"Normal?"

"Yes, that physical characteristic . . . so strange . . . *that* . . . that disturbs us."

"What are you talking about?"

Tibor stared at me, speechless.

"Haven't you noticed?"

"What? His hands?"

A rare smile appeared on Tibor's lips, and he murmured, "Yes . . . his hands . . . his hands, too . . ."

"Tibor, what are you talking about?"

Driven by a different energy, he stood up, worried. "After all, it's better like that."

"What?"

"Everything," he concluded, walking away, cold, impenetrable.

Despite my impatience and annoyance, I didn't insist: Tibor responded to questions only if he had already decided what the answers were.

At first, the floating houses were small, in order to resolve problems with sharpening, gluing, sewing, then they were of average size, and now Vlaam was about to tackle the largest one.

Counting the houses and the villagers, I calculated that if the Lake became angry, we wouldn't be able to take everyone with us. Far from it. This possibility made me feel guilty. Noura, with whom I dared to discuss this, replied simply: "Draw up a list!"

"Sorry?"

"A list of priorities. Determine who should be saved first."

"But . . . but . . . that's monstrous!"

"There are, I suppose, people you're more attached to?"

"Of course, you, Mama, Barak, Tibor, my sisters, my . . ."

"Perfect. Which persons seem to you the most useful?"

"Tibor, always, Barak, Vlaam."

"Well, there you are, you've finished a list! If you want advice for a second list, I suggest you select the young, sturdy people who will survive and reproduce."

"Noura! You'd abandon our elderly?"

"They've already had their share."

"Every life counts."

"In principle, yes, but in a community, no," she protested, as precise as a knife that slices.

I couldn't tolerate the prospect of a sorting. I was responsible for all the souls in my village, without exception. The solution consisted in accelerating the construction of the floating houses in order to provide a place for everyone. Consequently, I asked Barak and a few strapping young men who had rapidly completed their work in the fields to help Vlaam by chopping down trees, stripping them of their branches, and then cutting them into beams, girders, rafters, and planks.

Moons went by, and the floating houses grew more numerous. Sometimes, I worried when I calculated that we would never be ready; sometimes, I no longer understood why we were exhausting ourselves: one day seemed like the next, one night seemed like the next, nothing changed, and the idea that a catastrophe might occur became as abstract as it was absurd.

*

Everything began with silence.

That morning, under a clear blue sky, as we were climbing

up to the carpenters' village, Tibor turned to me and exclaimed, "Do you hear that?"

"What?"

"Nothing."

Uneasy, I looked at him without comprehending. He explained, "There's nothing to hear anymore."

That was what explained my feeling of oppression! The birds had suddenly fallen silent. Their silence stunned us like a terrible din.

This unexpected muteness altered the density of the air, the sunlight, the colors of the landscape. In a visceral way, I sensed that I was in danger.

"Look!"

Tibor was pointing to the hill. Behind us, pouring out of the caverns, clouds of bats were infesting the sky, blackening it with their incoherent zigzags—bats, which usually hunted at night and slept during the day.

A snake slithered through the grass, quickly, in a hurry. Then another. Five. Ten. From all sides, blindworms, asps, garter snakes, and vipers sprang out of their hiding places and raced up the slope. Rats, voles, and fieldmice followed the reptiles, suggesting a complete reversal: the prey were pursuing their predators . . . On the path where we were talking, shiny, squat beetles gathered and began an ascent as speedy as it was awkward: the path was covered with a line of moving carapaces, in whose elytra ephemeral rainbows glimmered.

In the village, the dogs began to whine; the pigs ran about, cried out, and attacked one another, tormented by an uneasiness they did not understand. A donkey brayed. Among all the animals, aggressiveness, fear, and trembling were increasing.

Tibor lost his composure.

"It's coming."

We scrutinized the surroundings. Nothing seemed to have changed; the Lake's horizon offered up its opalescent tranquility.

"What's going on down there?"

We hurried down to the shore to find out what was happening on the water's edge, where we perceived unusual greenish, grayish movements. Fat-bellied toads with bumpy skin, spat out by the waters, were landing on the shore, bouncing and making sounds like wet sacks, like balls with feet, croaking as they ran around. At a bend where the river joined the Lake, we pondered dark swirls: fish, giving up on the dead water, were trying to swim against the current, like salmon in the spring.

Tibor took my arm.

"There's not a moment to lose, Noam! Lead them to the floating houses."

This time I didn't reassure my villagers, I rushed into the main street and shouted, "The Lake is angry! Evacuate immediately! Everyone go to the carpenters' village. Hurry!"

Faces appeared on the thresholds of the houses, flabbergasted or skeptical. Though the Lake was spread out peacefully before us, as usual, squadrons of birds were arriving from afar, geese and ducks, in close ranks, flying at top speed in flocks so compact and inflexible that it seemed they were attacking us. At the edge of the village, wild horses, galloping as if possessed, almost blindly, swept by the houses, knocked against fences, and disappeared. Obviously, the animals discerned something we didn't.

More prompt than the understanding of the danger, the fear of it spread. It contaminated us in the blink of an eye. We no longer sought reasons; we thought only of fleeing.

I rushed to my house, grabbed Noura by the hand, and raced to the home of Barak and Mama, who, without a word, followed us, and then we climbed, out of breath, the steep path that led to the carpenters' camp.

There, the alert had also been sounded: men, women, children were hurrying from one place to another, gathering up their possessions.

An old woman let out an atrocious scream. People fell silent and stopped dead.

An enormous hairy mass came barreling among us. A gigantic bear, almost black, was crossing the village, swinging its legs as far and as fast as it could. It didn't look at anyone, it didn't see anyone, it just tore along, its muzzle pointed, its eyes half-closed, panting, terrified.

The bear's panic increased our own. If the king of animals whose superior divinity we revered was running away, there was no longer any doubt: the end of the world was approaching.

And then there was . . .

At first, we thought it was the silence, the silence provoked by the bear's sudden appearance, the silence intensifying the better to make itself heard; in reality, something was wringing out the silence, twisting it, forcing it to moan, torturing it, exhausting it, something that became a sigh, a murmur, a roar, a scream. This something that killed the silence was the Wind.

The Wind leaped, belligerent, ferocious.

An unprecedented wind. An unheard-of wind. A wind that was dizzyingly violent.

There is nothing more mysterious than the wind. Where does it come from? Where does it go? Starting from the unknown, going toward the unknown, it strikes, knocks, uproots, blows down, tears apart, pulverizes. I hated the winds in general, those brusque, capricious, superfluous demons, as impossible to foresee as they are to understand, but this one seemed to me the worst.

An ice-cold hand crushed my shoulder.

Tibor, standing behind me, his face livid, his eyes open wide, pointed to the Lake with his chin.

A giant wave, higher than a mountain, emerged from the gaping horizon and rushed toward us, resolved to engulf us.

2

The Wave moved forward, furious, regular, inexorable.

Death was about to befall us; I was sure of it, even as, along with the others, I tried to organize our salvation. Running to find a sack, flasks, piling up blankets, gathering provisions—all of these things frightened me less than waiting, motionless, open-mouthed, eyes rolled back, until I was eliminated. To avoid yielding to terror, I yielded to movement. Lacking the courage of despair, I thought it better to run myself ragged than to be petrified by fear.

As long as the Wave was perceptible only to our eyes, we somehow shared the illusion that we could escape a bad dream; when it attacked our ears, its din prefigured the violence that would stun us. First the booming, the rumbling grew, weighed down with blasts, vibrations, detonations, explosions; then it transformed into countless mixed, continuous thunderclaps, relentless, implacable.

Most of the villagers fled. Like the animals, they ran away from the Wave, trying to reach a high point in the valleys. This reflex doomed them. They would never be able to run fast enough, or far enough, or high enough.

"Here! Come back!"

I shouted myself hoarse to get them to turn, but they persevered, not listening to me, no longer hearing me.

Shall I admit it? By the look in Noura's eyes, I realized that the problem that had been tormenting me for moons—who to put in the floating houses when we were running out of room—had been resolved.

"To the shelter!" she yelled, her voice composed.

Noura astonished me. She was usually frightened by the tiniest inconveniences—a spider, a toad, a snag in the fabric of a dress—but that morning, she faced up to the tragedy boldly, as if she knew little fears but not the great one, as if she cultivated fear as a pleasure, as a game to lend spice to everyday life and then cast it off in the presence of real peril. A daughter worthy of Tibor, she remained energetic, concentrated, effective, and completely unaffected by any terrors preying on her mind. Pulling Mama along as Barak loaded sacks on his shoulders, she ordered my sisters to stay close to us. We rushed toward the floating house where Vlaam, his wife, and his sons had already taken shelter.

Constructed in the middle of the forest that had provided the trunks, the vessel measured a hundred and twenty feet long and twenty feet wide. Unlike our houses consisting of a single room, it had many separate rooms, small ones that could hold two people, medium-sized ones that served as storerooms, and the big one, which was for the animals. Although we had brought in fodder for them, the herds were still grazing in the neighboring pastures.

Barak popped up, goats squirming under his arms.

"Tie them up. I'll go get the sheep."

"Barak, we don't have time!"

"What do you know?" he retorted as he went out again.

Around the partitioned areas there was a wooden deck, which was itself surrounded by lashed-on decks. Under the cabin, Vlaam had built a giant, bulbous hold which would, he said, guarantee more buoyancy.

The danger was approaching. We could now clearly see the green crest of the Wave.

Noura suddenly appeared behind me.

"Where's Papa?"

I paled.

"Tibor!"

I bellowed his name over and over, hoping each time that

he would show up. Worry distorted Noura's face; she lost her composure.

"He went back to gather his things down there," she exclaimed.

"Madness! He'll never be able . . ."

I interrupted myself, ashamed to be alarming Noura instead of calming her. Her anxiety increasing tenfold, she began to tremble. I was about to leave the houseboat to look for Tibor, but Noura held me back.

"No! Not you!"

Her eyes filled with tears, which annoyed her, and hiding her emotion, she paced up and down the deck calling out to her father in all directions: "Papa! Papa!"

Nothing hurt me so much as the distress of the woman I loved. My powerlessness humiliated me more with regard to her than with regard to wrathful Nature. I should have been comforting her. Wasn't it my mission to ensure her happiness?

The catastrophe charged on. As high as a mountain, the Wave advanced unimpeded across the surface of the Lake; where it crashed into the shores, it brutally destroyed every obstacle in its path, slapping against the rocks, submerging forests whose treetops stood tall for an instant, then bent down like blades of grass.

Barak came out of the sheepfold and roared, "Where's Derek?"

I hadn't thought of him, even though he was part of our group.

"There!" Mama cried.

She pointed to the top of a nearby fir tree that Derek had climbed. Clinging to the trunk, tense, even paler than usual, he was keeping his eyes closed, convinced that not seeing the risk would eliminate it.

"Come down from there," Barak thundered.

Terrified, Derek didn't react.

Noura spoke to me again, "What about Papa?"

I turned back toward the Lake. I remained speechless, dumbfounded. I no longer had the strength to move the slightest muscle, even those in my lips. I understood what was going to happen: the Wave, a colossal beast full of claws and jaws that crushed, fractured, and ground up, would kill us with one blow, and then its waters would swallow us. Our vessel would serve no purpose, would not come back to the surface, would never float; long before, it would be wrecked, torn apart, destroyed by the crushing Wave; nothing but smithereens would remain.

Noura spoke sharply: "Noam!"

Pulling me out of my torpor, she pointed to someone climbing the path below us. The dark color of the man's cloak suggested that it was Tibor.

"Papa!"

A curious mental detour! Instead of waiting for the Wave, that is, for death, we were waiting for Tibor. We had shifted the danger. Tibor's late arrival eclipsed the prospect of our destruction. Blessed details! We no longer wondered whether the vessel would survive the Wave; we wondered whether Tibor would succeed in boarding it.

This time, I didn't hesitate: I rushed to meet him, took the bags that were slowing him down, and then returned in haste, with him hot on my heels.

Once he was on deck, Tibor, relieved, felt the bags that I was putting on the wooden floor. "I saved my main herbs and potions, as well as my tools. They'll be useful."

Noura was also delighted; abandoning her reserve, she hugged her father, caressed his hair. I was overcome by gloom: they thought they had won, but they would die in a few moments.

Barak continued to exhort Derek to move. But all he could get Derek, who was green with terror, to do, was open his eyes and shake his head to signal that he wouldn't budge.

In front of us, the ineluctable was about to happen. The great, supreme Wave was reaching our village. Clearly, it was going to ravage us. There was no reason to think the water would run under the vessel and lift it up: it would strike us head-on and pulverize us.

Everyone was screaming.

There was nothing left to do. We were merely witnesses of the disaster. We were waiting for the crash, the moment when we would fly to pieces. The end would provide us with deliverance.

When it fell on our village, the Wave encountered obstacles. The geography of the site opposed it. On its two rolling sides, the Wave ran against hard, protruding surfaces, which led to collisions, waves flowing in opposite directions; from the left, another wave came to crash against it, and the same happened from the right. The waves diffracted and smashed into each other. We watched, powerless, deafened, the struggle of these enormous masses that were colliding, becoming higher with each collision, then heavily falling, one after the other. The conflict was taking on colossal proportions. The rollers were tearing each other apart.

A lateral eddy invaded our clearing, turned inside it, and, with a terrible grinding roar, struck our vessel, shook it, and raised it up . . .

We were not torn apart; we were lifted on the crest of the maelstrom, even if at every moment suspicious cracking sounds indicated that our vessel would soon break up.

As we spun about, we passed near the tree where Derek had taken refuge.

"Jump!"

Barak opened his arms to the soothsayer. Derek, stimulated by this gesture, let go of the trunk to which he was clinging and threw himself into the void.

Barak caught him on his chest and laughed, happy amid the raging elements and shouting in his stentorian voice: "Look at this strange bird I've dug up!"

Hardly had he said this than Derek fainted, as if dismembered. Barak took him into the hold, stretched him out on a bed, and tied him down so that his body would not roll around or strike things when our vessel swerved.

The Wave went on its way, terrifying, untamed, and now we

were part of it. Around us, gusts of wind blew up cones of foam, and the waves raged.

Although it was constantly in danger of breaking up, our vessel was floating. No matter how great and constant our fear of being engulfed was, we were floating. We had found a temporary place in this chaos, among the unfinished, the vibrating, the vague and confused.

Four houseboats of a smaller size were escorting us. They could not be steered, choose a direction, or stay in one place, but they were floating, bobbing on the surface, lively and gay. We were warding off oblivion! Instead of thinking about the many deceased, shredded, dismembered, lacerated, under the Wave, I took pleasure in thinking about the survivors. We made a few signals to one another, giving us the feeling of leaving on a journey together.

But we hadn't taken into account the vehemence of the Wind and the Wave. They engaged in a ferocious, unremitting duel, of which we became the victims. They competed to see which could torture us better: the Wave, by tossing us from the heights to the depths, from peaks to troughs, or the Wind, irritated by the wall that the Wave created to block it, by opening hostilities with what it carried, whistling, manhandling, banging, jumping from shrill complaint to warning, from bellowing anger to an attempt to sweep away our roof, our shutters, our planking, ourselves. Nothing stopped these two furies.

I ordered Tibor, the women, and the children to take shelter inside the hull. Noura refused. I insisted. "There aren't enough ropes to tie you down! Only Barak, Vlaam, and I will stay on deck."

Noura tolerated my order to set an example, to respect my authority in public, but I was nonetheless very aware that since she had to endure this, she preferred, as I did, to observe what was happening to her.

Wind and Wave were each more aggressive than the other. As

soon as one danger spared us, another attacked. When we rose as high as a hundred feet, propelled by the Wave, the Wind sent us flying from the crest. When we came down again, plunging head-first into the void, afraid the boat would break up and then surprised to find ourselves still whole, after each looming mass of water, powerful gusts immediately tried to sweep us off the deck. As soon as the water gave up trying to tear our vessel apart, the Wind looked for ways to flatten it.

The four other skiffs gradually disappeared. Their lightness had transformed them into easy prey, projectiles that soared in the sky and whose return proved fatal. The Wave and the Wind quickly managed to finish them off. Our vessel, though, was resisting.

For how much longer?

We were hastening toward the abyss, tossed about by the frenetic turbidity, the madness of the flow, the fever in the air. We were rushing onward, without direction, without visibility, without being certain of anything except the worst.

"No!" moaned Barak, as he pointed to the strip of land toward which the Wave was carrying us.

I didn't understand what he was pointing out to me.

He explained, in a strangled voice: "The Cavern of the Huntresses."

The Wave was rushing with dizzying speed toward the cliff of pink-colored rocks within which I had spent such splendid nights.

Would it avoid it or smash into it?

We slid rapidly toward the rock wall. Its roughness grew more apparent, frightening. The wave carrying us along was aiming at it. There was no way to slow down, to avoid the cliff. The rock grew larger, waiting for us to strike it.

A gust of wind pushed our vessel to one side, a swell lifted us up, and the cliff receded, disappearing. The anarchic battle between the Wave and the Wind allowed us to evade it.

Then I witnessed the scene whose memory has haunted me for centuries.

Along the path that ran along the summit of the escarpment, a horse was galloping wildly, a woman riding astride it. The horse's mane and the woman's hair streamed behind them in the wind. I sensed that fear was tensing the powerful muscles of the horse and its rider.

Suddenly, the woman turned her head to see the Wave coming toward her.

My heart shuddered in my breast. I screamed, "Tita!"

She continued her desperate flight, spurring the animal forward with her shins. How could she have heard me, the deaf-mute Huntress?

Her relentless determination to cleave the air combined the sublime and the ridiculous. She would not escape the Wave that would devour her, but she did not accept her defeat; she would fight to the end, fierce, superb, untamable.

Looking carefully, I could see that Tita was holding something between the horse's back and her belly: she was fleeing to protect her child.

One last time, she turned back toward the Wave that was about to engulf her. Did she see me? Today, as I write these lines, I remain convinced that she did. That determined her act. If not, it would have been pure madness. Yes, she saw me! A lightning bolt shot through her terrorized eyes; she recognized me and felt a fleeting return of hope. Otherwise, how can we explain that she seized the child and suddenly, with superhuman strength, threw it as high as she could in the direction of our ship?

She didn't have time to follow its trajectory, to make sure I caught the flying child; the Wave was upon her, carrying her off into its tumultuous depths.

I looked at the infant in my hands.

It wasn't crying. It opened its sweet eyes wide, unaware of the surrounding cruelty.

I smiled at it. It returned my smile. That was how I made the acquaintance of my son . . .

What happened? Everything broke inside me. Though I had valiantly overcome violence of all kinds, the trusting face of the baby overwhelmed me. My strength exhausted, I collapsed.

Then the sky closed up, and everything sank into darkness.

*

No moon. No stars.

An opaque world. Black overhead. Black below.

And the Wind, the Wave, the din, the speed . . .

I don't know what is more terrifying, the danger you see or the danger you don't. On the one hand, darkness amplified the noises and shocks to frightening proportions, transforming a rustle into a roar, a jolt into an explosion; on the other, it offered respite for the sense of sight that the day had monopolized, harried, saturated.

We were drifting on at random. Bobbing on an unstable element.

Barak had taken the child and put it in the safety of the cabin, followed by Vlaam, who rejoined his family.

I remained alone with the spindrift, shaken. Tita's sacrificial devotion opened up unknown doors within me: it showed me my path. While nothing mattered anymore in this apocalyptic chaos, Tita had held her head high, flaunted her refusal, proudly asserted her dignity, employed all her strength in a single mission: to save the child. Up to that fatal moment, she had thought only of her duty, indifferent to her personal destiny, feeling no anxiety about her end, only worry for her son. I was certain that relief had won out over every other feeling when she entrusted this young life to me, just before being swallowed up by the murderous waters.

By killing Tita, the Wave had made her greater. If Tita was

dead in this world, she remained more alive and intense than ever in me. A single life would not suffice for me to carry on her light and devote myself to her son.

To our son . . .

How could I tell Noura? Barak was going to recommend that I lie—according to him, that was the solution to all complications—but I wouldn't tarnish Tita's memory by deception; she deserved for me to hold out our child and announce, "This is my son; I'll take care of him forever." I owed it to her. If I didn't do that, reduced to the status of a temporary lover, I would be no more than a transitory father, as well. Not an option. Both the gravity of the situation and Tita's honor demanded that the truth be told. Noura would understand. Moreover, wouldn't I be demeaning her, too, if I thought her incapable of understanding?

I untied the rope that attached me to the deck and slipped into the hold. I had hardly entered when Barak's robust hand grabbed me.

"Come with me," he murmured.

I followed him to Derek's room. He let me in and went away; the room was too small for all three of us—or rather, all four, since Derek was rocking the baby, who was asleep on his lap.

A flickering oil lamp allowed me to contemplate the child's sweet golden face, to admire the length of his eyelashes, to delight in his minuscule nostrils, his ears fringed with curls, his soft, moist mouth.

Derek pointed to him.

"Is he your son?"

Despite my emotion, I pretended to be surprised, not wanting to share any secrets with him.

"Why do you ask that?"

Derek scrutinized me at length, then concluded, "You're not answering, so he's your son."

Though I was annoyed, I kept my tone casual, "Oh? A woman on horseback threw him to us at the last minute, that's all."

He corrected me: "Threw him to *you*, according to Barak."

"What difference does that make?"

Derek grimaced and said in his reedy voice, "I'm disappointed, Noam: you don't trust me."

He was so on target that I exaggerated my denial. "Not at all! But when you create a tie that doesn't exist between this child and me, I deny it. Nothing more. No mistrust with regard to you."

Derek bent over the baby, delicately took his hand without disturbing his slumber.

"Look, Noam. You've transmitted your mark to him."

He showed me the baby's fingers. I shivered. He had two fingers stuck together. My grandfather Kaddour also had this rare characteristic. My father Pannoam did, too. And I had it. In our family, we saw it as the mark of the eldest sons. The skin enveloped the middle finger and the ring finger.

"This little detail will keep you from lying to me again," Derek declared.

My back against the wall, I bent my head, defeated.

"Derek," I begged him, "Noura can't find out about this."

He smiled, gratified that I had confessed, delighted that I was imploring him. I went on. "I slept with a Huntress during my exile, when I thought I was separated from Noura forever."

"I have no problem with that," he said, dismissively. "But Noura won't miss this physical abnormality! Her eyes are everywhere; she forgot how to be an airhead. She'll guess, she'll accuse you, and she won't forgive you."

I bit my lip, certain that his prediction was correct. Panicked, I examined the child's hands more closely.

"Can't this be camouflaged? Put a bandage on him . . . or a glove . . . or . . ."

Derek held up his hands encased in mittens and shook them in front of me.

"Something like this?" He snickered. "Funny! You're copying my mother . . ."

"Excuse me?"

"My mother tried to wrap up my hands as soon as I was born. She was hoping to hide her infidelity from her husband."

He slowly removed his mittens, and I found that he had the same abnormality I did.

I thought I must be seeing things. Apart from my father and grandfather, I'd never met a man with joined fingers. As I examined his peculiarity, the left corners of his lips twitched into a smirk. My disarray amused him.

"Oh, ho! Noam is beginning to suspect the thing that eluded him . . . Personally, I've known about it longer than you have."

"Known about what?"

He pointed to his fingers, mine, and my son's.

"About that!"

Stupor prevented me from formulating hypotheses; I could no longer think straight. I mumbled humbly, "Explain it to me, Derek."

Something was crashing into the ship. A mountain of foam burst onto the deck, the beams creaked, the planks moaned. Then our mad scud continued.

Derek slipped his mittens back onto his hands and leaned toward me.

"Not now, Noam; we don't have time, the walls have ears, let's keep explanations for later. However, I have a suggestion."

Then he whispered in my ear, "This child belongs to me."

Reflexively, I drew back, shocked.

"What?"

"For your peace of mind, Noura's, the child's, and the passengers', let's claim I conceived him with a woman and just miraculously got him back. Barak will be overjoyed to tell people about the rescue he witnessed."

His proposal displeased me. Could I refuse? It guaranteed that I could keep both the child and Noura's love; it would spare me countless pitfalls.

Before accepting, I felt the need to sink my teeth in a little. "You really thread your way between lies and truths, don't you, Derek?"

He changed color, froze. "What are you talking about?"

"The City of the Gods where no god lives."

He sighed and shrugged. "Oh, that . . ."

Seeing that he had no scruples, I added, "You led me to believe the gods were sending me."

His eyes shone with malice. He exclaimed, "The biggest problem is not that I said that, but that you believed it . . ."

His cruelty disconcerted me. He filled the ensuing silence by caressing the child. As soon as I gathered my wits, I wanted to be done with this tortuous exchange.

"You deceived me; you could at least say you're sorry."

"My expedients served your interests, didn't they?"

"What?"

"Thanks to them, we're here, alive, not dead underwater with the others."

He was right. I didn't respond. He took advantage of my silence to strike a final blow.

"Should I repent, Noam, that I made our survival possible? Should I be sorry I helped you save us?"

He was putting me in an awkward position. Like my father, he was good at reversing situations to his own advantage. He laid his hand on my shoulder, almost warmly.

"Noam, if you react badly to these little deceits, how can I reveal the others to you?"

"The others?"

"The lies still between us."

"Between us?"

"Everything I haven't told you."

"What are you hiding from me?"

"So many things . . ."

"Reveal them to me."

He stared at me gravely.

"As soon as you're capable of understanding them. Not before."

Without giving me time to protest, he swept up the child and said curtly, "This is my son?"

I reluctantly acquiesced. He kissed the babe's cheeks, nibbled on his nose.

"You're going to wake up in your father's arms, my boy."

The tenderness Derek showed him tore my son away from me more than our ruse did. Trying to calm myself, I stood up.

Derek asked, "What was her name?"

"Who?"

Derek urged me to speak more quietly. Despite the ambient roar, our words might be overheard. He whispered, "My wife."

I couldn't stand that he was drawing my secrets out of me, one after another—and even less that he was appropriating the Huntress.

"Your wife?" I repeated, stubbornly.

"The mother of my child."

Despite his angelic face, he was taking pleasure in annoying me, I was sure of that.

"Tita!"

I withdrew, uncomfortable, convinced that I had betrayed Tita once again. Hardly was I on deck before I turned around and hurried back to Derek.

"By the way, we named him Cham."

"Cham? Ah, already . . ." he mumbled, disappointed.

I'd guessed rightly: Derek wanted to name my son himself. I repeated, "Yes, Cham. Tita really insisted on it. He'll answer to it, you'll see. Let's keep it, in her memory. After all, she was your wife, the mother of your child, Derek . . ."

He stammered, caught in the trap, not knowing that even if Tita had raised her son, she would never have uttered his name.

When dawn broke and we saw again what was overwhelming us, we worried even more. Thousands of thick, gloomy clouds darkened the sky and churned along the horizon at a rapid pace.* Raising furious walls of water, the Wave and the Wind pursued their frenzied battle. They collided, pierced, lacerated, intensified, slammed, spewed, and lashed out at one another. Under their assaults, our vessel was constantly being damaged. Noises prefigured its breakup.

A greenish pallor had spread over the passengers' faces. They were all vomiting. Their anxiety was accompanied by nausea, vertigo, and muscle spasms. No one had experience with navigation, and still less with storms, especially since we didn't even know the sea or ocean existed—we knew only the Lake.

I confess that even though I was the head of the village, I didn't immediately establish myself as the master of our vessel. Like everyone else, I was bewildered, sweating, shivering, suffocating,

---

* It took a long time for humans to discover the faraway! If one of the most recent disciplines, meteorology, took millennia to be born, that's because it presupposed two breaking points.

First of all, an intellectual revolution: we had to stop interpreting phenomena rather than measuring them. Whereas Galileo, the founder of the modern approach, used mathematics to analyze and synthesize falling bodies, two of his students made it possible to understand the climate by creating measuring instruments. Castelli invented the rain gauge in 1639, and Torricelli invented the barometer in 1643.

Second, there was a regional break: choosing to think that what is happening here depends on an elsewhere. This was the end of a view that took the observer as the center and the goal. Meteorology forbade us from maintaining that *here* is the center and *elsewhere* the periphery. There is no longer a center. Everything derives from everything. The distant conditions the close. That was what people found difficult to believe, even if, today, the smallest image sent by a satellite convinces even the most obtuse holdouts.

It was necessary to abolish not only the boundaries of narcissism, but also those of nations. Scientists like Alexander von Humboldt, a polyglot and world traveler whom I met on several occasions in the nineteenth century, broke out of the local and pointed to the planetary dimension. Humboldt thought we lived in the "depths of an ocean of air." In his wake, representatives of ten countries met in Brussels in 1854 to draw up universal systems of measurement and to consider the possibility of sharing information, which led in 1873 to the founding of the International Meteorological Organization in Vienna, which was later incorporated into the UN. Distance continues to humiliate our feeling of our own importance.

throwing up. Sometimes, paralyzed with cramps, I could no longer stand. When I managed to do so, I was so dizzy that I fell down again. So I proved myself incapable of stopping those who, to put an end to their pain and fear, jumped overboard right in front of us. Psychologically, I had no influence over them; physically, I couldn't stop them—and for that matter, would they have even heard me over the commotion? Abida, my younger sister, her husband, and one of Vlaam's sons disappeared before our eyes.

I wasn't dismayed. I even think that, in the moment, I envied them . . .

Three people escaped the general malaise: Tibor, Noura, and Barak.

Tibor reeled and staggered, to be sure, but that hardly affected him. "Fascinating!" he cried that morning. Since I remained speechless, he explained to me that our adventure would give him an opportunity to do research. "For a new illness, a new remedy!" He advised us, after conducting a few experiments, not to lie down flat: being horizontal accentuated the body's disarray by amplifying the vessel's movements; it was better to remain seated, holding one's head up, or to stand, looking into the distance. Then he suggested that we use a procedure he had formerly prescribed for pregnant women: massaging the inside of the wrist, at a distance of three fingers from the palm, where the skin becomes softer, supported by internal ligaments. I quickly noted that my seasickness abated.*

Noura recovered her matchless reflexes and acted like a healer's daughter. Moving from patient to patient, she distributed mint to be chewed to fight nausea and designated the point on everyone's wrist that was to be regularly massaged. Since the

---

* How surprised I was, centuries later, to learn that Chinese and Japanese medicine advised Tibor's method! According to the system of acupuncture, this is point P6, between the wrist and the elbow, covered by two tendons that run along the inside of the forearm. The pression of the fingers—acupressure according to the Chinese, *do-in* according to the Japanese—particularly affects this point. A five-minute circular massage with the fingernail or the tip of the finger relieves nausea.

passengers found it hard to concentrate, she circled this point on the skin, using a vegetable dye. She took the opportunity to mark a second point, under the collarbone where it joins the arm: pressing this point gave a feeling of well-being.[†]

As for Barak, though he was subjected to the pitching and tossing, he moved about quickly, vigorously, at ease despite his stag's-bone leg, repairing the ship joints that were threatening to break as he went.

Amid this tumult, the Huntress's child attracted no one's attention, which removed a thorn from my side. I had informed Barak about the fable that Derek and I would tell people who asked questions, and my uncle firmly approved of it. On the other hand, the revelation of Derek's physical peculiarity intrigued him.

"How is it possible that he has two fingers joined together? That has distinguished the eldest children in our family for generations. Let's consult Tibor."

He arranged things so that we—the healer, he, and I—could be alone for a moment.

Afraid that Tibor might speak with Noura, I acted prudently: I told him that the preceding day, Derek had recovered his son Cham in a miraculous rescue.

"His son?" Tibor repeated.

"The son he had with a Huntress."

"Did he tell you that?"

"Yes."

---

† Tibor often resorted to these markings on the skin, because few people in our period knew anything about anatomy. So he practiced therapeutic tattooing. This technique, along with others, was later abandoned and then forgotten, particularly since those who might have been able to testify to it on their limbs had returned to dust. In 1991, an individual was discovered in Italy who had been preserved in ice for 5,000 years. Found in the Ötztal Alps in South Tyrol, he was named Ötzi. His body bore paintings that were at first thought to be ritual or ornamental. It took the persistence of open-minded researchers to notice that these drawings marked the acupuncture points of several meridians to the millimeter. A modern autopsy showed that Ötzi suffered from pains in the lumbar area and in his knees: crosses and dashes indicated the points where intervention would ease lumbar and knee pain.

"He's got some nerve!" Tibor cried.

Seeing his suspicion, I felt my secret was in danger. "It's beyond the shadow of a doubt: his son has the same characteristic he does."

"What?"

"His third and fourth fingers are connected."

Tibor paused and stared at me. "Like yours."

"Nothing to do with me."

Tibor looked at me for a long time, then reluctantly muttered, "Is that right?"

He didn't believe me. What did he know? How had he figured out the relation between Cham and me?

His features tensed; his skin took on a waxy consistency. He focused his eyes on me and reprimanded me: "Choose, Noam. Who are you talking to? To Tibor or to Noura's father?"

I paled. He continued, severe, "To Tibor, you can tell the truth. To Noura's father, you can't."

He grabbed me by the arm. "It's Tibor who's listening to you now. Noura's father is busy somewhere else."

I took his hands in mine.

"Thank you for freeing me. You're a better man than I, Tibor; you don't deserve to be misled. I conceived that child after I left the village, back when Noura was married to my father. Did I not have the right to do that?"

"Of course. But Noura won't forgive you for it. She wants to be everything to you. You're everything to her."

I acquiesced and murmured, "That's why we made up that story, Derek and I. Cham becomes his son."

"Do you find that credible?"

"Yes."

Tibor turned to Barak. "Do you?"

Barak blushed, fluctuating, waving his hands in the air. "Derek isn't a womanizer; that doesn't interest him. What did he say to you, Noam, every time he had the opportunity to get off?"

"'I prefer not to.'"

Barak ruminated on the mysterious formula. "'I prefer not to.' What an unusual man, this Derek! But to claim on those grounds that he's never touched a woman . . . let's not exaggerate!"

Tibor stood up, wringing out his cloak. "If that seems plausible to you, I won't say anything."

We looked at him, perplexed.

"You won't say anything . . . about what?"

Tibor's eyebrows twitched. "Anything."

He had clammed up. Pointless to press him. Nevertheless, I asked again, "Why does Derek have our characteristic, the joined fingers?"

"Ask him. The reason is surely at the root of all his misfortunes."

"His misfortunes?" Barak exclaimed.

"Yes."

"Do you consider Derek an unfortunate man?" I asked, astonished in my turn.

"A very unfortunate man, without a doubt! The poor fellow. . . ."

Barak and I exchanged a puzzled look. We thought Derek was bizarre, different, but in no way to be pitied.

"A very greatly unfortunate man," Tibor confirmed. "One reason I'm so wary of him . . ."

And he left.

Even if we were throwing up, we had to eat. Helped by Noura, I undertook to inventory the food we were carrying. This operation took time. Each person had provisions and considered them to be for themselves and their families alone, without any thought of adding them to a collective stock.

I fought to persuade people to pool our resources, to convince them that we would be stronger together than in groups of one or two. I expressed sorrow for those who refused to share: "Oh, that's all you have! That's too bad . . . when you compare it with the others . . . Well, good luck," and that led them to fear they would be denied access to the abundance.

Once everything was collected in one room, I established surveillance: Vlaam and Barak took turns guarding the door.

In reality, Noura and I felt a kind of shame. By dangling the collection of goods before their eyes, and then organizing the defense of the larder as if it were a monumental treasure, we lent credibility to the idea that our reserves would take us far. But we hadn't stockpiled much. Moreover, to parcel it out successfully, we would've had to know how many days it needed to last. Two? Ten? Forty? After forty days, we'd already be dead . . .

Given our doubts, the rationing changed its objective: start starving today so as to keep starving as long as possible.

"Provided that the Lake calms down," Noura said, a note of pleading in her voice.

"And that it goes down again," I added.

What we still hadn't foreseen was a serious shortage: water.

We were surrounded by it; it flowed under our feet, splashed over our heads, beat against our chests with every wave that washed over the deck; how could we have suspected that there might not be enough?

When we were hit by the spray, when we licked our lips, we discovered in the droplets a strange new flavor. We concluded that it came from the foam. The water, having been beaten, was degraded. The blows, slams, reversals, and mixtures tainted it, giving it this bitter, briny flavor. This same water, once it was calm, would recover the taste of the Lake . . . We knew only the water from the sky, the rivers, a sweet, pure, crystalline water that we'd been drinking since time immemorial. That there might be another kind, cloudy, salty water that might make us sick if we drank it, never occurred to us.

A second night fell upon us.

*

Violence is usually transitory. It's connected with a crisis. If it goes on for too long, death cuts it short. By obliterating everything, death puts an end, if not to violence, at least to the suffering that results from it. Ultimately, death is a tool in the arsenal of happiness, survival in that of torture.

Our storm went on and on . . . The alternation of liquid crests and troughs exhausted us. We wished our boat would break apart once and for all rather than continue to endure these confounded ups and downs. How many silences broken! How many respites immediately canceled out! How many lulls violated! False hopes wore us out. Total despair seemed enviable.

For days and nights, we had thunder both above and below us. Our senses were dulled by it. Our bellies cried famine and then rejected the small amount of food we gave them.

Mama, drained, no longer left her cubby. Only Barak was allowed in. As for Noura, she turned out to be a better leader's wife than I was a leader. Indefatigable, constantly available, she cared for everyone, listened to their grievances, tried to help. In the evenings, she joined me in our bed, and we made love ferociously and intensely, stimulated each time by the idea that it might be the last.

Derek, after sweating it out for a while, had returned to social life and talked at length with the passengers. With his child Cham in his bandaged hands, he gained an ascendancy over them. The hypnotic power of his voice calmed people, and he proposed reassuring religious activities: praying, singing, making offerings to the Lake.

Although I was suspicious and only too aware that Derek was proving to be a virtuoso of the fable, I refused to assess the extent to which his spiritual affirmations were well-founded. I let him intervene because he calmed and reinvigorated the group. As long as he comforted people, it mattered little that he was lying, that he was making it all up! Occupying the sickly weaklings we had become, he gave us goals, tasks—reciting this poem, chanting that hymn, throwing this or that object into the water—and persuaded us that we were intervening in our fragile, endangered destinies, shadowed by nothingness.

Although we had not discussed the subject, Vlaam shared my opinion. In contrast, Tibor observed this ascendancy with a disapproving eye.

"What an impostor!" he grumbled one evening.

"You provide relief for bodies, Tibor. Derek relieves minds."

"I don't relieve bodies by administering just anything to them. But he relieves minds by telling them just any old nonsense."

"Minds are more easily influenced than bodies . . ."

"More manipulable!" he replied, outraged. I found it difficult to decipher Tibor's behavior toward Derek. On the one hand, he pitied "that poor, unfortunate man," and on the other he couldn't bear to see or hear him. When I asked him to explain, he retorted, "Let's not talk about Derek anymore. He's a necessary evil."

To me, the way he doted on the child and consoled the villagers seemed a necessary good.

*

Suddenly, everything stopped.

The Wind dissipated, the Wave petered out, the noises sank into the waters.

This calm frightened us. It marked a sudden end. We'd have been less afraid had the wildness gradually lessened; yes, we would've gotten used to seeing it off, measuring it, encouraging its retreat. The abrupt end of hostilities made us fear a ruse: a supreme, definitive blow waiting in ambush for us behind this unexpected respite.

I went out on deck, cautiously.

It was dawn. The bright sun, reflected by the waves, dazzled me. Blinking, my eyes slowly adjusted to the flood of light, as aerial as it was liquid.

Around me, the waves had died down. In the exhausted sky, rinsed by the Wind, there were no clouds. No bird was singing or slashing through the blue. The silence seemed virgin, timid.

A soft, ambient lapping had replaced the din of the foaming downpour. I recognized the Lake that I'd known before, slightly more unsettled and throbbing, but without animosity.

Appeased, the heart of the world was catching its breath.

In unison with the physical lull, I felt a spiritual lull. Gods and spirits were no longer fighting with each other, Wave and Wind had died down, the sun was shining, the Lake resumed its dreamy life. The retreat of the aggressions provided me with a dense feeling of well-being, not joy—there was no sparkling inside me, or singing, or dancing—just a profound gratitude, a miraculous comfort.

Sometimes convalescence doesn't offer a return to normality, but rather the crossing of a milestone: the illness teaches; we escape from it more mature. That morning, I didn't just return to life, I re-learned it, I rediscovered it, I discerned its unsuspected riches.

Noura joined me, and, holding hands, we contemplated the panorama.

Water everywhere. An infinite expanse of water. Nothing but horizons. A circular horizon. Was the whole world submerged?

No more questions, please! A little happiness.

For the moment, Noura and I relished the crazy privilege of being alive, absorbing air, sunlight, the expanse, the warmth, the peace. Nonetheless, we divined that behind every delight lurked uneasiness—Would we someday walk on land again? When? Would we eat? Would the ship hold up?—but we put off worrying until later. Nourished by the quiet of the elements, we savored a first victory before engaging in new battles.

"I love you, Noam." She laid her head on my shoulder. "That's why I never panicked. I knew we would be okay."

Noura moved me deeply; she seldom expressed her feelings

so openly. I tried to answer her. I couldn't. Unlike her, and despite my love, I'd experienced fear, consternation, despair. I was receiving the confirmation of what I'd always supposed: Noura was stronger than I was.

"If the waters recede, we'll rebuild the world," she added. "And I want you to build this world in your image: just and straightforward, without lies."

I trembled. Noura idealized me with a passion. She was far from imagining how many concessions I'd already accepted, as a leader, as a husband.

Inside the ship, Cham was crying with hunger.

"Listen to the song of dawn," she said, smiling.

I closed my eyes, afraid she might perceive my dread. Lasciviously, she relaxed completely in my arms.

"Soon, our child will be the one babbling."

With a lump in my throat, I failed to say even a word. Several thoughts were running through my head in disorder: Oh, please don't let her suspect anything! Why isn't she getting pregnant?

Reality, that bully, drove away my happiness.

Little by little, the survivors came up to the deck and took in the situation. They didn't feel the intoxication that had initially numbed us, Noura and me; they looked around, defiant.

"Where's the land?" Vlaam asked.

"Will we be able to hold out long with our food supplies?" Tibor worried.

"The ship's in terrible shape!" Barak noted.

Mama extricated herself from the hold, and I thought I was hallucinating: her hair, now white as snow, had lost its shining chestnut color. She came toward us carefully, blinded by the sun, trying to gain her balance. At the sight of our astonishment, she sensed that something was off.

"What?"

Reflexively, she swept her long braids forward and saw her accelerated whitening. She squeaked, "Barak!"

He rushed toward her.

"Barak! What's happening to me?"

The colossus hugged her affectionately against his breast. "It happened the first night, my love. It suits you."

"What?" she stammered.

"It softens you. You're cute now. Actually, you look like yourself more than you did before."

"I look like myself?"

Beyond the lover's conviction, I saw the truth in what Barak was saying: before, Mama was beautiful; now she was cute. A softness tempered the sharp edges of her features, flirtiness replaced insolence, charm took over for authority, and the subtlety of her multiple tiny wrinkles reflected the delicacy of her soul, a wounded, experienced, valiant soul. The difference between the cute and the beautiful is the difference between a face that has endured defeats and one that is preparing to confront them.

"Let's thank the gods for having been pacified," trumpeted Derek. "Let us kneel down, put the palms of our hands flat on our heads, and give thanks."

Tibor shot me a glance that said: "He's at it again!" I pretended not to notice and got down on my knees like the others.

Derek hammered home abstruse formulas—had they been clear, they wouldn't have inspired everyone—that we repeated in unison, and then he intoned a hymn.

Once again, I admired the unparalleled splendor of his voice. Fleshy, mellow, it was able both to mute itself and to swell in volume, be lunar in the high notes and doughy in the low, tinting its timbre with a silvery luster. When he sang, Derek convinced me. His charisma relieved him of his shadows; he enchanted and calmed people. Did he become different? Or did he become himself?

Cham, bundled up, lay at his feet and listened to him with fascination. At that moment, noting his amazement, I didn't regret having entrusted him to Derek.

Alas, the following days and nights destroyed the harmony of that glorious morning.

Although we'd escaped the danger of the hurricane, we didn't escape the remaining threats. The inhospitable had changed shape: hunger, thirst, waiting, boredom, despair.

The calm after the storm produced a new trial. We were drifting on waters without shores. Every landmark had disappeared: nothing could be seen in the distance except more water. We couldn't say that we were lost because there was nothing left, neither route nor landmark. Only the sun gave us a clue, by its rising and setting. But what good was that? Not only did we not know where to go, but we were floating, not navigating; no oar, no sail would direct us this way or that.

The ship had suffered badly in the storm, and despite Vlaam's and Barak's repeated efforts, it was in danger of eventually breaking up.

A slow catastrophe thus followed the spectacular catastrophe. From then on, we were waging a war without violence or an enemy. We drifted, helpless, inactive, and isolated, in the middle of a boundless battlefield on which we wouldn't be carrying out an assault.

If a storm is a violent killer, a shipwreck is a cold-blooded murderer. Methodical, invisible, insidious, it takes its time. It tacks, twists, and turns, delights in our impatience, in our failure of nerve, in our bellies' screams for food, our throats burning with thirst. It's undeterred by delays, ever-expanding time, and sluggishness; on the contrary, it takes pleasure in them.

Many of those who had been steadfast during the worst of it now lacked strength. Having given their all during the brief battle, they no longer had energy enough for the long one. Wounds became infected. Diseases broke out. We discovered that saltwater doesn't quench thirst; on the contrary, it makes thirst excruciating, inextinguishable, and makes us want to drink again, thus accentuating a vicious, fatal circle.

Dehydration killed one of my brothers-in-law, who took advantage of the cover of night to drown himself.

Fortunately, rain had filled up some of the barrels. Mixed with water from the sky, the seawater lost a little of its saltiness and burned our mouths a little less.

Foodstuffs were running low. Rationing became not a matter of distributing food, but of controlling the shortage.

Deprivation was demoralizing us. Our faces became gaunt, our bodies lost their muscles, their fat. Gray complexions, chalky mouths, split lips, dry hair, swollen cheeks, reddened eyes—we looked like cadavers. Except for Noura, who could be restored to health by just an apple, or Derek and Cham, who triumphed over abstinence. Among us, Barak and Tibor, though weakened, continued their activities thanks to their altruistic energy, but most fell into a lethargy that minimized their movements, economizing even their senses of sight and speech.

One hope tore us out of our apathy: the Lake was changing. Now that it displayed a smooth surface enlivened by short waves, it was being cluttered by things that were gradually rising from the depths. Beams, branches, trunks, decomposing animal corpses, bits of people with rotten flesh whose scraps no longer looked human. Every day, shreds, remains, and refuse from the old world floated up. We were wandering amid detritus in an atmosphere infested with noxious odors. However, here and there we spotted branches where a few fruits remained, scattered pinecones from which we extracted the nuts. Barak regularly dove into that vast pond full of dead bodies and, taking care not to swallow any liquid, made his way around the carcasses, closed his nose to their toxic emanations, and brought us back something we could nibble on.

One morning, he and Tibor came to consult me.

"Noam, is it possible that we brought rats and mice on board along with our sacks of grain?"

"Why?"

"It's disappearing without anyone having entered the store-room," Tibor said.

"We're the only ones who go in there," Barak added. "One of us is constantly guarding the door. If we're away, Vlaam replaces us."

"I trust Vlaam completely," Tibor said. "We have rats."

"What?" I exclaimed. "Are those parasites feasting while we starve?"

Barak lowered his voice. "At night, while guarding the storeroom, I've heard little sounds. I've never looked into them because the ship creaks all over. This afternoon, I searched the storeroom from top to bottom, examined it, poked around . . . but I didn't find where they're hiding."

"On land," Tibor continued, "I would trap them. But considering the circumstances, I refuse to waste the smallest bit of edible food!"

I proposed to slip into the storeroom at night to surprise the rodents.

"Excellent idea!"

By moonlight, Barak let me in and stood guard at the door. I stretched out among the sacks of grain, still and silent, hoping my odor wouldn't alert the pillagers.

For a long time, nothing happened. Then I heard discreet scratching noises; they didn't sound like the patter of tiny feet on the floorboards or like gnawing, but their persistence none-theless indicated meticulous petty theft.

Patiently, without disturbing anything, I crawled closer. The rats hadn't smelled me, and the trituration continued.

I leaned toward the corner from which the sounds proceeded: a hand, introduced through a hole in the wall, was carefully extracting grain.

The thief was on the other side of the wall. A lightning bolt of reflection would have allowed me to determine who was lying there, but I didn't need it. The hand, which was immense, bore a highly recognizable sign: two fingers linked by the skin.

I grabbed the hand and held it firmly. A voice yelped on the other side of the wall. The hand, terrified, struggled to escape my grip.

"It's Noam!" I whispered to the wood.

The hand stopped resisting.

"Now, you're going to stop, and I'll come to you."

When I let go of it, the hand disappeared back through the hole.

I crossed the storeroom, this time without taking precautions. Barak opened the door for me.

"Did you capture the rats?" he asked in a low voice.

"Just one, a big one, a giant."

"No!"

"Derek."

Stunned, Barak fell silent. His friendship with Derek had just suffered a shock. Flabbergasted, he finally stammered, "The same guy who stuffs us full of sermons on solidarity? The guy who bores us with hymns about sharing? The guy who inculcates good and evil?"

I headed toward his tiny room. Just as I got there, Barak spoke to me, "Do what you have to, Noam! Don't allow yourself to be blinded by friendship!'

Good old Barak with his magnanimous heart! He added, "If you want the group to hold together, punish anyone who attacks it."

"That's exactly what I'm going to do."

And I entered Derek's room.

Sitting on his bunk, hardly visible in the darkness, he was holding Cham and feeding him grain. He whispered to me, "Normally, I chew it for him. Easier to swallow. And to digest."

I immediately deciphered the defense system that Derek was adopting and decided not to care. "Stealing to feed your son, Derek?"

He raised his head and shot me a perfidious smile. "*My* son? Very flattered . . . I believed he was yours."

After establishing his devotion to Cham, he trotted out the second argument in his defense: a threat.

He held the child up. "If he's not mine, I'll give him back to you."

I took Cham and sat him between my legs. Impassive, the infant closed his eyes. "I'll be able to take care of him, thanks."

"Of course!" he said approvingly. "And so will Noura. She dreams so much about a child to pamper. She just can't know who he is."

His third argument was a sucker punch to the stomach: blackmail.

I took a deep breath and tried to find internal calm as I explained to him, in a controlled tone, "I won't tolerate your behavior, Derek. You stole."

"Oh, so little."

"So little, but in so little time! We're soon going to starve to death."

"According to your argument, we have to all die together? At the same rate?"

"Idiot!"

"You insist on sharing everything, what there is and what there isn't."

"I'm the chief, Derek."

"You're the chief, so you do what you want."

"I'm the chief, so I don't do what I want."

"The chief is free!"

"The chief is responsible!"

"You're not aware of your privileges."

"I don't have privileges; I have duties. My mission is to maintain order so that someday as many of us as possible will be able to leave this ship. That's why I condemn your theft. You're going to confess it and apologize publicly."

"Never!"

"Tomorrow morning!"

"Never! I play a different role here. I give people hope; I comfort them. They need me. Like Vlaam, you'll come to terms with me because I prove useful."

"If the survivors learn that you've betrayed them, I don't think they'll have such a good opinion of you. Don't forget that you lecture them, that you command them to pray, that you communicate the gods' desires to them."

"Precisely. They won't listen to me anymore if I ask them to forgive me."

"I no longer want them to listen to you, Derek. I refuse to allow those for whom I am responsible to trust a liar and a thief."

He stiffened, stung, hate flaring up in his eyes.

"Take that back, Noam!"

"Never. People need to see you as you really are."

Anger made his limbs tremble. He stuck out his chin and sized me up. "Then Noura will see you as you really are."

I shivered in my turn. He pushed his advantage, "You're commanding me to speak? I'll speak."

He gave me a haughty smile. "You can't muzzle me."

The solution forced itself upon me. Without the slightest hesitation, I brandished my dagger. Since he was harming us, since he was harming me, I would eliminate him.

When he saw the weapon that was about to strike him, he screamed, his eyes rolling back in his head, "You're my brother!"

Carried by its momentum, my hand fell to strike him, but at the last moment, I turned the blade away, striking his chest a thump that stunned him.

I seized him by the throat and shook him. "What did you say?"

Motionless, sweating heavily, his face deformed by panic, he stammered, "You're my brother."

I strangled him, shouting, "You're lying!"

He sobbed, sputtering, hiccupping. "I swear it. I have proof: the mark."

And with his eyes he directed my attention to his joined fingers, just like mine. "I am Pannoam's first son."

I hesitated. He noticed, and he found, as he managed to swallow, the strength to add, "My mother conceived me with Pannoam."

"When?"

"Before you. Before he met Elena."

"I don't believe you."

"I'm your elder brother, Noam."

Disgusted, I let go of his neck and pushed away his body, which reeked of fear, cowardice, and slyness. I pressed my back against the wall, my head between my bent knees, murmuring: "No, no, no," like a child who's been punished.

Derek controlled his whistling breathing, cleared his throat several times, spat, coughed, and then pointed at me.

"It took you so long to catch on! I knew it the moment I saw you."

I wondered internally if some part of me hadn't in fact guessed it earlier; on the other hand, another part had immediately rejected it.

"You're certainly not the brother I dreamed of having, Derek."

My remark hurt him. Never had I wounded him so deeply, even when I called him a liar, a thief.

He moved as far away from me as he could and remained prostrate, still panting.

"Give me details."

He looked up, contemplated me, hesitated. After an interminable silence, he gave in. "I'm a bastard, and . . ."

"I thought that word was not to be uttered in your presence."

"That's true. I alone can utter it. So, I'm a bastard, conceived by my mother with a man other than her husband, an aberrant term that suggests a sin, an original degradation, an inferior birth.

But I take an immense pride in descending from Pannoam and my mother. I am the son of an illustrious chief and a chief's wife."

His assertions having somewhat reinvigorated him, he went on. "Azrial, my false father, knew it, and took it well. First, his son Vlaam had preceded me and would inherit power. He immediately forgave my mother because he was . . . how should I put it? He was . . ."

"In love with your mother," I breathed, annoyed that he was scheming even when facing an obvious fact.

He clucked. "No, in love with Pannoam! Yes, the more I think about it, the more I think that Azrial was infatuated with your father. My father. Our father."

"You're insane!"

"It's true! He never stopped talking about him, or offering him a place to stay when he needed one. He always brightened up when Pannoam was present; he sought his advice and prized it, and he was all about spending quality time with him. Had he been a woman, I'm sure he would have done just what my mother did . . . Azrial never reproached me for my ancestry; he treated me kindly, very kindly, as well as he treated his son—better, even. Ask Vlaam! Brought up strictly in view of his succession, Vlaam probably sometimes wished Azrial would treat him as warmly as he did me. I suspect my false father felt honored to bring up one of Pannoam's sons in his home . . ."

He hardened. "I adored my false father. A good man. Nothing like Pannoam. No?"

He stared at me, waiting for my reply. I avoided his eyes. I didn't want to talk about Pannoam. With anyone. Especially not with him. I turned the conversation in another direction. "Did you meet Pannoam?"

"He came back three times. When I was one year old. When I was five. When I was nine. I remember the last visit. He . . ."

Derek was lost in his memories. I pressed him: "He what?"

"He nothing!"

He struck the walls around him. The blows replaced his words. Once exhausted, he grumbled, "I hate Pannoam. An odious man. I'd give everything not to retain any part of him."

Tears moistened his eyelids. An impulsive sympathy swept over me.

"What did he do to you?"

Derek let himself slip to the floor, distraught, his mouth twisted, "And to you? Horrors like what he did to me! He couldn't help himself. His hunger for power and his selfishness won out over everything else."

"You're right," I conceded, without realizing it. "It took me so long to suspect it."

"I knew when I was nine."

Having said this, he stopped dead. Nothing more moved on his face, neither his lips nor his pupils. In the half-light, he seemed a statue. For the first time, I saw Tibor's wisdom: "An unfortunate man, a very greatly unfortunate man." And I feared that these pains might not proceed from what he'd revealed to me, but from what he was still concealing.

Confused, and burdened by my pity, I stood up, handed Cham over to him, and whispered, "I won't say anything, Derek. You, either. You stop stealing; I'll nail a board over the hole and say I killed the rat."

He struggled to return to reality, to assimilate what I'd said to him. His eyes glowed feebly, and in his high voice, he whispered to me like a child, "Thanks, brother."

Despite my newfound compassion, this nearness between us—blood brotherhood and the solidarity of a shared lie—led me to distance myself from him even more.

*

What were we waiting for?

On the surface of the liquid horizon, my eyes lost their

bearings. Nothing stood out on it. I was constantly confronted by immensity. The immensity of the sky above. The immensity of the water below. The immensity of the remote all around us.

But what was most oppressive was the immensity of the unknown. Where were we? Where were we going? Had all the land been submerged? Would the water ever go back down? We were surrounded by nothing but enigmas.

The unknown is the father of anxiety. Humans flee ignorance. If they don't furnish the void with acquired knowledge, they fill it in with their imagination. In the latter art, Derek was a virtuoso: he had transformed what was happening to us into a logical story.

According to him, the Lake was punishing the gods, the spirits, the nymphs, and the demons who hadn't respected it. It had chastened the Earth for having sullied it, the rivers and streams for having soiled it, Winter for having frozen it, the Wind for having annoyed, disturbed, whipped, and pawed through it. It had also punished the inferior beings that proliferated on its shores, those futile creatures that led their lives without worshipping it; thus it had corrected animals for only thinking of copulating, gorging themselves on food, and sleeping, and it cracked down on humans who, thinking themselves a species apart, had isolated themselves and begun to worship themselves, forgetting to worship it. The Lake had reminded everyone of its superiority by showing us its power. If it had massacred so many living things, it was to bring them back to deference, to devotion. Why had this apocalypse spared us? Because, among us, a few individuals did not participate in this frivolous insolence: they had heard the Lake's message; they had made use of their clear-sightedness and prepared themselves. At this point, Derek added the gilding of a legend to his story. The first heroes, Tibor and he, had received the Lake's signs. Later on, Noam and Vlaam had persuaded their people to make the right decision. Finally, the villagers had followed their commanders and confronted the ordeal. At the same time that he covered the leaders with glory, Derek confirmed each individual's merit, not solely their good luck, by whispering to them that they did not owe their survival to chance, but to their submission to their masters and, beyond them, to the Lake. Derek restored the self-esteem and pride of the wretched persons dying on the ship. We became the elect of the Lake.

Derek proved to me that he was what he had claimed to be: useful. Tibor, the solemn healer and rigorous mage, would never have dreamed up such a tale; as for Vlaam and me, we remained too pragmatic to integrate our actions into a divine, cosmic epic.

Being aware of Derek's fundamental duplicity gave me a distance on him that enabled me to arrive at a better analysis of what he was preaching. His cleverness confounded me. In him, cunning had espoused efficacy. By assigning an essential, admirable role to Tibor, Vlaam, and me, he didn't limit himself to seducing us; he also increased our power, our legitimacy. Why should we attack him? His specious verbiage consolidated our collective cohesion. Derek was protecting himself by protecting us; reducing him to silence would make us more fragile.

One point intrigued me: Derek hierarchized the universe. Before the flood, no one would have placed a god above, except by village or family preference. At that time, our world was turning out to be composite, rich, overabundant, multicolored, disparate. Gods, spirits, nymphs, and demons cohabited in it, with squabbles, but largely in harmony. Derek told us that this time of play and laughter among the gods was coming to an end: for the diverse cults, he substituted a single cult, that of the Lake, and he subjected us to a god superior to all other gods. A sovereign god.

This proved to be cruelly judicious. As our group increasingly demanded solid cohesion, since it required a strong chief and absolute obedience, Derek was describing to the villagers a reorganized kingdom of the gods. I noted without pleasure that his brilliance as a falsifier helped me as much as it benefited the community.*

"Why are there no more perch or pike in the Lake? Not even a trout?"

Barak furiously scratched his head as he examined the surface of the water. "A little fish would do my stomach good!"

The food shortage was getting worse. We ate less every day—so as to be able to feed ourselves longer. I had doubled the guards on the storeroom and the stable, so certain was I that hunger would lead some to break the rules.

"Isn't that a salmon, there?" Barak cried, pointing to a spot of foam.

There were so many moldy bits of the old world in the water that we couldn't distinguish anything.

Behind us, Derek said, "Let's pray to the Lake to favor us and feed us again. O Lake, act as you used to do!"

A few voices buzzed, and then, led by Derek, a sung invocation rose under the devouring sun.

Barak turned to me and said, with quiet irony, "I'm not going to pray to the Lake; I'm going to visit it."

And he leaped into the murky waters.

I went to the stable, which was emitting a dreadful but deliciously terrestrial odor, a mixture of manure, urine, goatskin, rotten wood, and salty hay. There were four sheep and two goats left, the other animals having died of fear during the hurricane. Since we could still feed them by gathering floating grasses, which we dried, I'd ended up barricading the doors, so worried was I that the hungry might kill the livestock. Their milk was

---

* Falsifying is not equivalent to lying. In narrating the divine act, Derek believed what he was saying, whereas he would never have believed one of his lies. Having an authentic belief in the gods, spirits, genies, and demons—a faith he shared with the people of his time—he respected them and feared them. When he described their acts, he didn't think he was inventing something, simply receiving it. Gods, spirits, genies, and demons spoke to him through his imagination. A passageway between one reality and another, it was not a power of creation but a power of restitution.

of more use to us than their flesh: in addition to my son Cham, there were three other young children among us.

At the back of a small room nearby, my nephew Prok, six years old, pale and woozy, his hands on his excessively swollen stomach, was breathing with difficulty. At his side, Tibor gestured to me to indicate that there was nothing he could do, then whispered in my ear, "He's hungry. I don't have any medicines for that."

"Barak is fishing."

"Fishing? Fishing for what? Since the water acquired that briny taste, the fish have disappeared. You'd think that, like us, the saltwater is poisoning them!"

Groaning, Prok stirred without opening his eyes, seeking a position that would hurt less. I looked dejectedly at this little boy whose mother, my sister Abida, and father had drowned during the storm.

"Becoming an orphan has weakened him," I sighed.

"He needs more than food to grow; he needs reasons to eat. People don't grow well without love."

I crouched and caressed his burning temples.

"I can't draw on our reserves; otherwise, in two days, we'll all look like him."

Tibor clapped his hand to his forehead. "It's intolerable, Noam! I didn't become a healer to watch a child die!"

"Do you think I became a chief to watch a child die?"

Mama came in and tried to calm us. "Don't exhaust yourselves pointlessly. I'll watch over him. If he dies, at least he'll die in my arms."

She sat cross-legged, gently hugged Prok to her. Was it the warmth of her caress? His grandmother's smell? He stopped moaning; his breathing became more regular.

The boy's reflexive reaction gave me renewed hope, and Mama noticed that. She warned me sadly, "Don't fool yourself, Noam."

Her eyes filled with tears, and she lowered her head, concentrated on Prok, and hummed a lullaby.

I was overcome by emotion; I'd known this sweet melody forever, because Mama used to sing it to me, and now, hearing it again, I was a month, a year, six years old, like my nephew. My adult intelligence recognized the miracle the lullaby represented: a throat, a little attention, and some tenderness succeeded in making peace and confidence rain from the heavens.

In Tibor's company, I returned to the deck, where Barak was climbing out of the water, empty-handed and cursing the debris that had stuck to his skin.

"Nothing alive in that molasses!"

Noura's voice rang out, "Look!"

Pointing over the ship's rail, she drew our attention to something happening in the distance. A liquid was spurting up. This liquid, at first condensed, blossomed into a cloud of droplets that hung in the air before dispersing. The phenomenon occurred again farther on. Jets of vapor under pressure were regularly piercing the surface of the water.

"Never saw that before," Barak growled.

Suddenly, an enormous, supple mass emerged from the waves, terrifying, an animal, dark with an endless back and a narrow muzzle, greater in volume than our ship.

Breathless, we wondered if we were having a nightmare. The monster, propelled by an invisible force, sliced through the water silently, despite its gigantic size. It spurted again and then dove.

I clung to the railing, frightened. "What is it?"

The giant reappeared, rising half out of the water. After a few instants of observing it, Tibor declared, "For a bigger Lake, a bigger fish."

"What? That thing is a fish?"

"What else would it be?"

We nodded our heads, gradually persuaded by Tibor's logic, which struggled against our resistance. He persisted,

"Everything's changing in proportion. If the Lake gets bigger, its inhabitants must, too."

"We're turning into a nutshell that ants live in!" Barak burst out.

The creature seemed to prove him right: if it came toward us, it would sweep us aside like so much dust! Fortunately, it moved away, with a peaceful fluidity, indifferent to our presence.[*]

"For the moment, this . . . fish isn't attacking us," Noura remarked.

"My dear, why do you think it would attack us?" Barak replied, indignant. "Because it's bigger than everything else?"

Despite the tension—or because of it—we smiled at Barak's irritation. Sensitive, he viewed any reflection on giants as a personal criticism. He continued vehemently, "It's so tiresome to hear this nonsense! Why would a large animal be hostile? A colossus has no need to bite, Noura. The most ornery animals are often small, puny things! Fear a flea or a mosquito more than me!"

"We weren't talking about you, Barak, but about that monster over there," I replied, trying to resist my desire to chuckle.

"Monster, huh? That's easily said! It seems very graceful to me, your monster. You saw its shiny skin, a superb gray, a little lighter on the sides? And the lovely fin at the end of its back? Personally, I like your monster. I'd like to paddle around with it."

"Well, then! Dive in, Barak!" I exclaimed.

His furious outburst calmed somewhat when he eyed the dirty water stirred up by the mysterious form. He grumbled, "Later."

"Later," I concluded. "You mustn't scare it. It's never run into a beast like you!"

"That's for sure," Noura added impishly.

We shook with laughter. A good sport, Barak laughed with us.

---

[*] This was a rorqual, a whale surpassed in size only by blue whales. This cetacean measures more than twenty meters in length and weighs, even if no one has ever been able to put it on a scale, more than forty tons.

A spark of gaiety passed through the eyes of Tibor, who was still watching the monster.

"Excellent news, my friends. If a fish like that lives around here, that means that there are thousands of others."

"What?"

"What do fish eat? Other fish. We're floating on a cannibalistic universe. Under our feet, the big fish devour the little ones. Soon we'll be fishing."

We applauded him, convinced that his analysis was correct. Noura shivered on contemplating the horizon that was growing brighter.

"Papa, how did the Lake create such an animal so rapidly?"

"As for that . . ."

Tibor turned away and, as he left us, said, "Ask Derek. There's no question he doesn't have an answer for. That's how to recognize people who don't know anything: they know everything!"

That evening, Mama told me that the child was no longer suffering: Prok had fallen asleep for good in her arms. As often at grave moments, she wasn't weeping—she wept only about minor events. She simply leaned on me to keep from collapsing. Framed by her silvery hair that she piled even higher than before, her features betrayed a profound fatigue, an exhaustion that distresses not only the body, but also the spirit.

"We should offer Prok to the Lake," she suggested. "He'll rejoin his mother and father who are already there."

Did she believe what she was saying? Was this little boy, inert and stiff, going to swim with strong calves toward his parents who were peacefully waiting for him in the depths? I guessed, by her empty eyes, that she didn't really buy that idyllic outcome. She was fighting chaos, rejecting the arbitrariness that leads us to be born and die, trying to do something that would preserve meaning. It was how she could continue to care for the child, for her daughter, for her son-in-law; if the only way they could go on living was through wishes, imagination, symbols, she would wish, imagine, symbolize.

She guessed what I was thinking.

"What do you know about it, Noam? No one knows."

"Of course. Death remains an unknown."

"So much the better!"

"So much the better?"

"People dress it up in lavish colors. They consider it good and just. But maybe it's a bitch!"

"I agree, Mama: we'll return Prok to his parents in the Lake."

"Good, it will be our way of loving them forever."

At that point, Derek arrived. He examined the boy. "Do you want me to take care of him? I can say some prayers for him and entrust him to the Lake in accord with the rites."

What rites was he talking about? Old ones that he was perpetuating, or new ones that he was inventing?

Mama stared at him. Like me, she instinctively mistrusted Derek. How would she react if she knew she was rubbing shoulders with the son Pannoam conceived with another woman?

She almost refused, but then, too tired, she accepted Derek's offer, which lightened her burden.

Derek looked at me questioningly. I acquiesced, as well. "Please, Derek, do it discreetly. The fewer people see his little body sinking into the water, the better."

Derek picked up the cadaver reverently.

Immensity is not plenitude; it's the true name of the void. When I found myself facing a profusion of water, an abundance of space, and an extravagance of light, I couldn't see anything but what it lacked: land, a point of reference. I no longer perceived anything but absence. I had become a nothingness detector.

Like my companions, I had known neither deserts nor seas nor oceans, having lived within a limited sphere around the Lake ringed by mountains, indifferent to what was situated more than a few days' walk away. I'd lived in a world that displayed its center and its limits. A vast, happy garden.

And now I was wandering aimlessly over an endless surface. I wondered who the foreigner was here. Was it the water? Was it us? Sometimes I thought it was the water, conquering, invading, outrageous, which had crushed everything and driven us away; sometimes I thought we were the parasites, the only solid things among the liquids.

On that morning, dying of thirst, I envied the sun, which didn't need to drink.

At my side, Noura was watching the sky. "There are clouds coming, over there. Not many, but . . ."

"What are you predicting, Noura? A storm?"

"Rain. To catch pure water."

I kissed her. She never complained; she looked for solutions. The exact opposite of the spoiled Noura who was crazy about dresses and jewelry and preoccupied by tiny, exaggerated ailments, she evinced robust health and passed that energy on to the others. Still, that night, we'd failed to go back to sleep after hearing the sound of the child's body sinking into the waves. Without admitting it to ourselves, we'd thought about the uncertain future and about our lovemaking, which, however intense, hadn't gotten Noura pregnant. She'd whispered, "My womb is just proving how wise it is. It won't shelter anyone until we're back on solid ground."

She was probably right . . . Mama had told me stories about women who copulated but didn't get pregnant, a deep-seated reticence suspending their fertility.

Derek came up to us, rubbing his hands. He appeared beyond himself with excitement. "Noam, I have good news!"

I had so thoroughly lost the habit of this kind of announcement that I didn't trust my ears.

"Sorry?"

His eyes shining, he repeated impatiently, "Good news. As I

was getting milk for Cham in the stable, I noticed that a sheep had died."

"How is that good news?"

"We'll eat the meat, Noam. I'll make a hotpot with pieces of mutton and the plants you find around the ship."

Noura was astonished. "What water will you use?"

"The salt water will give the stew flavor!"

He licked his lips, delighted. Noura laughed joyfully. I complimented him, "Thanks, Derek. Very good news."

"Let me cook it by myself. Don't say anything about it. Leave me alone to cook. Agreed? That way, I can organize a magnificent feast! It will lift everyone's spirits."

I happily nodded my assent. Noura pressed my arm, satisfied. Once again, I was delighted by Derek's altruistic side; he was an odd bird, capable of both the worst and the best.

Like Pannoam.

Like me?

The meal proved to be the most joyous we'd had since the catastrophe. Derek had done the cooking surreptitiously—though he hadn't succeeded in hiding the smoke—and, when he brought the stew on deck, the shipwrecked passengers couldn't believe their eyes.

No one dared reach for the food, not even Barak, who was usually so prompt to gorge himself, so precious and miraculous did this abundance of meat and boiled vegetables seem to us.

"Enjoy it!" Derek commanded. "There will be enough left over for this evening and tomorrow."

Tibor recommended that we chew thoroughly and absorb the food slowly. I don't know whether his advice was followed.

After this feast, everyone retired, some on deck, some inside the ship, for a nap made all the more necessary by the blazing sun beating down on us. Without a breath of air in the humidity, we lay sweating, motionless.

Noura begged me to let her have the room, the better to stretch out, and that suited me, because I felt myself about to fall asleep in the little bit of shade I'd found outside.

While we were drowsing, a cry rang out. I leaped to my feet. I ran and almost knocked over Noura. She was holding her hand over her mouth to control herself. She shot me a tormented look.

"Noura, what is it?"

"As I was passing Derek's room, I paused to thank him; I looked down, and . . ."

"And?"

"And I saw him asleep, naked."

"So?"

She looked at me, doubtful. I joked, "Was it the first time you'd seen a man naked, Noura?"

"He's . . . he's . . ."

She struggled to formulate what had caused her to scream. I said softly to her, "Was he as ugly as all that?"

She stared at me, reflected, then changed her mind.

"It's not important. I'm going to lie down."

"Shall I come with you?"

"No!"

She had replied angrily, as she used to do when we were sparring with one another, when she was blowing hot and cold. Why this turnaround? What had I done? What had I not done?

I shrugged, convinced that I'd soon find out.

As evening approached, at the hour when colors were fading, except on the horizon, which blazed with the setting sun, Derek invited us to a second feast. Happiness was in the air. We rejoiced to be sharing a pleasure, not a fear. Only Noura, who was still pouting, had insisted on eating dinner in her room.

Barak appeared on deck and took my arm.

"Come," he whispered. "Don't resist."

Even if I'd wanted to, I couldn't have, because his giant's grip drew me inside.

He went toward the stable he was guarding, unbolted the door, and showed me the animals.

"How many were there, before?"

"Six."

"Are you sure?"

"I'm sure. Four sheep, two goats."

"How many are there now?"

I had to count the animals twice to be certain: there were four sheep and two goats.

We exchanged a stupefied look, Barak and I, and then, gripped by a sudden fear, I rushed to confront Derek, who was enjoying his stew.

"Derek, no animal is missing. What did you feed us?"

He didn't flinch.

"You counted wrong."

"I counted perfectly well. What did you serve us?"

He stood up, unfolding his tall, scrawny body, and sized me up with scorn. "Did you like what you swallowed?"

I lost my composure, fearing something intolerable, and stammered, "Derek, don't tell me that . . ."

"You liked it! Everybody liked it! Don't pretend to be so delicate, please."

"You dared serve us . . . human flesh?"

"A human child's," he corrected me.

"But Prok . . ."

"Oh, that's enough of your scandalized act, Noam! And all of you around us! I could have kept it all for myself, and then I wouldn't . . ."

A wooden beam struck his head. Derek collapsed.

Holding the beam in his hand, Barak pointed to the body stretched out on the deck. "Put him to death!"

The other passengers repeated, spitting on Derek, "To death!"

*

Night is the kingdom of sounds. The vessel creaked, the waves lapped against its sides, the breeze whistled, we vomited.

No one admitted what Derek had imposed on us. He had defiled us. We threw up the meal we'd eaten, as much by a visceral disgust as by conviction. Humans don't eat humans. To be sure, we had heard people talk about warriors who ate the brains of their enemies to humiliate them, and we had also heard the story of a son who'd swallowed his father's heart to ingest his bravery, but we prohibited such actions: humans were defined above all by their respectful disgust for their fellows. If not, what kind of world would we be living in? Hunger was better than cannibalism! We preferred the death of an individual to the death of man.*

Mama and Barak turned out to be the ones most sickened, probably because they were the oldest. Had they not wanted to respect my function—to dispense justice, to punish—they would have thrown Derek overboard. Not only had this reprobate crossed a sacred limit, but the hold he had on people's minds,

---

* "Man" was us, the Peoples of the Lake. We recognized our fellows only when they were just like us. Like the Greeks, who later called "barbarian" anyone who didn't speak Greek, those who said "blablabla," we were suspicious of those who used a different language. We legitimately wondered whether their mouths were producing noises or meaning . . .

The foreigner is upsetting. Nothing is more spontaneous than the mistrust they elicit. They lurk beyond the frontier, not only that of the village or the country, or even the language, but also the frontier of the human. Was someone who didn't talk like us a human like us? People we didn't understand, who dressed differently, who acted in different ways—were they human?

There were two reactions to this uneasiness: disparagement and hospitality.

Hospitality gradually did away with the problem. Receiving strangers, giving them food and drink, providing them with a place to sleep, allowed us to domesticate them, to discover the commonalities beneath the thorny differences. Hospitality reintegrated foreigners into the human family—and in so doing, broadened it.

Disparagement, on the other hand, made us feel even more uneasy. Instead of reducing the distance, it increased it. Foreigners, corrupted by suspicions of stupidity, cruelty, and laziness, were seen as an inferior species whose faces were the only thing still human about them.

Hospitality is reflective, xenophobia impulsive. While the wisdom of hospitality gives us a path toward peace, xenophobic passion leads only to violence and war.

through his talents as a preacher and his fascinating voice, made his guilt all the greater. He alone could persuade people to attempt the unthinkable—he'd proven it in the past—and that transformed him into a malicious taboo-breaker. To the dangers from the outside—gusts of wind, backwashes, the heatwave—was added a threat from the inside.

"Death!" Barak had cried.

"Death!" the villagers had repeated.

I went to the small room where Derek, his hands and feet bound, was awaiting his execution. I had entrusted Cham to Barak, the only person who had deigned to take the child in, because the survivors rejected "Derek's son" with animosity.

Derek snorted in derision when he saw me: "Have you come to kill your brother?"

"You didn't leave me any choice."

Hindered by his skinny legs and his long arms, Derek kept trying to find a comfortable position. Annoyed by the swells, he said, without turning toward me, "There's always a choice."

"If I don't eliminate you, I'll no longer be their chief."

"My poor Noam, you've never been their chief: you obey them."

His condescension was getting on my nerves. Who did he think he was? Did he think he was so important that he could treat me with irony and pity me? I responded in the same tone, "My poor Derek, you've never understood what a chief is."

He shivered, shook his head, stared at the wall.

"I hate chiefs."

"They're necessary, though."

"You're just like your father! Our father . . ."

"In what way?"

"A chief. Nothing but a chief. Pannoam behaved like a chief before he behaved like a father. You, too! You put the chief before the brother."

Even if he was right—perhaps because he was right—I shot

him a scathing reply, "My brother! Who would put up with such a brother? You're not a brother; you're a disgrace."

He jutted out his chin, venomously. "How are you going to kill me?"

"Quickly."

"By what means?"

There were leather thongs in my pocket. I'd chosen to strangle him because I didn't want to see Derek's blood flow, and still less to clean it up. Strangulation provided a rapid, neat execution.

Faced with my silence, he stopped taunting me and, suddenly feverish, murmured, "Get on with it . . ."

Tears ran down his pale, delicate, childlike cheeks. His lips were trembling with anguish. Despondency made him seem younger, erased his coldness, his strangeness. I didn't like it.

"Derek, please!"

"What?"

"Die like a man!"

"And I have to help you, to boot . . ."

I was going too far by calling on him to toughen up, but I was loath to kill him. He sniffed, looking at me without ill-will. "The other man also demanded that I help him . . . 'Act like a man,' he said . . . And I tried to do what he asked . . ."

This time, I felt he wasn't lying, that he could no longer control himself, and that, terrified and sincere, he'd stopped playing a role.

I replied softly: "The other man . . . What other man? . . . Who are you talking about?"

"Pannoam."

"Pannoam wanted to kill you?"

Derek leaned back against the wall, closed his eyes, and took a deep breath. "I was nine years old. My mother thought only about herself, about her exceptional beauty. She loved herself passionately. She never took care of her children. Having brought them into the world was enough for her; she'd paid her tribute as a female by giving birth, and she showed us the minuscule stretch marks on her perfect body and blamed us for them. We were raised, Vlaam, my sisters, and me, by our aunts. My false father, Azrial, paid us more attention. A good cuckold! Dominated by his wife, but full of benevolence.

"Pannoam honored us by visiting us; he was the glorious chief, the one people talked about all around the Lake. They praised his village, which was growing; his craftsmen, who were becoming more numerous; his market, which attracted crowds. He'd acquired the status of the most venerated man of his time. Since my mother bragged about him, I knew he was my father. I gloried in this ancestry.

"My false father organized feasts and redoubled the kindness with which he treated my true father. Proud, I tried to parade alongside Pannoam as often as possible. I watched him: he was handsome, and I wondered if I would become as handsome as he was; he wore his hair long, had a magnificent beard, hair on his chest, and I hoped I would inherit all this; his voice resounded deep in the drum of his breast, and I shivered at the idea of sounding the same. I never left him. More than being my father, he represented my model, my god, my religion.

"Pannoam kindly allowed me to cling to him this way. He lived in a separate house that Azrial reserved for distinguished guests. One evening, he proposed something that made me faint with pleasure. 'Can Derek sleep with me?' Azrial agreed—he would have handed over his wife. When we got to the house, Pannoam suggested I take a bath. A servant brought jugs of boiling water and poured them into an oaken tub. He added donkey's milk. 'It softens the skin.' And I, like an idiot, was delighted; I savored his words as if they were nectar. As soon as the tub reached an agreeable temperature, he undressed. I'd seen dozens of people without clothes on, but seeing my father naked overwhelmed me. To be him! Strong, firm, virile. I felt intoxicated. Did he realize that? Fittingly, he encouraged me to get drunk. He grabbed a wineskin, and we got into the tub. On taking the first gulp of the wine, I coughed and spat it out. He scolded me. 'Act like a man.' So I drank. I drank without restraint. I was proving my strength to him. Did Pannoam drink, too? He gave me the impression that he did. When I started to confuse words, to have a feeling of well-being, and to get drowsy, he opened another wineskin and urged me to keep drinking. 'Act like a man.' I soon lost consciousness. And then, he finally did what he'd come for."

"What?"

"At noon the next day, I woke up in a bed. An excruciating pain had roused me from my sleep. I looked at the lower part of my body. There were linens stained with blood. I screamed, beside myself with pain. Azrial hurried to my side. Seeing my condition, he called out for Pannoam. The serving woman told him that Pannoam had left the house at dawn, with all his things, without the slightest commentary. Azrial leaned over me, lifted the linens, and saw what had happened."

"What had happened?"

"Pannoam had castrated me."

"What?"

"In the tub, taking advantage of my drunkenness and the heat that softened my flesh, he had cut open my scrotum and pulled out the testicles."

I drew back, horrified.

"But . . . but why?"

Derek reopened his eyes and met my stare.

"To erase me. So that all my life I would be mocked, scorned, defamed, insulted. To ensure that I would hate him, that I would tear him out of my memory. Who wants to be the son of a father who did that?"

His gaze searched me. I lowered my eyes.

He went on, "Above all, he did that to me for you."

"What?"

"To settle a succession problem. To keep you his only son. To transmit power to you. For you, Noam, for you."

*

In the middle of the night, people heard a plop when Derek's weighted body, wrapped in a shroud, sank into the water.

Although no one had wished to witness the operation, everyone was awaiting the event. As soon as the ship was rid of the traitor, they fell asleep.

When I rejoined Noura, she refused to let me lie down next to her.

"Go to Derek's room."

Having little desire to start a quarrel, I obeyed.

I don't know whether I dozed or stagnated in a prolonged stupor. My eyes closed, I was haunted by the images Derek had permanently imprinted upon me. An innocent boy. Pannoam, cruel and cold. The emasculation in the bathtub. The opalescent donkey's milk that turned scarlet. The unbearable, burning pain upon awakening. The condemnation to a life outside life. This unveiled a new side of my progenitor: his caprice had conceived a child, and his will gave birth to a monster. Once again, I tried to sketch a coherent, balanced portrait of Pannoam. I failed. I couldn't bring myself to see in him only a criminal. From whom I was descended. "Who wants to be the son of a father who did that?" And I owed him my power. "For you, Noam, for you."

At dawn, I went up on deck.

I was thirsty. I was hungry. I only drank, only ate air.

The sun, indifferent, slowly emerged from the liquid depths and gradually shed its light on us. Warmth was slow in coming.

Around me, nothing subsisted that was not broken, disconnected, diverted, unfastened, corroded, cracked, ravaged, annihilated. We were experiencing absolute impotence. No way out. No land to be reached. A bobbing shell. There was, of course, something solid under my feet, but it was so fragile, at the mercy of a too-vigorous wave, of a rope that failed. How long would it be before the shipwreck? Long enough to starve to death?

A furtive sound disturbed me. I turned my head.

I didn't place it immediately. Or, rather, it took me a minute to understand what its presence heralded.

A chickadee was looking at me, carrying a twig in its beak.

A chickadee?

The chickadee! The way it was observing me, the way it seemed amused by my bewilderment, its small size and discretion: I recognized the chickadee Mina. It was her! It could only be her!

I examined what she was carrying: an oak twig, very light, very green, very tender, recently torn off a young tree.

The message took shape in my mind: the shore wasn't far away. The chickadee provided me with proof.

I cried out in joy.

Frightened, the chickadee dropped the twig, flew off, and landed on a high spar.

"Thank you, Mina," I whispered as I held the precious twig in the palm of my hand.

A rustling of wings answered me. The chickadee, as if in a hurry, had taken flight and was leaving the ship.

I followed her with my eyes to determine which direction she was flying. No coastline was visible where she was disappearing. But I knew that it would be soon.

When the survivors got up and came onto the deck, I didn't tell them about the miraculous bird. I would have had to go back to Mina, to her death and her rebirth in the form of a songbird— all details that would make me vulnerable, and about which the others might laugh. Besides, tormented by fatigue, my anecdote seemed to me increasingly stupid, and I wondered whether I'd lost my common sense. Had thirst, hunger, and heatstroke made me delirious?

Since the surface of the water was covered with branches, leaves, and trunks, Vlaam suggested that we collect this debris, hoping to find a few acorns or hazelnuts in it. Barak dove into the water and brought back branches. After countless back-and-forth trips, we succeeded in gathering a pitifully small harvest.

We ate a little. Noura appeared, grabbed three acorns, and shut herself up in our room without even looking at me. Her behavior annoyed me more than it intrigued me. I had better things to do than work out the kinks in her moods.

Vlaam asked his sons to try to capture a whole tree trunk, a large one, and, as a kind of distraction, hollow it out to make a canoe. They reacted with enthusiasm. Never had I seen a team of carpenters so eager to cut, scrape, empty, burn, and smooth the wood.

When the sun reached its zenith, I studied the course indicated by the chickadee.

A shoreline was coming into view!

I shouted. The survivors came running. They scrutinized the horizon: there was no doubt about it; shapes were emerging. We were close to our goal.

Reality cooled our enthusiasm. We were approaching not a coastline but a multitude of rocks and small islands. Even those that were bigger than our boat were still too small to land on. They were more hills of earth than land.

"In any case," Tibor exclaimed, "I'm glad to see that the water level of the Lake is sinking."

This outlook stimulated the carpenters, who, excited by the project of reaching land, finished the canoe.

"Thanks to this canoe," Vlaam announced, "and all the others that we'll build, we'll be able to approach the islets. Surely we'll find a couple of things to eat . . ."

I agreed.

In late afternoon, a first attempt that I made with him in the canoe allowed us to harvest plants to cook and bark to chew on. For once we were eating food that wasn't salty.

Euphoria was spreading. I admit that I didn't share this ecstasy. How long would our vessel hold up? Wouldn't it crash against the reefs?

Despite the uncertainties, the atmosphere was relaxing.

Night fell. Noura continued to cold-shoulder me. Her behavior seemed to me so juvenile that instead of arguing, I avoided her. She noticed and closed up even more.

When the castaways went below for the night, I remained on deck.

Water and sky had been inverted. During the day, sparkles of light sprang from the surface of the water; at night, when it was dark, only the waves were completely black. Overhead, the stars were telling me a story that escaped me. What were they? Rips in a black veil? Was there a purer, more brilliant universe behind it? How far away from us? And the moon, the real moon whose irregular surface I examined, was there any way to reach it? Should I take that idea seriously?

A brilliantly effulgent shooting star crossed the celestial vault and illuminated it.

In this, I saw a sign.

Convinced that the castaways were asleep, I slipped below deck, lifted two planks covered with straw in the middle of the stable, and, taking precautions because the boat was rolling, descended into the hold. This place, which had no light, reeked of salt, damp beams, and rot. Groping my way forward, I followed the wall. I bumped into something alive, warm.

I moved closer to the gagged face and whispered, "Come on, Derek, follow me."

*

The canoe glided over the black water.

Moving more quickly than we were, clouds bearing shadows were covering the moon, absorbing the stars. Afraid that this darkening would hide my goal, a rocky island, I paddled faster.

Derek didn't turn a hair. To allow him to leave the ship and get down to the canoe, I'd untied his wrists and ankles, then retied them without any protest from Derek, who was aware that any rebellion would awaken the passengers and lead to his demise.

I hadn't been able to execute him. Discovering that Derek was one of Pannoam's victims had stayed my hand. What made him my brother was not our common blood, but our shared suffering. The fact that he'd been subjected to our father's cruelty had suddenly made him close to me and forbidden me to kill him. I'd asked him to trust me, and then I'd bound and gagged him and hidden him in the hold. At that point, I was just buying some time, without imagining where this deception would lead; the sudden appearance of the islets had provided a way out.

Behind me, in the bottom of the canoe, there was a pile of furs and blankets that probably belonged to Vlaam. Why not leave them with Derek, once we were on land?

Derek remained silent. His aquiline profile stood out against the increasingly dark horizon. He was giving himself completely over to fate—or to me. He'd put away his disturbing ability to convince people.

As I paddled, I thought about his characteristics. His feminine skin and hair, his powerful, clear voice, his inordinately long limbs . . . all that no doubt resulted from his emasculation. His loneliness, his isolation, his distance from other people, his reticence with regard to women, his "I prefer not to"—his mutilation also explained that. I felt compassion for him mounting in me. Yes, now that I knew what he'd been through, I was inclined to treat him with affection.

And yet, I was about to abandon him on a wild islet.

It was too late . . . Too late to love him. Too late to correct him, encourage him to be upright, to temper his cynicism, his appetite for vengeance, his taste for manipulation—defects that were the result of the violence he'd undergone.

We were approaching the shore.

"Give me a hand, Derek."

I untied him, and, silently, he helped us with the landing. We dragged the canoe onto a stretch of gravel. The darkness was growing deeper. We could hardly see each other.

Out of breath, Derek ventured to take a few steps. So did I. We had lost the habit of being on solid land, so much so that we pitched and tossed, walking less comfortably on land than on the boat.

"Are you going to abandon me here?"

He spoke for the first time since he'd confessed.

"It's a dangerous place," he added.

"In your case, the boat is more dangerous."

His silence indicated his assent. I defended myself. "I'm doing what I can, Derek, not what I want."

He cleared his throat. I went on. "You're my brother. Whatever crime you may have committed, I won't kill my brother."

"And yet I'll die on this island. From what? There are so many choices: hunger . . . thirst . . . boredom . . . another flood . . ."

"Like all of us, Derek! Nothing guarantees our safety."

"You can still hope to move forward."

"Tomorrow, you'll explore your domain. There are trees, animals, a spring. Leaving you here means I'm not executing you."

"No, you're condemning me."

I turned on my heel. Whatever else I did, I couldn't argue with him; his twisted mind always found a way to turn situations to his advantage, to give me a guilty conscience, to persuade me to do the opposite of what I had intended!

"Farewell," I said, as I walked away.

He didn't call after me or follow me. Had he finally grasped that he was no freer than I was?

I returned to the strip of land where we'd left the canoe. As I was moving it, I remembered the skins and blankets I wanted to leave for Derek. When I stuck my hand into the canoe, I was astonished. Nothing? Was the opacity of the darkness playing tricks on me? I ran my hand over the whole of the canoe.

Nothing.

Had we lost what was in the canoe as we climbed out of it?

Pensively, I looked around me, but the obscurity prevented me from locating anything at all.

"Are you looking for me, Noam?"

I almost fainted as recognized her voice.

"Ah, you're surprised . . ." she said, mocking me.

When the moon briefly peeked through the clouds, I saw Noura, her face pinched, trembling, her eyes shining with anger.

"You were avoiding me; I followed you."

"Noura, we have to talk."

"I'm counting on it; that's why I'm here. At least no one will hear us." Irritation altered the timbre of her voice.

"I'm listening," she said, in a menacing tone.

"Derek is my brother. My half-brother. I didn't kill him."

"I don't give a damn about Derek; he doesn't interest me. Tell me something else."

"But . . . but . . ."

"Why do you have a son?"

I wasn't expecting that line of attack. She snarled as she rushed toward me, pointing her finger. "Yesterday, I found out what Papa guessed a long time ago. When I went into Derek's room, I saw . . ."

"What did you see?"

"That he was castrated! He was sleeping naked because of the heat. A castrated male, whether human or animal, doesn't reproduce, so far as I know! Afterward, I examined Cham and realized that his mittens camouflaged linked fingers. Then I understood."

"Noura, I'm going to explain everything to you . . ."

"Of course, but your explanations won't change anything. I'm hurt. You betrayed me. When I was with Pannoam, I saved myself for you, I didn't sleep with him. You know that perfectly well because you deflowered me."

That annoyed me. "You didn't sleep with him because he couldn't do it."

"Because I didn't want to!"

"That's what you say."

"He'd tell you himself if he were still alive."

"It's easy to put words in a dead man's mouth!"

Her voice was scolding, tense to the point of cracking, threatening. "You'll regret this, Noam . . ."

We were interrupted by a thunderclap. A lightning bolt lit up the darkness. Rain poured down on us. Heavily.

In other circumstances, I would have rejoiced that the storm was giving us the fresh water we so needed, but that evening, on an unknown islet, facing an exasperated Noura pulled tauter than a bowstring, I cursed with rage. "Oh, come on!"

Hardly had I uttered those words when a lightning bolt from the sky struck the oak tree towering behind Noura. A violent cracking sound rang out, followed by a sizzle, and then the trunk separated, split in two by the celestial axe. Its two parts leaned away from each other, forming a V.

"Quick!" I shouted, grabbing Noura's arm.

I pulled her toward me just before one half of the tree fell where she'd been standing.

By reflex, I started to run, holding Noura by the hand, toward the place where I'd left Derek. Rocky outcroppings provided shelter.

Incessant lightning bolts zig-zagged through the darkness, allowing us to find our way, and, when we suddenly appeared, Derek called out to us: "Over here!"

From among the rocks, he was signaling to us. Without hesitation, we hurried toward him.

The Wind had picked up. With vigorous fury, it was adding its madness to the showers, lightning bolts, and booming thunder, whirling in crazy, chaotic spirals around the little island.

To protect ourselves from the turbulent elements, we advanced among the rocks until we finally reached a round cave that offered us sanctuary. Far above us, rain was coming in through a narrow crack. We found ourselves in a sort of immense chimney. Despite the water flowing into its center, we were able to keep dry while we waited for the storm to abate.

The storm grew even wilder.

"Thanks, Derek," I said.

Noura whispered in my ear. "Watch out for him. You saved his life; he'll never forgive you for it."

She withdrew her hand from mine, letting me know by means of this gesture that our dispute had not been settled, that our confrontation would resume later.

Derek rushed to stand under the water pouring into the center of the cave.

"Finally, something to drink!" he exclaimed.

He placed himself at the heart of the waterfall. His head thrown back, he opened his mouth wide to catch the liquid.

"Good idea!"

Noura joined him under the life-giving stream.

Then the incomprehensible occurred . . .

A ball of fire suddenly split the opening above them and headed straight for Derek, who collapsed, then rebounded on Noura, who, with a terrorized cry, was blasted in turn.

I leaped forward.

Too late!

Noura, rigid, was no longer breathing. Derek lay on the floor of the cave, also dead.

As I raised my face to the heavens to scream in pain, a second ball of fire burst into the cave and annihilated me.

A face was leaning over me.

I had trouble opening my eyelids, which were heavy, dry, stiffened. I could hardly make out the face. When I finally succeeded in letting in the light, objects were blurred by a sort of veil.

"Noam . . ."

More than my name, I heard the anguish that contracted the voice. The person speaking to me was trembling with a mortal anxiety. I felt the inverse. Life was coming back into my body, my blood was circulating, my heartbeat was slow and peaceful, my chest was twitching to the rhythm of my breath. One by one, my senses were loosening up: cold, lukewarm, bright, humid, hard, sweet, bitter, salty, sugary. This flood of sensations was intoxicating me . . .

"Noam?"

I smiled. I didn't know at whom, but I smiled. I wanted to express my gratitude; I wanted to reassure.

"Oh, my nephew, you terrified me!"

Barak's big, hairy head became clearer. Above me, my uncle was like a sun, his face forming the center, his mane the rays. Timidly, he stroked my cheek.

"You're not in pain?"

At that moment, I understood what had swept my mother off her feet. The gentleness of this muscular, powerful, impetuous giant radiated a peculiar grace. The fact that a hand made to deal a lethal blow was delivering a caress made its light touch all the more precious. That a temperament made for fighting manifested affection intensified its tenderness. That an energy made to be expended physically was refined, channeled, spiritualized into thoughtful concern made the attention overwhelming. Barak seemed to me to be pure love, because his raw natural aspect didn't suggest it at all.

"I'm all right," I said.

Entirely absorbed by the happiness of existing, I took deep breaths, concentrated on my bare arms and legs, which the beneficial warmth was reviving. I was amused by the prickling that Barak's fingers produced when he stroked my skin.

Then memory reared up, putting an end to this beatitude.

"Noura!"

The image of Noura dead made me sit up. Then I became aware of what surrounded me: I was not lying in that fatal cave, but on gravel, at the water's edge.

"Where am I?"

Barak grumbled, "It doesn't have a name, Nephew. Call it the place you escaped to three days ago."

"What?"

My last impressions went back only a few instants, not three days! Noura and Derek had been hit by lightning just a few moments ago. So had I.

I got up, tested my sense of balance, then scratched the back of my neck for a long time. Why wasn't I in the cave? Where were Noura and Derek?

My uncle asked me to sit down again.

"In the middle of the night, I heard a strange sound. Once on deck, I spotted you leaving in a canoe with someone. The darkness kept me from immediately recognizing Noura, but I assumed it was her as soon as I saw she wasn't in your room. I wasn't worried. You were sneaking off to one of these little islands, just the two of you, to . . . to do you know what . . . without being forced to contain yourselves. I have to admit, your mother and I sometimes get tired of making love like trout, in silence."

I didn't correct his narrative. It was better that he thought the second figure was Noura, since he believed I'd executed Derek.

"The thunderstorm broke out," Barak went on, "and there were terrible gusts of wind, waves for a full night and the following day! The ship almost broke up. Wind, cloudbursts, rolling, a calamity! Fortunately, Vlaam and his sons were able to repair the damage as fast as it occurred. After the storm let up, we saw that we hadn't drifted far away, luckily. I could still see your islet. I explained your escapade to everyone, and we waited for you. But after a day had passed, I borrowed a canoe from Vlaam. And I found you here."

"Here?"

"Yes, here."

"Not in the cave?"

"What cave?"

A mad hope lifted my spirits. Maybe Noura was still alive? Maybe she was waking up at this very moment?

"Follow me."

Threading my way among the rocks, I retraced the same path, followed by Barak. We reached the large rock chimney. Anxiety petrified me; I was probably going to find nothing but bodies struck dead by lightning.

The sanctuary was empty. No trace of Noura or Derek.

"But . . ."

"What, Nephew?"

"We were there. How did I get out?"

Barak pointed to the residue of mud flows leading to a hole in the rock wall at ground level.

"The torrent carried you outside . . . I picked you up just on the other side."

A few feet away, through the hole, I saw the place where I'd regained consciousness.

Circumspectly, fearing the worst, I crouched down to be sure that Noura's body hadn't been caught in a crevice of the rock.

Nothing obstructed the channel leading to the strip of gravel. Barak's firm hand gripped my shoulder.

"I'm afraid the current carried her away, my boy."

He was right. Noura, slender, light, must have glided like a piece of bark as far as the outside and slipped into the waves rather than landing on the narrow beach.

Barak couldn't get me to return to the ship before nightfall. Incapable of believing that Noura had simply evaporated, I looked for her everywhere, among the rocks and trees, under the bushes.

In every place I'd already searched, churned up, I expected her to suddenly appear. Noura, dead? Noura, gone? I couldn't accept it. Not only did my uncle put up with my agitation, but he helped me search. He had no illusions regarding the possibility of finding Noura, but because he was devoted to me, he accompanied me as long as my denial required.

At twilight, when cold penetrates the bones before it does the landscape, I agreed to get into his canoe—mine had been swept away by the hurricane. After three strokes of the paddle, I stopped Barak.

"Let's look just one more time!"

"Look at places we've already gone over and examined ten times?"

"You never know . . ."

"Yes, my boy, we do know!" he murmured compassionately. "You could stay on that island for a thousand years and scrutinize it from every direction: Noura is no longer there."

I bowed my head so he wouldn't see my tears.

Noura's absence overshadowed everything. That evening, I didn't ask myself by what miracle I had survived a lightning bolt, or how I had been able to remain inanimate for such a long time without dying of thirst or hunger. I would ask those questions only much later . . .

*

A strange atmosphere prevailed on the ship over the following days. On the one hand, hope was reborn: in addition to the fact that we had collected rainwater and brought food from the islands, we were on the lookout for the increasingly numerous birds in the distance, messengers from a nearby land. On the other hand, Noura's disappearance had destroyed us.

She left behind her the dazzling memory of a strong woman—despite her slender figure—who had shown an inflexible determination during terrible moments, breathing her daring into the survivors, supporting them. To each of them, when horror prevailed, she'd brought a smile, a word, a meal, help, consolation. She had in no way failed to carry out the mission she'd given herself: to lead our community to victory. As a result, her death before the dénouement cast a pall over the course of her life, all but giving the lie to optimism. If the person who had never doubted that our travail would have a happy ending had not lived to see it, then what was the point? Did we have to persist in our stubborn hope? Holding on didn't make us any more powerful . . . Courage didn't fend off death. The survivors shared my sense of helplessness; with me, they talked about Noura's actions, her solicitude, her beauty, her light. I wasn't sure whether this alleviated my sorrow or made it weigh on me even more heavily. Grief overwhelmed me.

As for Tibor, he reacted the same way I did: he rejected reality. It seemed to him that Noura had always overcome everything; she'd escaped childhood diseases, healed from adult illnesses, avoided being buried along with her first village in a mudslide. She'd emerged from a failed marriage holding her head high, triumphed over the anger of the Lake and the Wind, withstood thirst and hunger. Noura incarnated the survivor *par excellence.* Noura couldn't die. Especially not before he did. This solemn, tough, thoughtful man had already been deprived of his home, his wife, and his sons, and now he had lost the only thing he had left that was alive, close to him, beloved: his daughter.

In countless little ways, Mama and Barak sought to cheer me up, to revive my desire to move forward. While Barak had adored Noura, Mama had treated her with respect, despite her jealousy; discerningly, she had avoided attributing Pannoam's vile actions to Noura, and she had later accepted her with grace as a daughter-in-law, considering her up to the task. Mama and Barak shared my suffering by projecting into it what they would feel if one of them were to die.

Vlaam also raised my spirits. Rather than competing with me for power, he advised me to reinforce mine.

"I consider you our chief, Noam. Even if you're a widower, you're still a chief."

"I don't want to be chief anymore, Vlaam! I was trying to govern so that Noura would admire me. But now . . ."

"She would've hated it if you abdicated. She loved you, Noam, but she loved you as a chief."

How right he was! Noura cherished power. Seduction depended on it; love belonged to a different register—her feelings had developed afterward.

Out of fidelity to my late wife, I forced myself to lead the survivors, to maintain the cohesion of our group, to impose unfailing patience without excess or dissension.

On that morning, the sun was shining brilliantly. An oily surface, uniformly smooth, was rising and falling like some creature's respiration, while a gentle wind, almost a breath, pushed us toward a horizon where birds were flying.

Tibor joined me, unshaven, frowning, his eyes dull. More prostrate than impassive, he leaned on the ship's rail.

"I'm stupid, Noam. Since your return, I've been denying Noura's death. My mind refuses to admit that it's true."

"Your mind is sparing you . . ."

"What?"

"By keeping you from understanding, it's keeping you from suffering."

The succession of silky waves carried our vessel forward. We were advancing effortlessly. In a hoarse voice, Tibor protested: "My dreams keep whispering to me that she's alive."

"She's living another life," I said, contemplating the flocks of birds.

Tibor rubbed his temples, his forehead wrinkled with worries.

"I bring misfortune, Noam. I don't protect the people I cherish; they all come to tragic ends. Burial, suffocation, lightning . . ."

"You don't kill people, Tibor; on the contrary, you take care of them. How many men, women and children have you saved with your talents as a healer?"

He weighed my remark, then said, "Not only have I lost my daughter, but I've also lost my faith in my intuition. But my intuition tells me she's not dead."

I felt the same thing. Instead of admitting that to him, I clung to my role as a wise comforter.

"Tibor, I want to ask something of you . . ."

"Yes?"

"Allow me to become your son and your disciple during the years that remain to us."

Tibor turned toward me. For the first time in days, an emotion passed through his pinched features. His pupils dilated, and the corners of his lips rose slightly.

In a way that was at once pompous and awkward, he put his rough, noble hand on my shoulder. "Do me the honor of becoming my son, Noam. I will teach you everything I know."

A magnetic force was transmitted from him to me, from me

to him, a force that united us, transformed us, a force that had the tension, thickness, and intensity of an indisputable fact.

At that moment, Barak shouted: "Land! Land!"

In the distance, a vast coast was coming into view, broad, high, green, solid, inviting. The ship's passengers screamed with joy: we were saved.

*

Some kinds of fatigue are rewards, others hindrances. During the period when we were rebuilding the village, we had to select our fatigues carefully.

On the one hand, enthusiasm filled our days; the tasks to be done required all our strength right up to the last moment, when we collapsed into bed, dazed, exhausted, fulfilled. On the other hand, at the cold hour of waking, we no longer thought about what we had done, but about what remained for us to do; then despondency reared its head. That fatigue came in the morning, not the evening; it affected the mind, not the body; it was not exhaustion but weariness.

Blessed exhaustion . . . oppressive weariness . . .

Building houses, arranging them, clearing meadows, fencing in land, planting, weaving, braiding, turning, scraping, chopping, piercing . . .

Starting over . . . The very idea was distressing. When we start over, melancholy restrains joy: we think more about what we lack than what we're creating. Whereas when we're just starting out, we go for it.

I struggled against listlessness by devoting myself to my two-fold role, that of leader and that of father. I revealed the truth to everyone by introducing the child I'd conceived with a Huntress after Noura married Pannoam. This news didn't shock anyone—Noura alone had found it intolerable—and Mama immediately gave me her assistance, seconded by Barak, who had never had a child to dote on. When I caught the three of them playing on all fours, I had the feeling that Cham was becoming their grandson, the issue of their love.

We had landed on a propitious coast, rich in trees, grasses, moss, and game.

The villagers rejoiced that the Lake, finally calmed, had withdrawn. Every day, they organized prayers, sang hymns of gratitude to it, and laid offerings on its waters, some soaking their amulets in them to win its favor. According to them, the flood was nothing but a fit of rage. Once that fury was past, the water had sunk, letting the land reappear. Because we had drifted for more than a moon, we hadn't found our former village. Oh, well. It made more sense to remain here than to look for it. Where would we look, anyway? If the Lake had spared us, we shouldn't go against its clemency; we should agree to settle where it had put us.

Tibor and I didn't share this opinion. The Lake had not gone down after having risen; it had remained higher than before. The rocks, islets, and islands we had passed during our voyage, and the territory on which we settled, couldn't be reduced to lands that had emerged from the receding water; they were mountains that the water had never reached. How else could the green forests, the floral luxuriance, and the presence of animals be explained? All that had not previously been under water.

Tibor and I had concluded that the Lake, salty and swollen, had conquered a new space. In the course of this invasion, it had carried us toward higher land. Our village, our fields, forests, springs, and caverns, the landscape that we had known, our past remained forever destroyed, submerged, inaccessible. Even if we had tried to get our bearings, to move, we couldn't have undertaken a return voyage. Our world was lost.

*

"Cham, get out of that burrow, please."

Even though he loved to hunt, Cham observed the soil, dug in the dirt, picked up pebbles. If we passed near a hole, he jumped into it to see what was inside. And if we walked by a cave, there was no stopping him: he rushed into it, felt the wall, examined it, used his flint to chip the stone.

"Look, there are colored streaks," he cried, marveling.

I found his fervor touching. I associated this penchant for the mineral with Tita, who had lived in the Cavern of the Huntresses and had brought him into the world. Though Cham didn't know it, something deep within pushed him to rediscover his maternal habitat.

"What a pink . . .!"

That morning, Cham had come out of a burrow with salmon-pink rubble that he put in his shoulder bag along with some yellow debris.* In the evening, as was his habit, he would examine and try to transform them, either by striking them or by heating them. Tibor encouraged him, saying, "Cham's curiosity about stones is like my curiosity about plants. The spirits whisper thousands of things we don't hear. He'll discover important secrets." Tibor often left his own research and helped the child light fires that would alter the appearance and texture of the fragments.

I admired my son. He was ten years old. He captivated. As I'd imagined when I laid my head on his mother's belly, he had Tita's bravery; proud shoulders; sculpted, swift muscles; and olive-colored skin. Every father has this conviction: I was convinced—naively, sincerely—that my son was the best, a judgment shared by Mama, Barak, Tibor, and Vlaam, the latter determined to see his eldest daughter marry him someday. Must I explain? After the flood, we were counting on four adolescents to perpetuate the human species.

Naturally, a wife had been proposed to me. Two, even, of

---

* Copper ore and gold ore

child-bearing age. Faced with my half-heartedness, I'd been advised to marry one of the prepubescent girls, with the promise that she would be reserved for me. Even though I hadn't used Derek's expression—"I prefer not to"—my attitude had been the same: I'd declined the offer. I felt incapable of marrying anyone at all. After Noura, my heart had closed off. To be sure, I continued to cherish Mama, Barak, and Tibor, and my love for Cham had grown even greater, but what I felt for them was an already-present affection, devoid of sensuality.

Though love always has a body, it doesn't always have a sex. I loved my mother's heavy, soft flesh, which I didn't hesitate to hold close to me; I loved Barak's powerful build, his gleaming skin, his well-rounded limbs and smell of leather and camphor; I loved Tibor's ascetic face, the gray of his irises, his aquiline nose and hollow cheeks, and his ashy, bristly hair; and as for Cham, I idolized him as a model of earthly beauty, from his pure forehead to his nimble feet, passing by way of the promise of his slender figure. But the delight I took in seeing them, being around them, smelling and touching them, expressed neither a desire nor its satisfaction. Though my attachment didn't disregard their bodies, it was distinct from attraction and sought no sensual pleasure.

Living with a woman required the return of sexuality to love, a constraint that seemed to me as pointless as it was impossible. Noura had taken me so high that lower summits no longer attracted me.

Shall I admit it? In this distaste, I was cultivating a new form of my passion: faithfulness to Noura beyond death. Each time I thought about it, I felt an intoxication that reminded me of our ecstasy. Refusing to give myself to women by invoking Noura gave me a kind of intense, almost physical pleasure . . . As for the rest, like any ordinary man would do, I'd found a tree, similar to the Beech of my adolescence, climbed into it, forgetting everyone else, and relieved my tensions by indulging in pleasure.

"Papa, there's a herd down there!"

His arm stretched out, without the slightest trembling, Cham pointed to the teeming thickets shaken by convulsions. Animals were hiding in them.

"What do you think they are, Cham, wolves? Boars?"

He watched carefully. Impossible to tell what was provoking the activity.

"Shall I go see?" Cham asked.

"No, I'll go," I said, fearing that he might be charged by a wild boar protecting her young.

"You never let me go first. Why even bother taking me hunting? I'm not a kid anymore, you know!"

I looked at him: he may still have been a kid, but his angry eyes, his indignation, and his desire to fight with me were those of an adult. He moved me.

"Go ahead," I murmured.

He smiled, turned on his heel, and went down the slope. The stirring in the branches stopped when he walked around them. He disappeared into the foliage. His voice rang out, "Papa!"

In his tone, I perceived no trace of fear, just astonishment. Nonetheless, I hastened to join him. Her pointed to the clearing.

"Look . . ."

In front of us, about twenty people carrying bags—men, women, and children—were staring back at us.

Tibor had been right: the Lake hadn't covered the entire world; it had simply enlarged its empire. The territory we'd landed on contained every possible kind of living creature, including humans, and we'd just received proof.

The nomads joined our village. They used a somewhat different language, which hindered our communication, but I finally understood that they periodically migrated, camping for a few moons here and a few moons there, long enough to exhaust the game and fruit in an area, then moving on.

Talking with them confirmed me in the belief that humans,

living in bunches, were prospering elsewhere, without ever having dealt with our catastrophe. They'd heard about the flood . . .

"It happened a long time ago, right?" asked their leader.

It had been ten years. To us, that seemed close in time; for them, it belonged to the distant past. They proved to be curious about it, probably because their regulated, monotonous life did not include such interesting disasters.

Our villagers recounted our trials. The nomads listened, delighted.

I discovered then a paradox I would encounter again and again over the centuries: people believed the story while, at the same time, not believing it. The ambivalence didn't bother them. The boundary between fiction and reality dissolved, and they mixed for the pleasure of all, without anyone protesting. Both those who listened and those who recounted the events moved in a space freed of restraints, a place where facts were less important than beauty, moral instruction, and emotion. The plausible won out over the real. If it served the narrative, even a probable improbability was better than a true truth that spoiled it.

That is how our villagers came to say that our voyage on the water had lasted forty days. Where did they get that number? Nobody had counted the days. "Forty" seemed about right because "thirty" would have seemed paltry and "fifty" outrageous. The number forty, given by an initial windbag, was repeated so many times that it became canon.

In addition, our villagers claimed that the water had covered the whole earth. But that was merely an impression produced by the circular horizon; moreover, had they reflected on it, they would have realized that they had landed in a region that had never been submerged. Still, they described a universal, complete, radical flood, and their listeners, without wondering why they hadn't been drowned ten years earlier, acquiesced, ready to spread the story in their turn.

Going back to Derek's interpretations, our villagers explained the causes of the flood. The Lake, disrespected and angry, had decided to punish the disrespectful and had eliminated them. Nonetheless, so that its power might be recognized and feared, it had to have witnesses: it had chosen to spare a few carefully selected humans who were less forgetful, less dissolute, less thoughtless. These latter were the elect. They refounded the world on sound, pious bases, and their children, their grandchildren, and all the generations to come would commemorate the supremacy of the Lake forever.

I saw how a myth was born. Its father was meaning, its mother exaggeration. It assumed that nothing happened by accident and that events contrasted with one another. The mind lent order to chaos, and sensitivity added art. Necessarily, the fable unfurled an intelligent design that no contradictory or superfluous detail could blur.

At the cost of meeting these requirements, the legend was established and traveled from consciousness to consciousness, authorizing anyone to embellish, enrich, or complete it: multiple variations would be understood as additional clarifications.

The more our villagers recited the story of the flood, the more important my role in it became. At the time, as I witnessed the elaboration of the legend, I wasn't credited with more than I would've tolerated, but I sensed that after my death, the sky would be the limit.*

---

* Once writing had been invented, my story also appeared in books. The Mesopotamians were the first to put it in writing, in several versions, the most complete of which is found in the *Epic of Gilgamesh*. There I am described as a sage who saved his friends and family, his livestock, and indeed all animals, by carrying them away on a boat. Amid countless fanciful references, one detail disturbed me: I am said to have been rewarded with immortality and to have gone, to take advantage of it, to Dildmun, the land of abundance (today the island of Bahrain in the Persian Gulf). This detail—which is authentic, as you will soon see—long made me fear that my secret had been revealed. But providentially, after several invasions, there was no one left who could read Sumerian, Akkadian, or Assyrian, which ensured my tranquility. Furthermore, with distance, I see that the only true part of the Mesopotamian narratives is the one that's considered the most implausible . . .

In their turn, the Jews reworked our adventure in the book of Genesis, the

*

"You don't age, Noam!" Mama exclaimed for the nth time, ecstatic.

I couldn't return the compliment. Mama was slowly, humbly declining. Far from rebelling against the passing years, she accepted growing heavier, more hunched. She pleased people as much as ever, if not even more, because she was radiant: an internal light, that of her joyous soul, occupied her eyes, structured her face, justified the pattern of her cheerful wrinkles and her shining, immaculate hair. Mama was jubilant to see me leading the village, to comment on her grandson's conquests, and especially to be unconditionally loved by Barak.

He, too, was getting old. His mane was now salt-and-pepper, deep folds marked his leathery skin, but unlike Mama, he resisted ageing, standing straight, forcing himself to run, taking care to keep his actions quick and sharp. I sensed the effort behind his behavior, but I didn't disapprove: my giant of an uncle owed it to himself to remain a colossus.

As for Cham, he had reached his adult height. He was blooming, carefree. Since we now knew that the world was big and populated, he no longer felt the pressure to reproduce himself, to

---

Bible's opening pages. They give my name—Noam becomes Noah—talk about my son Cham, and complicate the chickadee Mina's involvement by transforming her into two birds, a crow and a dove. Endowed with genuinely poetic inspiration, they add a rainbow that appeared at the moment we landed on *terra firma*, a multicolored sash that would testify eternally to the new alliance between God and humans (funnily, the rainbow was a reminder for God as much as for humans!). Even if I admired rainbows long before the flood, I still love them as a symbol. Those cosmic garlands are beyond us, splendid and forever out of reach, urging us to be humble.

As for the Greeks, they distanced themselves more from the memories that were peddled for millennia. They named me Deucalion and Noura Pyrrha. Still later, the philosopher Plato mentioned the flood in his dialogue *Timaeus*, and, for political reasons, transformed the flooded Lake into the island of Atlantis.

To be sure, none of these texts is presented as a report on the flood or on me. No one was concerned about precision. Only the meaning of the fable mattered.

fill out our community. He was discreet when it came to girls and spent the rest of his time satisfying his curiosity about minerals.

Since his first efforts, he'd made enormous progress. He could now successfully extract veins of copper or gold from the rock and then transform them. Whereas, as a child, he was content to shape the metal by hammering it cold, he had since invented copper metallurgy. We liked to watch this process. For us, making a stone pass from a solid state to a liquid state was tantamount to a miracle; to be sure, we suspected that the heat of a fire caused this melting, but we couldn't look at fusion as an ordinary operation. And the return to a solid state by cooling fascinated us in the same way.

"Cold is one of Nature's most formidable spirits," Tibor noted. "When it attacks water, it changes it to ice. When it attacks liquified stone, it transforms it into metal. I classify it as a solidifying spirit."

"What about Heat?"

"Heat is a destructive demon. It burns, dries, reduces to ashes, annihilates. Anyone who approached the sun would die. We have to constantly monitor and control Heat to prevent it from doing damage."

With copper, Cham made arrow points, rings, bracelets. At first, he made tools and even weapons, but they proved weaker than similar items made from flint, bone, or antler; they were soft and didn't hold up. Cham, obeying the virtues of metals the way Tibor obeyed those of plants, specialized in the manufacture of small, precious objects.

He continued to accompany me when I went hunting, like a worthy heir of his mother, finding a gut-level satisfaction in running, jumping, climbing, exhausting his vigorous muscles. He wore a perpetual smile that he lost only when strangers took us for brothers.

"You don't age, Noam." That night, Tibor, at whose home I was having dinner, was scrutinizing me.

"You don't either, Tibor. You look exactly like the Tibor I met back in the day."

"That's normal. I've always looked old. Say rather that I'm finally as old as I looked."

Speaking without affectation, he was on target. I admitted it. Wrinkling his forehead, he narrowed his eyes.

"You, on the other hand, aren't ageing."

That sentence, which I heard often, was usually meant as a compliment. But for Tibor, it was the statement of a problem. Instead of dodging it, I weighed his remark and solemnly reaffirmed it. "It's true, Tibor—I'm not ageing."

He perceived my uneasiness. Taking him into my confidence, I dared to confess something: "Tibor, it gets even stranger than that: I repair myself."

He shrugged. "We all repair ourselves; Nature demands it. The living defends the living. We get over indigestion or a headache, bleeding stops, we scar and heal."

"The other day, you remember, I injured myself," I said. "My bowstring broke just as I was aiming. The arrow cut my skin."

"I remember; I bandaged it for you. The cut was longer than your thumb. A nasty wound. How is it, by the way?"

I removed the bandage and showed him my right arm. He pushed me away, grumpily. "Stop fooling around. Give me the arm that was hurt."

"This is it," I replied, without moving.

Intrigued, he examined my right arm, my left arm, and then returned to the right. His fingers palpated me. Perplexed, he drew me closer to the fire in order to see more clearly.

"No!" he breathed. "Not a single mark. No one heals like that!"

"I told you . . ."

Tibor remained silent, and then pensively, as if I were no longer there, he took his hallucinogenic herbs out of a sack and crushed them in a concave stone.

"Tibor, not in front of me!"

"Sorry! It's automatic . . . I'm preparing them for tonight."

He stared at me, suddenly inquisitive. "I don't understand, Noam. I've treated you in the past. Before, you didn't heal that way."

"Before what?"

"Before the flood."

A weight settled on my chest. Tibor's remark overwhelmed me. Even if he was formulating what I'd been feeling for a long time, I rebelled: "Why would the flood have changed me? What did I experience during the flood that you or the others didn't? I pitched and tossed like you, vomited like you; I suffered from hunger and thirst like you; like you, I thought my last moment had arrived; I . . ."

"Stop! What happened on the island?"

The acuteness of his thought dazzled me. He was designating the sole moment I'd been apart from the group. What should I reveal to him? Everything or only part of it? Everything—that is, the presence of Derek? Or only what concerned Noura and me?

He raised an eyebrow: "You're thinking about it, Noam; that means you're going to lie to me."

I took a deep breath and decided to tell him every last detail of our expedition, including my deception of the survivors—my decision not to execute Derek because he was my brother and Pannoam's victim. After I related the hideous scene Derek had described, Tibor interrupted me: "I immediately guessed that he'd been emasculated. When I asked him whether he'd had an accident—angry swans sometimes attack little boys' testicles— he snapped at me. Afterward, we avoided one another. I was going to tell you my suspicions when you claimed he was Cham's father, but I feared that Noura would hear about it."

"Noura found out. That's why the worst happened."

He stared at me, speechless. I told him about Noura's cry upon seeing Derek naked while he was napping, her exasperation with me, her hiding in the canoe so that we could talk. I told him about the storm, our escape, the cave, the ball of fire that struck Noura and Derek, about rushing toward them, seeing that they were dead, and then being struck by the lightning, too. I mentioned the black hole, the three forgotten days that I was unconscious, during which the water had carried me out of the chimney-shaped cave, and then waking up in Barak's arms.

"Were you hungry or thirsty when you regained consciousness?"

"No . . ."

I realized how unusual it was to emerge from a faint this way.

Tibor exclaimed, "That's it! That's when something happened! In the cave. During those three days and three nights. After being struck by lightning."

"Tibor, how do you explain . . ."

"I don't explain anything, but I'm getting closer to the mystery. Knowing doesn't mean eliminating the mystery, just demarcating it. Knowing means first of all knowing what we don't know. I have to remove the superficial layers, the ones that are resolved, to touch the real heart of the mystery."

He stood up, examined the contents of the house around him, and sighed.

"I'm leaving, Noam. After what you've just revealed to me, I'm going."

"Why?"

"I'm going to find out what happened in that cave."

"I'll go with you."

"Out of the question. This will take time, and you're governing the village. Mainly, I have a mission."

"What?"

"To verify that Noura is dead."

*

My son was in love. I didn't know the girl he was infatuated with because she lived in a village four days' journey away. Like most young people, Cham and Falka had found each other during the harvest festival, which brought together already-constituted couples and hearts that were still free. Falka had ignited an instantaneous crush in Cham; since then, he either talked about her excitedly and at length or remained silent, languishing, thinking about her.

His passion pleased me as much as it worried me. Was he being carried away reasonably? A woman who charms doesn't necessarily make a good wife . . . I'd broken the tradition according to which parents arranged their children's marriages in advance, and without their input. Why? I refused to act like Pannoam: social position didn't constitute sufficient reason, and my marriage with Mina had produced such gloomy years for me that I certainly didn't want to inflict that fate on Cham. Still, I felt guilty about it. Can a son choose better than a father?

Impatient to be wed, Cham urged me to meet Falka. I quickly agreed, hoping to reassure both of us.

When I entered the room, where the clan had prepared a reception worthy of a chief, I immediately perceived Falka's uneasiness. As we moved toward her, she contemplated Cham, then me, then Cham: her eyes kept jumping, flabbergasted, from one of us to the other. When I spoke to her, she melted with pleasure. Her cheeks turned bright red, and she lowered her eyelids and constantly touched her hair, lips, and neck as we talked. Moreover, she didn't chat: she cooed, clucked, sighed, smiled, perished, and her eyes were laden with emotion when they slid over my face. I noticed that even her breast was becoming flushed, dotted with scarlet blotches. Very fortunately, Cham, blind, didn't notice that he'd disappeared from the ardent eyes of his intended, which saw only me.

As soon as I could, I left the house to escape the intolerable cosseting. My son had fallen for a coquette! Even though I'd long kept my distance from women, I clearly understood that Falka found me seductive. I pleased her too much. If the two of us had been left alone, she would've leaped into my arms.

Annoyed, disappointed, irritated, I decided to be frank with my son: he was falling for a flirt who loved men rather than a man, who preferred love to the lover; Falka would cheat on him, lie to him, and if he persevered, he'd be in for humiliation, treachery, and cruelty. I was beside myself with fury. If Cham didn't understand, he would at least obey me: I would demand that they separate!

Tirtsa, Falka's mother, came to find me behind the house.

"Is it possible?" she murmured.

I looked at her, incredulous, frowning, cold. She spoke again: "Why does the father look as young as the son? You're his brother, aren't you?"

I contradicted her with an exasperated gesture.

"Falka is terribly upset, Noam. We all are. But, for her, the turmoil is verging on anxiety: what she likes in the son, she sees in the father. That disturbs her. I'm telling you this because she won't dare admit it to you."

Astonished by these words, I stared at her. Tirtsa, who was elegantly slim, had a gaunt face with deep-set eyes; the dark circles under them and the multitude of wrinkles circling them gave her gaze an incredible intensity. Her awkwardness in this moment proved her sincerity.

"You seem to be only a year or two older than your son."

"My mother, my uncle, my village will all testify that I've been raising him forever."

"You look the same. Your maturity appears only in what you say, your attitudes. I've never seen anything like it."

I looked away. What could I say in response? How could I explain the inexplicable? For the first time, my prolonged youth was a problem. What had been, up to this point, the pride of my family was now in danger of destroying it. Now I was disrupting my son's life.

Intelligent, Tirtsa respected my silence and then asked, "If Cham and Falka marry, where will they live?"

"Under my roof."

"I refuse to allow my daughter to live under your roof!"

Her face bitter, she insisted. "Don't impose that on her. I don't want . . . your privilege . . . your weirdness . . . to confuse Falka, constantly lead her astray, or worse . . . transform her into . . . someone else."

I was stunned by what Tirtsa said.

"Falka adores Cham," she added. "How could she not carry his double in her heart?"

Thanks to her perspicacity, I foresaw my duty. I bowed before her.

"My son will marry your daughter. They love each other. My daughter-in-law belongs to an august clan. They'll make their home in my house. And I will go on a long journey."

"Immediately?"

"Immediately!"

"Long enough for them to have a child?"

"Long enough for them to have one or two children. Long enough for them to establish their marriage on a firm basis. Long enough for me to wither."

"Thank you," she replied simply.

She held out her hands toward me so that we could seal our agreement. I executed the ritual. We experienced the relief felt by responsible fathers and mothers.

She withdrew her hands and asked me, looking deeply into my eyes: "Tell me: are you really Cham's father?"

"I swear that I am, Tirtsa."

"So you're my age?"

"Yes, I'm your age, Tirtsa."

She shivered and rubbed her bare arms to warm them. In spite of myself, my attention lingered on her dry fingers, veiny at the joints and swollen by inflammation, as they massaged the withered skin on her elbows.

Realizing that I was looking at her, she gave me a sad smile.

"Bon voyage, Noam. I, too, will be glad never to see you again."

Tirtsa went home.

Very uneasy, I collapsed on a stone bench. An injunction was going round and round in the depths of my soul: Don't be like Pannoam. Through a series of suspicious links, events were urging me to steal from my son, a slippery, dangerous slope. Of course, unlike Pannoam, I didn't desire Falka; but on the other hand, if she developed the slightest interest in me, I would bring unhappiness on Cham. Would we become, from generation to generation, men who stole fiancées and broke sons? I rejected that fate; I refused to reproduce it.

If Falka, alerted by the wise Tirtsa, detected the causes of my coolness, Cham, for his part, did not. On the day after the wedding, he urged me to delay my expedition: "Stay, Papa! Don't leave just when I'm the happiest." I gave a dozen good reasons to travel all over the world; I would have invented a thousand more to avoid confessing the only one: to have done with the curse on our dynasty, which set selfish fathers who were thieves and sensualists against altruistic sons who were robbed and unhappy.

*

I spent two years roaming around the region, lavishing my skills as a healer on the natives. I missed Mama and Barak terribly. I hoped to run into Tibor, whom, strange to say, no one remembered seeing.

These years gave me the chance to discover that this territory had not a shore but a coast: you didn't come back to your point of departure if you walked along the water's edge. The world no longer consisted of a closed circle. This revelation unsettled me: the Lake was a sea.

During my peregrination, I developed an aversion to the sea that lasted for centuries. The child of brooks, rivers, and the Lake, a man of pure, running, transparent water, I saw the sea as a usurper—and especially as a graveyard. It was nothing but the cemetery of the flood. If it smelled bad, if its bottom wasn't visible, that was because thousands of carcasses lay in its depths; it was composed only of excrement, of destroyed, rotten, putrefied, corrupted, eroded bodies stirred constantly by its rising and ebbing tides, its unstable waves with their foamy slaver. Sometimes, it still threw up skeletons, their bones bleached white. The iodized air over this cesspool was an exhalation of the breath of the dead. And I thought that the salt, that brackish stench that made the liquid undrinkable, oozed from the rotting cadavers.

Talking with the bold men who were increasingly venturing forth on the sea, I noted that death continued to prowl around us. Not only did frightening monsters rise up from the waves, but devastating storms broke out over them. What should we see in this turbulence? The memory of the flood? The forerunners of a new cataclysm? A reminder or a threat? In any case, when the Wind howled, when the waves roared, the sea was denouncing the sins of earthly beings, warning them that if they behaved badly, it might no longer contain its rage. The noise made by the sea, its constant rumble, the surf's scream tortured me and reminded me of my insignificance.

By the end of my trek, I'd perfected a technique that would help me live alongside Cham: ageing myself. A powder dulled my skin. Using charcoal sticks, I accentuated my features to the point of putting wrinkles on my forehead, around my mouth, and at the corners of my eyes. Using brushes made of animal hair, I darkened the contour of my eyes so as to create bags under them, and then I emphasized the hollows. Then I used iron oxide to add red blotches and traced a violet vein on my temples. Finally, I applied chalk dust mixed with grease to whiten my beard, mustache, eyebrows, and hair. Leaning over the ponds that served me as mirrors, I taught myself the art of makeup before the theater came into existence. Since I'd succeeded in making myself look the age I really was, I could go back to Cham.

My appearance disconcerted him when I turned up in the village, but he was overjoyed. He proudly displayed his two infants, and Falka, who was more in love with Cham than ever, welcomed me affably, without her earlier uneasiness, treating me like a venerable elder.

I decided not to live with them and instead moved into a nearby house whose inhabitants had been decimated by dysentery. Two motives led to this decision: not making things awkward for the young couple and concealing the process of putting on my makeup, which occupied a large portion of my time each morning.

Confronted by my ageing, Mama and Barak often seemed skeptical. Due to insight? To affection? Did they know that their Noam would never be subject to the humiliations of time? Or did they want to believe it? When my makeup was successful, they limited themselves to a sideways glance, reluctantly murmuring, "You look tired today," almost as a reproach, without empathy or concern. On the other hand, as soon as the pigments began to disappear as a result of sweat or a long hike, they exclaimed: "How handsome he is, our Noam!" Looking back, I think they guessed that I was following a unique path; in any case, seeing that I didn't want to talk about it, they respected my silence.

Mama fell ill. Lost all energy. Stomach cramps. A lump that could be felt under her belly. I worked furiously to prepare infusions and decoctions for her, but I noted with frustration that despite the medicinal plants, her condition was steadily declining. Her appetite disappeared. A yellow tint spread over her skin. Drinking became difficult.

Mama didn't complain. She'd understood. She was resolute. Just as she had accepted old age, she accepted death. Better yet, she welcomed it.

"What good would it do to moan?" she said to me one day,

during a bout of fever that racked her with shivers. "Death will be a relief."

One thing warmed her up: a smile. While in reclusion, bewilderment and disappointment clouded her face, but it cleared as soon as one of us approached her. She, who lacked the strength to keep up a long conversation, was still able to keep smiling. Nothing diminished the joy in her eyes when she contemplated Cham or his children. As for Barak and me, we became as necessary to her as the air she breathed, and in the smiles that we exchanged—a grin that stretched from ear to ear—the intensity of our love circulated.

Outside the house, the strong, invulnerable Barak wept secretly, like a little boy who's done wrong, but as soon as he returned to Elena, his face lit up with a warm, radiant smile more beneficial than any fire.

One night, Mama stopped fighting.

At dawn, as I entered her room, I found her cold body and alongside it Barak, on his knees, chanting sacred formulas.

I knelt down and joined my prayers to his. During the moments of silence, I sent my love to Mama, and I saw, through the subtle movements of Barak's lips, that he, too, was continuing the dialogue; then we returned to the ritual prayers.

Barak didn't shed a single tear. Because of me? Because Elena, even inanimate, forbade him to sob?

When we had recited our prayers several times, Barak raised his head, his gaze enraptured, and spoke to me for the first time that day. "Do you have any idea, my boy, how lucky we both are? You had Elena as your mother, and I had her as my wife. Do you know any men more fortunate than we?"

He smiled, his eyes bright, his features peaceful, his breathing serene, and I understood that far from finding an outlet for his feelings of loss, he was absolutely sincere in showing his gratitude. On this morning when fate had deprived him of the love of his life, he was exultant rather than regretful.

"She died in my arms. Nothing could have made her happier. Nothing could make me happier, either. Except for dying in her arms."

He reflected, then corrected himself: "No, that would have made her suffer . . ."

He looked at her, overcome with passion.

"So everything's okay," he murmured.

The villagers came to the house to pay their final respects. The attachment to Elena felt by each of them moved me deeply. Barak noticed.

"What did you expect, Noam? We deserve nothing for loving her: Elena was loveable!"

Seeing Vlaam, his family, the old people, the children, the shepherd, the potter, the water carrier, the crude, the kind, the egoists—they all bowed before her, and I no longer wondered who loved her but only whether there was anyone who didn't.

I was transfixed by grief. The villagers had lost someone they were fond of; I had lost my mother. Each of us had neighbors, but she was the only mother I had. All pains being equal, there was still something unique about mine . . . Maybe I would fall in love again, form a new friendship, welcome new children or grandchildren into the world, what did I know? But I would never replace the irreplaceable. No one would ever love me as she did, and I would never love anyone the way I loved her.

Dejected, I went home for a moment. When I emerged again, I was told that Barak was digging Mama's grave, below the village.

I joined him.

The sun was setting. The soft, mauve light of dusk was slowly veiling the landscape. Nuances took the place of contrasts. The countryside was slowly fading into night.

Barak had chosen a strange place: the center of a clearing. I saw him standing next to a mound of brown soil, dropping his tool.

"You're just in time, Nephew. Let's put her in her last bed."

Mama had been wrapped in a thin, elegantly woven shroud with embroidered edges that didn't conceal her shape; one might have supposed that she was playing a trick on us, and that she would soon rise up from her veils, laughing.

With great care, we lowered her into the grave. The size of the hole complicated the operation.

Once we had laid her to rest, Barak arranged the wrappings by smoothing out the wrinkles and eliminating the folds. He seemed to be preparing her for a visit.

We climbed out of the grave.

"Shall I cover her up, Barak?" I asked, picking up the hoe.

"Wait."

He wiped his forehead, ran his fingers through his beard and hair. Looking at his hands covered with mud, he grimaced and then, with a sigh, resigned himself to his untidy appearance. The sun, which was about to sink below the horizon, bronzed him entirely. I found him magnificent.

He looked hard at me, came toward me, and wrapped me in his arms. Then he returned to the edge of the grave and pensively cried out, "What if we added a few flowers?"

"Do you want me to bring some from my garden?"

"Please."

Detecting from his imperious tone that this detail was important to him, I walked away with long strides. After ten paces, I heard Barak call out to me. "I have no penchant for suffering."

I turned around without understanding. Barak continued in his thunderous voice: "So long as I can see her and touch her, I can hang on. But as soon as she's under the ground, I won't be able to stand it. Forgive me, Noam."

And, before I could react, Barak lifted his dagger to his throat and cut it. Blood spurted from the wound.

As I heard his body fall, I rushed toward him.

Barak lay in the bottom of the grave, dead, holding Elena in his arms. He was smiling.

*

We see the departure of our elders as normal, a normality that provides neither balm nor consolation, but instead leaves us with the feeling that nothing will ever be the same.

Life goes on, but it becomes more fragile. Our confidence, shaken, seeks its supports without finding them. The danger we'd always perceived—the loss of those close to us—ceases to be part of an indefinite future; the horror is no longer coming, it has happened.

The death of Mama and Barak was not reducible to the demise of two persons; it amounted to the dissolution of more. With them, my past, my childhood, my youth, cheerful and carefree, had disappeared. Worse yet, I had lost my protectors. Some might laugh: how were an old lady and a fallen giant defending a strong, healthy man like me? By loving me. By giving me their unscathed tenderness, their pure attention to my peace of mind, their pure desire for my balance, their pure affection from the first time they saw me. You'd have to have known me as a child to detect the little boy who still lived within me. And now, that was over! Mourning commanded me to grow up.

No matter how old you are when you learn that your parents are dead, that day kills the child. To become an orphan is to become the widower of your childhood.

I shouldn't have complained: I was nearly an old man when misfortune called on me to grow up. Unlike so many unlucky people, I didn't experience this tragedy in my early years.

Sometimes I was astonished by the magnitude of my distress, and I scolded myself: Accept sadness, Noam; it's not something that can be avoided. Tell it to limit itself to its place. Let sadness remain sadness, nothing else! Still, my sorrow, like a river overflowing its banks, carried along a myriad of emotions: boredom, nostalgia, loneliness, disgust, fear of the future, disenchantment, the bitter fear of never again vibrating, never again climaxing, no longer feeling delight.

"I have no penchant for suffering," Barak had said as he committed suicide.

Neither did I. I couldn't endure the unendurable. During the first moons of my mourning, I no longer exercised any power over myself; my moods flooded and drowned me without my agreement or control. Then, from time to time, I succeeded in resisting this surge, in controlling myself, if only slightly. Oh, at first I won only brief victories, but I sensed that they were opening a breach for a reconquest. Happiness is decreed before it's experienced.

"I have no penchant for suffering," my adored uncle had cried. So I decided to be happy.

I committed my energies to my family. Playing the role of the elder, the function that had earlier been performed by Barak and Mama, gave me the pleasure of keeping them alive by continuing their work; in it, I savored the contentment of a reinvigorated loyalty, and I loved it.

My son ruled the community with a light hand and devoted himself, in addition to his family, to his metallurgy.

Like nascent spring, happiness once again peeped over the horizon. At first willed, it was now experienced. I no longer had to force myself. Two years after the twofold demise, we were finally passing through a peaceful period. The felicity of being a father and a grandfather filled my days. Ageing now seemed to me a kind of hygiene, especially since to my makeup I had gradually added feigned stiffness, slower movements, and clothes suggesting that I was putting on weight, that my abs were weakening, that my muscles were turning to fat.

My grandchildren were growing. Cham was maturing; I was declining. How I loved that period!

Alas, a single morning would put an end to it all.

An immobile sun, unbearable. Stuck at the zenith, it had devoured the sky by making it pale, allowing it to regain its color only at the horizon. Under this sun, everything seemed inert, stunned; the breeze was out of breath; dust no longer had the energy to rise.

This full sun projected pools of shade onto the ground, and it was cooking my skull. I couldn't wait for the intense heat to decline in the evening—I had to cool off.

Walking with slow steps, I made my way toward the river. The tall, dry grasses, already consumed by the summer, lay flat on the ground. Only a viper here, a lizard there still evoked life.

Having arrived at the flats where the river widened before resuming its flow toward the beach, I took in the panorama. In the distance, the sea sparkled with a metallic sheen. Its diffuse radiance forced me to squint to tolerate the glare.

Nature was inclined to silence. Birds chirped ridiculously in the nearby treetops, but far higher, in the pallid ether, the slow, indefatigable eagles were soaring soundlessly.

I observed the mountain stream that nestled in the hollow of this narrow, rocky cirque. Whereas elsewhere plants lay shriveled on the ground, on the bank they were stirring again. Lapping, a slight trembling, little waves, shaking. The water was calling to me, irresistibly; it represented the quivering beneath the crushing heat.

To escape the contagion of the torpor, I undressed and entered the rapidly flowing, cool, limpid water. There, I came back to life. At the heart of icy currents, I felt the strength of the renewal, the intensity of life reasserting itself. Waves of impatience shook my body; I began to swim, to dive, to do pirouettes, to splash the water with my arms, to beat it, to float. I savored my strength: I rejoiced in my suppleness; I intoxicated myself with pleasure.

Despite the time that was passing, the hunger that urged me to eat, I couldn't tear myself away from my acrobatics, from the inexhaustible attractions of physical exertion.

A silhouette appeared on the bank. Cham crouched and caught sight of me.

Joyously, I waved him over.

Leaning forward, watchful, his eyes nearly closed, he was observing me.

Laughing, I repeated my invitation.

"Come on!"

He rose, took off his clothes, and entered the water, grimacing at the dramatic contrast with the torrid air. Then, with a few strokes, he swam toward me.

"Good, isn't it?" I exclaimed.

He nodded. His calm, his gravity made me a little impatient. Instead of enjoying himself, he was staring at me.

"Papa, how is it possible?"

"That this feels so good? We don't care, Cham!"

And I splashed water on him. He accepted my roughhousing without cheering up. I felt like a child again, facing an adult. He persisted, solemnly. "Papa, how is it possible?"

He pointed to himself.

"Look, my skin lacks firmness, my muscles are fading, I'm getting fat around the middle, my hair is falling out, and the part that isn't is turning white. Explain that to me."

Still carried forward by my enthusiasm, I mistook his meaning and tried to reassure him, "You're normal, Cham. What's happening to you happens to everyone."

"Everyone?" he objected.

Sobered, I understood what was going on. My time in the water had washed away the traces of my artificial ageing, and my excitement had done away with my borrowed demeanor. Cham was becoming acquainted with his father as a youth, the age I was when I conceived him with Tita. I suddenly felt more naked than naked in front of my son.

To my embarrassment, he saw that I had finally comprehended. He went on. "This is not the first time I've thought about this, Papa. Certain details make me suspect, almost every day, that you're deceiving me."

"I'm not lying to you, Cham; I'm protecting you."

He looked at me for a long time.

"I believe you, Papa. You're trying. I understand that better now. Explain it to me."

"I can't explain it. It's . . . it's . . . it's a curse."

"It would have been a blessing if you'd passed it on to me and my children . . ."

The candor with which he expressed his confusion—and, beyond that, my own—overwhelmed me.

"Cham! I . . ."

What could I say? The situation was inexplicable for both of us.

"Let's go back to the bank, please," he suggested.

We got out of the river and lay down, naked, on a flat rock, our faces turned toward the burning sun. We followed the movements of the kites as they rigorously cultivated slowness in the azure sky.

"Does it pain you to see me getting old?"

Cham touched me in my deepest depths. I resolved not to deceive him with stories.

"Yes. A father always sees his child through the lens of his memories, but it's obvious to me that you're ageing, Cham. At the beginning, stupidly, I was angry with you. I almost whispered to you, 'Stand up straight, take care of yourself, take better care of your skin, your hair, your teeth,' but I restrained myself. You're being subjected to the ageing process. Just like I'm being subjected to the fact that I . . . am not."

Cham looked into my eyes.

"It's falling apart, Papa. Despite your numerous efforts to appear old—thank you for them—you're fooling people less and less. People are talking behind your back, asking questions . . ."

"Who? Falka?"

"Falka, the villagers, the visitors, everyone. People ask me questions, harass me, and, because I don't give them an answer, it's getting worse, it's spreading. Now some people are starting to . . ."

He didn't dare finish his sentence. I encouraged him to continue. He admitted it: "They're beginning to hate you."

"What?"

There was no need to beg for further information. What I'd feared for a long time was happening. I jumped to my feet.

"I'm leaving, Cham."

He grabbed my heel and held on.

"No."

"It's the only way to keep me from ruining your life, to keep me from poisoning you."

"I know. You already did it once."

I mumbled, "You . . . you guessed?"

"Not at the time, but after you returned, I was struck by your sudden ageing—in two years, you'd gotten twenty years older—and I talked about it with Falka. Then she told me about her confusion when she met you, your anger, your coldness, and then your departure."

Tears welled in his eyes. He was struggling against his emotion.

"I hated the years you were gone, Papa. I assure you—I was completely joyless. I started loving my children the day I introduced them to you, when I saw how pleased you were. Don't abandon me . . ."

"Come now, Cham! What other solution is there?"

He bowed his head.

"I'm sorry. I'm listening only to my own selfishness."

"I don't care that you're selfish. You're my son, Cham, my only child. If I can satisfy your selfishness, I'll be the happiest father in the world."

He raised his head and fixed his eyes on me.

"Leave and stay."

"What?"

"Go live secretly at a distance from the village. Not too close, so that no one will run into you or recognize you. Not too far, so I can visit you often."

I held out my hand to shake his and seal our agreement and asked him, "Do you have someplace in mind?"

"I was thinking of a cavern that . . ."

Despite the tragic nature of the circumstances, I broke into laughter.

"A cavern? You really are your mother's son!"

*

I lived in the cavern for thirty years.

I will sum up this period in a few words: natural plenitude, human emptiness.

Natural plenitude, because I merged with the elements, the protective rock, the fertile soil, the water that I received, like dawn, with gratitude, the cold that perked me up, the heat that made me languid, the plants whose properties I tracked, the animals I venerated as much as I delighted in eating them. Hunting requires respect for and knowledge of animals: game can be flushed out if it has been previously waited for, studied, understood. Although hunting ends with death, it's preceded by patient attention, an authentic knowledge of the adversary, and a fundamental respect for its abilities. To be sure, the kill is abrupt . . . But doesn't that abruptness constitute the ultimate respect? We have to kill without tormenting, execute rather than torture. I've never killed proudly, but I've always killed well— quickly and for good reason. The savage I became during this era drew on Barak's lessons. I embraced Nature.

Human emptiness because I waited for Cham for six days and saw him again only on the seventh. My son never came with his hands or his mind empty: he brought me fruit, vegetables, grains; he showed me his latest jewelry made in gold, a material to which he was gradually becoming accustomed; he gave me news about the village, his children, their wives, their husbands, and then his grandchildren . . . Cham had a talent for telling stories. The chronicle he kept for me for thirty years enchanted me, so exquisitely did he sketch the characters, the stakes, the intrigues. Through the quality of his language and observation, he transformed every place into a setting, every situation into a stage, every event into an adventure, every narrative into suspense. His supreme gift was the ability to elevate each individual into a character; he made me care about people I'd never seen, would never visit, but whose happiness I rejoiced to learn about and whose death I mourned. Cham described little; he suggested. He didn't judge; he presented. A universal sympathy bound him to people whose vices and virtues he evoked with equal tenderness, aware of their complexity. Unlike the stories people tell children, there were neither good characters nor bad ones in his story, which developed the good and bad in every individual. I, who'd been brought up by a strange hero, a father as luminous as he was dark, as valiant as he was wicked, was gripped by this journey into ambiguities. Once we enter the human labyrinth, we no longer want to leave it; we want to explore it. Similarly, once ensconced in Cham's narrative, I didn't want to finish it; I wanted to savor it. To the recluse in his cavern, Cham generously brought his world, which proved to be so rich, so diverse, so exciting, and so full of dramatic contrasts that for me it became the world. Writing didn't exist yet, but when I consider the domination Cham exercised over me with his weekly gazette, I suppose that in another period he would've made a magnificent author.*

---

* Could he have produced a body of written work, an *oeuvre*? Cham had the talent to do it, and I was the reason why. An *oeuvre* requires means and cause. Cham became a storyteller to improve the confinement he'd imposed on me. He'd received his narrative art as a gift, but he constantly stimulated it, as much by a guilty conscience as by love. Affection mixed with culpability. Later on, I found that great creators always made fire by mixing noble and ignoble fuels. Both are necessary. Pure and impure. An *oeuvre* isn't made by an angel, and not by the Devil, either.

Cham created his great novel for me. It was addressed to me. I heard it. It really existed, even if there's no trace of it now. Before writing existed, geniuses wrote on the wind.

My cave was located in a region the natives considered inhospitable; they never went there, on the pretext that there was no water. In reality, my den concealed a well, which allowed me to live there peacefully.

What did I think about during all those years? I probably didn't think; I contemplated. Everything absorbed me, the mobile as well as the immobile, the silent and the noisy, from the dust floating in a ray of sunlight to the clouds piling up in the distance, from the whisper of the rain to the cawing of a crow. An odor sufficed to occupy me, especially since I'd decreed that there were neither good ones nor bad ones: I filled myself with the yellow fragrance of broom, the swampy stench of the toad, the greasy aromas that rose from meat turning on a spit. Everything provided me with entertainment.

I discovered the kingdom of the night. Instead of sleeping, as the activity of the village had forced me to do, I examined the firmament. I was, I admit, rather proud of this: no one scrutinized the sky! As soon as it got dark, people drowsed, flowers closed their petals, no animal turned its eyes or nose toward the inedible ether. Even nocturnal animals, owls and bats, kept their eyes on the ground, obsessed by hunger. If the earth was a belly, the sky was a spirit. Sometimes, alone in the world, my head thrown back, I murmured to the stars, "Don't worry; I see you." And a fit of vainglory allowed me to consider myself exceptional.

At first, I felt an aesthetic pleasure in looking at the stars, and then, as time passed, I began to search for connections among them. Did I have before me, each evening, different stars that placed themselves at random, depending on their desires, like sheep in the meadow of the sky? Or were they governed by some order? In the past, with Barak, I'd located the evening star, that light source that shines more brightly than the others, and also two groups, the Big Tadpole and the Little Tadpole. I undertook to push my investigation further and decided to reproduce the sky at my feet.

A vast field of hard-packed clay represented the celestial vault, and stones the stars. Often, between gazing at the true sky and my ersatz one, I developed aches, cramps, and a stiff neck. I also got discouraged, because I was finding more chaos than order. To be sure, the stars followed a path not unlike that of the sun, rising on one side and setting on the opposite one; however, though the dome moved in an identical fashion over my head, some of the stars strutted all night, and others only a few instants; some appeared only in the summer, others only in the winter. The seasons changed everything: the sun didn't rise year round alongside the same stars.

Gradually, I understood that there was an underlying, hidden logic that escaped me. Observing the sky confirmed me in the belief that the manifestations of the lights were neither fanciful nor arbitrary, but I remained unable to detect the principles.

On the ground, I drew the constellations, connecting the stones by lines scratched in the clay. This system later helped me to identify them in full daylight and then name them to aid my memory. When I chose these nicknames by making risky analogies with animals, I was aware of their artificiality. The only way to tame the unknown is to reduce it to the known. As the first, I called Ursa Minor, the "Little Bear," the Little Tadpole and Ursa Major, the "Big Bear," the Big Tadpole. Likewise, I designated as "the Horse" a group that I succeeded in reducing to a body endowed with four legs and a neck, which became, a few centuries later, among the Chaldeans, the constellation of the Lion—I, of course, had never seen a lion. As for a heap of stars whose number and clarity fluctuated depending on the moment, and which reminded me of a hen and her downy chicks, I called it the constellation of the Chicks, whereas a few millennia later it would be passed down to posterity as the Pleiades, the Greek astronomers seeing in it the seven daughters of the Titan Atlas. Finally, one constellation was described in several ways, so difficult did it seem to give meaning to its path: sometimes I called it the Sheep—as the Sumerians were soon to do—and sometimes the Hunter, because I discerned a bow aimed at the Chicks—an idea that occurred to the Greeks, as well, who called it Orion.

Had I elaborated, without realizing it, the first map of the sky? Had I, with a dreamy lack of awareness, initiated stellar catalogues?

I didn't know what I was looking at when I looked at the stars—who knows, even today? Not only was I unaware that I was living on a planet, but I guessed even less that I was observing other planets. The objects circulating above me weren't related to our earth. To my eyes, there was no infinite universe, just a wall behind which the sun, the moon, and the stars slid, a blue wall in the daytime, a black one at night. To my eyes, there was no unlimited space, but rather a closed, finite world. To my eyes, there was a center: where I was. Neither I nor the ground on which I sat cross-legged were moving; it was the celestial dome that pivoted.

On several occasions, however, I felt an uneasiness, a dizziness that in hindsight I consider premonitory. I trembled when I asked myself a question: if the stars were attached to the vault, or if they pierced it, as some claimed, what was behind the vault? In my terrified mind, space opened up again, stretched out, conquering new fields, then others, and then others, like the Wave of the flood that had pushed us forward, and I exhausted my brain constantly trying to imagine the expanse after the expanse, an area without boundaries. This perspective chilled me, ridiculed me, humiliated me, and, miserable, I interrupted this parade by shaking my head. Impossible! In fact, the notion of the infinite was tormenting me. Thinking only in images, I didn't conceive of the infinite, which can't be represented, only conceptualized. It's available to reason, not the imagination. Mathematics and philosophy, which had not yet been born at that time, did not allow me to reflect on the infinite, although they already made demands on my understanding. Even if I responded only with panic and demoralization, I sensed that a continent of new, different ideas was waiting for me somewhere.

Cham was getting old, the landscape was evolving, time was passing.

And I, over whom time glided, was participating in a dialogue with a cosmos that escaped time. An incorruptible human was staring at incorruptible stars.

I ventured little outside my territory. Since I no longer concealed my perpetual youth, I avoided letting villagers identify me or new people notice my anomaly. Like a phantom or a wild animal, I fled, accustomed to camouflaging myself as soon as I spotted a human figure. I would have feared the elite tracker, the one who lies in wait, watching, during the daytime, but people hunted less and less; agriculture and husbandry sufficed to feed them.

Twice a year, I went as far as the edge of the village to meditate before Barak and Mama's tomb.

An extraordinary thing had happened there: two trees had sprouted on the little hill where I'd buried my uncle and my mother; they had grown admirably straight for several years, and then, when they reached maturity, they had interlaced; more than interlacing, they'd penetrated each other. How else could I describe this incredible fusion? The main branch of one of them, thick, broad, and robust, had entered into the trunk of the other. The latter had not only tolerated the intrusion, but had strengthened it by healing around it, adding rolls of bark that formed links. The accord was sealed.

I was moved by the contemplation of these fused trees. Barak and Elena—it could only be they—were continuing their story. Their passion had succeeded in reemerging from the earth, mounting toward the sky, and reuniting them definitively. As plants, they'd accomplished what humans fail to do: make one out of two. Love would never perish . . .

For three decades, I went in the spring and at the end of the summer to pay them homage, without telling Cham. I spent the day sitting between the two of them, in their kindly shadow. I stroked them. Sometimes I hugged them—I trembled when the bark against which I pressed my cheek prickled me the way Barak's coppery beard used to, and I broke into tears when the sweet, heavy perfume of the flowers delicately enveloped me, because I felt Mama holding me in her arms. Despite the intensity of these emotions, I returned strong and confident. So eternity existed. And so did a happy life.

Noura never left my thoughts. During the first years, remembering her overwhelmed me; later, it enchanted me. There was no need to summon up precise features or to tell myself stories. I was content to imagine her, to act under her gaze, to see her face vaguely.

From time to time, I wondered if Tibor was still part of our world, if he was still roaming it in search of his child. His sudden departure disconcerted me as much as it had before, and I hoped for him that he'd finally accepted the death of his daughter. This man, so wise, so knowledgeable, so reflective, had known only one madness, Noura.

Like me?

During those three decades, I lived in the present, but I had the fuzzy sense, deep inside me, in a zone inaccessible to words, that I was waiting. For what? I didn't know . . .

It was Cham who one day told me what it was.

I saw him coming in the distance. How he was dragging himself along! His hunched, gaunt silhouette seemed as light as the dust on the path. He was struggling against a wind that could hardly bend the dandelions.

"Poor Cham!" I exclaimed. "He no longer looks like himself."

The stupidity of my judgment didn't occur to me. It was obvious that this Cham no longer resembled Cham as a young man, but why was I according more importance to one physical condition than I did to others? Cham had been himself at every age of his life, at three months, at five years, at twenty, and now at sixty-five! Would one condition serve as a reference point? Had I reproached the thirty-year-old Cham for not reminding me of the ten-year-old Cham? Like many people, I foolishly thought that childhood was a preparation and old age a decadence. According to this prejudice, Nature devoted twenty years to building an individual who benefited from their physique for ten to twenty years, and then it spent the following decades destroying them.

Cham reached me, out of breath and sweating. Our embrace confronted me with his emaciated shoulders, his sharp shoulder blades. I joked, trying to hide the pity he inspired in me.

After a few pleasantries, I expected him to begin his captivating gazette. Alas, he remained silent, rubbing his hands.

"What, Cham?"

"Falka died, Papa. Five days ago."

"What did she die from, my boy?"

He stared at me with a little surprise.

"Old age."

His reply threw me off balance. Not having seen Falka again over the past thirty years, I had to refresh my images in an instant, trade a radiant woman for a moribund old lady.

Cham examined me. His silence was eloquent; his silence cried: "I, too, am declining, Papa. I, too, will die soon."

I started nervously walking around the clearing where we met each time. I was ashamed of myself, of my youth, of my inability to transmit it to him; I felt sorry for him, for Falka, for all those beings who are subject to time. Why was I spared? It was hell!

When my body had rid itself of anger, I sat down near Cham. He smiled at me kindly.

"Come back to the village with me."

"No, Cham, let's avoid . . ."

"You won't bother me. Everyone who ever met you is under the ground, Papa, except me. You can come back."

"Your children? I took care of them when they were young. They'll recognize me."

"Of course they'll recognize you: you haven't changed! And precisely for that reason, they'll conclude it isn't you. No one is supposed to be exempt from time. I'll present you as a cousin; that will justify the family resemblance with Noam, my late father, who died, don't forget, thirty years ago."

His plan seemed convincing to me. I shivered.

"Cham . . . I'm afraid."

"Of what?"

"Of going back. I'm so used to my solitude. Could . . ."

"It's too hard for me to come here. Too far. It exhausts me."

I rushed toward him. "Forgive me."

"If you don't come back with me, you'll stay alone, and so will I. I won't be able to handle that, Papa."

And that is how I came to live once again alongside my beloved son.

Cham was right. The villagers never suspected that the dashing, robust, tanned, athletic features of the twenty-five-year-old who turned up in their village concealed the father of old man Cham. The few people who had seen me long ago enjoyed joking about the resemblance, more charmed than astounded, and thought I was "almost as handsome as Noam." I noticed that my reputation had flourished since my disappearance, raising me from the status of a hero to that of an idol. I was venerated as a sage, a just man, a founder. It was explained that I had foreseen the flood—I had only listened to Tibor's worries—that I had constructed a prodigious boat, of unparalleled solidity, into which I had loaded, in addition to people, pairs of animals to preserve all the species. To hear them tell it, I hadn't left anyone behind, and they no longer remembered the people who had died. From a lethal calamity, they had drawn a triumphant epic.

I immediately blamed Cham for having allowed this nonsense to prosper.

"I tried to correct them, Papa," he replied, sincerely. "I really insisted, especially since you explained everything to me on several occasions. But my qualifications didn't interest them. They listened to me out of politeness, kept silent for a decent time, and then started up again, more exaggerated than ever. People don't need the truth; they need legends."

Cham was getting weaker. Despite my care, my potions, my herbs, his energy was flagging.

People end as they begin, by needing help. Old age returns to infancy. The family order is inverted: the young care for the old. Every forebear is transformed into the child of their descendants.

That didn't happen in my case. I remained my son's father right to the end, until he drew his last breath. In private, we didn't hold back: Cham showed me his love, and I received it and gave him mine, without limits. How many hours did we spend lying on a mat in the half-light, talking about this and that, rejoicing to hear our voices blend, taking advantage of being together? I savored my son's presence voraciously, knowing that death would take him from me in the near future. The prospect of that loss showed me what really mattered. So much distress underlay my happiness! The coming void urged me to enjoy the full present. Every instant was gilded with nostalgia in advance: someday, all this would no longer exist.

On one of these afternoons spent sheltered from the sun, in the soothing silence of the house, my son fell asleep forever as he leaned against me. I sat motionless for a long time, stunned. I had taken him in my arms when he was a baby. Now I was still holding him in my arms as an old man. The difference? He no longer responded to my smiles . . .

I buried Cham alongside Barak and Elena, at the foot of the trees that had intertwined. Then, once the family members and I had sung the prayers, I felt like an outsider among these people who saw me as a vague cousin whose company Cham enjoyed. My role was coming to an end. I had to disappear.

How long would this ageless body force me to exist?

To me, sorrow seemed normal; I believed I could get over my sadness, no matter how acute it was. On the other hand, beyond all pain, I was tormented by a burning question: Did I still want to live? Like this? I considered doing what Barak had done. My world was dying, and I wasn't! Escaping everyone else's calendar, no longer wasting away along with those I loved: far from granting me a privilege, it was torturing me instead. This prolonged youth, absurd, insolent, ferocious, stupid, was a burden that grew heavier as it gradually isolated me. I cursed the genies, the spirits, and the gods for having conceived for me a new kind of solitude, temporal solitude. While everyone knows reclusion in space, I, and only I, was experiencing confinement in time. How can you live with a person without sharing their vulnerability? How can you watch your beloved wither without withering yourself? How can you survive the death of your son? And, of course, of future children?

I received no answer.

Not from the gods, not from the spirits, not from the demons, not from myself.

This silence suspended the fatal act. Torn by too many questions to answer them with a dagger, and without decreeing or wishing it, I continued to live.

Or at least that's what I thought.

*

After thirty years of immobility, I left, a bag slung over my shoulder.

The world had changed. Families were becoming sedentary, something that, paradoxically, the roads themselves testified to. In the age of the hunter-gatherers, one saw hardly any permanent paths, because no travel took place regularly enough to leave its mark on the ground. Now that humans had stopped moving around, paths appeared everywhere, furrowed by feet, marked by walking sticks, worn by wooden clogs, earthen paths beaten by peasants, their flocks, and merchants or suppliers moving from market to market. Villages were growing and becoming more numerous. There were fewer and fewer nomads.

As I wandered, I realized that my independence was increasingly out of place. The idea that an individual might succeed in meeting their own needs—food, lodging, clothing, medical care—flabbergasted those I met. They belonged to complex communities in which labor had been divided, skills distributed, knowledge fragmented. A person who raised livestock no longer wove; one who wove didn't care for animals. The end of autonomy! Each person counted on others. Helplessness stalked them. The specialization of know-how had done away with the ability to actually do something. People depended on one another, doomed to collective life.

I felt like a survivor from a world that had disappeared, a world where individuals stood on their own two feet. In the past, everyone knew what others knew; now, everyone mastered their own task, and left the rest to others. The ancient world had been the time of shared knowledge: the new world was that of shared ignorance. From then on, villagers differed from their neighbors thanks to an expert competence and resembled them only by generalized incompetence. They were unified by countless shortcomings and divided by expertise.*

* I'm always reticent when people talk to me about progress. The more things people as a whole know, the less knowledge the individual has.

In 1950, I had the good fortune to meet Albert Einstein in the United States. Better yet, I may have saved his life . . . An avid sailor, the great physicist was sailing alone on a lake in New Jersey, near Princeton. A nasty gust of wind suddenly capsized the boat, and an awkward movement on Einstein's part threw him into the water, almost knocking him out. I dove in and brought him back to the shore. Once he'd recovered, I helped him recuperate his boat, repair it, and put it away, and then we had a bite to eat. I've never been around a more charming individual, or a clumsier one. Why

Thanks to specialization, craftsmen made rapid progress. Whereas Cham had limited himself to working with pure copper and pure gold, blacksmiths and jewelers were experimenting with alloys. By mixing tin with copper, they obtained a metal that was more malleable when it was hot and stronger when it was cold: bronze. The result greatly improved things. Thanks to bronze, because of it, everything changed: people traveled to oversee the trade in raw materials—our region was rich in copper, but not in tin—and the sale of tools, daggers, swords, and helmets.[†]

One village, Biril, had achieved excellence in working with bronze. A leader of a new kind ruled it. His name was Zeboim. He was cruel and wanted everyone to know it.

Zeboim ruled this immense village on the seacoast, a complex fortified with walls made of logs and into which the only entry was through two gates under constant surveillance. Zeboim himself lived in a vast residence surrounded by pavilions watched over by guards. Everything helped make people feel his importance. When Zeboim appeared at ceremonies, he wore a mask made of gold that made him impressive, superb. This stratagem surrounded his physiognomy with mystery. Not knowing his features and aware that he sometimes walked among them anonymously, without his metal mask, people in the streets were careful

---

did this superior mind have ten fingers? He didn't know how to use them—except for playing the violin—and had no practical sense. Although I found him touching, I compared him with the men of my youth: if they encountered difficulties, they would all have handled it better than he did. Einstein didn't notice anything around him; he knew neither the flora nor the fauna of the lake, couldn't distinguish between the plants that were edible and those that were poisonous or had medicinal qualities; he didn't know how to predict a thunderstorm or squall, how to sew up a rip in his clothes, light a fire, or make a flint knife, let alone use it. As for laying traps for rabbits or otters, the idea would never have passed through his brilliant brain! He displayed an exhaustive ineptness.

Specialization preserves those who don't know how to do very much. Ultimately, civilization has made it possible for geniuses and morons to survive. The moron isn't good at anything, and the genius is good at one single thing.

† For the poet, it's gold that changed the human species. For the moralist, it's money. For the historian, it's bronze.

about what they said and did. Zeboim frequently punished his subjects for having spoken ill of him or criticized something he'd done. The executions took place in public. A crier summoned people. Before a very orderly crowd, Zeboim, wearing his shining mask, sat on a throne. As the villagers watched, wavering between horror and excitement, the executioner cut off the guilty party's head, which was then put on display at Biril's gate until the vultures and crows had devoured it.

Zeboim ruled by terror. He recruited mercenaries. The official pretext? The defense of this wealthy, much-envied village. In reality, Zeboim's enemies were inside the village walls, at its heart, and his troops ensured internal order. Then, as the intoxication of power led Zeboim to imperialism, his army began the conquest of neighboring communities.

How much of this was caused by Zeboim, and how much by bronze? Inequality between the villages grew. The raids I'd witnessed in the past resulted from temporary poverty or from envy; now the violence flowed from the system itself. Technology led to wealth, wealth led to power, power led to weaponry, and as weaponry improved, aggressiveness erupted.

Shall I admit it? This excess looked to me like salvation: I decided to enlist as a warrior in Zeboim's army. Young, vigorous, experienced, unscrupulous, I rented my body to the party that guaranteed me a bed, food, clothes, and laundry.

He hired me. Or rather Kurk, his spokesman, his visible part, the one that exercised command, ruled over the soldiers, and led the attacks hired me—Zeboim remained hidden inside his fortress.

I lived among brutes whose company was particularly insipid. They imagined themselves to be immortal and weren't, throwing themselves into the fray with jubilation, intoxicated by an illusion of superiority, convinced they would emerge victorious because, from altercations to brawls, they never stopped fighting. When I was with them, I was immersed in triviality. They drank, feasted, swore, spat, strutted, copulated, hurled abuse, and then died with a cry of astonishment in the middle of a battlefield. The crudeness of these oafs made such a contrast with Cham, my son, with his subtle language and refined analyses, that these boors offered me oblivion. I, who had cared for others, was hurting people! I, who had healed, was exterminating! I, who had saved my people, was melting into an anonymous group, a soldier among soldiers, without concerning myself for an instant about the cause for which I was fighting . . . Was it me? No. What was I punishing myself for? I was seeking the erasure of the Noam who came before, the Noam who had wanted to be good, loving, responsible, and who had succeeded only in suffering atrociously. I was deserting the camp of pain. Better to cause it than to endure it.

I proved to be an excellent mercenary. Indifferent to the blows that struck me and rapidly recuperating from wounds and contusions, I was the ideal warrior. Having set out on a frenzied race, I'd driven death out of its lair, and I was running in front of the dangerous beast, hoping that it would catch me.

Alas, I was going faster than it was . . . I killed but wasn't killed. Ever.

I became gloomy. Something had disappeared. Those I loved, Noura, Mama, Barak, Cham, Tibor, but also something essential, impalpable: Nature's enchantment.

Plants were now staked and fields fenced. What a shock! Humans told plants how they should grow and animals where they should live. Stakes and fences! A revolution . . . The land was becoming agricultural, the animals alimentary. Forests and prairies were being destroyed, the former burned to provide fields, the latter fenced to serve as pastures. Peasants with callused hands were breaking their backs, hunched over the humus, clearing the land of vegetation and then of stones, breaking, softening, removing clods, hoeing, plowing, seeding it. They didn't venerate the soil; they used it. Animals, frightened, fled the flames and tried to live far away from humans, whereas before they lived with them. Their suffering didn't stop there: humans created two races, domestic animals and wild animals. Resisting enslavement, wild animals were condemned to exodus and then to hiding, whereas the worst awaited the docile beasts that had the misfortune to show a little tameness and sociability. After determining which animals would eat and reproduce in captivity, farmers locked them up for good and killed the wild ones. Nature allows only the strong and aggressive to survive, but humans practiced an inverse selection. I noticed this every time I passed by flocks in their pens: the domesticated goats, sheep, and bovines were never as big or robust as their wild cousins.

The landscape was changing. Of course it was: it had changed authors. Earlier, Nature had created it; now humans were getting involved. Our coast, the result of millennia of labor by the elements, including the flood, was beginning to be punctuated by roads, meadows, slash-and-burn fields, plantations, fences, specialized forests, villages, ports. Wheat, barley, houses. Wheat, barley, palisades. Wheat, barley, granaries. Wheat, barley, stables. Wheat, barley, houses . . . Nature invents with prolixity, displaying an endless, eloquent imagination; humans burn, grid, simplify.

When columns of smoke rose into the sky, I trembled all over: my contemporaries were burning more than a parcel of land, they were destroying a way of living on it. Nature henceforth belonged to humans, who not only colonized the territories but also seized their living species, vegetal or animal, depending on their needs.

In the old days, we subsisted thanks to hunting, fishing, and gathering. Like the plants and animals, we moved about as Nature's guests, without privileges and burdened with serious handicaps—very slow growth, a long period of dependence on our elders, no superior physical qualities, no fur or scales. Living beings amid other living beings, we remained transitory visitors. This equality was broken. Humans now thought they were above the Nature they were transforming. From then on, there would be two worlds: the natural and the human. And the latter invaded the former shamelessly.[*]

A man of the Lake, I had traversed a Nature without barriers, where matter and spirit mixed. The blade of grass, the walnut tree, the hare, the stream, the rock, the cloud, the wind were all animate, endowed with intentions and feelings. I could communicate with them through observation, meditation, reverie, dreams, song, dance, drugs, trances. No impenetrable wall existed between us. But humans constructed it. With a view to possessing objects, bodies, phenomena, they emptied them of thought and reserved understanding for themselves alone. They conquered the cosmos by making it hollow. I had lived in union with Nature; they separated me from it. Humility was eclipsed, and harmony, as well. My paradises were lost.[†]

Then my desire to put an end to it all chose a final means.

Of average size, slightly hunched, with a thick neck, Kurk had such robust limbs that his clothes always seemed tight in the arms and legs. A multitude of amulets made of bone, teeth, and bronze

---

[*] In Genesis, one of the narratives that were devoted to me later on, this radical break is emphasized in a few lines. According to the Biblical text, God says to Noah before he boards the ark: "Take with you seven pairs of all clean animals, the male and his mate; and a pair of the animals that are not clean, the male and his mate; and seven pairs of the birds of the air also, male and female, to keep their kind alive on the face of all the earth" (Genesis 7:2–3). He entrusts Noah with guarding, not owning animals! And when they disembark, God establishes a covenant with "you and your offspring after you, and with every living creature that is with you" (Genesis 9:10). This means that there are three on earth: God, humans, and animals. The separation of the human from all other living beings, in the eyes and with the guarantee of God, came to pass. Unthinkable for the Peoples of the Lake.

[†] I have the impression that poets still live in this lost paradise. Is that why, for centuries, I've been reading them so much? Many individuals born long after me feel the same thirst. This inclines me to suspect something that I'll talk about later: we don't necessarily live in the period where we think we reside. Many of us live, in our innermost selves, in a universe different from our reality. Otherwise, how can we explain the appetite for literature on the part of some people, and depression on the part of others? The accidents of birth force us to pass through a world unconnected with the one that our unconscious continues to inhabit.

hung on his bulging chest, creating a proud and superstitious display whose jingling signaled its presence. You heard Kurk even when he remained silent, a rare occurrence, since his pungent, guttural voice constantly screamed. Two details summed him up: sweat and the veins in his neck. His armpits and thighs ran with sweat, and a sort of vapor oozed from his sticky hair, his forehead with its deep furrows, and the wings of his pug nose, covering his tanned face with an oily consistency. I never knew Kurk to be dry; sweating expressed his fever, his frenzied need to be moving, his eagerness to serve an unpredictable tyrant. As for the veins in his neck, they stood out, violet, contracted, palpitating, serpentine, testifying to an energy on the brink of eruption.

From the start of my acquaintance with Kurk, I satisfied him by showing myself to be a redoubtable warrior. He liked me. I won his confidence, and he occasionally delegated to me a few minor tasks of command. Entirely devoted to Zeboim, he had sacrificed any family life. With no wife or children of his own, he dreamed about Zeboim's wife and children; by substitution, Kurk referred to them, moved, as though they were his close friends and relatives. Zeboim had three sons and three daughters who were reaching maturity; having become a widower, he had married a splendid second wife. "No need to put gold on her sweet little face; she's radiant," Kurk repeated over and over. "I've never seen a more beautiful woman." Although she didn't hide behind a mask, she went out very little.

I listened to Kurk; he had a need to talk, and I needed to substantiate our camaraderie.

Finally, the Battle of Letomi came. Zeboim coveted that modest village. A river descending from the mountains passed through it and would ultimately allow him to continue his expansion eastward by canoe.

The battle turned out to be so unequal that I felt sorry for the inhabitants of Letomi. With simple sticks and stones, they tried to stop us, professionals equipped with helmets, swords, and shields. In no time, they gave way under our blows. As soon as the last of their men fell, I carried out my plan. Above the carnage, I turned toward Kurk. Spattered with blood, he smiled at me and cried, raising his fist in the air, "Letomi belongs to Zeboim!"

He spoke as if he'd won the victory for his own benefit.

I addressed him in a loud voice: "You're going to die, Kurk."

Convinced that I was joking, he laughed out loud.

"Of course I'll die, but not just yet. Tonight, there's wine for everyone!"

"You're going to die, Kurk. Now."

In a flash, I thrust my sword into his belly. His rheumy eyes opened wide with surprise. He staggered.

I withdrew the sword. He faltered. With a clean cut of my blade, I slit his throat. Blood gushed from the wound. He collapsed.

The mercenaries hadn't had time to intervene. Aghast, they looked at the body of their commander lying at their feet.

"What the hell, Noam?"

They hated Kurk, but they nevertheless obeyed him. Not only did they live under his orders, but they died under his orders. If my act didn't sadden them, it did stun them.

"Arrest me," I exclaimed.

"What?"

They understood even less.

"Arrest me. Otherwise, you'll be suspected of complicity. The blame will fall on me, not you. Zeboim will punish one mercenary, not all of you."

The least dull-witted of them finally reacted. I was tied up.

As I had expected, the case was dealt with quickly and efficiently. Zeboim didn't waste his time simulating justice. He refused to organize a hearing and announced that I would be immediately executed on the public square.

The herald had only a few minutes to summon a crowd, the executioner to set up a block, and the drums to roll before I was pushed, bound hand and foot, toward my death.

Dusk was falling, but the sunlight had been so hot that it lingered everywhere, a little reddened, on the walls, people's faces, and the ground that I was staring at.

Walking at the pace of the death knell, I felt an unprecedented relief. I was being reborn. Dying returned me to myself. I was rejoining the Noam who lived in accord with his principles, the Noam who had loved Mama and Barak, the Noam desired by Noura, the Noam of my son Cham, the Noam who had come to earth only to care for and preserve life. As I moved toward the executioner, I suddenly remembered Tibor and I, on our ship during the flood, leaning over little Prok as he died of starvation. Tibor had been indignant: "I didn't become a healer to watch a child die!" Then I'd gone him one better: "Did I become chief to watch a child die?" I had been that Noam, a leader, father, lover, physician. These last years, despair had led me away from myself without bringing me anything other than the habit of killing. Does one reject the past without it taking revenge? Noam's revenge turned out to be mild: dying like myself, because I no longer knew how to live like myself.

The executioner struck me behind the knees to make me fall. I anticipated what would follow by voluntarily rolling over near the wooden block used for decapitations. There I knelt and laid my head on the wood.

In front of me, on a dais, stood Zeboim, haughty, his arms crossed, wearing his gold mask, with his sons and daughters lined up alongside him.

The executioner raised an enormous bronze axe, and the drums subsided. A woman, lively and light on her feet, joined Zeboim and slipped her hand into the crook of his elbow. By her loving, submissive attitude, I inferred that she was his second wife.

A cry escaped my lips.

"Noura?"

Surprised, the woman looked around to see where that name had come from, and spotted me.

"Noam?" she stammered.

The executioner's axe fell.

EPILOGUE

Noam looks up.

He has just understood: the book puts an end to an enigma that's been irritating him for thousands of years . . . the Black Sea.

His temples burning, he slams the volume shut, stands up, needs fresh air. He's suffocating. Quick, walk, move his arms, shake himself, regulate this body on fire! He opens the window.

The crisp fragrance of the pines that surround the house calms his lungs. The buzzing of the cicadas sweeps over him in a beneficent wave. A pure, washed-out blue sky spreads out peacefully, and Noam draws from it, by looking at it fixedly, the strength to take in what he's discovered. The Black Sea . . .

For weeks, the Ark's library has offered him a refuge within the refuge. To escape the boredom produced in him by his companions, Marmoud, Charly, Hugo, and the lethargic James, Noam spends as much time as possible in this enclosed space whose walls are covered with books. On the vast mahogany table, he continues writing his manuscript, and then, when fatigue disperses the words, making his sentences laborious, when his overstretched brain turns his work into that of a shepherd vainly trying to collect scattered sheep into a flock, he gives up, sets his notebook aside, and sinks into the hollow of the sofa to read.

Bequeathed by a literary connoisseur, this is a library for survivalists. Although it includes practical manuals on hunting, camping, and cooking, it also contains literary works on catastrophes, from Homer's *Iliad* to Camus's *Plague*. Intrigued, Noam has perused hundreds of recent novels depicting plagues, tornados, tsunamis, earthquakes, pandemics, post-nuclear society, Nature cooled-off, Nature burnt up, extraterrestrial exile, and the cosmos in which machines have rid themselves of their inventors. This morning, he found, at the top of the wooden ladder, a shelf containing scientific books. Spotting a study on the flood, he grabbed it gingerly, warily.

For centuries, he's been consulting what scholars write about the flood without having learned anything new. More precisely, he's learned a great deal about the authors, but nothing about the flood.

Humans relate everything to themselves. Events don't just happen; they happen to *them*. Or rather, they don't happen; they're *destined* for them. A calamity, no matter how hard it is, turns out to be a message intended for them. It matters little that animals die, that plants wither, that deserts sterilize fields and forests, all this is addressed to them, and to them alone. Who is speaking to them through typhoons and cataclysms? The gods when there were lots of them, God since he's become a bachelor, and Nature, now that God has gone away. An intelligent entity still teaches them a lesson. The gods, God, Nature take revenge on humans for their arrogance and urge them to be modest. What a paradox! Presumptuous beings affirm that Power encourages them to be humble, but in doing so they lack humility because they make themselves the center and purpose of creation!

This morning, Noam began reading this study on the flood reluctantly, fearing that he might find only a contemporary formulation of the eternal foolishness.

An hour later, he's dumbfounded: this compendium gives him the keys to understanding what he experienced several millennia earlier.

Noam leaves the window. Feverishly, he paces the room, turning quickly around the table. The Black Sea . . .

In 1993, two marine geologists, William Ryan and Walter Pitman, who were exploring the entrails of the Black Sea, found inexplicable sediments: they should have been in a freshwater lake, not a salt sea. Six years later, an oceanographer, Bob Ballard, detected a beach a hundred and fifty meters below the surface. What? A seacoast at the bottom of the sea? All this testified to a major rise in the water level. But the beach revealed something even stranger: the petrified animals and shellfish with which it was strewn belonged to species that had evolved in fresh water. Thanks to carbon 14, it was possible to date them: seven thousand eight hundred years old. On the other hand, the species, not far away, that required a salty environment were seven thousand three hundred years old. A sea had thus replaced a lake!

Starting with this discovery, other information made it possible to reconstruct what happened.

There had been a lake—the Lake, thought Noam, who has relived, through the lines he's written, the enchanted universe of his youth—fed by the streams of the Ukrainian plains. And it had earlier been lower than the nearby sea, the Mediterranean. When the ice age ended, the warming climate caused the planet's glaciers to melt significantly. Consequently, the level of the seas and oceans rose. Four degrees of warming sufficed to make the Mediterranean a hundred and thirty meters higher. From the Mediterranean, which overlooked it from the south, the Lake was protected by higher land, because the present-day straits of the Bosporus and the Dardanelles were not straits then but isthmuses, strips of land that formed a wall. When, under the pressure of the water, the natural dam of the Bosporus collapsed, thousands of cubic kilometers of water flowed a hundred and forty meters down into the Lake and surrounding countryside, where thousands of people drowned . . . The result of this outburst was a less salty body of water over eleven hundred kilometers long from west to east, and six hundred from north to south: the Black Sea.

Next, the study said what Noam had already concluded: the flood had not been universal but local; while some individuals had survived by fleeing, mountain populations hadn't been affected. In the absence of writing, no one recounted the facts, and the devastation reverberated from memory to memory, repeated, commented on, deformed, enriched, clarified, fantasized.

"He's going to call! Let's stay here. Not enough time to go down."

Outside, Marmoud is shouting to Charly and Hugo on the way back from a climbing exercise. Noam automatically heads for the window to close it and thus ensure his peace and quiet.

The three paramilitary men are arguing excitedly. Noam hesitates. In addition to not wanting to interrupt them by suddenly appearing, he prefers to eavesdrop on their conversation from the sofa along the wall.

"I bet he's announcing when it will start," exclaims the young Hugo.

Noam has mixed feelings regarding the survivalists he's met. He thinks they're wrong as often as they are right. He doesn't confuse them with the apocalyptic prophets he's run into over the centuries, who belonged to civilizations that believed because they didn't know. Today, the situation is reversed: people know but don't believe. Or worse yet, they don't believe *what* they know. Though the warming of the atmosphere and its consequences are based on science, they accord it neither belief nor attention. In Noam's view, only the ecologists and the survivalists have the merit of believing what they know.

Marmoud, Charly, and Hugo go above and beyond. From rational concern, they've moved to fundamentalism. In the name of tomorrow, they bully people today and want to precipitate the disaster for which they've prepared themselves. They're not guided by altruism, but rather by aggressive egoism.

Hugo's phone rings.

"D.R.!"

They huddle around the telephone. When he hears them greeting one another, Noam imagines that D.R. has appeared on the screen. The leader's metallic voice says resolutely, "Zachary's cell will take action in three days. It will coordinate the attack on five nuclear plants in the United States."

"Yes!" screams Marmoud.

The three terrorists shake hands and bellow their battle cry.

The voice continues, biting: "Observe the greatest discretion! Even showing your joy could attract suspicion."

"Don't worry! We're alone at the refuge."

"No one is ever alone!" D.R. retorts, his tone cutting.

Noam shivers, hopes the conspirators don't notice they're standing near an open window . . .

Clearly, they don't care, because Marmoud goes on: "What about us?"

"You'll wait."

In the deformed timbre of this voice, an intonation disconcerts Noam.

While Marmoud insists that the operation planned for Lebanon should begin sooner, Noam approaches the window, propelled forward by a sudden fear. He feels an urgent need to confirm or disprove his intuition.

Marmoud doesn't give in, argues, explains how his team has a plan for everything, even the unexpected. He proposes, "We'll blow up the Chabrouh Dam the day the Americans take out the nuclear plants."

Noam sneaks a look, and, amidst the necks leaning over the screen, he sees the man the Lebanese militants are imploring.

"I prefer not to," replies Derek.

PUBLISHER'S NOTE

T he *Passage Through Time* presents an enormous challenge: telling the history of humanity in a purely novelistic
form, entering history through stories, as if Yuval Noah
Harari had met Alexandre Dumas . . .

For the past thirty years, Eric-Emmanuel Schmitt has been
driven by this titanic project, by an aspiration that has ended up
tracing a life path. While writing his other texts (novels, short
stories, theater, essays), he has continued to work on it, amassing
historical, scientific, religious, medical, sociological, philosophi-
cal, and technological knowledge. At the same time, he has let his
imagination create powerful, touching, unforgettable characters
to whom we become attached and with whom we identify.

From this synthesis of his intellectual training and his talent
as a writer arises a unique work that leads us from one world to
another through cultural fractures surrounding moments when
accidents, evolutions, or revolutions change civilizations. And
each time, the present sheds light on the past, just as times gone
by reveal the contemporary era.

This incredible passage through time begins with the Flood
and continues in our own time. Through their love affairs and
their struggles, the key characters embody major events or
transformations.

Each of the eight titles in this immense publishing venture
is connected with a decisive age of human history: 1. *Paradises
Lost* (the end of the Neolithic and the Flood) will be followed
by 2. *Heaven's Gate* (Babel and Mesopotamian civilization; 3.
The Dark Sun (Egypt in the time of the Pharaohs and Moses); 4.

The Light of Happiness (Greece in the fourth century BCE); 5. *The Two Kingdoms* (Rome and the birth of Christianity); 6. *The Age of Myth* (Medieval Europe and Joan of Arc); 7. *The Age of Conquests* (the Renaissance and the discovery of the Americas); and 8. *Revolutions* (political, industrial, and technological revolutions).

Eric-Emmanuel Schmitt is one of Europe's most popular and acclaimed authors and playwrights. His many novels and story collections include *The Most Beautiful Book in the World* (Europa, 2009). In 2001, he was awarded the French Academy's Grand Prix du Théâtre. Schmitt divides his time between Paris and Belgium.